Praise for

"Reminiscent of Elmore Leonard, Arnote's style is hard-boiled and lean, with fast-paced action and gritty characters."
—*Winnipeg Sun*

"Guaranteed to please all fans of nonstop, cliff-hanger suspense novels."
—*Mystery Scene*

"The characters are unforgettable, the milieu unmistakably authentic, the suspense relentless. In Willy Hanson, Arnote's created one of fiction's most enduring heroes."
—Ken Goddard

"This novel of love, greed, power, and revenge is set against a uniquely intriguing backdrop."
—*Ann Arbor News* on *Hong Kong, China*

"A stylish thriller... there is adventure here as well as romance, played out against the well-evoked, exotic scenery of Hong Kong."
—*Publishers Weekly* on *Hong Kong, China*

"Arnote is a godsend to thriller fans."
—Molly Cochran, coauthor of *The Forever King*

"Arnote has a sure instinct for suspense, lurid scandal, brutal violence, and sexual excess!"
—John Farris, author of *Sacrifice*

"If you crave original, pulsating suspense, put Arnote on your menu!"
—Ed Gorman, author of *The Marilyn Tapes*

By Ralph Arnote from Tom Doherty Associates

WILLY HANSON NOVELS

Evil's Fancy
Fallen Idols
False Promises
Fast Lane
Fatal Secrets
A Rage in Paradise

Hong Kong, China

FAST LANE

RALPH ARNOTE

A TOM DOHERTY ASSOCIATES BOOK / NEW YORK

NOTE: If you purchased this book without a cover you should be aware that this book is stolen property. It was reported as "unsold and destroyed" to the publisher, and neither the author nor the publisher has received any payment for this "stripped book."

This is a work of fiction. All the characters and events portrayed in this book are either products of the author's imagination or are used fictitiously.

FAST LANE

Copyright © 1998 by Ralph Arnote

All rights reserved, including the right to reproduce this book, or portions thereof, in any form.

A Forge Book
Published by Tom Doherty Associates, LLC
175 Fifth Avenue
New York, NY 10010

www.tor.com

Forge® is a registered trademark of Tom Doherty Associates, LLC.

ISBN: 0-812-54035-2
Library of Congress Catalog Card Number: 98-23523

First edition: December 1998
First mass market edition: September 2000

Printed in the United States of America

0 9 8 7 6 5 4 3 2 1

Eddie and Avis—Joplin's Best

And—Angelique

FAST
LANE

1

"Jason, we have to talk." Amanda Granger spoke as she entered their bedroom. She found Jason finishing up packing for his early morning business trip. He was fussing with a couple of neckties, holding them under the bright light of a lamp.

"Damn! Lately it seems that I can't wear a necktie twice. They seem to be a magnet for specks of God knows what." He tossed the ties onto a chair in disgust and then turned to make a new selection from a rack that must have held at least a hundred ties.

Amanda's eyes narrowed. Jason's lack of warmth puzzled her. Something had changed over the past few months. Whatever it was, he wasn't sharing it with her. "Let me help you, Jason," offered Amanda, not wanting him to get any more upset.

"I can manage quite nicely, Amanda. How about doing something useful, like pouring me a brandy."

Amanda sighed, then sat on the edge of a chair and watched him. He always seemed to get very uptight when preparing for a business trip. "Jason, we have to talk," she repeated, sober-faced. Her wide-set brown eyes fixed on his new selection of ties.

"So, damn it, talk. You talk and I'll listen. If you don't mind, I want all this packing done so that I can hop right out of bed and head for Columbus in the morning. Every minute is valuable. You know how I feel about trip preparation, Amanda."

"You make it difficult to talk, Jason. It didn't used to be like this." She persisted: "I'll wait until you've finished. I want your full attention."

Now it was Jason's turn to sigh heavily. He sat on the edge of the bed and stared at her in mock attention. "Okay, shoot. What is so important that won't wait until I get back?"

"You are going to be a father, Jason." She broke into a smile and waited for his reaction, hoping for him to mirror her own feelings of elation.

"How do you know that?" The question came without any detectable hint of feeling at all. It was as if she had told him the pot roast was overcooked.

Amanda avoided his fixed stare and looked down at the carpet. Maybe she had misjudged him, she thought, and decided to brave her way through the conversation. "I've been feeling . . . just a little different lately. So I went to Dr. Wilson today, and he confirmed that I was pregnant." She lifted her eyes to again meet his. "Oh, Jason, isn't it wonderful?"

Jason broke his gaze, stood up and walked to the window. He stared for a moment out into the darkness. "So what are you going to do about it?" he asked, still not looking at her.

"Do about it? Jason, I said we were going to have a baby. What on earth do you mean?"

"Relax, there is no need to get upset. I guess you rightfully think this is wonderful." He paused, nervously fidgeting with a necktie. "I just think we should think it through. I seem to remember that we agreed to wait five years for this, certainly until after I've got my promotion. New York, remember?" He hesitated before turning to face her. "It's just that we are awfully busy now, getting our life in order."

"Busy! Did you say busy? I can't believe this." She rose from the chair and walked over to face him. "Maybe you're busy, Jason, doing whatever it is you do day after day, and lately night after night. But I have nothing but time."

He looked past her, not meeting her eyes. "Only this morning you told me how busy you were. You are a full partner in our success, Amanda."

"The country club, the ladies' golf program, the charity drives, entertaining our . . . your friends. That is what I'm busy at. It's secondary, Jason, all make-work to fill in the gaps." She felt a tear trail down her cheek. "My God, Jason, it all means nothing compared to the fact that we are going to be parents." She turned and moved toward the door, not believing that he would let her leave the room in her present mental state.

"We'll talk about it when I get back, Amanda. I have this gut feel that our having a child right now does not fit with the program. Think about it."

Amanda strode from their bedroom and dashed downstairs. She closed the door of the den behind her, sprawled on the couch and began to weep.

2

The sign clearly read, MERGE TO THE RIGHT—1,500 FEET. Jason Granger glanced at the side mirror of the red Corvette and spotted a big van sport utility vehicle as it pulled parallel to his rear wheels. He shoved his foot down on the gas pedal but permitted the big SUV to keep pace as they both moved over the crest of the hill. He was careful not to let it actually pass.

Now, only a few hundred feet ahead of them, a huge construction crane occupied the fast lane in front of the van. Granger floored the accelerator, still determined not to let the driver on his left pass.

There was a squeal of brakes as Granger easily sped ahead. The SUV swerved to tuck in behind him, knocking over a row of plastic orange cones, coming perilously close to the massive construction crane.

Inside the SUV, Sonny Houston glanced at his ten-year-old son, whose knuckles tensely whitened as he gripped the dashboard. He continued to tailgate the Corvette. "Relax, boy. The son of a bitch cut us off. He dissed us with that fancy car of his. We're gonna teach him a lesson, boy."

Houston lightened up on the accelerator of his special-built four-wheeler, letting the Corvette move away and finally permitting several cars to move between them. Houston glanced at his gas gauge. He had just filled up. There was no question that he would outlast the Corvette moving ahead of him.

It was early A.M. on the turnpike through central Pennsylvania when the red Corvette turned into the Blue Mountain Service Plaza. A quarter of a mile behind, Sonny Houston and his son watched the car park next to the fast-food complex. At this early hour there were only a half dozen other vehicles in the parking area. When the driver got out and disappeared into the service building, Houston parked next to the Corvette.

"Come on, son. We'll get some coffee and doughnuts."

"Can I have some soda pop, Dad?"

"You can have whatever you want, son." After exiting the van, Sonny Houston opened a small awl on a Swiss Army knife, paused to feel the sharp point of the awl and then began to drag it along the side of the sports car, digging a groove in the glossy finish the entire length of the car.

The boy grinned at his father. "You fixed him good, Pops, didn't you?"

"Not quite yet, son, not quite yet. When a man shows you disrespect, it takes more than a little scratch in the paint to get even. You'll see," promised Houston as they walked inside.

The brawny Houston, who towered over his young son, surveyed the nearly empty facility and then headed for the rest room. Inside the bathroom, he bent over and looked under the line of stalls, finally spotting the white sneakers and blue trousers he had seen getting out of the sports car. "You wait right there by the door, boy, and let me know if anyone is coming."

Houston flung his bulky frame against the door of the occupied stall, which popped open in the face of the startled occupant. "Yep, you're the bastard that cut me off on the pike. You could have killed my little boy."

He looked down at Granger for a second, and then smashed his fist into Granger's face. Then he grabbed Granger's head and slammed it repeatedly into the wall behind him. Finally he let the groaning man slump to the floor. A puddle of blood quickly formed on the white tile. Turning away, Houston walked to his wide-eyed son, who still kept vigil near the door.

Young Tad Houston grinned at his father. "You really fixed him, didn't you, Pops?"

"He won't show us any more disrespect, son." They exited the men's room. He glanced around. An attendant behind the counter prepared food for the morning ahead. A couple of early customers sat, in the distance, engrossed in morning newspapers and their coffee. Houston walked over to a vending machine, fed in some quarters, and waited until two cans of soda clunked down into the chute below. "Let's get the hell out of here, son."

Tad Houston climbed inside the big four-wheeler and sat at attention next to his father. He didn't like to see his father this angry. Experience had taught him that it was best to be silent when his father was venting such rage. He glanced furtively down at the Corvette parked next to their vehicle. The ugly scar along the side now marred the sleek image of the fast car.

Tad thought of the groaning man they had left behind. He had glimpsed the puddle of blood spreading beneath the wall of the booth, and wondered how badly the man was hurt. "Sure thing, Pops, you fixed him real good."

"Shut up, boy!" Sonny Granger scowled menacingly at his young son. "You used them words a while back. What'd I tell you about rattling on and on and making a fool of yourself. I heard you the first time. Now shut up! Now put the whole thing out of your mind, boy. It never happened. And don't go tellin' your mama. Hear?"

Tad squirmed in his seat and managed to shake his head in assent. He resolved to put the whole thing out of his mind.

3

After ignoring the telephone for a dozen rings, Amanda Granger decided to pick it up, despite the fact that she was in a hurry to meet her committee at the country club for brunch. They were to make final plans today for the Ladies' Golf Outing. "Hello, this is Amanda."

"Would this be the residence of Jason Granger?"

"Yes, but he isn't in right now."

"Would you happen to be a member of his family? This is Officer Sandusky of the Pennsylvania State Police."

"Oh . . . I'm Jason's wife. Has something happened?"

"Mrs. Granger, first of all I want to say that Mr. Granger is probably going to be alright, but he has been taken to a hospital in Carlisle. Seems he was assaulted at a turnpike rest stop near Blue Mountain."

"Oh, my God!" Amanda paused, jolted by the unlikely news. "Are you sure you are talking about Jason?"

"Yes, ma'am. He was able to give us his name and showed us some identification. Then he passed out on us. The EMS boys thought it best to take him to Carlisle. He lost quite a bit of blood. They have a good hospital in Carlisle, ma'am."

"Who did this? Who assaulted Jason? Do you have anyone in custody?"

"No, Mrs. Granger, not yet. We're working on that. He was evidently assaulted in the rest room at the service plaza. We're questioning people there. So far, no luck. It was pretty empty at that time of morning. I'm anxious to talk to him about it as soon as he is able."

"Able? I can't believe this!" Amanda paused, trying to organize her thoughts. "Do you have a phone number for the hospital?"

"I sure do, ma'am. I'm sorry I have to give you the news this way." Officer Sandusky paused for a moment and then gave her the hospital telephone number. "By the way, Mrs. Granger, he carried a registration card in his wallet for a red Corvette. I take it that it is his automobile."

"Yes, he drives a red Corvette."

"We found the car at the plaza and towed it to the state police facility near Lewisville. We'll impound it in a security area there until you notify us when it can be picked up. I'll give you a number to use when you're ready to do that."

"Thank you, Officer. I'll talk to Jason and get back to you as soon as I can."

"That'll be fine, Mrs. Granger. Good luck. I hope you find him okay."

Amanda Granger hung up the phone, feeling very upset about the news. Jason had made the decision to drive to Columbus from Harrisburg for a business meeting only late yesterday evening. The weather forecast was perfect, and he had been itching to give his new Corvette a real road test. She had almost made the trip with him, but he had talked her out of it. On tap was her scheduled meeting at the club. Now she wished she had gone. Whatever happened might not have happened with her along.

Amanda began at once to alter her plans for the day. First she called the hospital number in Carlisle. Yes, Jason Granger was there. She was transferred to a nurses' station.

"Mrs. Granger, he is in intensive care at the moment. I'm sorry I can't connect you."

"Intensive care? My God, what's happened to Jason?"

"Just a moment, Mrs. Granger. I see the physician on duty. I believe he was here when Mr. Granger was admitted." There was a short wait as the nurse explained the phone call to someone.

"Hello, Mrs. Granger, this is Dr. Lavin. I'm afraid we can't disturb Mr. Granger right now. He has suffered some trauma but seems to be in stable condition right now. I suggest you make arrangements to come to the hospital, Mrs. Granger. . . ."

"I see. . . . I'm about twenty-five miles from Carlisle, I think. I'll be over there as quickly as possible."

"Perhaps that would be best, Mrs. Granger. Can you tell me a little about your husband? Is he on any medication for anything at all?"

"Oh, no. Jason is a health nut. He's a very fit person. He jogs every day and watches his diet. Frankly, I've never known him to have anything other than a common cold."

"Not taking any medication at all?" There was a pause before the doctor continued. "Hmm, that's very good. He's been moving and talking now and then. I think you being here might help him."

"I'm on my way, Doctor. Will you be around the hospital for a while?"

"Yes, at least for a couple of hours. If I must leave for some reason, he will be in good hands. By the way, Mrs. Granger, do the words 'git-go' sound familiar to you? When

Mr. Granger talks once in a while, he says something that sounds like 'git-go,' over and over again."

"My God, Doctor, it sounds like he is delirious."

"Well, I wouldn't put it quite like that. He is resting, Mrs. Granger."

"I'll be right there." Amanda Granger hung up the telephone. "Git-go?" she mused to herself. The simple expression had no meaning at all to her.

She called the country club and left word that she wouldn't be there for the meeting. She began to fuss with her long dark hair, then decided it wasn't important.

Within minutes she headed for her BMW in the driveway. " 'Git-go.' That's crazy," she spoke aloud as she shook her head. "Dear God, make Jason be okay when I get there." She was amazed at the spontaneous thought in view of last night's argument. The thought of Jason's anger over her condition still infuriated her. A restless night's sleep had done nothing to dampen her feelings.

Amanda Granger wheeled the black BMW onto the turnpike. She realized that the hospital was closer than she figured and decided she would arrive in fifteen or twenty minutes. She tried to imagine the energetic Jason lying in intensive care. It was hard to do. Jason, a bit over six feet tall, took pride in his athletic build and worked at keeping himself fit.

She had met Jason when he was a linebacker at Penn State, and soon found he had an intellect that matched his strong athletic abilities. Until recently, their short marriage had been a whirlwind of happiness and success. But his out-of-hand rejection of fatherhood jolted her and left an uneasy feeling that she could not shake. She had been sure he would be ecstatic.

"We're like two thoroughbreds," Jason had said long before they were married. "We'll have children as exceptional as we are. Think of it, we'll probably conceive a governor." Obviously he didn't feel that way now. Her pregnancy was, after all, his doing as much as hers. They had talked occasionally about having a family, and he had never seriously reminded her of the vague "five-year pact" they had once talked about.

Amanda frowned at her recollections of last night. She again tried to picture Jason, delirious, in intensive care. Beaten up? She tried to picture Jason in a fight—in a rest room along the turnpike, at that. It made no sense.

But then, Jason did have a temper. He controlled it well, even in his football days. If an opponent got the best of him on a play, he would grin, and never panic. He would systematically plot revenge that usually came much later in the game, revenge that more than once brought forth a stretcher for his tormentor. Yes, Jason always got even.

4

Blair Lawton paced the hotel room on the outskirts of Columbus, Ohio. It was almost noon. Jason should have been there long ago. In a half hour it would be time to leave for the meeting with the Harmony Mutual presentation. Jason's test sales program lay completed on the desk. She had worked late into the night organizing the final draft, making certain that all Jason's notes were incorporated into the presentation.

Jason's plan was unique. The test in the Columbus division of Harmony Mutual was to be a template for other divisions if it proved successful. Jason was regarded a genius. Of course it would be successful. They both expected that it would rocket him into top management, and big money. And, of course, she would follow him.

Blair fidgeted with the ribbon tie to her peignoir and let the flimsy garment drop to the floor. She glanced at the clock on her night table. There would be no time for their usual games. She felt uneasy, then angry. Punctuality was high on Jason's list of priorities.

She opened the drapes and eyed the parking lot below. Not a single red Corvette among the scores of cars. Blair turned and studied the clothes she had laid out for the meeting. Jason had selected them. She walked to the full-length mirror, picked up a brush and pulled it through her long blonde hair several times. She looked critically at her body. Jason had told her many times that every square inch of it was perfect. She smiled. Jason wasn't the only one who had told her that. Of course she worked at it, though on this day, she had missed her morning jog. Jason would be very critical about that if he knew. She decided that that would be one of the things she wouldn't tell him.

Now she was dressed. If they were to make the meeting on time, Jason would have to arrive at once. She sat on the edge of the bed and stared out over the parking lot. There was still no red Corvette.

She began to think about what to do. Hesitating for a moment, she decided to dial Jason's home in Harrisburg, steeling herself for an unwanted conversation with Amanda Granger. She breathed a sigh of relief when an answering machine responded to her call, decided not to leave a message and hung up.

Waiting until the last possible moment after dressing, Blair stowed the report in her oversized Coach bag and walked to the rental car in the hotel parking lot. Before leaving, she circled the lot, looking vainly for Jason's car.

A few minutes later she pulled into a VIP space at Harmony Mutual, carefully noting that Jason's red Corvette was not there either. She rode the elevator to the conference room floor and announced herself to the receptionist.

"Ah, there you are, Ms. Lawton. We've been expecting you. The conference has been canceled. I'll buzz Harvey James. He feels terrible about everything."

"Really!" Someone should have told me before I flew out, she thought. "Is Jason Granger here?"

About that time, Harvey James entered the reception area, looking very serious. "I'm sorry, Ms. Lawton, we have been trying to reach you." The regional manager looked strangely sober. Blair remembered a much more cordial Harvey James on previous visits. "It seems that Jason has had some sort of accident, or more correctly, suffered an assault at a way station in Pennsylvania."

"No! When?"

"Sometime early this morning, near a little town called Blue Mountain. He's in intensive care at a hospital in Carlisle. By the way, our home office has been trying to reach you."

Blair slumped into a chair in the reception area. "That's incredible! We finished our work in the office late yesterday evening. He opted to drive out in his new Corvette. I flew out . . . this morning." Blair told a little fib, and immediately wished she hadn't. She'd have to be more careful. "How badly is poor Jason injured?"

"I really don't know. Mrs. Granger is at the hospital in Carlisle now. We expect to hear from her or the home office soon." Harvey James studied the face of Granger's striking assistant. There had been some rather nasty rumors about the woman, but he had always chalked them up to the wishful thinking of several associates. The tall, willowy blonde was a hard-driving businesswoman. He knew from previous meetings that she possessed a mind far quicker than most. "Ms. Lawton, several of us are about to go to lunch. Please join us. I'll have any calls transferred to the restaurant."

"Thank you, Harvey, but I'd better get back as quickly as possible. Carlisle is just a short drive from Harrisburg. I'll catch a flight back. I won't rest until I know more about Jason. Amanda Granger must be devastated. Poor woman." Blair dabbed at the corner of her eye, hoping she had sounded sincere. The last person on earth she gave a damn about was Amanda Granger.

"I understand." James patted gently on her shoulder. "Perhaps everything will be alright. If you change your mind, let us know. We won't be leaving for a few minutes."

"Thanks, Harvey. If you talk to the office, tell them I'm on my way back."

Blair immediately got on an elevater and returned to the parking area downstairs. Inside the rental car, she stared at the clock on the dashboard. She pulled a cellular phone from her purse and called the airline. There was a plane leaving for Harrisburg within the hour. She made the decision to be on that plane.

As Blair drove to the Columbus airport, her thoughts turned to Jason, and then immediately to the red Corvette. Where was the Corvette now? Had it been in a accident? Harvey's report had been rather sketchy. An assault? Who would assault Jason? Had the Corvette been searched by the police? Her usual steely nerves failed her. Her fingers clenched and unclenched against the steering wheel as she sped faster toward the airport.

Jason was a damn fool this time, she thought. His childish obsession with the sleek Corvette defied good reasoning. Now she had no options. She had to get into the Corvette before anyone else. She sighed. Better for it to have crashed and burned than be subjected to a thorough search. Reaching the Corvette was a top priority.

Once on the plane, Blair called her office back in Harrisburg. She reached Kathy Taylor, an assistant who split her work between herself and Granger.

"He must be hurt pretty badly, Blair. Amanda Granger is at the hospital. She says Jason hasn't come around yet. Isn't it terrible?"

"Yes, it is. That poor woman must be going out of her mind. Look, Kathy, the day is about shot for me. I have a car at the airport. As soon as we land, I'll drive over to the hospital. I think Amanda needs some support." Blair startled herself with her feigned sincerity.

"Good idea! I'll tell everyone you'll keep us posted."

Blair hung up, hoping that Amanda would stay at the hospital until she arrived. Retrieving Jason's Corvette must be the farthest thing from Amanda's mind right now. Maybe she could help with that little problem.

5

Jason Granger moved his head ever so slightly and moaned. He opened his eyes for just a second, fearing the pain any further movement would cause. He caught a glimpse of Amanda in profile, sitting near the end of the bed reading something. He closed his eyes and wondered just where he was and what exactly had happened. Where was the Corvette?

He had awakened in the midst of a dream, a horrible recollection of disjointed thoughts. There was the face of a small boy, nose flattened against the window of an SUV trying to pass his Corvette. He was staring down at him, terrified, as they both approached the big orange construction crane. Then there was a screech of rubber as the big SUV pulled behind him. The license plate, GITGO 7, was framed inches away from his rear bumper in his side mirror for the longest time. Then the vehicle had slowly faded from view in the traffic behind him. Later, there was the man who must have been the driver, snarling at him in the men's room. And now here he was, obviously in a hospital.

He groaned again as he moved. It was hellishly painful to move.

"Jason, are you awake? Jason, dear, can you hear me?"

Sensing his movement, Amanda arose and walked over to him.

He steeled himself, not willing to face her just yet, not until he knew how much she knew.

"You are going to be alright, dear. You're in the hospital in Carlisle. You're going to be alright." She leaned over to kiss his cheek.

He let his eyes flicker open. Amanda's loving attention made it clear that she was her normal self. She was unaware of what was going on. "Amanda . . . damn, it hurts to talk."

"Then don't try. The doctor says you shouldn't do much at all for a few days. Get your rest, Jason." She kissed him again.

"I . . . guess I was mugged . . . robbed maybe." His effort ended with a wince of pain.

"Well, you must have fought him off, Jason. You still have your wallet and everything else, as far as I can figure. I'll bet whoever it was looks worse than you do." Amanda smiled. "Now you get your rest. I'm going to talk to Dr. Lavin."

"Amanda . . . where's my Corvette?" He tried to smile weakly.

"Aha! Now I know you're feeling better. Your new pride and joy has been impounded by the state police near Lewisville until I tell them what to do with it. Evidently it's okay." Amanda turned away from him, hearing someone enter the room. "Well, look who's here, Jason. Blair, so good to see you."

The two women embraced briefly, Jason Granger staring silently at the unexpected visitor.

"Thank you, Jason, for the airline miles I collected for the absolutely useless trip to Columbus. Harvey James sends greetings and says not to worry about a thing. The presentation can wait."

Jason closed his eyes and forced a weak smile.

Amanda eyed the vivacious Blair Lawton, dazzling in the

form-fitting business suit. She wasn't aware that Jason was to meet her in Columbus. "Thanks for coming by, Blair. You can tell everyone in the office that Jason will be back in the saddle in a few days."

"Is there anything I can do, Amanda? Anything at all?"

"I don't know what it would be."

"How about the new Corvette? I heard you guys talking about it when I came in the room. It's only about thirty minutes away. If you drop me off there, I'll bring it back, if you can get it released. It would be a shame to have that new beauty towed. I'll park it right outside his window here. It will be a morale booster for Jason and will be one minor problem all taken care of. How about that?"

"Did you hear that, Jason?" asked Amanda.

He opened his eyes and nodded his assent. "Good idea," he mouthed.

The short trip to Lewisville found the two women gabbing a lot, mostly about Jason. Amanda decided that she liked her. She could sense that businesswise, Blair was very sharp, and no doubt she had her own ambitions. Amanda had always felt just a wee bit jealous of her, but that ebbed now. After all, if there was anything between Blair and Jason, would they have traveled together? It was certainly nice of her to offer to pick up the Corvette. She no doubt had other ways to spend her time. Before they reached Lewisville, Amanda decided to consider Blair Lawton a friend, at least for the moment.

A patrolman took them to a small chain-link compound to the rear of the state police headquarters. The red Corvette gleamed inside, parked among several other vehicles. "These are mostly DUI impounds," explained the patrolman. "We get our share along the pike."

Amanda took the keys and handed them to Blair Lawton. Blair was gaping at the red Corvette. "Oh, my, look at this." She ran her finger along the scratch that ran from the rear to the front of the otherwise-gleaming new sports car. She tried to buff it away with the flesh of a finger, but the fresh scratch would need much more attention than that. "That's too bad, but it could be worse."

"It was that way when we found it, according to the report here." The patrolman was studying the paperwork.

Amanda shrugged. "Nothing we can do about that. Jason will have a little problem to take his mind off his troubles." She turned to say good-bye to Blair. "Thanks a million, Blair. Now I know why Jason says so many good things about you. You've been so helpful."

"We gotta get Jason back on the job, Amanda. Poor guy. Let's keep in touch," Blair replied, sounding as if she truly meant it.

She watched Amanda's car as it proceeded toward the next exit of the turnpike so she could make a U-turn back toward Harrisburg. Then Blair climbed into the red Corvette, turned the key in the ignition, slumped back into the bucket seat and listened to the purr of the engine. "Warm it up 'til the tach drops down to a normal idle." She remembered Jason's words when he first let her get behind the wheel. She pulled slowly away from the fenced compound and drove to a vacant area near the on-ramp for the turnpike.

Glancing about to make sure that she was absolutely alone, Blair opened the console next to her and carefully lifted out all the contents. She then tugged at the shell that lined the compartment of the console, slipping it completely out. Jason hadn't bothered to resecure it with the screws.

Peering into the opening, she first lifted out several small videotape cassettes and slipped them into her purse, breathing a sigh of relief that they were still there. Then she reached down and to the rear of the dark compartment and withdrew a soft leather case about four inches wide and seven inches long. Its flap was held secure by a by a row of snaps.

Her curiosity couldn't be contained. She had to have

another peek. Carefully, she slid her finger under the snaps and opened the broad flap. Several layers of felt were crisscrossed over the contents. Blair folded them back one by one to reveal six separate compartments, each brimful with various assorted delights. Jason's little drugstore was still intact. Blair fondled the small cocaine packets and then fought off the urge to celebrate her good luck. Such celebration would be much nicer with Jason. She wondered what the tiny orange capsules were. It looked like Jason's last trip to New York had brought back a surprise.

Blair put the leather case into her large purse alongside the videotapes and then dropped the liner of the console back into place. She followed the turnpike to the nearby off-ramp, crossed an overpass and then reentered to head back toward Carlisle. She checked her side mirror carefully and then tromped heavily on the gas pedal, watching the speedometer soar quickly over the hundred mile-an-hour mark, then immediately eased up until the needle crawled back to seventy. What a kick! No wonder Jason was in love with the Corvette.

A gleaming white Cadillac inched alongside her. The driver gaped boldly at Blair at the wheel of the flashy car, then gave her a quick thumbs-up signal of approval. She tromped heavily on the pedal and roared ahead, slowing down only when he was a speck in her rearview mirror. She had an aversion for old fools puffing fat cigars.

Her thoughts went to Jason, so obviously struggling with his pain back in the hospital, and she decided to visit him when she dropped off the car. It still wasn't clear to her what exactly had happened. The whole incident seemed bizarre and out of character.

Blair circled the Corvette slowly around the parking lot of the hospital. Feeling confident that Amanda's car was not there she pulled the Corvette into an open space that would be visible from Jason's window.

Entering his room a few moments later, she was surprised to see that Jason had been elevated to an almost sitting position and that he appeared to be wide awake. "Jason, what a wonderful surprise! You look almost normal." She smiled. "That is, you look about as normal as it is possible for you to get."

"They gave me some new stuff for my aching head. Whatever it is has me in another world. How's the Corvette?"

"Just fine, Jason," she beamed. "Everything is just ducky."

Jason sighed. "That's a relief. I worried that the cops would get a little nosy."

Blair nodded. "We learned a little lesson, didn't we, Jason? Remember the lecture you once gave me about being cautious? Maybe it's time for me to give you the same speech."

"I read you, Blair. By the way, how did you get along with Amanda?"

"Famously. I think she really loves you, Jason. She's more than a little worried about what happened to you. I hope you have some kind of a rational explanation for it."

"I'll give it some thought."

"Are you going to tell me?"

"Of course. It's all a little foggy in my mind right now. Give me a little time."

Blair smiled broadly. "Well, Jason, I have something on my mind that is not the least bit foggy or difficult to understand." She sat on the edge of his bed, bent low over his face and kissed him. "We, you and me," she touched the tip of his nose for emphasis. "We are going to have a baby!"

Jason stared blankly off into space behind her. He groaned a little and held his head for several seconds before speaking. "My cup runneth over."

"Jason! What a nice thing to say."

He shrugged, again gazing into space beyond Blair, then smiled weakly. "Some people have all the luck."

Blair hugged him, not knowing whether to attribute his lack of enthusiasm to the lie she had just told him or to his pain. "Don't worry, honey. Everything will work out just fine," she said. She rose from the bed. "Jason, you need your rest. I'll be back soon." Blair walked from his room as he closed his eyes.

Yeah, he thought to himself. Everything will be just fine. How did she come to that conclusion? His carefully planned life was quickly becoming a shambles. He pressed his call button to ask for a painkiller, wanting desperately to sleep, hoping this was all a nightmare.

6

Tad Houston watched as Eddie Foxworth grasped his hands above the knot in the rope. The look on his freckled face was filled with determination as he stepped backward away from Dagget's Pond, until the frayed rope was as taut as it could be. Taking a deep breath, he ran toward the pond as fast as he could and hurtled himself over the pond, letting go when his forward motion stopped. Eddie plummeted into the pond with a big yelp and a splash. He disappeared under the water for a moment and then came up flailing his arms and spitting water. "Oh! It's so cold! Did I make a record?" He gasped for breath and then swam to the edge of the pond.

Tad Houston shook his head decisively at his friend. "Nah, you didn't even come close. I've gone lots farther than that!"

"Oh, sure! You're just saying that. Let's see you prove it."

Eddie climbed up on the bank of the pond and sat next to Tad on a fallen trunk. "You can't even climb a tree without getting your arm busted."

Tad looked at the heavy cast on his right arm and then stared, misty-eyed, across the pond. A small creek wound its way from the lip of the pond to the Delaware River about a half mile away. He had lied to Eddie. He had told him he had fallen from a tall white pine he had climbed on his uncle's farm. "I got this crazy old cast on my arm. The doc says if it gets wet, it will get soft and my arm won't heal. I have to leave it on for maybe a whole month."

"Is it heavy?"

"Yeah. Dumb thing I did, wasn't it?" Tad dropped his arm and let it thump against the log.

"Well, I'm going to jump one more time. Now watch, I'm gonna go for a record." This time he let go at just the right time and splashed down a few feet from the far bank.

"Wow!" Tad said admiringly. "I'll give you a record for that."

"Pretty good, huh? I thought I was going to hit the rocks on the other side for a minute."

"Well, it wasn't that good. I'll beat it when my arm gets well." Tad got up from the log, and looked at the sun, now low in the west behind a stand of pine. "I got to get home. Pops will be mad as the devil if I'm not on time for supper."

"Shucks, that's no big deal. So you just eat cold supper."

"Not at my house. At my house you'd go right to bed without your supper. That's the way they do in the army, you know."

"Really? Was your dad in the army?"

"Yep. He crossed over the enemy lines once and shot a lot of guys, and got back without a single scratch. That's why we follow the army rules around our house."

Eddie stared at his friend. He had asked his own father once whether he was ever in the service. He had said that he was lucky enough to be just the right age and grow up between the wars. He felt glad for a moment. "Well, we don't have any army rules around our house."

"That's alright. Sometimes I wish we didn't, to tell the truth." Tad frowned and then looked away from his friend. He hopped off the log and started running up the winding path through the woods toward the farm where he lived, Eddie tagging along behind.

Reaching a paved country road, the two boys split off in opposite directions toward their separate houses. Eddie turned around and called out. "Hey, Tad, I'm sorry you fell out of that dumb old tree!"

Tad turned and waved the heavy cast toward his chum and then started walking slowly to the old farmhouse just ahead. He wondered what Eddie would think if he told him there was no dumb old tree. On the way to the doctor, Pops had told him to tell the doctor the story about falling from a tree. He remembered that he was still in pain then, and he promised to do as he was told. His mother was not to be told the real story, either.

It was all Eddie's fault anyway. He and Eddie had been sitting on the porch. Eddie was bragging about his dad catching all these shad down on the Delaware. Eddie was always bragging about his dad doing this and that. So he had told him the story of Pops getting dissed on the turnpike and then ripping the big scratch on the Corvette just to get even.

His heart jumped as he looked ahead to their farmhouse. Pops's truck was in the driveway. He hoped dinner wasn't on the table yet. Tad started to run.

It had just been a week to the day since Pops suddenly loomed behind him as he was telling Eddie the story of the scratch on the Corvette.

"Tad's telling little lies lately, Eddie. Are you teaching him to do that?" He had startled them both. Eddie had jumped up and lit out for home.

Pops took him immediately to the barn and began slapping him around. Pops wound up and cuffed him real hard on the side of his head, causing him to trip backward over a wagon tongue. His arm cracked audibly as it struck the top of a milk can. Pops jerked him to his feet and smacked him one more time before he noticed the arm.

"Now look what you've done, Boy. You've made a damn fool of yourself." Tad stopped just before entering the house. He remembered every word clearly. He had to go without dinner that night, even after they got home from the doctor.

He remembered Mother bringing him cookies and milk late that night after Pops fell asleep. He repeated to her the lie he and Pops had concocted about him falling out of a tree.

Tad was amazed that his mother believed him. After all, the barn was close to the house and there was all that screaming and yelling. He remembered seeing the glass of milk shake in his mother's hands, and saw her glance nervously at the bedroom door. Then he realized that she was as afraid of Pops as he was.

Despite the milk and cookies, he stayed wide awake for most of the night. The awkward cast made it difficult to be comfortable. Once, after having fallen asleep for only a short time, he was startled awake by his recurring dream. He was standing in the door of the rest room of the turnpike rest stop. There was the loud grunting and smacking of his father's fist as it pounded on the driver of the red Corvette. Then he saw the man's head as it hit the floor beneath the stall, and watched the spot of red blood grow larger on the white tile.

He jumped to a sitting position in bed and sat tensely, wondering if he had made any noise. Jeepers, he thought to himself, he hoped Pops would never hit him like that. Then he was reminded by the heavy cast that Pops had indeed hit him just like he had smacked the man. Breathing hard, he realized that it was just a matter of time until Pops would hit him again, because Pops made so many rules, and he just couldn't remember them all.

It was early in the morning and he still had not fallen asleep again. He closed his eyes tightly and refused to open them for the longest time, but still no sleep came. Thoughts of the repetitive dream always came back.

7

Dr. Uriah Wilson was a little more than Amanda Granger's gynecologist. He was a family friend and a frequent golf partner of Jason's at Quaker Ridge Country Club. That is why she felt impelled to bring the news of Jason's tragedy at Blue Mountain to the doctor's attention. He had listened intently to her story and promised to call Jason at Carlisle Hospital, and also to make some inquiry about his condition from colleagues he knew there.

Now he was sitting across from her at his office desk poring over notes on a pad in front of him. Her first examination since he had diagnosed her pregnancy had just been completed. He looked away from his notes, rubbed his short beard thoughtfully and then fixed his gray eyes upon her and began to speak. "Amanda, everything appears perfectly fine." He broke into a slight smile. "Your blood pressure is a trifle high, but nothing to be concerned about right now. We'll keep our eye on it. As near as we can tell, you are still a full seven months away from delivery. There is still time for plenty of golf and exercise. Perhaps you should try to make the most of that."

Dr. Wilson focused his eyes on her, waiting for a response. She seemed oddly quiet, far from the bubbling enthusiasm she exhibited when first informed of her pregnancy.

"I have a question." She hesitated, staring over his head at a wall filled with pictures of his family and several framed diplomas. "I want to ask you a hypothetical question. At least it is hypothetical at this moment."

"What is it, Amanda? Hypothetical questions are the easiest kind to answer because they are not real. Fire away."

"What if I decided . . ." She hesitated and looked away from him, struggling for the words. "What if I decided to terminate the pregnancy?"

"Amanda! I am a little shocked. Are you seriously considering doing that?"

"I . . . I don't really know. I feel confused right now, and won't know for a while. But I intend to discuss it again with Jason."

The doctor narrowed his eyes and looked across the top of his glasses at her. "Discuss it with him again? Amanda, you are in perfect health. Nothing could look any better than it does for the moment. I recommend that you think about a step like that very carefully."

"But what if I did? How long . . ." Her voice faltered as she turned again to avoid his gaze.

"If you make that decision, it is best done as soon as possible. The thought pains me, but I would recommend you to a specialist in that sort of thing, someone who has a perfect track record." Now it was the doctor's turn to be at a loss for words. Right now he wished she and Jason were not such close friends. "I made a decision long ago, Amanda, not to perform that procedure unless it were an absolute emergency."

"I understand." She forced a smile. "For the time being, we'll keep the question a hypothetical one."

"Good girl, Amanda. I like to here that." He slid his chair back and stood up, now avoiding her eyes. "Amanda," he began slowly, "I am here to talk to, you know. If there is anything to discuss you know it would be confidential."

"Thanks. I know and appreciate that. Let's just forget about it for now, okay?"

He walked her to the door, shook hands warmly,

and closed the door behind her. He stood quietly looking out the window. He felt startled and shaken by her question. Perhaps she was bothered by some anxiety she did not want to share with him at the moment. He considered people like Amanda Granger and Jason among the most solid and dependable he knew. Perhaps the matter would come up with Jason, as soon as he put his present troubles behind him. Strange, he thought to himself, that a man like Jason would have a fight with someone.

Outside, Amanda sat, teary-eyed, in her car. It was stupid of her to bring up abortion with Uriah Wilson. What must he think of her? Damn Jason! She was the one who was pregnant. She wanted the baby. There was no good reason not to have it. She tightened her grip on the wheel with her left hand and turned on the ignition. Maybe Jason would change his mind. The beating he had taken might have affected his outlook about everything. Perhaps when he felt better, his attitude would change. But it was a fact that throughout their marriage, once Jason ventured an opinion, he almost always stuck to it.

Amanda glanced at the clock on the dashboard and decided there was still time to visit Jason in the hospital before going to the club for dinner with friends. Perhaps the news that she was doing so well would please him if he was in a better mood.

She immediately spotted the red Corvette in the parking lot where Blair must have left it. As near as she could tell, it was parked right outside of Jason's window. That was thoughtful of Blair. Perhaps that would raise Jason's spirits.

Inside the hospital, she made her way quickly to Jason's room. The door was only slightly ajar. She entered quietly without knocking, not wanting to disturb him if he were asleep. The privacy curtain was drawn partly around his bed, obstructing the view from the door. She tiptoed in and gently swung the curtain back.

Blair Lawton sat in a chair near the head of the bed. Her body was twisted so that her torso was bent low over Jason, their faces almost touching. Blair turned her head and looked at her blankly for just an instant, and then broke into a broad smile. "Jason! Look who's here, it's your darling Amanda."

Jason's eyelids fluttered open and he raised his hand and waved weakly. "Hi, doll, what a great surprise."

"Well, at least you got a greeting. That's more that I could get out of him." Blair sat straight up in her chair. If she was one whit nervous about Amanda's sudden appearance, she hid it well. She pointed to a file folder lying on the bed. "I brought him some stuff from work to look at, just in case he was feeling up to it, but I think our boy is still feeling pretty rocky."

Amanda slid back the privacy curtain and walked over and kissed Jason quickly on the forehead. "Are you feeling better, Jason?" She couldn't rid herself of the feeling that she was an interloper, that she had interrupted something.

Jason shook his head. "I'm a lot better, Amanda. In fact, I may be getting out of here in a couple of days." He winced as he turned his head. "I still get these beastly headaches from time to time. But I am much better." He extended a hand toward her over the covers.

She decided to ignore it. "Well, you look better," Amanda insisted as she glanced out the window. "I see Blair parked your new jewel right where you could see it. Good work, Blair. That should get him on his feet." She fought off her little spasm of jealousy and beamed at her husband's assistant.

Blair responded by getting out of her chair and preparing to leave. "Amanda, I'll leave you two guys together. At least you're getting some conversation out of him. I'll leave the folder here, Jason, just in case you get bored." With that said, she picked up a small purse and walked out of the room, blowing a kiss their way as she left. The too-short dark knit skirt neatly molded her buns as she walked down the hall.

"She does wear clothes well, doesn't she, Jason?"

"I suppose so, but not as well as you."

"That's nice of you to say, Jason, even if it isn't true." She gave him a rather tepid smile as she sat down in the vacated chair, pushing it back slightly from the bed. Her instinct kept her from duplicating Blair's closeness. "I had an interesting conversation with Uriah Wilson, who says I'm fit as a fiddle and doing very nicely at two months." She watched his face closely, trying to read his real feelings.

"That's good, Amanda. You've always been a healthy one." It was said matter-of-factly, without expression. He could have been talking about Chowder, their dalmatian, after a visit to the vet.

She leaned forward just a little. "I do have another little bit of news from Dr. Wilson. He seems to have some sort of a hang-up. He doesn't do abortions." She studied his face, waiting for a flicker of some kind of emotion. "The poor fellow seemed shocked. I'm sure he's disappointed in us, Jason."

"That's too damn bad. He gets paid to do what he does, not for meddling in his patients' lives." He stared out the window, eyes on the Corvette. He wondered if the cocaine and videotapes were still hidden under the console, or whether Blair had removed them. He rubbed his forehead. Had Blair told him, and had he forgotten?

"Don't become so hostile, Jason. He offered to find a competent colleague if we made that decision."

"If? I seem to recall us making that decision." Jason continued to stare blankly out the window.

"Jason, I have a lot of problems going through with it." She lied: "Besides, the doctor said that I had some time to consider it."

"Problems with it? It's a very simple procedure. It's done every day, all day, everywhere."

"Damn it, I'm not worried about the procedure. I'm

worried about the stupidity of it." She faced him, but he kept his eyes out the window as tears welled in her own eyes. She dabbed at them futilely. Tears kept coming. "Jason, I want this baby. It would be so wonderful."

Jason remained stone-faced but shook his aching head slowly from side to side. He closed his eyes and remained silent.

Amanda's tears ebbed as her anger grew. "You're the one who was plunging into sex repeatedly lately, knowing neither of us were using protection. I guess I thought you had changed your mind." Amanda again dabbed at her eyes. "Of course, having a baby might keep me away from the country club. It would certainly keep me off the golf course now and then. For God's sake, Jason. We're young. We're not poor. Now is the right time."

"Do me a favor, will you, Amanda? Trust me. There will be a better time, in just a few years." He shrugged and turned away from her. "This is giving me a headache. Do you mind if we talk about something else?"

"I'll tell you what, Jason. I'd rather not talk about anything then. I hope you feel better tomorrow. Good night, Jason." With that she quickly strode out of the room.

Jason sighed heavily as he swung his legs over the side of the bed and then stretched his arms. Why, he wondered to himself, had everything turned so sour in his life. He had trouble getting a civil word out of anyone. It all started with that stupid encounter he had on the turnpike. Blair pregnant, too? What in the hell was going on? Everything was rosy just a few days ago.

He pictured the small boy with his nose mashed against the window, looking positively petrified. Then came the memory again of the SUV tailgating the Corvette, and its peculiar license plate, GITGO 7.

He looked at his wristwatch. Gary Steven, the security chief of Quaker Ridge Country Club, should have called back by now. Jason put through a call.

"Mr. Granger, I just got the information a few minutes ago. By the way, how you feelin'?

"Just fine, Gary. So what did you find out?"

"I told the police what you said to tell them, Mr. Granger. I told him that this vehicle had parked several times in a space that was assigned to a member, and I wanted to know who it was."

"So what did you find out?" He was impatient. The man was always so long-winded about things.

"I got the complete dope. Got a pencil handy, Mr. Granger?"

"Yes, yes. So what did you find out?"

"The vehicle is registered to a guy named Sonny Houston. He resides at a rural address near Milford, Pennsylvania. Here it is."

The man labored through the address several times as Granger wrote the information on the back of the file folder that Blair had left with him. "Gary, do you have any idea where Milford, Pennsylvania is?"

"Funny you should ask, Mr. Granger, because I just happened to look it up in the road atlas. Sometimes it pays to be curious, you know. It's in the far eastern part of Pennsylvania, up near Port Jervis, where the three states come together. It's pretty country, Mr. Granger. I used to spend some time up there."

"Thanks, Gary. I'll tell the boys at the club that you do good work."

"I'm at your service, Mr. Granger. You want that I should go on with the investigation?"

"Absolutely not, Gary. I can pick it up from here. It's a small matter. I'll probably drop the guy a letter. I would appreciate it if you would keep our little investigation between just you and me. Understand?"

"Gotcha! Mum's the word. I hope you get well real fast, Mr. Granger."

Jason hung up before the man could launch into some other matter.

He looked at the address he had written on the folder and then smiled for the first time since he had been in the hospital. Soon, Mr. Sonny Houston was going to come to a lot of grief. And he would never know the reason why.

8

Tad Houston sat at the breakfast table eating the scrambled eggs and sausage that his mother had fixed for breakfast. Pops had insisted that she serve extra-size portions because they would not be stopping for lunch. This suited him just fine. It was one of his favorite breakfasts.

He looked out the kitchen window at his father strapping the new Coleman flatback canoe to the top of his van. Recent rains had caused the water to rise in the Delaware, and the gentle rapids a few miles south of them would be a good test for the craft.

He looked at the heavy cast lying in his lap. It was still another ten days before the doctor would remove it. "Mom, don't worry about us. The arm is okay. I can feel it now. I even use it all the time. The dumb old cast just gets in the way. I'll be just fine. That's what Pops said."

His mother looked skeptically at the awkward cast. She had argued uselessly with Sonny when he insisted that Tad go with him on the canoe's test run.

"Don't make a little momma's boy out of Tad," he had told her. "It's high time he quit babying himself over the arm and started doing some chores around here. The arm's just fine. He and Eddie even went fishing yesterday."

"Sitting on a bank, waiting for a cork to bobble isn't the same as canoeing in the rapids, Sonny," she had replied.

"That's nonsense!" he had roared. "I saw him tossing a

ball with it the other day. You want him to grow up like a little sissy boy? Not in my house, Elizabeth!"

Whenever he called her Elizabeth, that was a signal that the conversation was over. He had made a decision and that was the end of it. She stood behind Tad and rubbed her fingers through the boy's crew cut. "Just be careful, son, promise?"

"Sure, Mom! Don't worry. I can handle a canoe. It's easy."

Sonny Houston entered the kitchen just as Tad was downing the last of his breakfast. "Come on, boy, let's get going. We're wastin' time now." He pointed his finger at his wife. "Now remember, Bessie, pick us up in the pickup down river below the bend at Bushkill at three o'clock. We have chores to do around here before dark. You got that straight?"

"I'll be there, Sonny. Just you be careful."

The two of them walked outside in the dim light of the early morning as she watched from the kitchen window. Sonny tested the tension on the lines holding the canoe one more time, and the two then climbed into the powerful 4×4. Within seconds they were out of sight around a bend of the road and headed for the Delaware.

Sonny Houston stopped to fill up the gas tank at the country store. While Sonny tended to that, Tad ran inside, told Mr. Lester to fill the coffee thermos and bought a half-dozen doughnuts, just as his dad had instructed.

Back inside the SUV, he put the thermos in the holder on the dashboard and dipped his hand in the sack to withdraw a chocolate-covered doughnut. About that time his father let out a long string of curse words from somewhere behind the SUV. Tad froze before he could take a bite from the doughnut. When his father ran a string of bad words together like that, real loud, it meant he was really mad.

"Tad! Get your butt out here. Now!" he roared. Trembling, the ten-year-old opened the door and stepped down from the van.

Sonny Houston was down on his knees near the rear of the van on the driver's side. He was running his finger along the highly polished deep green finish of the van. "Come here, boy. Look at this."

Tad gaped, wide-eyed, at the side of the SUV. A long thin streak was gouged in the paint all the way from the headlight in front to the taillight in the rear. Low on the driver's side door a large *X* had also been gouged deep into the finish. Tad was speechless as his mind went back to that other day about three weeks ago when his father had put a similar mark on the red Corvette. Finally words came. "Jeez, Pops! Who did that?"

Sonny glared at his son. "Now I wonder," he said in a whisper. He looked up to see if anyone could overhear. "We both know the answer to that, don't we, son. We both know all about scratches, don't we? Where's that new pocketknife, boy?" Sonny's hand shot out and slapped the chocolate doughnut from Tad's hand. His father immediately stepped on it with his heavy boot.

Tad tensed up, fighting to make words come. "It's in my tackle box, I guess, Pops. I keep it in there all the time, just like you said."

His father glanced toward the window of the country store. Mr. Lester was looking their way, probably wondering what was going on. Sonny Houston bounced to his feet from his crouch, still glaring at Tad. "You get in the van and fetch it. Right now! You wait inside the van for me. I'm going inside to settle the bill with Mr. Lester. When I get back, we're going to have long talk, boy."

Tad choked up and ran to the SUV. He climbed in back and found the shiny new combination knife and fish scaler right where he had put it. He moved into the front seat and sat quietly, holding the knife in his hand.

Sonny Houston soon climbed behind the wheel, started the engine and then turned to stare at Tad. He reached over and snatched the shiny new knife from his son. He studied it carefully for a moment and then opened the blade. Tad watched as he scrutinzed the sharp tip. "Whatcha been cuttin' on with your new knife, boy?"

"Eddie and I were cutting on some willow sticks down by the pond," he said truthfully. "That's the only time I ever used it."

"You lie, boy. You been diggin' at paint. I'll just have to keep this." Sonny snapped the blade closed and stowed the knife in his jacket pocket.

"Pops, I didn't . . ." Whap! came the slap of the back of his father's hand across his face. Tad buried his face in his arms and cowered against the door. The tires squealed as the SUV lurched forward and out into the road. Tad was hoping at least that his father would turn toward home, but he didn't. When he looked up they were headed for the rapids on the Delaware.

They had driven for about fifteen minutes before his father spoke. "I don't want you lying any more, Tad. Bessie and I didn't raise you to be a liar. I think you better stop hanging around with Eddie. Your mother and me come from fine stock, but I don't know about Eddie. Is he the one that's teaching you to be a little liar?"

Tad, afraid to speak, shrugged his shoulders and shook his head negatively.

"What's the matter? Cat got your tongue? When a man asks a question, a real man snaps right back with the answer." Sonny glanced at him, affecting a friendly smile. "Your mother and I are raising you to be a real man, not some fool to go digging around on things with a pocketknife."

"Pops, I didn't do it," declared Tad, then flinching, waiting for another slap that didn't come. He turned cautiously to face the same forced, friendly smile from his father.

"Let's bury the hatchet for now, son." Sonny reached over and rubbed his tousled hair. "That's what men do, boy. They bury the hatchet and go on. We'll talk about it some other time."

Within a half hour Sonny Houston pulled the SUV into

a grove of trees alongside a wide bend in the Delaware River. Two other vehicles were parked nearby. It was a popular spot for early morning fishermen. Sonny got out of the car and began to untie the lines holding the canoe in its rack. Tad stood watching, awaiting instructions from his father.

Sonny stepped back suddenly when his eye again spotted the long streak on the side of the SUV. Once again he stooped and stared at the vandalism, deep in thought. He had driven to Port Jervis late yesterday evening. He had never been away from the van for more than a few minutes. He had seen no one come near it and was sure that if it were done the day before, he would have spotted it when he had gotten home.

He shook his head and stared soberly at Tad a few seconds before speaking. "Okay, son, I'm going to ease the canoe off the roof of the van. I just want you to steady it until I get under it, so I can carry it over by the river."

It looked easy enough. The river bank was less than fifty feet away. Nevertheless, Tad felt himself grow very tense. He father was unusually quiet and would glance from time to time at the scratch on the SUV. He knew that he was still thinking about the scratch and he would hear more about it when they were alone on the river. "A jerk. That's what he was, Pops. Whoever scratched our van was sure a jerk, Pops."

"There you go again, boy. I told you we'd talk about it later. A bunch of new lies don't cover up the first one." Sonny grinned his phony smile at Tad.

"Aw, Pops . . ." he stammered. "I didn't do it. I swear it!" He swiped his good hand across his cheek trying to stop the tears from rolling down his face. He glanced back at the road through the trees and wished he could go home.

"Now, son, that cryin' isn't very manly. What you gonna do when we get around the bend on the white water. You gonna start cryin'?" His father shook his head, feigning disgust. Then he turned away, positioned himself under the center of the canoe and hoisted it above his shoulders.

Quickly, he moved it to the water's edge and lowered it until the canoe was partway in the water on a shallow shoal. "Okay, son, start bringing the supplies over and stow them aboard like I taught you."

Tad ran back to the van and fetched the two knapsacks, stowed them in the canoe and then returned for the paddles and the coffee thermos. His dad positioned the canoe further out in the water so that all they would have to do would be to give it a gentle shove. "One more trip, Pops. I'll get the fishing rods and the tackle box."

"You won't be needin' your rod, son. You been lying too much lately. Just bring my rod, and stow yours back in the van."

"Aw, Pops! Shucks, I want to go fishin', too. Mom said—"

Whap! The sharp slap across his face from his father knocked him on his back into the canoe. The heavy cast on his arm thumped heavily against the wooden seat. "You mind your tongue, boy. I've had enough lyin' and back talk for the day." He glared at Tad, still on his back in the canoe, then shook his finger at him. "Now you mind what you are told. You stay right there and wait 'til I get back. I'll get my rod and lock up the van."

Tad struggled to a sitting position in the bottom of the canoe and watched his dad walk back toward the SUV. He glanced at the road when a car passed through the trees, and longed again to be home. He closed his eyes, rubbed at his arm around the cast and wondered if the blow had re-injured it.

As he opened his eyes again, he felt a gentle movement. He then realized that he was a full twenty feet from shore and starting to drift rapidly in the current away from the shoal.

Tad froze, fearing the wrath of his father if he were to cry out. Then he shouted in desperation. "Pops! Pops! I can't stop it! Help! Help me, Pops." Now he was caught in the swift current. He grasped a paddle and tried to rudder his way toward the shore. But his grip did not hold and the paddle fell in the water. He now scooted faster toward the rapids.

Then he heard his father yell and saw him run from the van and splash into the shallow waters of the shoal. Quickly, he disappeared as he stepped into the deep water. Tad saw his father's arms flailing as he came up and then watched as he swam back toward the shoal. Now the canoe was several hundred feet away, scudding rapidly on the water toward the rapids around the bend.

Miraculously the canoe raced through the first short stretch of white water without capsizing. He could see the water boiling downstream. Using all his strength, Tad worked his way onto a seat. He tried to steer with the remaining paddle so that at least he would not go broadside into the rapids ahead.

By luck, or miracle, he again managed to clear a hundred yards of white water. The canoe skimmed along the New Jersey shore of the Delaware and then slowed as the width of the river broadened.

Tad knew that the worst of the white water was ahead. The canoe slowed as it was driven behind a sandbar. Slowly but surely, he could see, he would again drift into the open current. Try as he might, he didn't have the strength to drive the canoe up on the sandbar.

He watched, helpless, as their new canoe drifted around the tip of the shoal and then began racing toward the boiling rapids ahead. He looked around him. There had been several bends in the river since he had drifted away. He reasoned that his father would have no way of knowing where to look for him. He saw dense forest across the river on the Pennsylvania side. The shore road had evidently moved inland for a stretch, as it often did in the rugged terrain.

He stretched his arms. To his surprise, the soggy cast

slipped off. He looked at the arm. It felt okay, but it was strangely white and thin. He again grasped the paddle and tried his best to guide the canoe away from the white water ahead.

Now he could actually hear the thunderous roar of the rapids. The canoe met them head-on and then breached as it struck one of the boulders near the shore. Tad plunged into the water and struggled desperately to hang onto the tossing canoe. Just before the calm water appeared ahead of him as the river again broadened, his hold on the canoe with the weakened arm gave way and he watched helplessly as the craft moved further and further way.

"Pops! Pops!" He screamed, but quickly stopped as he realized he was totally alone in the swirling cold water of the rapids.

Sonny Houston drove slowly down the shore road. Whenever the road neared the river, he got out of the van and explored the shoreline. The boy had done a damn fool thing. He was convinced that Tad had purposely tried to get away from him.

Finally, there it was! He spotted the canoe drifting slowly into a narrow backwater. It was empty! He watched as the current pinned the canoe against the shoreline.

Sonny Houston splashed through the shallow waters of a narrow cove and finally stood next to the canoe. One of the knapsacks that he had lashed under a seat was still there. Everything else was gone.

He looked back up the river. It was fully five miles from the point where they had put the canoe in the water. It figured that Tad was somewhere out there. "Damn fool kid!" He cursed aloud as he dragged the canoe high and dry.

He looked out over the water. It was a lot rougher than he had figured it to be. No wonder the kid didn't make it. He sat down on a log near the shoreline. He had to figure out something to tell Bessie. He shook his head.

He muttered to himself. "Stupid kid!" He would convince Bessie that the kid had turned from God's ways a long time ago.

9

The bar at the country club was crowded with hangers-on from the luncheon where an announcement had been made to Jason's peers about his promotion to vice president. On the morning after his release from the hospital, CEO Dillon Archibald had surprised him with the luncheon.

Jason made his way to a phone booth, anxious to break the news to Blair. She picked up the phone on the first ring. "Blair, I have some big news." As Jason spoke he realized that he hadn't yet told Amanda about his promotion to the corporate headquarters in New York. But then, Blair was part of the new structure. She should logically be told first. He'd get to Amanda later.

"Yes, Jason, you're keeping me in suspense. Are you still on the line?"

"Of course. I'm just thinking that a telephone call doesn't do this justice. How about dinner tonight? I'm thinking about the Olde Pitt House, about seven."

"You devil! You are keeping me in suspense. You're going to ply me with drinks and spring your news on me then, right?"

"Blair, my big news is also your big news. Keep that in mind. Not quite what we anticipated, but close." Jason stopped talking, remembering that Blair had advised him not to trust the office phones.

"Of course I'll meet you, Jason. I'll bring along some

papers for you to sign. Where have you been all afternoon? Everyone has been looking for you."

"It can't be anyone who matters. I've been with the New York boys out at the club. Just a little game of golf. Talk to you later."

Jason hung up abruptly. He stared out across the eighteenth green, just outside the clubhouse from where he used the telephone. The New York contingent was still gabbing in the bar. Reluctantly he dialed his home number. After several rings, the answering machine greeted him. He breathed a sigh of relief. He really didn't want to go all through the details with Amanda yet. He almost hung up, but decided to leave a short message. "Hi, Amanda. It's me. The New York boys are a pain in the ass. They're still hanging around. It looks like dinner, so don't wait up. Bye, now."

After hanging up, it suddenly occurred to him that there was no sweet sentiment, no affection voiced in the short message. It further occurred to him that it was that way all the time now with Amanda. He'd no doubt hear about that later.

The Olde Pitt House was a hideaway in the wooded hills about twenty miles south of Harrisburg. The quaint old restaurant was located in a fieldstone building dating back to Revolutionary War times. It had a special significance for him and Blair. He had taken her there after an office Christmas party almost two years ago. His striking new assistant was intelligent, bold and blatantly provocative.

"I don't know much about this business," she had admitted openly. "But you are going to teach me. You're the fair-haired boy around here, you know."

He had tried to laugh it off. "I guess that makes my wife the fair-haired girl."

"Yes, but that's another life. She can't help you with Harmony Mutual. Besides, I'm going to be right by your side a hell of a lot more often than she is." Driving through the countryside he recalled how she had first nestled close and touched his leg as she spoke. "Besides, a man like you needs a sounding board, someone to trust. Someone to slice through the office politics and take care of every little need. I'm very good, Jason."

She was good. So good that they had wound up at a motel along the Pennsylvania Turnpike that night.

It was pitch dark before Jason pulled the Corvette into the parking area surrounding the Olde Pitt House. Spotting Blair's white Mercedes, he slipped into the open space next to it. Blair hadn't waited for him before entering the restaurant. In fact, she almost never did.

Inside, he found her sitting at the dimly lit, oak-planked bar in conversation with a ruggedly handsome gentleman many years her senior. She seemed to be doing all the talking. When Jason sat down next to her, she patted his leg in greeting without even looking his way. He wondered how she was sure it was him.

"And that is why I think he would make a very poor governor," Blair said, and then turned toward him. "Jason, Clyde here breeds trotting horses and votes Democratic."

Jason extended his hand to the man. "Nice meeting you. I must say that trotting horses have always mystified me, as have most Democrats."

The man smiled faintly, obviously not thrilled by Jason's sally at humor. "Well it's long past time for me to go, young man. I'll leave you here with your remarkable young lady." He waved gently at them, got off his bar stool and walked toward the door, exchanging parting pleasantries with the bartender.

Jason brushed a kiss along Blair's cheek in greeting. "I'm sorry if I interrupted anything. You seemed to have the old fellow mesmerized."

"Jason, please, not here." Blair drew away, glanced

around the room, then whispered. "Kissing in public is a no-no. Believe me, I'm yours Jason, to kiss any place you want to, but not in public. Sitting here at the bar is a little like being onstage. We've got too much at stake. Agreed?"

"Agreed. It is a small world, I suppose."

"Yes it is. Do you know, for instance, that our trotting-horse man plays golf at the club?"

"No kidding? I surely don't recognize him. How do you know that?"

"Jason, men tell me about anything. He told me. You might check the membership list for Clyde somebody. I'll bet you'll find him."

"Let's get a table. I've got exciting news." The hostess led them to a remote table in a quiet alcove, conveniently furnishing almost total privacy. They were able to sit at right angles to each other. "We can at least rub knees in complete obscurity. Or is that a no-no also?" Jason paused. "I've been promoted."

Blair stared at him, her cobalt blue eyes looking larger than ever. "So, when do we move to Manhattan?"

"I'm leaving in about two weeks. I figure to bring you in the home office in about six months. I'm going in as vice president. They're dumping Chris Cannon. That's a secret."

Blair glanced around to make certain they were no longer onstage, leaned toward him and planted a kiss fully on his mouth, sending her tongue exploring for just an instant. Then she spoke. "No good, Jason. It can't happen that way. I must go when you go. There's no way they bring me in later when it's obvious to the world that I'm pregnant. The good old boys back there would never let it happen."

"But in six months . . . I'll be in charge," Jason insisted.

"Jason, stop it! I won't hear of it. You can swing it now, Darling. Just fire somebody." Blair stroked his cheek and kissed him again. "Do you think I could honestly bear to stay away six months? It can't happen, Jason. I think you need a little refresher course in Blair Lawton." She brushed his ear softly with her tongue.

"I'll see what I can do," Jason murmured under his breath.

"I guess you don't understand, Jason. Take it as a promise. I'm leaving for New York when you go."

"You're being unreasonable, Blair."

Blair patted his cheek affectionately. "I know you'll work it out. By the way, I have a surprise for you later on."

"Later on?"

"Yes, I'll spring it on you when we get to the motel."

"Really. I didn't know we were going to a motel."

"Jason, I want to start with our videotapes. I promise you a fun night, Jason."

"What about Amanda. She expects me."

"You forgot one thing, Jason. Amanda doesn't exist in my world. I don't give a damn about Amanda. Remember? You'll have to handle her, Jason."

Jason sighed heavily, amazed at the erotic intensity Blair radiated. Actually handling Amanda was hardly a problem. She didn't seem to give a damn anymore. "Okay, you win. I'll find a way. Did you bring along the white stuff?"

"Yes, it's all yours, doll. It's off my list of vices until we have our kid. I knew you'd see things my way, Jason." Blair paused to gently caress the nape of his neck. "Don't worry yourself to a frazzle. I don't want a VP title right off the bat. Just something with a desk close to yours. Oh, Jason, it's going to be fabulous."

Blair opened her purse, produced a tiny Ziploc bag filled with white powder and slid it across the table. "It's play time 'til tomorrow, baby. Have a little appetizer." Blair began to study the menu. "As for me, while you're doing that, I think I'll start with the escargot."

"Order me a dozen blue points. I'm going to use the phone, if you don't mind. Amanda expects me. I'd better tell her I'll be very late."

"Suit yourself, darling. I'll order the appetizers and ask for a wine list."

Jason made his way through the candlelit dining room to the hostess podium and inquired about a telephone.

"Local call, sir? If it is, just use this." The woman smiled warmly and produced a telephone from within the podium.

As he dialed the number, he prayed that Amanda would not pick up. But she did. "Hi, honey. It looks like a late night with the New York gang. It turns out they want to go out to dinner and nail down a ballpark budget for next year. They just don't know when to stop." Jason paused, waiting for her reaction. There was none. "Sorry, honey. Don't wait up."

"I'll be fine, Jason, just fine. Thanks for letting me know." She then hung up abruptly.

"Bitch!" he muttered under his breath. He stared across the dining room to where he could barely make out Blair sitting in the dark alcove. His hand slipped into his side jacket pocket and fingered the plastic bag filled with cocaine. Then he smiled and made his way to the men's room.

Amanda stared at the telephone number she had scribbled down from the caller ID screen. It wasn't Jason's office and it wasn't the club. The number was totally unknown to her. From whatever phone Jason had called from, there had been no background noise. If they were going to have dinner after their golf game, why wouldn't they have it there at the country club? Her hand shook as she dialed the strange number.

"Hello, the Olde Pitt House. May I help you?"

The Olde Pitt House. Amanda was stunned. She hadn't been there with Jason in years. "Where is your location please? I have a reservation there tomorrow, but I can't quite place where it is."

"We're east of Harrisburg on 641, near Mechanicsburg. May I check your reservation?"

Amanda declined and hung up after rejecting the idea of asking for Jason. Why in the world would he take the home-office brass to the Olde Pitt House? The obscure little inn was hardly a logical place. She recalled the several times she and Jason had been there. It was quiet, candlelit, very romantic and unbusinesslike. She glanced at her watch. She had nothing to do. Why not take a little drive?

Within an hour, she had pulled into the parking area next to the Olde Pitt House. There was the red Corvette. But the car parked next to it was the one that most interested her. It was Blair Lawton's white Mercedes. There were only a half dozen other cars in the area. She parked on the other side of the one furthest from Blair's car. Amanda turned off the lights and waited . . . and waited.

Fully an hour passed before Jason and Blair came out the door. The two paused in the center of the parking lot to clinch affectionately. Jason's hand slid up her nylons to cup her derriere as they kissed. Jason spun her around and around as he danced her to the Corvette. They clinched again for several minutes.

Amanda watched spellbound and trembling as Blair tried to push her way across the console into Jason's lap inside the small car. Finally their two torsos merged and then became one for several minutes. Then came the sound of the ignition, and the lights flashed through the woods. When Jason backed the car up, Amanda held her breath. He very nearly backed into her. Then came the sound of acceleration and the spray of gravel from the spinning tires. The Corvette disappeared into the night.

Momentarily, she toyed with the idea of following them. The thought of doing that over the strange narrow roads at night frightened her. But she had seen all she wanted to see.

She pulled up next to Blair's Mercedes for a moment and noticed that the window was rolled down. Amanda, unable to resist, glanced back toward the quiet inn and then peered inside the open window. She was amazed to see the keys still in the ignition. She reached inside the car and pulled them from the ignition. With all the fury of the anger she felt, she flung the keys into the dense woods beyond the parking lot.

Amanda drove slowly back to their home. Tears came frequently as her rage refused to ebb. She knew for sure now that she would have her baby, and in the morning she would start planning her future with the child, her child.

10

Sergeant Evan Knight stood behind his desk in his Pennsylvania State Police station. It was located near the rain-swollen Delaware River. He began to pace slowly back and forth, finally pausing to scrutinize again the couple who sat in the two chairs across from him. The couple had just told him a chilling story.

"Now, Mr. Houston, your son, Tad, disappeared about nine o'clock this morning from a canoe on the Delaware. It's almost four P.M. Am I to understand that no other authorities have been notified until now?" The officer waited for an answer, watching the woman now clinging to her husband's arm, her face showing her pain and anguish, staring in the distance outside the window.

"I tried to tell the boy to keep away from the canoe, until we got the supplies stowed. Bessie here can tell you that the boy had a willful streak. Sometimes he just wouldn't listen."

Bessie Houston turned from her stare and frowned at her husband. "Tad is a good boy. He is kind of like all boys, but he is a good boy." She fixed her attention on Sergeant Knight. "The boy was out there with a broken arm." She wrung her hands and became misty-eyed.

"Folks, I want to help you as much as I can." He eyed Bessie, sensing that the woman was very much on edge.

Then he addressed Sonny Houston. "Now let me get the picture as clear as you know it. The boy went adrift on the river early this morning and you have not reported this to anyone until now. Is that right, Mr. Houston?"

"I drove and walked the shoreline for a lot of miles before I found the canoe washed up on a shoal. That took a long time. I figured my boy was somewhere on the river. He needed help, sir. I wasn't about to stop looking." Houston paused, obviously irked at the repetitive question. "You ever lost a son, Mr. Policeman? Let me tell you, your mind ain't on anything else."

Bessie Houston wailed in her anguish. "Sonny, don't say that! Don't say Tad is lost. He'll be home. Oh, God! Sonny, tell me he'll be home!"

Sonny Houston tried to put his arms around her in a move to comfort her. Bessie squirmed away from him. "Don't you do that. The boy has a broken arm. I didn't want you to take him to the river."

Sergeant Knight watched the squabbling between the couple, still wondering why they had waited so long to report the missing boy. "If you people don't mind, I've got to get a search party together. We don't have much daylight left. Mr. Houston, if only you had contacted us this morning we would have had a hundred men searching along the river in a matter of a few minutes." The sergeant's eyes switched to Bessie Houston, who was now weeping openly. He touched her shoulder. "Ma'am, we're going to do everything we can to find your boy. The way I figure it, if the canoe survived, it is possible that your son did also."

"Now, look here, Officer, I scoured a hell of a lot of that river. The Delaware is out of its banks, pushing up through the woods. The narrows have white water like I've never seen before. How can you figure little Tad is still alive?"

The policeman gaped at the boy's father, amazed at the negative run of words in front of the distraught mother.

"Mrs. Houston, I would like for you to stay in the office here with Officer Amy Clark." He nodded toward a policewoman who had just entered the room.

"Mr. Houston, I see that the New Jersey police are outside now. I want you to come with me into the next room. They are joining some of our boys around a map of the Delaware bottoms. I would like you to point out exactly where you last saw the boy and where you found the canoe."

Sonny Houston stood silent, watching the flurry of activity in the police station, as the New Jersey State Police entered the building. Reluctantly he began to follow the group into the next room. "Why the New Jersey Police, Sergeant?"

"The Delaware has two sides, Mr. Houston, and there are a lot of shallows here and there. That boy could be safe and sound. We've got to make every effort to try to find him."

Houston shrugged. "I've done been down that river." Shaking his head, he watched the policewoman walk into another small office with Bessie, and then followed the group into a room where a dozen men were staring at a large map of the valley pinned to the bulletin board.

Sergeant Knight studied the boy's father carefully. By his actions and attitude, he seemed to have given up on the possibility of finding his son. Of course, if the man were to be believed, it had been a long day and he had every right to be weary and despondent. Still, to remain silent and not ask for help for seven hours? Evan reasoned that the father was in shock, or not very bright. Otherwise his behavior certainly didn't match the gravity of the situation.

Sonny Houston studied the map for several minutes. "Right at this spot," he said, pointing to a bend in the river, "is where the canoe got away with Tad in it." He traced the water's edge for several miles before his finger stopped. "And right here is where I found the canoe, trapped in the reeds on a shallow bank."

One of the New Jersey troopers walked over to the map

and scanned the area pointed out by Sonny Houston. He shook his head and speculated aloud. "That's about the worst stretch of the river this time of year. It's over flood stage the entire way." Obviously perplexed, he turned to face Sonny Houston. "What the devil were you doing out there in water like that, Mr. Houston?"

Houston shrugged again and didn't answer. He watched silently as the group swung into action. Calls went out to fire departments and local police along the river to organize search teams and plans to walk the entire shoreline. Until pitch dark, it was agreed that several flat-bottomed shad boats would work their way down river, staying in communication with the men on shore.

Sergeant Evan Knight walked to the window where Sonny Houston was staring listlessly at the search parties being organized outside. "I know most of these men. They are fine men, sir. They'll bust their butts to find your boy."

Houston just nodded, not saying a word.

The sergeant walked outside to join the others, unable to rid himself of the feeling that Sonny Houston knew more about the disappearance of his son than he had told them. He certainly didn't act like a bereaved man. Knight made a decision to assign one of his men to to keep tabs on Houston for a while. If the boy weren't found alive soon, he would make a point of questioning the couple separately. The odds of the boy surviving looked pretty slim.

11

The simple round clock on the wall told Amanda Granger that it was five minutes before ten. The old Western Union clock was yellowed and mounted slightly askew, obviously a relic from some other time and place. The rest of the small reception area was clean and furnished with spartan simplicity. There were four straight-backed wooden chairs and a large wooden desk clean of clutter. A rather sophisticated telephone and a long yellow legal pad were all that sat on the surface.

A young woman sat at a keyboard staring into a computer monitor. Upon Amanda's entrance to the room she had flashed a brief smile and kept at the word processing until she had finished her thought. Now she turned to face her and produced another warm smile. "Good morning. I'll bet you're Amanda Granger."

"You've got that right. I guess I'm a few minutes early." There was something about the receptionist that made Amanda feel very much at ease. "I love your blouse. It's just perfect."

"Well, thank you! I can't say it's my choice. Mr. Hanson's much better half gave it to me for my birthday. She's a jewel."

"How nice! How long have you worked for Willy Hanson?"

"Only a few months. Actually, I don't work very hard. He and Coley Doctor insist on doing everything themselves. I have to pry work out of them." The receptionist smiled again and turned again toward the computer screen.

Amanda thought otherwise. The young woman had an aura of warmth and intelligence that would not tolerate idleness. She would bet that she carried her load.

The door to the inner office opened abruptly. A broad-shouldered man emerged, trim for someone who appeared to be in his mid-forties. He was well over six feet tall. Blondish hair was invaded by flecks of gray. He looked straight at Amanda with blue eyes that held her own without blinking.

"You've got to be Amanda Granger. I'm Willy Hanson." He grasped Amanda's extended hand firmly. "I'd appreciate it if we get right to it, Mrs. Granger. We're all a little pressed for time around here this morning. Why don't you come right on in." He turned toward the receptionist. "Penny, I'd like you to bring your handy little notepad and join us. Coley will be late this morning. I'd like him to get a full report on our meeting with Mrs. Granger."

Willy Hanson led them into a small office similarly furnished with bare necessities. The only decorative flourish was a massive poster on the wall featuring two basketball players intensely fighting under the basket. There were identical large oak desks at opposite ends of the room, which slanted to face the door. Two leather-upholstered chairs faced each desk.

Amanda Granger sat in one of the leather chairs and swept her eyes around the sterile room. The lack of decorative touches surprised her in view of the two private investigators' high-profile reputation.

"Mrs. Granger, if you don't mind, what led you to seek our help?" Willy Hanson eyed the woman carefully. She was attractive—in fact, almost flawless. She was dressed in a tailored suit that had cost her a lot of money. Her eyes engaged his own squarely, evincing some intelligence to go along with her beauty.

"The Manhattan phone book. I recognized your name in the Manhattan phone book. I remembered reading about you in the papers, Mr. Hanson. I closely followed the case where you and your partner pursued a serial killer all the way to Hong Kong. The weekly news magazines also carried the story. I'm an avid reader, Mr. Hanson. That is why the listings under private investigators jumped right out from all the others in the phone book. In fact, I didn't recognize any of the others." She smiled a gentle smile.

"Coley Doctor and I have to be very selective with the cases we take on, Mrs. Granger. We're busier than we should be." Willy leaned back in his chair, clasping his hands behind his head. The woman's dark brown eyes remained fixed on his own. "Tell me a little bit about your problem. If we can't help you right now, I'll steer you to someone who can. Fair enough?

Amanda leaned forward. "Mr. Hanson, I want a divorce. I want to nail my husband in the act of adultery. I want to take him for everything he's got."

Willy broke his eye contact with her. He hadn't expected her candid intensity right off the bat. "Everything he's got," echoed Willy, thinking immediately that he had another messy divorce case if he wanted it. It was Coley Doctor's specialty, not his. "That is a lot easier said than done, Mrs. Granger. Adultery is not the big rigamarole that it used to be. Also, we're pretty expensive. How much has he got?" Willy decided to try scare her off.

"Enough, Mr. Hanson. Enough for you, and enough for me and my child."

She had hit a soft spot. "I didn't realize there was a child involved. How old is the kid, and where is the child right now?"

"He's right here." The woman patted her abdomen. "We are at minus seven months and counting." For the first time Amanda Granger let a tear slip down her cheek from the corner of her eye.

"Really." Willy, taken aback, whispered the word, and then sat for a moment in thought. "Mrs. Granger, in view of the child and what having a father might mean in the future, have you exhausted going the route of outside counseling? If not, perhaps I can help locate such a person."

The woman was now dabbing at the corners of her eyes, trying to stem the tears. "Jason will not hear of it. He's in the midst of a big career move right now and insists that we have the child aborted. In fact, the more we talk about it the more insistent he becomes." Amanda paused. A fleeting image of Jason embracing Blair Lawton in the Corvette crossed her mind, as it did many times each day. "Anyway, I'm quite sure I don't love my husband anymore."

"Do you live here in Manhattan?" Willy asked softly. He felt sorry for the woman. She was quite a dish. It always amazed him that such women frequently had husbands who looked over the fence and saw greener pastures.

"No. We live in Harrisburg right now. We're here looking for an apartment. Jason has been promoted to a vice president's position at Harmony Mutual." Her voice wavered. "Oh, Mr. Hanson. It could have been such a happy time. But it isn't. I want out. There will be no changing my mind, Mr. Hanson."

Willy decided the woman said it like she meant it. "Okay, Mrs. Granger, tell me something about Jason's philandering. Penny here will record your statement if you don't mind, so that we can play it back for Coley Doctor. This is more his specialty than mine."

They both watched Penny until she cued them that the recorder was ready to go. Amanda first told them about the surveillance of Jason and Blair she had done at the Olde Pitt House in the parking lot, relating the whole story. She told them about the conversations in which Jason was insistent about an abortion. She brought up Jason's run-in at the turnpike rest stop and his subsequent hospitalization, adding the tidbit that Jason and Blair Lawton were cheek to cheek when she surprised them at the hospital.

Willy questioned her further after she had finished and decided as he did so that Coley would probably want the case if she was willing to pay the fee.

"Mrs. Granger, where are you staying in Manhattan?"

"At the Waldorf. Jason is with me. At this moment, he doesn't suspect that I really intend to go this far. No matter what, I am returning to Harrisburg tomorrow. I have no intention of joining his search for an apartment."

"You obviously have to call me, Mrs. Granger. Call me at three this afternoon. If Coley and I decide we can help you, I'll let you know then. Coley will no doubt want to confer with you before you go back to Harrisburg."

The woman stood and thanked Willy profusely. "Please help me, Mr. Hanson."

"I'll try. By the way, please call me Willy. Coley and I are pretty informal. We enjoy being on a first-name basis with the people we are trying to help."

Willy watched as Penny showed Amanda to the door. The woman was a real looker. He wondered about Jason. What would his side of the story be. No question that his interest was piqued. Besides, the woman was able to pay for a few simple days of investigation. It was right up Coley's alley.

"I admire that woman," Penny volunteered when she returned to his office.

"Why?" Willy asked, eager for another opinion.

"For being so determined to have the baby. The guy can pay, and he should, until it hurts."

"Oh, really? There are two sides to every story, Kiddo. Amanda there may well be perfect. But the fact seems to be that as dazzling as she is, this Blair babe has won the big battle for her husband, whether he really wants that or not."

12

"How did it get there?" Sergeant Knight asked the question all the others in the search party were thinking. He read the name of TAD HOUSTON aloud to the group. The identification label on the knapsack was encased in plastic but had still gotten wet. However, the name of TAD HOUSTON was quite readable.

The search party stood in a narrow ravine leading away from the Delaware on the New Jersey side of the river. The knapsack lay on the ground, clearly visible from the flat-bottomed shad boat at the water's edge. The knapsack was fully three feet above the apparent high-water mark, clearly identifiable by the moist tree trunks and vegetation laid flat by the rampaging river.

"Somebody had to take it out of the canoe and put it there," Sergeant Knight observed. "This gives us reason to hope that the boy is still alive. Get on the horn and pass word back to headquarters. The Houstons should be informed." Evan thought of the disconsolate Bessie Houston as he spoke. There was reason to hope now.

After making certain the shad boat was well secured to a tree, the search party began to work its way east up the ravine. It was slow going. Sergeant Knight called back to the officer holding the radio. "Tell them to bring the search parties just north and south of here to this area. We'll all fan out and conduct a search until we reach the road. Tell them to hurry. We're about to lose all daylight."

Knight loosened the tie that held the flap down on the knapsack. Inside were several articles of clothing, a Met's baseball cap, and a big combination knife and fish scaler in what looked to be a new leather sheath. There were a couple of cereal bars and several chocolate bars. None of the items inside were wet. Why, he thought to himself, if the boy were alive, why would he abandon the knapsack?

He studied the wooded cove carefully. Perhaps the canoe had drifted into the cove and the boy had come ashore with the knapsack and placed it high and dry. Evan frowned at his next thought. Maybe the kid went back to the canoe, boarded it and somehow drifted again into the swift current. He decided to keep that thought to himself. The dry knapsack gave them the only cause for hope they had. South of here the river narrowed and the rapids became much more treacherous.

Two more boats carrying a dozen men soon pulled into the small cove. From a map of the area, Sergeant Knight estimated it was about a mile to a road paralleling the river. The group formed a line with about fifty feet between each person and reached the road in less than an hour. There had been no sign of the boy anywhere. The road was frequently traveled. He could have hitched a ride from here.

But did the boy even know there was a road beyond the dense woods? And why would he leave the knapsack behind? Evan Knight had the search party fan out again and work their way back to the shad boats. When they were almost there, one trooper, working near Knight, bent over and picked up a cereal bar wrapper. "Hey, Evan," he called excitedly. "This is the same kind we found in the knapsack."

The full contingent zeroed in on the area where the wrapper was found, but their search, conducted well into the darkness, found nothing else.

"We can't give up," Evan told the others. "I've talked to headquarters. None of the other search parties have found a damn thing. We'll rework the area with some dogs, as soon as we can get them here."

Evan rang up headquarters again and asked to talk to Sonny Houston. He was told that he had taken Bessie home to catch some sleep. Strange man, he thought to himself. If it were his own kid that was missing, he would damn well be tramping the woods with the search party.

13

Tad scrambled up the embankment topped by bustling Interstate 80. Big semis and their heavy loads rolled by in a steady stream. One emitted a deafening honk on an air horn, causing Tad to freeze as he climbed over the iron guardrail. He decided to walk eastward along he highway, staying outside the guardrail, away from the steady stream of traffic.

Tad rubbed at the mosquito bites and scratches from the

brambles on his legs. He had slept most of the night in an empty barn. At least he thought it to be empty until he was awakened by movement of a young heifer staring him in the face about sunrise.

He had walked though the dense bottomland all the way from where the canoe had gotten away from him, except for one ride he had hitched with a Jersey farmer. The man was nice enough but had asked too many questions, so he sneaked away when the farmer made a gas stop. Besides, he wasn't going in the right direction to get Tad to Aunt Sarah's house. Now he was all mixed up. Finding Aunt Sarah might take a long time. More important, he was hungry. The few apples and tomatoes he had filched along the way tasted nothing like Mom's pancakes and syrup.

He reached into his pocket and pulled out a five dollar bill and two ones still damp from the river. So he did have some money to spend when he found a diner.

The iron guardrail ended abruptly as the shoulder of the road fanned out to a broad area where tractor trailers were lined up with drivers snoozing in their cabs.

"Hey, kid! Where ya headed?"

Tad looked up to see the unshaven face staring at him from the cab of one of the rigs.

"No place," Tad stammered. "Just taking a little walk."

"You off one of the rigs?"

"Yeah, my pops is back there." Tad waved toward the long line behind him as he lied.

"Well, you better hustle on back there. No kid of mine would be roaming along the road. Now you get on back to your rig!"

Tad stopped walking for a second and then burst ahead in a run. He had no intention of moving toward Pennsylvania. He turned once to see the man still staring at him from his cab, but he just kept on going.

Soon he came to an exit ramp off the busy highway. He plodded wearily up an overpass to the connecting road and then walked northward over the highway. He figured Aunt

Sarah's house was just a few miles from the Delaware and he reckoned that he was not far away. Of course it had been a long time since Bessie had driven him there once on a Sunday outing when Pops had gone away alone for a day.

Aunt Sarah was real friendly. She had taken them to visit some friends and then into downtown Morristown and bought him a new pair of jeans. Aunt Sarah had a way of laughing at just about everything. She only got serious when she talked to his mom about Pops. He could remember her saying once, "I swear, Bessie, I don't know how you live with my brother. You must be a saint. He and his military ways! I'd be telling him where to get off."

His mother always defended Pops. "I could have done a lot worse, Sarah. He comes home every night and there is always enough to get us through the hard times. He's put up with a lot, you know." Tad had no idea of what she meant by that, but he had heard her say it a number of times.

Tad walked rapidly down the blacktop road, bursting into a run once in a while, buoyed by the friendly image of Aunt Sarah in his mind and the thought that he would see her soon. So preoccupied was he that he didn't hear the bakery truck approaching behind him until it had slowed down next to him.

"Hey, kid! You lost or something? Hop in, I'll give you a lift." The man looked friendly. He smiled broadly at Tad from under a cap that proclaimed that he worked for BEST BAKERY IN THE WORLD in big letters above the visor.

Tad instinctively backed off a few feet as he continued to walk along the road. He could smell the aroma of fresh bread coming from the truck and remembered seeing the truck many times in the past.

"Come on, boy. Get in here. Look what I've got." The driver lifted a big cinnamon bun from the seat beside him, the kind with raisins and thick white icing.

It was too tempting for the hungry Tad to ignore. He

climbed in and sat beside the driver, taking a firm grip on the sticky bun.

"Where you headed, pal?" The driver eyed him several times as they picked up speed.

Tad stopped in the midst of a bite to answer, "Morristown."

"Morristown! Say, boy, you are lost! But lucky for you I'll get there later this morning. Just stick with me, kid."

"Really! You going to Morristown? My aunt lives there."

"Just relax, son. We'll have you there soon. Have another cinnamon bun." The driver looked at the small boy as he rubbed at the bites and scratches on his legs. Maybe, he thought, it would be best to turn him into the police. He was a long way from Morristown. And he didn't know whether to believe the boy or not. He was obviously exhausted. He fell off into sleep soon after finishing the second pastry. The warm van no doubt felt very good to him.

When Tad woke up, the driver was not in the truck. Out the window he could see that they were parked in a supermarket parking lot. He could see the driver pushing a hand truck toward the store.

Down the block a group of people were standing on the platform of a small train station. Then he remembered that Mom had once taken him to Aunt Sarah's on a train from Port Jervis. The sound of a commuter train came from somewhere up the track.

Tad glanced toward the market. The bakery man had disappeared inside. Tad opened the door, then stepped down from the truck and started running as fast as he could toward the station. He arrived just in time to follow the last commuter onto the train, and heard the door slide shut behind him.

He stood on the platform between the two cars for a long time and watched the trees and fields flash by the window. The door slid open to the passenger compartment and a man dressed in a black uniform and shiny visor peered down at him.

"Son, it's against the rules to ride between the cars. You get yourself inside there." The conductor reached down and grasped his hand and led him into the passenger compartment. "Where's your ticket, young man?"

Tad couldn't muster a thing to say and only shrugged, looking past the conductor into the crowded train. He was trapped.

"Where you going, young fellow?" The conductor eyed him carefully, noting the torn jeans and the generally unkempt appearance of the boy.

"Morristown, sir," That's where I'm goin', Morristown."

The conductor scowled at him. "Morristown? Young man, you can't get there from here. You come with me, lad." The conductor took him by the hand and led him down the aisle to the end of the car where he made him sit on a seat next to him. "What's your name, boy?"

"Eddie, Eddie Foxworth," he lied, giving him the name of his best friend.

"Well, now, that's a fine name." The conductor scrutinized the boy. "Where'd you get on my train, boy?"

"When you stopped, just a while back. I just thought it would be fun to take a ride."

"Fun? What about your mom and dad. What would they think about you sneaking a ride on my train?"

"Mom wouldn't care. Pops wouldn't like it at all." His voice trailed off as his eyes lowered to the floor. "Pops was in the army once. He went to war, won it and then came home."

"Sounds like he's a good man. Betcha he'd be mighty upset about you riding my train without a ticket." He studied the boy who was still staring at the floor. "When we get to Hoboken, Son, we'll call your folks. They'll be mighty glad to hear from you. Okay?"

"Yes, sir. Where's Hoboken?"

"It's the final stop, son. Can't go no further without running right into the Hudson River. Now you just sit there quietly. I'll do my job and when all the passengers are off the train we'll go to the stationmaster's office."

Tad watched as the conductor worked on some papers, which he pulled from a big leather briefcase on the seat next to him.

"Hoboken! Last stop, Hoboken!" A voice came over the intercom as the train slowed perceptively until it finally stopped. The conductor rose from his seat and disappeared through the door that led between the cars.

Seeing his chance, Tad bolted from the seat, walked rapidly back through the car and became a part of the crowd that surged out of the train onto the platform. In the station he followed the mob of people down a crowded staircase.

Ahead of him people were lined up at a turnstile, beyond which he could see another train. When his turn came, he quickly ducked under the turnstile and ran ahead and joined a throng of people entering another train. Jammed among standees, he heard the doors close, and within seconds the train sped ahead into a long tunnel.

After several stops, most of the people had left the train. He waited until the last person had gone from the car and then got off. He climbed what seemed to be an almost endless flight of stairs and finally emerged on a crowded city street and walked with the crowd for several blocks. He paused for a moment and looked skyward. There, only a short distance away, was the Empire State Building. The tall spire had been pointed out to him many times. He was in New York City! The sign on the corner told him that he was at Broadway and Thirty-fourth Street. Tears began to clog his eyes. How would he ever find Aunt Sarah now?

14

Coley Doctor kicked his feet up on the oak desk, leaned back in his chair and listened to the tape recorder while he sipped tenatively at the blazing hot coffee. He closed his eyes and tried to visualize Amanda Granger as Willy had described her to him. The woman on the tape sounded sure of herself and quite a bit more vindictive than most women who came to him in those circumstances.

He liked it that way. She sounded like a woman who had made up her mind. There were no pangs of speculation about whether or not she was doing the right thing. Amanda Granger wanted to dump the bastard.

Coley stood up and stretched his long arms. Doing so allowed the six foot seven, black private investigator to touch the low ceiling of their office easily. He fidgeted with his belt and scowled downward. He prided himself on maintaining the fitness of his elongated body, keeping it close to the fine edge he sported back in his All-American basketball days. The trace of tightness in his beltline would not be helped by the idle hours to be spent slouching around in cars and tediously waiting and watching for another errant husband to hang himself.

The relationship between private eyes Coley Doctor and Willy Hanson dated back a half dozen years. Coley, black, ghetto-born NBA reject, and Willy Hanson, early retired Manhattan CEO, were about as different as two business partners could possibly be.

Coley was at home amid the roar of the big cities, places like New York, L.A. and Miami. Willy lived each day as fast as he could to return to his home on the yacht *Tashtego*, now moored in Weehawken across the Hudson. Living with longtime friend Ginny Dubois, who skippered the *Tashtego*, he would have much preferred a life probing far-away places via endless sailing adventures.

The fame of the two men grew when they were successful in solving several cases that grabbed headlines nationwide. What started as an effort to merely assist a few friends with their problems wound up as a money-making investigative team much in demand.

Coley decided to tell Willy that he would like to take the Amanda Granger case. The strong resolution of the woman to get the job done, apparently at any cost, should enable him to move quickly. The case was not without its interesting points. Why would a man who seemingly had everything want a beautiful mate to abort a first child? It was his experience that, usually, suburban commuter dudes prided themselves on having their woman periodically pregnant and immersed in the politics of the local school board and the usual snooty country club.

The last few words of Amanda's tape filled the small office as Willy Hanson entered the room. He stood quietly at his desk listening to the recording with Coley until its conclusion, visualizing the striking woman he had seen utter the words. "So what do we do, Coley? Is life so dull that we should treat ourselves to another messy divorce case?"

Coley stared at his partner. He had thought many times that Willy was generations removed from his proper niche. If there was a Camelot, he should have lived in those days. His penchant for the pursuit of noble and low-paying causes had pushed them to the brink of disaster several times. But so far truth, justice and the American way had always triumphed. His admiration for his partner had no end, but just once in a while he wished Willy would be more receptive to making an obviously fast buck from people who could afford to pay. "Let's go for it, Willy. If the guy is so far off base as she claims, we should be able to wrap it up in a few days."

Willy nodded without enthusiasm. "Coley, I really didn't expect you to turn down this damsel in distress. I am sure the fact that our new client could easily pose for the cover of *Elle* had no bearing on your recommendation."

"Willy, I've become immune to all such frivolous thoughts. My mind has a steel partition between matters of business and matters of pleasure. Besides, I only have your word that she is a dish. And sometimes your taste is pretty weird."

"My first impression of Amanda Granger is very good, Coley. I felt, for a first meeting, she was very candid. But let's don't get overpowered by that. There are two sides to every story. Try to stand in the other guy's shoes before we let her drag the guy into court. If there is a living saint on this earth, I haven't seen him or her yet."

His partner's moralistic little lectures always puzzled and amused Coley. "Willy, who the hell do we work for, Amanda Granger or her husband?"

"Amanda Granger, of course."

"Then I'm going to nail the bastard."

Willy grinned broadly. "That's the spirit, Coley. As I see it, you'll be able to handle this one yourself. Amanda's due to call in half an hour. Meet her someplace and have your own chat with her. I have some business uptown. If you feel like I do after talking to her alone, we'll go about the business of nailing the bastard."

Amanda Granger was already at the Essex House when Coley arrived. Willy was right. She was a dazzler. She sat sipping at tea, holding an unopened paperback book in one hand and staring off into the distance, apparently deep in thought. Coley walked directly to her table. "Amanda Granger, I'm Coley Doctor."

Amanda looked up, startled by the quick appearance of the tall investigator, and then offered her hand without getting up. "Please sit down. And thank you for being on time.

I am anxious to get started on this. Have you heard the tape I made for Mr. Hanson?"

"As a matter of fact, I just finished listening to it a second time." Coley glanced down at the paperback book, a current best-selling mystery.

Amanda fondled the book thoughtfully for a moment. "I've found myself with gobs of free time lately." She paused and broke into a bright smile. "But I guess all that free time will come to an end in about seven months."

"And I gather that your husband, Jason, doesn't share your obvious happiness."

He watched Amanda's bright smile darken to a frown. "No, he does not." She shrugged and continued quietly. "And even if he did, it wouldn't matter. He will never experience fatherhood with this child. Never!"

The intensity with which she spoke precluded further discussion of the matter for the moment. "Where is Jason right this minute?"

"He's apartment hunting right here in Manhattan."

"I would think that would be a task you would share."

"Why? Just as I told him this morning, it's his apartment, not mine. I'm staying in Harrisburg. He thinks it's just until the baby comes. He hasn't yet figured out that it's forever."

"Then he doesn't have an inkling of your plans for a divorce?"

"Mr. Doctor . . ."

"Please call me Coley."

"Coley, he avoids all serious conversation about the matter. I suppose he thinks I love him and need him. He's so wrong. Whatever we had between us is gone." Amanda's eyes met his for several seconds. The tall man brought to mind the huge photograph on the wall of the office she had left earlier in the day. It was a blowup of a basketball player slam-dunking a shot. Another player was sprawled on the floor under the basket. "I'll bet that's you in the big basketball blowup on your office wall, Coley."

"Actually that's me on the floor. I keep that on the wall to remind me that I got beat by a hotshot freshman when I was a senior. That photograph explains why I am here, Amanda. It explains why I am a lawyer and a private investigator, instead of trying to live being a nobody in the NBA. It's a reality check. I'm lucky. The photographer did me a big favor."

Amanda's intensity eased and she smiled. "Coley, did you ever get the inclination to tell someone that you are the player making the slam dunk instead of the guy dumped on the floor? You really can't see either face very well."

Coley grinned. The woman had a lot upstairs to go with the fancy bod. "It never occurred to me, Mrs. Granger."

"Really? Well, that's the difference between you and my husband. He'd lie every second of the day if it made him look good. I can't live with him anymore. Now he has reduced himself to a nothing. Do you understand that, Coley?"

"Yep, I sure do." Coley produced a small notebook from his jacket and again met her eyes squarely. "Now I want you to give me a few details, a starting point. Who is the other woman and where can I find her? If what you say is true, if I follow her, she will lead me to Jason. In an affair like this, I have more success following the woman. Tell me all the gory details. . . . Take your time." Coley smiled again. "You know I charge by the hour."

"By the hour?"

"Yes, it's something I learned in law school."

Amanda smiled. "Well, then, I suppose I should have brought a stopwatch. But who cares? It's Jason's money." Her smile turned to bitterness. "Actually it should be very easy for you to find them together. You see, when Jason was promoted, he saw to it that Blair Lawton was promoted with him. He always insisted that they work well together. It took me a long time to discover that they must do everything very well together."

"I suppose then she's staying at the Waldorf," Coley ventured.

"No, Jason isn't that stupid. She's staying at the Sheraton in midtown. At this very minute, she's out helping Jason find us an apartment. Isn't that a kick! But then he says Blair knows New York very well, and it would be better if I rest up for dinner while they do all the chasing around. What a sap!" Amanda became misty-eyed, and couldn't mask the tremble in her voice. "Coley, it could have been such a happy time." He voice trailed off for a few moments. "I suppose she'll be at dinner tonight. It's sort of a company thing."

"And where is that going to be?"

"At the Water Club, someplace on the East Side."

"Very nice! Too bad you're not in the mood to enjoy it." Coley hated to be indelicate, but he had to ask the question. "Are you absolutely sure that they wind up in the same bed once in a while?"

"Not a doubt about that, Coley. I take care of his dirty clothes and check his pockets before I drop his suits off at the cleaners. I can and will make a long list of evidence for you. On the tape I told you how I played detective at the Olde Pitt House near Harrisburg. I'm a poor detective, Coley. It's a wonder I didn't get caught."

Coley paused and sipped at a cup of coffee. Amanda had ordered tea and pastry before he arrived. He pulled a card from his pocket. "Amanda, I want you to be in touch with me every day at this number. When you dial, no one will answer. There will be three distinct beeps. Bring me up to date after the third beep. I'll get your message within a short time. Bring me up to date on anything you think I should know. If it's a real emergency, call Penny at the office. Don't hesitate to speak with Willy Hanson."

"Thanks, Coley. If you don't mind, I'm going back to the Waldorf and rest up for dinner like a good little girl." She smiled again. "Maybe I'll treat myself to a massage."

"Good idea. By the way, I'll be somewhere in the Water Club tonight. If you see me, act like you don't." Coley rose as she prepared to leave. "Also, you haven't asked me about our fee. Aren't you curious about that?"

"Mr. Hanson already warned me about your atrocious fee. As I told him, I really don't give a damn about spending Jason's money. Good luck, Coley." She shook his hand warmly and walked away.

Coley followed her svelte silhouette until she was out of sight. He wondered again, Why would a guy be a chaser with a woman like that at home? He couldn't wait to find out more about what made Jason Granger tick.

15

Tad Houston counted out four dollars and twenty cents for the two hot dogs and a soda. He pushed the money gingerly across the counter, aware that the cashier was studying him closely. Kids were not uncommon in the Times Square Hot Dog Heaven, but this one looked pretty unsure of himself. "Is that going to fill you up, son?" she asked, trying to pry a word or two out of him.

"Oh, yes, ma'am! I usually eat just one, and it isn't as big as these." Tad turned quickly away from the counter and carried his meal to a shelf along the big window facing the street.

He finished one hot dog and washed it down with his soda. It seemed like every time he glanced back over his shoulder, the cashier was looking at him. He grasped the remaining hot dog, then bolted out the door and walked rapidly across Forty-second Street until he reached Eighth Avenue, continuing to munch away at the hot dog. Soon he became aware of a chill in the air as the wind whipped down the canyon of buildings ahead of him. He thought of the sweater he had left behind with the knapsack. It would surely feel good—but then, it was all wet and heavy. He didn't want to lug it all the way to Aunt Sarah's house in Morristown.

He was tired. He remembered the friendly face of the conductor on the train and wondered if he should have stayed with him. He decided to look for the place where he had climbed the stairs after getting off the train in New York. There were the same such stairwells on virtually every street corner but none seemed to be the right one and he always climbed back to the street.

It was now pitch dark, and the persistent wind became colder. Tad ducked in and out of storefronts looking at the stuff in the windows. There must have been a million cameras, he thought, along with endless displays of jewelry and radios. Some windows were filled with pictures of naked women, kind of like those he and Eddie had seen in a magazine they had found along the highway. He began to shiver and decided to move on until he found the train back to New Jersey.

"Hey, kid, it's cold out here. How about a movie. We can warm up in there."

Tad turned to face a tall man with long, disheveled hair. He wore a tattered leather coat. Tad could see teeth were missing as the man grinned down at him. The man had blocked his path back to the street. As he tried to pass him, the man grabbed his arm, his recently broken arm.

"You have money to pay our way in? We'll be nice and warm in there. I promise you."

"No! I have no money." Tad tried to twist away from him.

The man glanced around, then bent down to speak. "That's okay. I will pay. I will pay for both of us and I will keep you warm."

"Oh no you don't, you bastard!" A voice shrieked from

behind them. A tall dark woman with a long mane of black hair muscled herself between them and shoved the point of her elbow into the man's ribs. "Not tonight, you perverted old fool." She then kicked him squarely in the shin, and he dropped his hold on Tad's arm.

The man turned and saw that several people had stopped to see what the commotion was. In a burst of energy, he made his way to the sidewalk and hurried down the street, leaving the woman and the boy behind him.

The woman knelt and the boy felt her arms around him. "That man is evil. He is no good. Did he hurt you?"

Tad shook his head. The woman grasped his thin arm, and stared at him. "Where is your mother?"

Tad shrugged. At that moment he couldn't find words.

"Cat got your tongue, right?" The woman held his arm tightly. "Are you a bad one, also? Do you know that man?"

"No. He hurt my arm. . . . Do you know how to get to New Jersey?" Tad stammered.

The woman held him at arm's length by his shoulders and studied him with her great dark eyes. "New Jersey? My, my, you are a lost child, aren't you?" She glanced down at the watch on her wrist. "Well, now, what are we going to do about that?" she mused quietly. The night was young in her business. She hadn't turned a trick yet.

"Please let me go. I don't want to cause any trouble." The woman was strong and still held him in her grip.

"Trouble? There will be no trouble for you, because you are coming with me."

Still gripping his hand, she led him across Forty-second Street until she got to Ninth Avenue and turned the corner. After a couple of blocks, she climbed several steps and unlocked a door. Inside they climbed several flights of stairs. There she opened another door and led them inside. "This is where I live, child. It isn't much, but the last time I looked, the rent was paid." The woman released her grip and Tad scrambled into a chair near the door, which she locked behind them.

Tad gaped at the woman. He had never seen a woman dressed like that. How did she ever walk with shoe heels like that? he wondered. She had on black stockings and a short dress that actually showed her underwear as she walked.

The woman saw him squirm in the chair and then glanced down at her legs. She started to laugh. "Oh, my heavens, I'm sorry, little man." She pulled a robe off the back of a door and put it on over the unusual street clothes. "My name is Carlota, little man. What is yours?"

"Carlota . . . I never heard a name like that." The woman seemed friendly enough. She smiled a lot.

"Carlota was an empress. My mother named me after an empress. Did your mother name you after someone?"

Tad stared down at her long spike heels, avoiding her eyes. "I . . . I'm Eddie, Eddie Foxworth," he lied.

"And you live someplace in New Jersey?"

"Yep. I live in Morristown."

"Morristown? That's quite a ways from here, Eddie. I think the first thing we better do is call your parents." Carlota reached for a telephone on the table next to her.

"It's no use, I don't know the number." Tad became very nervous as she picked up the phone anyway.

"A big boy like you don't know your phone number. Shame on you." She eyed the boy carefully and decided he must be at least ten years old. She was convinced he was not being totally honest with her. "What's your daddy's name? Is he called Eddie, too? Eddie Foxworth?"

Tad squirmed and nodded his head in assent as she dialed information.

"Operator, I need the number of Mr. Eddie Foxworth in Morristown." There was a long pause as Carlota waited. The she put the phone back in it's cradle. "There's no such number, Eddie. You're not joshing me are you?"

"Nope, honest I'm not."

Carlota studied the small boy, dreading to call the police. She had enough problems with them and didn't know what they would do about Eddie. The temperature was dipping into the low fifties outside. She decided she would wait until morning before deciding what to do. "Eddie, you look like you haven't slept in a long time. I'll get a blanket and some pillows and you can snuggle up on the couch for the night. "How about that?"

Eddie looked at the comfy-looking sofa and remembered the cold wind outside. He shook his head up and down in agreement with her. "Miss Carlota, I would like that very much. It is cold outside and my arm is sore. It was broken and the cast fell off."

"Let me see that arm, Boy." She scanned the arm closely and saw the sallow color compared to the other arm. "It looks like its going to be okay, Eddie. It just takes time. How'd you break your arm, son?"

"My Pa . . . I fell down in our barn." Tad was sorry for his slip of his tongue.

"I bet your pa beat you, didn't he, boy?" She lifted his arm and studied him carefully. "You got bruises all over yourself."

"I fell down in our barn. I really did." Tad got up from the chair and walked over to the sofa and sat down.

"We'll talk more about that in the morning. It's time to get some rest. You like brownies with walnuts?"

"Sure do!" He watched her walk to the refrigerator. She poured a glass of milk, took two large brownies out of a sack and placed them on a saucer. "Here you go, Eddie. No more questions tonight. I'm going to stay home from work and you are going to get some sleep."

"Where do you work, Miss Carlota?" Carlota smiled and looked down at her long nyloned legs protruding from the robe, ending in five-inch golden-spiked heels. She didn't think there was anyone in the world anymore naive enough to ask that question.

"I try to make people happy, Eddie. Maybe we'll talk

more about that in the morning. Maybe then you'll tell me more about your folks."

Tad rolled over on the sofa and snuggled down under the blanket. He felt warm and incredibly tired. "Good night, Miss Carlota. You're sure good at your job. You've made me happy already."

Carlota lit a cigarette and watched the young boy drift into a deep sleep. To her surprise, she felt a tear roll down her cheek. She couldn't think of the last time that she had actually shed a tear. For a few fleeting moments, Empress Carlota, Ninth Avenue whore, really felt human again.

16

Jason had luxuriant dark hair with just a few flecks of gray at the temples. Broad shoulders and a narrow athlete's waist made Jason Granger an appropriately handsome escort for the beautiful Amanda. Coley studied the small group as they were seated at a window table in the Water Club. If Amanda were anything but happy about being escorted by her husband, she certainly didn't show it.

Amanda had told him a little bit about Dillon Archibald, the CEO of Harmony Mutual, now seated at the head of the table. He was a tall, portly man somewhere in his sixties. Impeccably dressed in a steel gray silk suit, he looked like a CEO should look. His thick gray hair and neatly trimmed mustache showed frequent attention by some lucky barber. A size-fifty waist showed that he partook of the good life that his success had allowed.

Conversation among the party of seven seemed animated, and Amanda sparkled the most among the three women. One rather matronly woman must have been Archibald's spouse. The sleek-looking blonde sitting between two other men had to be Blair Lawton. She sat rather sober-faced, her eyes seldom straying from Jason Granger.

Coley figured that Blair was low on the pecking order of those at the table and knew her place well. He predicted to himself that as she became more sure of herself beyond the cocktails and wine, the others would find themselves drawn to her in conversation. Blair Lawton carried herself confidently. Earlier, the close-fitting dinner gown she wore turned many heads as their party was shown to their table. A thigh-high slit was a little too much, but on her it looked perfectly regal. Coley could understand Jason's attraction to her. But still, if he had to choose one woman over another, just on scenic qualities, it would be Amanda.

Amanda puzzled him. She radiated smiles to the others and looked at Jason with apparent fondness now and then, even affectionately touching the nape of his neck several times. It was all an act. In public she would be the sugary-sweet, doting wife right up to the time she dropped the bomb on him. He had slightly misjudged her. Amanda could be a clawing cat beneath the sugar coating.

Coley's vantage point from the bar was very poor, so he welcomed the entrance of Penny Wine, the only other employee of Hanson's Private Investigation, Inc., besides Willy and himself. "You're late," admonished Coley. "Our client is swilling cocktails, and our pigeon is making goo-goo eyes at his amour, and vice versa. You've missed all that."

"Look, Coley, having dinner at the Water Club is super, but next time don't wait until the very last minute to let me know about it. You're lucky you're not eating alone and even luckier that my boyfriend is willing to tolerate my breaking a date for our noble cause."

The maître d' seated them at a table preselected by Coley. It put them some distance from the Harmony Mutual group but at an angle that facilitated surveillance, with a low probability of being noticed. The instant they were seated he saw Amanda glance casually at them. He was glad Penny had accepted at the last minute. A solitary diner at the Water Club would attract attention, especially one with his six foot seven frame.

Penny completed a quick study of the group. "Your Mr. Jason Granger must be hot stuff. I thought Amanda was a knockout in the office today, but Blair Lawton looks like a movie star. I take it that is the CEO at the head of the table."

"I'm sure it is," agreed Coley. "The other two twerps haven't got enough miles on them."

Penny periodically glanced at the group as Coley ordered from the waiter. "Incidently, that sweet, chubby little wife of our CEO better keep her eyes on hubby. He's mesmerized by Blair Lawton."

"Really, Penny? You amaze me by picking that up so quickly. Stick with me, kid, and you'll make a fine private eye some day."

"Coley, honestly now, did you notice that before I told you?"

"No, frankly I didn't, but I've noticed a few other things. Are you catching Amanda, with the saccharine smiles and the little love pats and whispers she is giving Jason? What's all that about?"

"Easy! She's setting him up. When she serves him with divorce papers someday soon, it will totally shock the office bigwigs. She's making it tough for him. Of course she must be irritating the hell out of Blondie. Jason will hear all about that in bed, from both of them."

Coley grinned at their protégée. "Maybe I just better call it a night and let you play detective."

"Stick around, Coley, at least until the check comes." Penny suddenly rolled her eyes at the table by the window. "The bombshell is going to the powder room. Dig that gown. There isn't a stitch on underneath."

"Really?" Coley fought off the temptation to peek as Blair passed behind them. "Why don't you follow her into the ladies' room and have a close look."

"At what?"

"At Blair Lawton. Maybe she'll say something useful. Ladies' rooms are a harvest of information for a detective. Women get careless with their casual talk in there. It's a well-known fact."

"How do you know that, Coley?"

"You'd be surprised. I've been in lots of mysterious places."

"Disgusting!" Penny faked a grimace. "But I'll take a peek, anyway." Penny rose from the table and started on her brief expedition.

Coley followed her with his eyes until she turned a corner out of sight. He decided Penny Wine was a future star for their little company. She had a lot of curiosity and enough brass to make her tough. He'd have to give Willy a good report.

His eyes shifted to the Harmony Mutual table. Their main courses had arrived, but Jason was continuing to talk to a group that had become very sober-faced. Amanda was still fawning over him by stroking the back of his neck. She was carrying her sugar and spice bit a little far, he thought.

Statuesque Blair Lawton passed behind him and returned to her table. This time Coley gave her the once-over. He agreed with Penny. The gown couldn't have a stitch under it.

"I caught you peeking, Coley." Penny whispered as she returned to the table. They both watched Blair slink to her chair. "Jeepers, Coley. She makes me feel like a man."

"That's nonsense, kiddo, and you know it." Without being flashy, the diminutive, dark-eyed Penny was a sleek looker herself. "So, what did she say in there?"

"It was pretty dramatic, Coley. First she said, 'Hello,' and then she said, 'It's a nice evening.'"

"That's fascinating."

"You didn't let me finish, Coley. Then she said that it

was too bad she had to waste the evening on a bunch of jerks."

"Really?"

"Yes, really."

"Now that's interesting!" Coley let his eyes wander over the group. Jason was still speaking, and the others were eating. "What's your gut feel? Do you think she meant to include Jason in her bunch of jerks?"

Penny shrugged. "Coley, I didn't crawl inside her mind. My guess would be that sitting through a seven-course dinner across a table from Amanda Granger fawning over her husband is driving her nuts. She's probably pissed at Jason for bringing her along."

Coley nodded at her assessment. "Our hero has finally finished his little speech. He's catching up with his entree. Blair is starting to gush and glitter. Our old CEO is hanging on her every word. No one else has cracked a smile in five minutes. You know, I get the feeling that nobody's very happy over there."

"So what's our next move?" Penny was looking at her wristwatch.

"Now isn't that something! I take you out, spend a couple hundred bucks for a fancy dinner, and you're watching the clock. You've probably got a late date with your boyfriend," Coley guessed. "You're one of those two-date-a-night babes."

"Bingo! That's right, Coley. Business is business and pleasure is pleasure. I keep them separate so I can make you and Willy happy."

"I guess you told Clifford all about tonight."

"Wrong, Coley. Business and pleasure. Remember, I don't mix them." Penny grinned at Coley. Actually she liked him a lot and thought for a moment if Clifford were nonexistent she would have to alter her rules. "Hey, look at this."

Dillon Archibald had arisen from his chair, as did Blair

Lawton. The two of them, chatting quietly as they walked, left the dining room area and disappeared through the barroom door.

Coley's curiosity got the best of him. He rose and made his way toward the bar. He found Archibald using a public phone with Blair standing by. Coley decided to stand at the bar.

The bartender approached. "Can I help you, sir?"

"Just stretching my legs, and I do love cashew nuts. I saw them when I came in. In fact, I make a list of bars that serve fancy nuts." Coley helped himself to a handful.

"Enjoy yourself, sir. They are a temptation." The bartender eyed him closely. "By the way, are you one of the Knicks?"

"I wish I was, sir." Coley was about to launch into a story about his basketball days but was distracted by the Archibald and Blair show. He had finished his phone call and the two were huddled in conversation. Dillon Archibald, the CEO of Harmony Mutual, had his arm around her and his right hand was neatly and firmly cupping the left bun of her derriere. Coley quickly glanced away and caught the eye of the bartender, who shrugged and smiled at the cozy scene. "I think in my next life, I'd like to be a bartender," Coley offered.

"Not much we don't see or hear," observed the bartender. "It keeps the imagination working overtime sometimes." He slid the bowl of nuts toward Coley and once again glanced at the errant hand of Archibald, which he reckoned must be getting quite warm by now.

Finally the CEO made his way to the men's room, and Blair Lawton returned to her table. Coley rejoined Penny Wine.

"So, what's up?" Penny asked eagerly.

"Damned if I know. He used the house phone, and then they talked after he hung up. The old boy had the palm of his hand glued to her fanny during the entire conversation. Want me to demonstate?"

"Coley, I'm going to tell Willy you're harassing me."

"Sorry! Just trying to help you visualize the picture. It's a joke, Ms. Wine, just one of my little jokes."

"I'm going to tell my boyfriend, and maybe he'll demonstrate. Clifford moves a little slow sometimes, Coley. Hey, the old boy is asking for the check."

Coley signaled for the waiter. "I'm going to put you in a cab right now, so you can get home and try to motivate Clifford. I have another cab waiting and I'll put a tail on them when they leave."

"Which one are you going to follow, Coley?"

"Blair Lawton. I ain't no fool."

Coley paid the check and they left for the cab line. Penny pecked a goodnight kiss on Coley's cheek and then ducked into a cab. "Good luck, Coley. Tell me all about it in the morning, okay?"

"Only if you tell me all about you and Clifford," he teased as he slammed the door of the cab.

Coley crouched down in the backseat of the taxi he had hired for the evening. Punchy, the driver he often used on such investigations, listened carefully as he gave him instructions. "I think they will all get in that limo over there. When the blonde in the snug white gown gets out, I'll get out and you'll hang around. Got that?"

"I got it. There will be no problem. You are a lucky man."

"Why am I a lucky man, Punchy?"

"Because you just have one girl after another. I saw you put the chick in the other taxi."

"You don't know how wrong you are, Punchy. I'm thinking about becoming a priest."

"Don't try it. They would have to throw you out of the church. Hey, looky here." Punchy nodded toward the limo ahead. Everyone got inside the limo except Blair Lawton. She waved good-bye and then got her own taxi.

"I follow the taxi, not the limo. Right?"

"Right." Coley was puzzled. Why didn't they just drop

Blair off? She might have been low on the totem pole, but that was no way to treat an employee. Coley decided that Mr. Dillon Archibald was too big for his britches.

The cab picked up Thirty-fourth Street, moved across town, turned north and dropped Blair off at the Sheraton Center.

Damn, thought Coley, she's just going to hit the hay. I should have followed the others. "Wait here. I'm going to mosey inside for a few minutes. We'll probably pack it in when I get back."

Punchy nodded, pulled snug to the curb, turned on his off-duty light, took a crossword puzzle magazine from behind the visor and waited.

Inside the hotel Coley spotted Blair riding upward on a long escalator. Hopping aboard, he followed her several levels before she got off and quickly made her way to a cocktail lounge. A hostess seated her alone at a table with a splendid view of Broadway.

Now what? Coley wondered why, after the fancy dinner and all the cocktails and wine, she was still motivated to have a nightcap by herself.

His speculation ended quickly. Harmony's exalted Dillon Archibald strode confidently into the lounge, spotted Blair immediately and joined her. Coley sat down at an obscure table, ordered Perrier, and kept watch on them. Within minutes Archibald was slobbering over the back of her hand and working his way up.

Seconds later, he signaled a waitress, tossed several bills on the table and stood up. Blair grasped his hand and led him from the lounge to a bank of elevators just off the large atrium. Moving quickly, Coley arrived in time to see them boarding an elevator going up into the many floors of guest rooms. He stood and watched the elevator doors close, deciding not to get on. He preferred to keep Blair Lawton at a distance for the moment.

Coley retraced his steps to the escalator and began the ride down to the lobby. Blair had surprised him. Now he wondered if Amanda were right about being so cocksure Blair was having an affair with her husband. Of course it might be a case of Blair climbing right up that corporate ladder as fast as she could. Opportunity had knocked and she had wasted no time. Maybe Jason was just a very temporary stop on her ascendancy.

At ground level, Coley decided it was time to call it a night. Then he had a thought that made him chuckle aloud. The CEO's apparent dalliance opened the possibility that Blair Lawton might allow Hanson's Private Investigation, Inc., to kill two birds with one stone. Mrs. Archibald might be very interested in what was going on somewhere upstairs. Of course, Willy would probably question the ethics of that idea.

17

Amanda Granger sat at the dressing table brushing her hair vigorously. Neither she nor Jason had yet said a word since returning to their room at the Waldorf. Jason, stripped down to silk boxer shorts, sat on the edge of the bed drawing deeply on a cigarette.

"I think you ... we made a mistake, Amanda. All old Archie wanted to do was have a little nightcap downstairs. He is the top dog, you know." Jason stared at her, blowing a series of small smoke rings.

Amanda slapped the small hairbrush on the palm of her hand and faced him, eyes blazing. "I wish you wouldn't smoke in here, Jason. It's not good for the baby. Also Jason, you're drunk. Dillon Archibald was watching you very closely. You've done yourself a favor by calling it a night."

"Bullshit! If the CEO wants to have a little nightcap, you have one. It was pretty thoughtful of him. He just wanted to relax with us after the others had left." Jason fell silent and then lit another cigarette, taking another deep drag.

"Put out that damn cigarette, or I'm going to sleep in the lobby."

Jason smirked. "Worried about the baby? Well, I'll tell you something, I'm not!"

Amanda jumped from her chair, strode to the bed, and jerked a pillow and a blanket off of it. Tossing them on the couch, she wrapped herself in the blanket and huddled facing away from him. "Good night, Jason. I'm flying back to Harrisburg in the morning. I don't give one damn about Dillon Archibald."

"Now that's being pretty stupid. He thinks you are pretty slick."

Amanda turned her head toward him on more time. "I've got news for you, Jason. Archibald thinks anyone in a skirt is pretty slick. You better watch him with your protégée. He could hardly keep from drooling every time she opened her mouth." She again turned away and buried her head in the pillow.

"You're nuts, Amanda. You're seeing the wrong kind of doctor. You'd better see a shrink. He'd tell you that you need a good screw."

Jason looked at his watch and stared out the window, yearning to be anywhere but where he was. Blair had left him without even a glance as she departed in her own cab. It was almost two A.M., too late to go out with the load of booze he was carrying. Amanda was apparently sleeping soundly.

He picked up a newspaper he had already paged through several times. He had ignored the local news. The business and sports pages had been thoroughly digested during the day. HOPE FADES FOR BOY MISSING IN CANOE MISHAP. He had missed the story buried deep within the news section.

A ten-year-old boy, Tad Houston, had evidently drowned

in a canoeing accident near the Delaware Water Gap. Search parties had been unsuccessful in recovering the body of the missing boy lost in rapids of the river swollen by recent rains. The paper reported that the distraught father, Sonny Houston, had returned to his farm near Milford, Pennsylvania, after a twenty-four-hour search failed to locate the boy. Authorities were amazed that anyone would take a canoe into the raging river at this time of year and held little hope that the boy would be found alive.

Sonny Houston? Milford, PA? Jason sat upright trying to clear his head. That was the guy that had beaten him up on the turnpike! That was GITGO 7. He had a vivid flashback of the young boy, nose pressed against the window during the speed duel on the highway. The same kid might be dead now! He still had a debt to settle with his dad, but he certainly couldn't wish this on the youngster.

His drive to Milford a few days ago for the purpose of tormenting Houston had been rewarding. He had followed him all the way to Middletown. Digging a scratch on the showy SUV as it sat parked at a mall was just a start to the hell he planned for Houston.

Jason rose from the bed, glanced at Amanda nestled in the large sofa, her back toward him. She was breathing evenly. She could always sleep through a hailstorm, he thought, envying her for the moment. He walked to the window, lit another cigarette and stared up Park Avenue. Save a couple of taxicabs, the elegant canyon was vacant.

He thought about Blair, alone over at the Sheraton, and then smiled. Actually, it was a good thing for Amanda to go back to Harrisburg in the morning. She had impressed the brass around Harmony Mutual. She had served her purpose.

He rubbed at his sore neck. It was still a sharp reminder of his encounter with Sonny Granger on the turnpike. He decided to pick up another prescription in the morning for the periodic spasms of pain. His thoughts returned to Sonny Houston and then he broke into a smile despite the pain. He would play upon his grief and really torment the bastard now. He picked up the newspaper article again and reread every word. If the boy's body had not been found yet, there was a possibility that it might not be found for weeks.

Jason rubbed at his sore neck and began to concoct a plan. He decided that he would send Houston a demand for ransom. Of course, he would never try to collect any money. He'd just make sure Sonny Houston threw away a bundle of his own. This simple little sport was going to be fun, a pleasant diversion from his problems with Amanda.

Jason thought back to his first impulse after Gary Steven, the country club security man, had supplied him with Houston's address. He picked his wallet off the nightstand and quickly found the address, which he had scribbled on a scrap of paper. He could have gotten in touch with the police and filed assault charges. But that would interrupt his own life, especially the almost daily affair with Blair. He really wanted no part of talking to the police. Now, time had gone by. Houston could deny any involvement. The only witness was probably dead.

He started to pace in front of the window, chain-smoking another cigarette. He paused to look at himself in the mirror. He was sweating with excitement, and also yearning, yearning for Blair. He looked at his watch. It was still a good five hours before he would see her. He'd surprise her early at her hotel. Perfect! he thought to himself. Amanda certainly would not be in the mood to have breakfast with him. She'd be busy arranging a flight home to Harrisburg.

Jason spent several hours staring at the ceiling. What in the hell had become of his life, he thought. Since the day Blair had first walked into his office, everything had changed. He heard Amanda moving on the couch. His beautiful Amanda! Why didn't he care for, or love, her anymore? He realized that her turning into a shrew was probably his fault. Maybe he should talk about the baby with her. But what about Blair? How in the hell was he going to handle that?

Once he fell asleep for what must have been just a few minutes. At six o'clock, he took a shower and dressed for the day, trying not to awaken Amanda. Just as he was opening the door to leave, he heard her.

"Good-bye, Jason."

"I can't sleep, honey. I'm going down for an early breakfast."

"I'll see you in Harrisburg," she said icily.

He quickly shut the door and hurried to the elevator. It was the first time in ages that he had left her without an exchange of kisses.

Within minutes he was in an elevator at the Sheraton gaping at himself in the mirror. He looked like hell. The door refused to open when the elevator stopped. He repeatedly jabbed at the button before he realized Blair was on a security floor. Absolutely nothing had gone right since last night's dinner.

Jason returned to the lobby, found a house phone and called Blair's room. It rang a half dozen times before she picked up. "Sorry to bother you, Blair. I couldn't sleep. Amanda's been pissed all night. I need a key to get on your floor."

After his torrent of words, there was complete silence for several seconds. Then Blair spoke haltingly. "You poor, poor man! I . . . I take it you are in my hotel."

"Yes, yes, I need a key."

"Of course, Jason. Go to the desk, I'll have them give you one. Don't make a scene, Jason. You sound so upset."

"Don't worry, I'm okay." With that he hung up and proceeded to the front desk in the lobby.

Upstairs, Blair Lawton moved furiously to straighten up the room. In an ashtray was the remains of one of Dillon Archibald's cigars. She quickly pulverized it and flushed it away. She scanned the room rapidly, stuffed a couple of brandy snifters under some pillows in the closet and then sat nervously by the phone continuing to look for evidence of last night's tryst. The phone rang. It was the front desk.

"Yes, yes, please give him the key, it's okay." She quickly unlocked her door and then went into the bathroom to freshen up. She spritzed perfume in the air. Dillon Archibald had left only a couple of hours ago. As she ran a brush through her hair, she heard Jason shut the door to her room.

"Jason, I'm in here. I'll be out in a second." She took a quick look at the mirror and wondered how observant Jason would be. She decided no clothes would be better than the rumpled nightie. She steeled herself and opened the door.

"Jason, you dear man. Let me hold you." She crossed the room and clasped her arms around him. They stood silently, embracing for several seconds, as his hands caressed her nakedness. "You do know how to surprise a woman, Jason. I've been dying for you all night long. Slip out of your clothes and get comfortable. I have a special treat for you."

18

"Sonny, I don't know how you can even think about insurance already." Bessie Houston gaped at her husband, sitting at the kitchen table. He was paging through an insurance policy, reading aloud some of the provisions when he needed her help for understanding. "In fact, I wasn't even aware that we had a policy on Tad. I thought only you and I had coverage." Her eyes, swollen by many hours of weeping over the loss of her son, filled again with tears. "Please, Sonny, let's put it aside for now. Tad might show up any minute, you know." Then more tears belied her words and she, too, was losing hope.

"Bessie, it's time for you to shut up." Sonny laid the

policy on the table and looked directly at her. "Someone around here has to be strong and face the facts. I saw the river that day. There is no way the boy is alive."

"That isn't what the troopers said! They found Tad's knapsack on the shore!" She looked pleadingly at him,

"Well then, if the troopers are so damn smart, where is Tad? Those troopers better mind their own business. Tad's gone, and that's that!"

Bessie Houston stared out the window. "Sonny, I've got to say something that's on my mind, something I never thought I would ever say to you." Her voice sounded measured and firm now. "We both know that Tad's not yours. When we got married, you said that didn't matter. I know now that it does matter. How can you sit there not knowing where Tad is, and talk about getting a little bit of money?"

"You hold your tongue, woman! That's a lot of blubbering nonsense. Now, I'll hear no more of it in my house!" Sonny slammed his fist on the table. "By the way, Bessie, who else have you told that Tad isn't mine?"

"No one, ever," she whispered, knowing the secret was safe with his sister Sarah.

Sonny slapped at the insurance papers on the table. "There's fifty thousand dollars here, and you damn well better stop jabbering nonsense." Sonny lowered his voice. "I miss the boy as much as you do, Bessie."

Bessie continued in a hoarse whisper, forcing himself to say what was on her mind. "You busted little Tad's arm, Sonny. He went to heaven with a busted arm."

Sonny Houston's face grew red with fury. "Now you listen to me, woman! Tad told you a damn lie. He's been lying about everything lately. I see now that he's been whining little lies to his mother. Now that's the end of that conversation. There will be no more said about it in this house." Sonny's voice had raised to a shout. Bessie was now bawling openly.

Houston lowered his eyes, pretending to study the terms of the insurance policy and then spoke in his normal tone of voice. "Just leave the policy to me. I remember when Jed Turner down the road lost his wife. He just took the policy into New York, showed it to the insurance folks and they forked over a check right there."

Distracted by a noise from outside, Sonny turned, looked out the window and frowned. "There's that damn newspaper reporter again. I'll handle him this time, Bessie. It's time he learned some proper respect. If these clowns don't stop nosing around, I'll have to set up a defense perimeter. You got any idea what that means, Bessie?"

Bessie shook her head and ran upstairs as Sonny went to answer the doorbell.

"Sir, I'm Cletus Lang of the *Journal*. I was here with the group of reporters a couple of days ago. How are you doing today, Mr. Houston?"

"How am I doing? Now what the hell you mean by that! My wife is upstairs bawling in grief, and here you come asking stupid questions. Maybe you ought to have a shotgun taken to your ass." Houston shoved the screen door open and stepped out onto the porch.

"Now, now, Mr. Houston, everyone feels terrible about your son. I'm sorry, sir. I guess it was a stupid question. Obviously you are still bitter and grieving over the accident, just as anyone would be." The reporter stepped down off the porch to put some distance between himself and Houston.

"You going to beat it, or am I going to have to throw you off my property?"

The reporter backed away another half dozen steps. "I'll leave, sir. Once again, I'm sorry about little Tad." Lang hesitated, reluctant to ask the real question he came to ask. Finally he decided that he could probably outrun the stocky Houston if he had to. "I do have one puzzling question, Mr. Houston. You see, I'm doing this story for my paper, and I'd like to get the facts straight. Everyone for miles around is grieving with you, sir."

"What's your question?"

"Well, sir, the police say they've found a witness who says you had a violent argument with the boy just before the accident. The witness says you slapped a doughnut out of his hand and shoved him down to the ground. The boy cried. Is that true, Mr. Houston?"

Houston glared at the reporter, wondering who had seen them that morning. "Whoever said that will rot in hell for lying. Who was it?"

"I wish I knew, sir. I don't know where the police got their information."

Houston clenched his fist and started to step off the porch when he heard Bessie shout from an upstairs window. "Sonny! Please don't! Now you get going, Mister, and you never come back!"

Houston froze with one foot off the porch. "You heard what the lady said. Git!"

Cletus Lang hustled to his car. He started the engine, watching Houston still rooted to his spot. He rolled down his window. "I am sorry about Tad!" he shouted, then waved and sped off down the road.

Sonny started to walk back into the house, wondering if Bessie had heard what the reporter had said to him about the spat between him and Tad. Probably not, he decided, or she wouldn't have butted in.

He thought again about the reporter. It was now midafternoon. The daily paper would have been delivered to their rural mailbox long ago. The box was located at a junction about a quarter of a mile away from the farm. He climbed into his van and drove the short distance. The paper was there. He sat in the van and turned every page, looking for a story about Tad. Finding nothing, he felt more at ease and began shuffling through the several pieces of mail.

There were the usual ads, a couple of bills and one small envelope addressed in a crude scrawl. Inside was a short, handprinted note on scrap of paper.

TAD'S RETURN WILL COST YOU TWO HUNDRED THOUSAND DOLLARS. GET THE MONEY TOGETHER IN SMALL BILLS. FURTHER INSTRUCTIONS WILL FOLLOW. TAD IS FINE.

Houston stared at the note, reading it over and over again. The plain white envelope had no return address. It was mailed from New York City just a day ago. He jammed it into an empty rear pocket and buttoned it closed. He sat in the SUV for a long time, wondering what to do. Finally he shrugged his shoulders. Nothing, that's what he would do. Nothing.

19

Jack Slade had been an Amtrak conductor for too many years. He often figured that he had logged well over a million miles, ninety-nine percent of it in northern New Jersey. He knew every intersection, every creek and every lamppost between Port Jervis and Hoboken. The run back to Port Jervis was nearly over on this day and only a half dozen commuters remained on the train. He took the shiny conductor's hat off and put it on the seat beside him, stretched his legs and waited for the last stop. Soon he would make it for the last time, now just weeks from retirement.

One of his daily routines was collecting discarded newspapers from the several cars. They now lay in a neat pile on the seat beside him. Tired at the end of a long day, he stared vacantly at the small photograph in the paper on top of the pile. His interest piqued, he bent over to study the picture more closely. The small headline read, HOPE FADES FOR BOY LOST IN THE DELAWARE RIVER.

Slade rubbed at his eyes and stared at the photo. It was the boy! The hair was combed neatly, but it was the same disheveled, towheaded boy who had escaped his train in Hoboken. He read the small accompanying news story. The boy had been missing since the previous Thursday. He had disappeared in a canoeing accident on Thursday. He scrambled to produce a pocket calendar from his jacket. Quickly he verified that he had taken off that Thursday. He had definitely seen the boy in Hoboken on Friday! The name, Tad Houston, didn't ring a bell, though. He had given him another name—Eddie, Eddie Foxworth. He remembered it because it was like pulling teeth getting the kid to give him his name. Said he was going to Morristown.

He pulled a flashlight from the briefcase he always carried and studied the photograph. The combed hair couldn't disguise the strange, wistful look. There was little doubt it was the same boy he had detained next to him before he ran away. He'd bet money on it. Slade checked the date on the paper. It was today's *Bergen Record*. The boy was certainly alive and well the day after the accident.

The train soon reached the end of the line in Port Jervis. Slade stuffed the newspaper into his briefcase. He consulted his daily calendar again, this time running down a list of phone numbers he kept on the last page. He decided he would call the New Jersey State Police. He didn't know what else to do.

The officer in charge listened intently to his story after Slade identified himself. "Where are you right now, Mr. Slade?"

"I just finished my run in Port Jervis, New York. I'm calling you because the paper said the boy, Tad Houston, was missing somewhere along the Delaware in New Jersey." There was a long pause as the officer on duty took notes.

"Sir, we have an investigative team working near there. They are working with the Pennsylvania State Police on a search of the river. They can be in Port Jervis in less than half an hour. They would like to talk to you, sir."

"No inconvenience at all. I'll wait right here. I would imagine that the boy's folks would appreciate this information. They must be frantic by now."

"We'll see to it that they are informed, Mr. Slade. There have been several other calls, sir. We don't want to build them up for a letdown. Our boys would like to speak directly with you before talking to the parents. You sound pretty certain of your identification."

"I am, Officer. The boy is a dead ringer for my passenger." After hanging up, the conductor once again studied the boy pictured in the paper, nodded confidently and began his wait for the police.

Meanwhile, back on Ninth Avenue in New York City, Carlota paced the floor of her third-floor walk-up. She had left Eddie around twelve to turn a couple of tricks with nooners. She had spent most of the weekend with Eddie, turning down business so that she could give the boy some attention. She had extracted a promise from him to stay until she got back.

Actually, the kid had a hell of a cold and a fever. He was just starting to feel better that morning. Now he was gone. Carlota tried to tell herself that she had done the best that she could with the boy, who had totally clammed up about revealing any more of his past existence. It was obvious that Eddie had been traumatized by some recent experience. He needed professional help. Tomorrow she had planned to turn him over to Mary, a social worker who had been kind to her on a couple of occasions.

Now it was growing dark. She was missing business again. She shrugged and tried to get Eddie off her mind. The boy had been so naive, and so needy and appreciative of her attention. God knows, the dingy pad of a Ninth Avenue hooker was no place for the kid. She had helped him about all she could, anyway. It was time to get to work. The rent had to be paid.

Her thoughts were interrupted by noise in the stairwell, and then a loud knock on her door. Carlota opened the door as far as the safety chain would allow.

"This your youngin'?" A large woman with frizzled graying hair held Eddie by the shoulders. Eddie looked disconsolately down at his feet. The woman scowled unappreciatively at Carlota's long, nyloned legs and the attire that revealed her profession. "The boy's got no business out in the street."

Carlota loosened the chain, opened the door and knelt down to put her arms around the boy. "Eddie, I told you not to go out. Look at you. You're all dirty and bleeding. I'll bet you've been in a fight."

"That ain't the half of it, lady. If I hadn't come along they would have drug him right upstairs at the crack house down the block." The woman was still scowling at her. "You should be ashamed of yourself. This is no place for a boy with some manners to live." She shook her head at Carlota in disapproval.

"Thank you for bringing him back." Carlota looked down at her own garish streetwalker's garb. "I'll take good care of him. I know you don't believe that, but I will."

"Boy, is this your place? You want to stay here?" The chubby woman still grasped on of his shoulders.

"Oh, yes! I'll be fine." Eddie glanced up a Carlota, trying to smile. "I got lost. All the buildings look the same around here. I knocked on this lady's door down the street."

Carlota took his hand and led him inside. The woman who had brought him up the stairs, turned without another word and walked down to the sidewalk, shaking her head all the way in apparent disgust.

"Eddie, look at yourself. What am I going to do with you?" Carlota led him to the sofa and sat down beside him, stroking at his touseled hair. "Eddie, this is no fit place for you. You should be in school. You should be home with your dad and mom. I've cleaned you up, got rid of your cold and shared my food with you. I can't do any more, Eddie. You've got to go home."

Tad squirmed on the couch and stared at the floor. "I'm afraid, Carlota. I'm afraid to go home, even if I could."

"Tell me about your mom and dad, Eddie. Don't you think they miss you?"

Tad held the hand which she extended toward him. "First of all, my name ain't Eddie. I'm Tad."

"Really now, you've been telling fibs to your Aunt Carlota? Shame on you, Tad. I didn't know my little friend told fibs."

"My dad calls me a liar all the time, even when I ain't." Tears escaped from the corner of one eye. "I can't go home, Carlota."

"Tad, listen to me. This is no fit place for you. Maybe if I take you home, you can come back and visit some day. How about that? I bet your mom is really worried and wants to see you."

Tad shook his head affirmatively. "Yep, Mom would like to see me. Maybe even Pops would, but he would beat me."

"Oh, Tad, whatever for?"

"He beats me all the time, when Mom ain't looking. He hates me! And that's the truth, Carlota." Tad looked at her pleadingly. "You know what?"

Tad was squirming and looking at the floor again agonizing over what he was about to say.

"What, Tad. What is it? You can tell me."

"Pops broke my arm!" He burst into tears and hugged Carlota tightly.

She sighed and held the boy close for a long time. "Tad, where do you live? We have to figure out a way to do something about you."

"I live in Pennsylvania. It's a long ways."

"Uh-oh! You told me another little fib. You said Morristown, in New Jersey, I believe."

Tad looked her and smiled through his tears. "That's where my aunt lives, Aunt Sarah. She's nice. That's where I was going."

"And you're telling me the truth now? No more little fibs?"

Tad bobbed his head up and down.

"If I were to take you to Morristown, could we find Aunt Sarah's house?"

"Oh, sure." Tad nodded confidently.

Carlota stood up and looked at her garish dress in the mirror. "Well, Tad, if we are going to see your Aunt Sarah, I guess it's high time to clean up my act." She remembered going to Morristown by train once to work a convention. If her memory was correct, it was only an hour or two away. "If you promise not to run away from me again, we'll go see Aunt Sarah in a couple of days and have a talk with her. Okay?"

"That's fine with me, Carlota."

"Tad, what's Aunt Sarah's last name?"

"It's Houston, same as me."

Carlota stared at her image in the mirror again, wondering what it was that had drawn her to the boy. She wasn't fit for hell, much less motherhood. Fleetingly, she pictured her own mother and her father, who had both beaten her. She realized then why she had to help the boy.

20

Coley was curious. Fighting his lack of sleep, he rose early that day and returned to the Sheraton. It was six A.M. when he spotted one of the hotel security people he knew. "Jimbo, still on the payroll. I thought you'd be sick of this job by now. Say, buddy, you've put on a few pounds." He eyed Jimbo's ample gut and shook his head in mock disgust. The man was retired NYPD, and Coley had known him long before he took the private security gig.

"This ain't no picnic, Coley. You'd be surprised what goes on in a place this big. It ain't nothin' like the old precinct downtown, but it keep's me going. What are you doing here at this ungodly hour?"

"Same thing as always. One of my sweet, devoted clients has a husband that persists in violating the solemn vows of matrimony."

Jimbo smiled. "Is that still a crime? Hell, that's par for the course these days. What room are they in?"

"I don't know, and your front desk won't tell me. I thought I would park myself near the elevator bank and wait for her to come down to the lobby."

"Hopefully with the pigeon, I assume." Jimbo shook his head. "It won't work, Coley. This place is big. There's a lot of ways they can bypass you. It would be much easier if you had her room number."

"Yes it would, old pal. Blair Lawton. I bet she has a fancy room."

"Still shooting hoops, Coley?"

"You bet! How about a little one-on-one?"

"Just a minute, Coley. I'll see what I can do." Jimbo produced a scanner from a belt loop, talked quietly to someone for several seconds and then fastened the scanner back onto his belt. "I'll have to go up with you, Coley. She's on a security floor. There's a clubroom at the end of the hall up there. You can plant yourself there and see all the elevator action. Please, Coley, no trouble. I ain't supposed to do this kind of thing."

"Gotcha! I don't intend to say a word to anyone. It would be best if they wouldn't notice me at all."

Jimbo stared at the six foot seven black private eye and shook his head, smiling. "You ain't exactly invisible, Coley."

"Us blue-ribbon private eyes have a special talent for blending in with the woodwork."

"That I gotta see! Let's go." Jimbo led the way to an elevator, produced a pass key for the security floor and led him to the clubroom. A cheery-looking young hostess was serving Danish and coffee. Jimbo winked at her. "Take care of my friend here. If there's any trouble, hit the panic button."

Coley settled down into a big wing chair and hid himself behind the pages of the *Wall Street Journal*. His position allowed him to peek out the door and have a clear view of the nearby elevator complex.

Behind the fourth door down the hall from the clubroom, Blair Lawton breathed audibly and deeply, then gasped and bucked wildly, and finally thrashed beneath the covers in uncontrolled abandon, and then lay still. When Jason started to move again, she screamed and started laughing in delirium as she fought to push him away from her.

"Stop! Stop, you fool!" She threw aside the cover and slapped roughly at him. "Jason! There is no more left. That's it. That's all! I need a breather." She struggled to a sitting position and then bounded from the bed and collapsed into a chair across the room.

After a few moments Jason rolled over and grinned at her. "Let's take the day off, Blair. How about another hit. Where the hell do you keep the stuff?"

"Jason, my dear superman, it's almost seven o'clock. We're due to have breakfast with Dillon at eight. Try to pull yourself together. Time to think about business, the new financial plan. Remember?"

Jason folded his hands behind his head and stared at the ceiling. "My God, do you realize I haven't slept a single wink all night? And I'm charged, Blair! Raring to go. Life is better without sleep. Just imagine what everyone is missing when they waste their time sleeping."

"You're crazy, Jason. But that's what I like about you. Don't change, Jason. But right now, you must get serious. You'd better shower first. I don't want you passing out on me."

"I have the usual perfect solution. We'll shower together." He leered at her.

"Oh no you don't." Blair bounded from the chair and into the bathroom, locking the door behind her.

Fifty minutes later the two of them stood fully dressed for the day, inspecting each other meticulously.

"You know, Blair, we're totally superior people. Look at us. A night without sleep and we look like gods."

"Dream on, Jason. You've forgotten that I've had a night's sleep," she lied, trying to recall when Dillon Archibald had left her room. "Are you ready for Mr. Archibald?"

Jason was scrutinizing himself in the mirror, tying and retying his necktie. "Yes, let's get out of here, quick, before I collapse."

They left the room and headed for the elevator. Coley was stunned as he watched Jason and Blair waiting. She had gone to her room with Dillon Archibald and now emerged from it with Jason Granger on her arm. They were both slickly groomed, obviously recently showered.

He opened his jacket slightly to activate the tiny Leica. Ah, a perfect shot, he thought. Of course, it was of little use. The two of them were just standing in front of an elevator. No touchy-touchy, no kissy-kissy. The shot would be interesting to Amanda, but it would serve little purpose in a divorce case. He had missed the real shot behind her closed door. It wasn't predictable or cricket for a woman to go to bed with one man and wake up with another. It just wasn't fair.

He hated the thought of having to report all this to

Willy. A maid could perhaps have been bribed to turn the pass key. A couple of quick clicks of the Leica, and the case would have been made for Amanda. It would have been over almost before it had started.

21

"When you've got something important to do, Bessie, you do it yourself." Sonny Houston raised his voice and enunciated each word distinctly. "Do you think you can call someone on the telephone and get fifty thousand dollars? It'll never happen, Bessie. That's just plain dumb! I'll go in and explain everything in person to the insurance company. I want you to stay here and box up all Tad's belongings so I can haul them to the dump. We can't have you whining and bawling over all that stuff forever."

Bessie groaned and closed her eyes tightly, trying to hold back tears that never seemed to stop flowing for any length of time. "There is precious little, Sonny. The boy didn't have much. I can get it all together in a couple of boxes. There ain't no hurry, Sonny."

"I said, now!" Sonny slammed the flat of his hand on the kitchen table and watched Bessie jump and then tremble as her eyes again flooded with tears. "Look at yourself. The boy's gone, damn it! I'm tired of coming home from the fields and finding you blubbering about Tad. I spent all yesterday setting up a defense perimeter out there so we can be warned when our property is invaded, and then come in to find you whining again."

She stared up at him, dabbing at the corners of her eyes with a napkin. "Sonny, whatever are you talking about? There's nobody bothering us."

"You don't know, woman. There is things happening that is concern for a man. And I'm taking care it. You have nothing to worry about, nothing except to pack up them boxes and get them out of here." Sonny bent over the table until his face was inches away from her. "Tad's gone," he whispered. "He's under a lot of water. He ain't never coming back. You got that, woman?"

Bessie sat rigid as stone, cowed by fear of being struck. That's the way it usually ended when they had a bad argument. Then, to her great relief, he stood erect and walked away from the table. He stuffed some papers in his pocket, put on his leather jacket and walked out the door.

Bessie Houston watched the SUV wind down the farm road away from their house until it turned left on Route 6 and vanished from view behind a row of willows. She sighed heavily and then walked slowly upstairs to Tad's bedroom to begin packing the boxes. She dreaded starting the chore.

A hamper of dirty clothes stood on the upstairs landing. She had gathered them earlier in preparation for taking them to the washing machine in the cellar. She stared at the clothes basket and decided to get started with that chore first. She welcomed almost any task coming to mind that would delay eliminating the last vestiges of Tad that lay scattered around his room.

She picked up the bulky load and then paused in front of their bedroom. She saw the coveralls that Sonny had worn all day yesterday when working on what he called his "defense perimeter," whatever that was. Occasionally she had glanced out the window and spied him in the distance. He had been running a single strand of new barbed wire around the cleared ten acres surrounding their farmhouse. The fields were sloppy with mud and water in the low spots, and the coveralls were heavily soiled from Sonny's long day in the field.

She wondered idly about the "defense perimeter." They didn't keep stock anymore, and Sonny had long ago decided that tending to livestock on the small farm was not worth the effort and expense. Use of the farm was now limited to keeping chickens and growing corn, tomatoes and green beans, which they sold to passersby in a stand Sonny had erected on Route 6. Their only real trouble had been with marauding crows. The strand of barbed wire would scarcely address that problem.

Bessie sat the clothes basket on the bed. She took the coveralls off the hook on the door, folded them quickly and set them on top of the pile. She was distracted for a moment by the bulk of one of the rear pockets. Mechanically, she unfastened the button, reached in and pulled out an envelope, which bore a Manhattan postmark but no return address. It was addressed to Sonny in a crudely lettered scrawl.

She started to lay the envelope on the dresser, then picked it up again. It had been ripped open. Her curiosity got the best of her. To her knowledge, Sonny had not been in New York City for months.

She read the short note, which was written in the same hand-lettered scrawl as the address.

TAD'S RETURN WILL COST YOU TWO HUNDRED THOUSAND DOLLARS. GET THE MONEY TOGETHER IN SMALL BILLS. FURTHER INSTRUCTIONS WILL FOLLOW. TAD IS FINE.

Bessie's hands trembled as she tried to fold the note and put it back in the envelope. She sat on the edge of the bed and read the note again. TAD IS FINE. The last line of the strange note brought a smile to her face that vanished almost at once. Why hadn't Sonny told her about the note? What had he done about it? They didn't have two hundred thousand dollars. Even if they sold the old farm, they couldn't raise that kind of money.

She again folded the crude note carefully and forced it into the envelope. She tucked it under her dress against her bosom. She buttoned the rear pocket of the coveralls and tossed them once more on top of the dirty clothes. If Sonny brought up the note she would tell him only that she found some bits of ruined, soggy paper in the washtub.

Now what? she wondered. She felt her heart pumping with excitement. Sonny would be furious if he knew she had explored his pockets. He would surely hit her. She just knew it. He had done it many times for much less provocation. Yet she had to talk to someone about what she had discovered. What did Sonny intend to do?

Slowly she started her trek down to the cellar with the clothes basket. All at once she made a decision. Tomorrow she would tell Sonny she wanted to visit his sister in Morristown. She had done it before, and Sonny always seemed to encourage her visits. In fact he would probably drive her there if she asked him. He would even agree to her staying over night a day or two. He had left her alone with Sarah before. Sarah was a highly educated woman. She would know what to do.

The trip into New York gave Sonny Houston a lot of "think time." He drove east on Route 6 and decided to turn south along the Delaware until he could pick up Interstate 80. His choice of routes took him alongside the still-high Delaware where Tad had disappeared. He studied the shoreline closely as he drove and reaffirmed his belief that there was no way the frail boy could have survived.

After circling the towering building that housed the Great Eastern Life Insurance Company several times, he pulled into a parking garage nearby, cursing under his breath at the sign that advertised a nineteen dollar minimum.

Once inside the marble-floored lobby, he approached an information desk.

"I'm here to collect on some insurance."

"Yes, sir. Would that be a commercial policy or survivors' benefit policy?"

"My boy died and I want to get the money."

The attendant of the information desk looked at the massive scar-faced man who had expressed himself so bluntly. Of course he had seen others like that. Recent loss of a family member affected people strangely sometimes.

"I'm sorry, sir. You will want to visit our claims division. It's on the fourteenth floor. The elevator is right over there, sir. Do you have your policy with you?"

"Now, I wouldn't come here without it, would I?" Sonny scowled at the man, turned and walked to the elevator. Upstairs he was given a number and seated in a row of chairs where a couple of other people were waiting. Soon he was escorted to a cubicle where he sat across the desk from a claims examiner. Without speaking he shoved the policy across the desk.

The woman studied the policy for a few moments and then spoke. "You are the beneficiary, Mr. Houston?"

"Yes, Tad was my son."

"I'm sorry, Mr. Houston." The woman began filling out a claims form. "And now, sir, tell me about the deceased. I will need a statement from you, identification and a notarized copy of the death certificate."

"Death certificate? There ain't none. The boy drowned last week."

"Oh, my, that recently? I am sorry, sir. The funeral director usually supplies copies of the certificate from the coroner's office. When was the funeral, Mr. Houston? I know it must be difficult for you at this time." She met Sonny's unblinking stare and silence. "If you will just fill out the claims form, I will give you a copy and a receipt for your policy and we will pursue the matter for you, sir."

Houston scowled at her. "I'm afraid you don't understand. There wasn't any funeral. My boy Tad is somewhere in the river. I come here to get my money."

The woman stood up with the policy in hand. "I'll make a copy of this, Mr. Houston, and then let you talk to my supervisor. In view of the fact we do not yet have verification of the boy's death, there may be some waiting period."

"I guess you didn't listen too well, do you?" Houston

started to raise his voice. "I am here in person to verify that my boy is at the bottom of the Delaware River. I've paid payments every month, all of Tad's life. I've driven through deep snow in the winter to get them to the post office. I want the money now!"

"Of course, sir, I understand how you feel, but we need an official notice of death." She saw sweat beaded on the man's brow. "Sir, I will be right back. I think it might be helpful if you speak to my supervisor." The woman walked away, leaving Houston sitting alone.

The supervisor came back with her, holding an envelope in his hand. "Mr. Houston, here is a copy of the policy and a receipt for the original. I personally will expedite the paperwork and see that a check is drawn when we have accumulated all the necessary verification."

Houston glared at him, snatched the envelope from his hand, turned on his heels and left the office muttering curses that were not completely audible.

The supervisor walked to the door of the office where he could observe Sonny Houston waiting for an elevator. He impatiently pushed the elevator button repeatedly, still muttering profanities to himself. The broad-shouldered man gave every appearance of being unstable, even menacing. When he finally disappeared into an elevator, the supervisor breathed a heavy sigh and turned to face his claims administrator. "He wasn't very civil, was he, Ms. Clausen?"

"No, sir, I found him a little frightening. But then, he did lose a son. The poor man hasn't had time to adjust, I suppose."

Outside, Sonny Houston strode rapidly to the garage where he had parked his SUV and paid the parking fee, emitting a string of curses at the attendant. "You got a license to steal, haven't you? I'll tell you something. It won't be long until people rise up and take care of thieves like you."

To his surprise the attendant smiled at him and then shouted across the garage. "Hey, Carlo, we have man here with a complaint about our prices."

A huge man, brandishing a tire iron, acknowledged Sonny by sticking one middle finger up in the air and grinning broadly.

Sonny Houston climbed into his SUV and pulled out into traffic, mumbling aloud. "And Bessie wonders why I'm building a defense perimeter. Damn! She damn well better learn why!"

22

Willy Hanson propped a foot on the edge of his desk and listened intently as Coley brought him up to date on Blair Lawton's busy night. "Amazing, Coley, absolutely amazing. What's this world coming to? I'm a little surprised with Dillon Archibald acting that way in these days of so much sexual harassment litigation. The old boy has quite a professional reputation. He pulled Harmony Mutual out of the doldrums by spinning off everything but their big insurance operation. They got tangled up in a health-care project that got them in a lot trouble. Dillon Archibald received lots of kudos in the financial press for straightening them out."

"Really?" Coley looked at his friend with admiration. "How do you know all that, Willy?"

"Easy. While you've been reading the sport sections in the tabloids, I've been reading the *Wall Street Journal*. There was quite an article about the old man a couple of days ago. The same article mentioned Jason Granger, his new vice president. He must be a fair-haired boy with Archibald."

"I guess that elevates Granger's assistant to his fair-haired girl. How stupid of me not to have figured all that out." Coley's mind did a vivid retake of Archibald's hand neatly cupping Blair's derriere.

"Coley, have you thought of the possibility that

Archibald might have gone to her hotel that night for some legitimate business purpose? It's done sometimes, I guess." Willy finished the question with an unbelieving shrug.

"I can't believe you said that, Willy!" This time it was Penny chiming in on the conversation. "Considering the amount of booze we saw them drink, and that he was drooling and pawing her and getting away with it, you can bet that there was no business on the agenda."

"Now that we have the woman's point of view, Willy, what do we do next?"

"Coley, I'll pick up the tail on Jason if you don't mind, and you continue with Blair Lawton. Given the facts, we should meet out there somewhere." Willy waved his arm toward the world outside the window. "Let's try to get this thing over with fast. Even if we don't nail them in the sack, we might be able to build up a solid case with an overload of circumstantial stuff if we keep a tight log on both of them. Use your microtapes and ears. We paid a lot of money for fancy listening equipment and haven't got a nickel in return."

"Since you guys get all the excitement, what menial chores do you have mapped out for me, Willy?" Penny grinned sarcastically. She never gave up trying to play the role of a real private eye.

"Patience, my dear Miss Wine. Your time will come. But for now I want you to dig up everything you can on Jason Granger, and while you're doing it, let's look at the bio on Dillon Archibald. If we are going to get this thing out of the way in a day or two we've got to know more about these people."

"Oh, goody," groaned Penny. "I get to go to the newspaper morgues and the public library."

"And then you've got to hang around the office. Amanda Granger is supposed to check in this afternoon. Don't say anything about Coley's discovery this morning. Amanda Granger seems to be in full control of her emotions. It's a little awesome how she has accepted her role as a jilted woman. Nonetheless, we don't want to precipitate a homicide."

"Aye, aye, sir." Penny saluted Willy whimsically and left Coley alone with him. To her, Willy was a mysterious, rather aloof character who lived year-round on a sailing yacht named the *Tashtego*. It was skippered by a mysterious woman named Ginny who had never once visited their office in Manhattan. Both Willy and Ginny seemed to want to keep Willy's business totally isolated from his private life on the yacht. Coley had told her once that Ginny was beautiful, and the salt of the earth, but never discussed her further.

Penny's thoughts were interrupted by the telephone. It was Amanda Granger. The connection was not good. There was a strange droning noise in the background. "Amanda, this is Penny. Willy and Coley are still here. Just a moment."

"No need to interrupt them, Penny. I can barely hear anything on this phone. I checked out of the Waldorf and am on a plane to Harrisburg right now. I can't stand being part of his life anymore. He can find an apartment in hell as far as I'm concerned. I did my last good deed for Jason by going to dinner last night. Dillon Archibald may be a financial genius, but socially, he's an adolescent creep."

Penny chuckled. "I guessed as much. I got that impression, even at a distance. Coley caught him with his hand glued to Lawton's butt."

"He'd better be careful. I think Cora Archibald might use a machete on him. She's a tough cookie."

"Really! Is there any message you would like for me to pass along to Willy or Coley?"

"There is one thing—the real reason I called. Jason has decided to live in a company-owned suite for a while in Manhattan. So he's not looking for an apartment anymore. I guess my situation put the kibosh on that. In fact, he's driving back to Harrisburg tomorrow to pick up some necessities."

"I hate to ask the question, Amanda, but do you think Blair Lawton will be making the drive with him?"

"I really don't know. He's been a clam. The only reason I know about him driving to Harrisburg is that it was brought up in dinner conversation last night. He drove his sexy little Corvette to New York. It wouldn't surprise me if he took Blair with him, if only for a playmate during the four-hour drive."

Penny chuckled again. "You're a very unusual woman, Mrs. Granger, staying so calm about it all. If he belonged to me, I think I'd do something drastic."

"No danger of that, Penny. I have a wonderful life ahead of me . . . without Jason. Bye now."

Penny thought she heard her voice falter when she mentioned Jason, but it could have been the connection from the airplane. She returned to Willy and Coley and promptly reported the news.

Willy grinned appreciatively. "I suppose I'll have to rent a fancy set of wheels to keep up with a Corvette."

"What if Blair Lawton rides with him? Do I get to ride in your fancy car?"

"Absolutely not, Coley. In that event we'll take two cars. We can pull a switcheroo now and then so they don't get used to either of us. This little trip could be just what we are looking for. Keep your camera ready and the ears out. We could wrap up this case tomorrow."

Coley frowned. "I'll bet you're gonna rent one of those snazzy new little BMW sport jobs you've been looking at. How about me? I suppose I'll have to rent one of those discreet little Chevys, something that sort of blends into the scenery."

"Bingo, Coley! We are of one mind."

23

Empress Carlota stared at her image in the mirror. She had ransacked her closet to find something that wasn't a badge of her profession and finally settled on a print dress, almost knee length, and a loose, heavy-knit man's wool sweater that one of her tricks had left behind.

Suzie's phone rang and rang. Carlota knew she was at home or the answering machine would have been on. The Park Avenue workhorse wasn't about to miss a trick.

"Hi, honey." A husky, low, chain-smoker's voice, both sleepy and sexy, finally answered.

"Sorry to disappoint you, Suzie. It's just me, Carlota. Am I interrupting anything?"

"Mm . . . let me check. Nope, the SB went home to his wife and kiddies. The bastard didn't even say good-bye. I hope he left a C-note on the dresser or he's in big trouble. What's up with you, Empress?"

"How's your old limo these days? I got an emergency."

Suzie chuckled in her raspy cigarette voice. "Doll, the last time I drove it, it was leaking oil like crazy. But she still goes. Better put a case of oil in the trunk if you're going very far. You're welcome to it, babe."

"Thanks, Suzie." Carlota breathed a sigh of relief. The "limo" was Suzie's beat-up old Ford Escort that she had accepted in lieu of payment for a night in the sack with an NYU law student. But it still ran, and it was legal. It was just what she needed for the trip to Morristown. "I'll probably have it back before dark."

"No problem, Empress. If the old crate dies on you, just take the plates off and let it sit. Keep it as long as you want. The old Ford reminds me of my date last night."

"Really?"

"Yeah, old man Hornaby must be about eighty. He wants to die in the saddle. He works hard at it. Some night he's going to make it. Nice old guy. He always tells me to be sure and lift his bankroll before the coroner gets there."

"Now there's a real gentleman, Suzie." Carlota giggled. She and Suzie swapped a lot of stories. She had long ago decided that she didn't have a best friend, but Suzie came close. "Thanks again, Suzie. You got one coming if I can ever help."

Carlota hung up and turned to see Tad, wrapped in a blanket, staring wide-eyed at her from the old sofa that had become his personal pad. "Young man, it's time to put on your clean duds. We have our chariot ready."

"This means I'm leaving you for good, Carlota?" Tad made no move to leave his position on the couch.

"Tad, baby, you make it sound terrible when you use words like 'for good.' You can come back to see me some day. Maybe I'll even come and see you." Carlota couldn't look at him when she said it. After all, what was the real likelihood of Tad's folks permitting him to come see a Ninth Avenue whore? "Now get your clothes on. Tell you what. You can be in charge of putting the oil in the engine when it needs it. You know how to do that?"

"Sure do! Pops showed me how to do that a long time ago." Tad turned glum again. He hoped that he was just going to see Aunt Sarah and maybe Mom some day. Pops wouldn't like the way he lit out and hid.

A few minutes later Carlota and Tad walked rapidly toward the parking lot that held Suzie's old Ford Escort over on Eleventh Avenue. A very large woman with frizzled, unkempt gray hair waddled down the steps that led to the door of an old brownstone. Tad recognized her at once as the lady who had led him back to Carlota's the day he got lost.

The woman reached the sidewalk just ahead of them and walked in their direction. Not slowing down, Carlota spoke a cheery good morning that was returned by an icy stare from the woman.

Soon out of earshot, Tad spoke. "Gee, Aunt Carlota, she ain't very friendly, is she?"

"No, Tad, but she did take the trouble to bring you home to me. We have to cut her some slack, I suppose."

"Cut her some slack?" Tad looked puzzled. The woman's disapproval of Carlota was very apparent.

"Yeah, Tad. We've got to assume that she means well. I guess she just doesn't like me. We'll have to live with that, Tad."

"Well then I don't like her either." Tad looked back and frowned at the woman, now a hundred feet away from them. Carlota quickened her step and soon they were seated in the dented and dusty old Ford Escort.

Driving made Carlota very nervous. She had never done it often enough to be comfortable. At Seventy-second Street, she turned left and soon gingerly merged into heavy traffic on the West Side Highway. The George Washington Bridge would lead to Route 80 in New Jersey. Finally she felt relaxed enough to glance at Tad, now sitting quite erect with his hands propped on the dashboard. She smiled at him. What had his father seen in the bright young boy to brought on such harsh discipline. "Do you like school, Tad?"

"I like reading, and I like science. But I ain't too good at arithmetic. Mom says I'll get better at it."

"What does your dad say?" Carlota glanced at him again and saw his expression change.

"Pops thinks I'm real stupid, I guess."

"Oh, come on, Tad. You know what? I think you're exaggerating."

"Nope," Tad shook his head vigorously. He stared far away up the Hudson River. "It's sure a lot bigger than the Delaware."

The drive through suburbia went quickly, too quickly, really, for Carlota. When the road sign appeared indicating the exit ramp for Morristown, she felt herself getting quite nervous at the prospect of meeting Tad's aunt. What if the boy hadn't assessed her properly? The woman had every right to blow her stack over her delay in reporting the missing boy. Even though the lad had not been honest with her about his name for a long time, that didn't explain why she hadn't turned the kid over to social services or the police.

The aunt might not understand that her own experiences over the years had destroyed her confidence in the system. She might not understand that she was drawn personally to the boy from the day she rescued him from the jerk outside the lobby of the X-rated movie palace. She glanced at Tad. He was now on the edge of his seat as they pulled off the exit ramp.

"This way, this way!" Tad shouted excitedly, pointing down the street to her left. "It's still quite a ways off, but this is the way you go."

Carlota drove for several miles, slowing down once in a while when Tad wanted to look down a side street. She began to wonder if the boy really knew where he was going. Morristown was bigger than she had pictured it. She was about to give up on her effort when, all of a sudden, Tad became very tense.

Tad twisted toward her with a pained look on his face. In fact, he was choking back tears. Finally he forced out a few words. "It's right back there, Aunt Carlota. Sarah's house is on that last side street."

"Wonderful, Tad! I knew you could do it. Let's see if we can turn right here and go around the block." Carlota drove slowly around the block and finally pointed the old Escort down the street Tad had indicated. "Okay, Tad, which house is it? You'll have to tell me."

Tad responded by ducking below the level of the window and curling himself into a fetal position. "Keep goin'! Keep goin'! I can't go in there, Carlota." He looked up at her, eyes running withs tears.

"Tad! You sit up and show me which house. Now, come on. You're acting silly." She stopped the car, held her foot on the brake and pulled him up on the seat next to her.

Tad pointed down the street and then buried his face in her lap. "It's right there," he mumbled, "by the big van." He twisted and looked up at her in agony. "That's Pops's van, old GITGO 7! I can't go in there.... He'll beat me good. Please, Carlota, go! Drive fast."

Carlota surveyed the block ahead carefully. Then, patting Tad gently on the shoulder, she held him below the level of the window and drove by.

"Young man, we've got to go someplace and talk. You've got nothing to be afraid of. I'll walk right in there with you."

Tad screamed, "No! No! No! I won't go in there, Carlota. Not in a million years."

"Now, Tad. We'll just see about that." Carlota drove ahead several blocks and then pulled into the parking lot of a fast-food restaurant. "Let's have a hamburger and talk everything over. What do ya say, Tad?"

Tad sat erect in the seat. He looked Carlota right in the eye for a second and then flipped the door latch. He jumped from the car, ran away as fast as he could and disappeared into a walkway between two buildings.

"Tad, stop!" She called after him in vain. Carlota quickly parked the car, and went to look for him.

She walked down the alleyway where he had vanished and looked along the backs of all the buildings in what was a narrow strip mall. She circled the area several times on foot. Finally she went into the McDonald's. There was no sign of Tad. Desperately, she opened the door of the men's rest room and peered inside. No Tad anywhere.

She walked slowly back to the old Escort and reparked in such a position that she had a view of the entire mall. She felt that Tad had to be hiding. She would wait and watch. The boy had to be somewhere nearby.

Carlota's eyes dampened. Her efforts to help the boy,

like everything else in her life, had met with failure. Tad was different from her other failures, though. He had trusted her implicitly, and she had failed him.

She looked at her watch and decided she would wait right there for a long time. Perhaps later, she would go back to the house Tad had pointed out. If the van was gone, the least she could do was to introduce herself to Aunt Sarah. Maybe together, they could think of something to do.

24

In some ways the red Corvette was a blessing. Early that morning Willy had watched the parking valet bring the car into position at the exit of the hotel. He quickly maneuvered his racy BMW Z3 roadster into position so he could watch for the Corvette to emerge with Jason Granger behind the wheel.

It was easy to follow the flashy car through the still-empty streets of Manhattan at that hour. Granger made his way to the East Side Drive, went north and finally exited into the tunnel under the apartment buildings and crossed the George Washington Bridge to New Jersey.

Willy was puzzled. If Granger was on his way to Harrisburg, he was going the scenic route, not the obvious short way using the turnpikes. Well, what the hell, he thought, perhaps Jason relished a spin through the Poconos with his new toy. He wondered about Blair Lawton. He would have bet money that she would be making the trip with him.

He wished Granger would slow down. He was pushing eighty or better most of the time. The state police were notorious along this stretch of Route 80. If he were to be stopped, Granger would probably be lost for the day.

In about forty minutes, Granger surprised him with a

last-second turn onto Route 208, leading him straight north. Now, this was confusing. Every mile in that direction took him further from Harrisburg. The road twisted around more than the interstate, creating the necessity to follow much closer. It required a lot of concentration. Granger seemed hell-bent on getting somewhere in a hurry.

A half hour later they were still snaking their way north through Stokes State Forest in the mountainous northwest corner of New Jersey. Jason led him streaking through the Delaware bottoms and then crossed the river into Pennsylvania. Suddenly he slowed to a virtual crawl after he had raced through the small town of Milford. He crossed Interstate 84 and picked up Route 6. Suddenly he pulled to a complete stop.

Willy had no choice but to speed by the Corvette, now parked in front of a large rural mailbox. At a bend in the road after he lost view of the Corvette, he made a quick U-turn and crept back to a point where he could focus on Granger through his small roof-prism binoculars. To his amazement, Granger had also made a U-turn. He was leaning out the window of the Corvette and putting something in the rural mailbox. Having done that, the Corvette quickly pulled away and headed back toward Milford, a couple of miles away.

Willy's curiosity couldn't be contained. The second the Corvette was out of sight, Willy pulled to a stop in front of the mailbox. The box stood at the end of a farm road which ran far into the distance. He could see the roof of a farmhouse among a grove of trees. Large letters on the box indicated that it belonged to HOUSTON.

Going against the grain of conscience, he looked all around and then reached in and snatched the small envelope from the box. He had to know what message Granger could have for the isolated farmer. "Mr. Houston, whoever you are," he mumbled to himself, "I'm going to borrow this for a while."

There was no address on the envelope, just the name

HOUSTON scrawled in big letters. He slipped the envelope between visor and roof. He roared away, realizing that it already might be too late to pick up the Corvette.

Luck was with him. As he approached Interstate 84 he saw the gleaming red Corvette curling around the cloverleaf of the on-ramp. Willy trailed him by a couple of hundred yards until Granger exited at the first available off-ramp. From there, it was a winding drive down a lonely country road and then a steep climb to the top of what appeared to be one of the highest ridges in the Poconos. Granger was certainly getting no closer to Harrisburg.

The taillights of the red Corvette far ahead of him began to blink. Granger slowed down and then made a sharp left off the mountain road. Willy slowed down for several seconds and then moved cautiously ahead. A large carved wooden sign overhung the driveway to the left, proclaiming that the weathered log structure beyond was the CRESTVIEW HIDEAWAY. Then, in smaller letters below, it read BED, BREAKFAST AND LIBATION.

Parked among half-a-dozen other vehicles facing the rustic structure was the red Corvette. From the looks of the fancy cars lined up in front of the Crestview Hideaway, it attracted an affluent clientele.

There was one exception. Far off to the right, partially obscured by pine boughs, was a small vintage Chevy Cavalier. He could make out the faint image of someone sitting in the Chevy behind the tinted windows. As Willy watched, the window on the driver's side slowly lowered. A hand extended and motioned in his direction, a large black hand. A face appeared, wearing a huge grin.

It was Coley Doctor! That could mean only one thing. Blair Lawton was also inside the Crestview Hideaway. Coley had followed her there. All of a sudden Jason Granger's mad dash into the wilds of the Poconos was explained. The Crestview Hideaway was a trysting mecca for Blair and Jason.

Willy's eyes came to rest on the white envelope he had pilfered from the strange mailbox. He had actually forgotten about it, absorbed by his chase to the Hideaway.

Coley slid into the seat next to Willy. "Fancy meeting you here, old buddy. You were sure right on about predicting we'd meet later in the day. I take it the red Corvette belongs to Jason Granger."

Willy nodded his affirmation, and eyed the lineup of cars in the parking area. "Which one of those belongs to Blair Lawton?"

"The white Mercedes. Didn't surprise me a bit. Blair Lawton is kind of the white Mercedes type. She's some piece of work. I followed her swiveling tail all the way from her hotel to the garage."

"What do you want to bet Dillon Archibald is paying the tab?" asked Willy.

"No bet, Willy. Right now that broad is sailing through life on a free ticket. With her brains and her body, she can go through life finding a sucker a minute."

"I'll accept your judgment about the body, Coley, but how do you know about her brains?"

"Just call it my natural flair for assessing the human female, Willy. She's a take-charge operator. You should have seen her at the Water Club. She started out being a quiet little prissy miss, and before the evening was over she had everybody charmed out of their pants, including Dillon, our legendary CEO. You should have seen her handle the registration clerk at our little inn here. She got him to switch their suite to the best in the house, despite the fact that some guy had a deposit on it for a month."

"Coley, do you think Jason is with her yet?"

"Hell, yes. Would you keep that one waiting?"

"What are we doing sitting here and talking, then? Let's check the place out." Willy started to open the door of the Z3.

"Relax, pal. I've rented the room next door. I've glued

'ears' to the wall and the tape is spinning. How about some breakfast? They have country ham, buttermilk biscuits and all kinds of goodies."

"Bingo! Coley, you're a wonder. I'm starving. Let's have some breakfast." Willy glanced again at the sun visor and the purloined envelope. "Oh, Coley, I forgot about this. When Granger was driving up here he went about twenty miles out of his way to put this letter in some farmer's mailbox. I got very curious."

Coley looked at the small, thin envelope as if it were infected with the plague or something worse. He stared at the name, HOUSTON, scrawled on the outside. "And the farmer was nice enough to give it to you?"

"Well, not exactly, Coley. I took it."

"You took it out of the mailbox? Willy, I'll bake some brownies and bring them to Leavenworth with a lot of nice new books."

"But aren't you curious?"

"Of course, I'm curious. But that don't give us the right to break the law." Coley held the envelope up to the light. "Here, Willy, you open it. We'll just take a little peek and then you can drive all the way back and put it where you found it. I sure hope no one saw you.

Willy grinned. "I knew you'd see it my way, partner." Willy took a pocketknife and worked it along a gap in the adhesive that sealed it. It took him a while because he was trying to preserve the integrity of the envelope.

Finally, he was able to get a finger inside and slip out a long narrow slip of paper. Scrawled in a peculiar combination of printed caps and cursive lettering was a short message.

LITTLE TAD MISSES YOU VERY MUCH. ON WEDNESDAY 10 A.M., PUT THE TWO HUNDRED THOUSAND UNDER THE FRONT SEAT OF YOUR VAN ON THE PASSENGER SIDE. JUST FORGET IT IS THERE. FORGET ABOUT WATCHING

THE VAN TOO. LITTLE TAD WON'T BE RELEASED UNTIL
THE MONEY IS PICKED UP.

Willy stared at the message. "What in the hell do you suppose this is all about, Coley? This doesn't make any sense at all."

Coley gaped at the scribbled message, trying desperately to jog his memory. Something about it rang a bell. He smiled and then frowned intensely as he reread the message. "Willy, the trouble with you is that you spend all your time with the *Wall Street Journal* and the *New York Times*. You should read the tabloids."

"Okay, Coley, I'll bite. Why should I do something stupid like that?"

"Well, then you would know that a few days ago, a little boy named Tad Houston was drowned in the Delaware River. I admit, I didn't follow the story very closely. We'll have to go back and pick up some old papers. I don't believe they ever found the boy's body." Coley shrugged in disbelief. "It's hard to believe that Jason Granger, the rising star of Harmony Mutual, would be involved in anything like this."

Now Willy sat shaking his head, gaping at the envelope in Coley's hand. "But he is, Coley. I saw him put this in the mailbox with my own eyes. There was absolutely nothing else in the box!"

"Holy mackerel! Here we are minding our own business, just trying to trying to help some nice, sweet lady get rid of some jerk and he turns out to be a kidnapper. I still don't believe it, Willy. What do we do?"

"We think of the kid. Nothing else matters right now. If this kid is still alive, there may not be much time left. As much as I don't believe that Jason Granger fits the profile of a kidnapper, we've got to follow through."

"I agree, Willy. We've got to get to the appropriate police right away with this." Coley looked back at the old inn. "Let's get in there and pick up the recorder. Maybe we'll get real lucky. Maybe they've been going at it like rabbits. He sure didn't waste any time getting up to her room."

"Yeah. I'll call the office and have Penny pick up all the back issues of the papers that have anything in them about the drowning."

Upstairs now, they tiptoed down the hall and entered the room next to the suite rented by Blair Lawton. Willy immediately spotted the listening device that Coley had taped to the wall. On the floor was a miniature recorder and a set of earphones.

Coley picked up the earphones and held them between them to share the perfectly clear sounds coming from the other room.

A series of low moans from Blair Lawton was followed by continual heavy breathing, interrupted by an occasional squeal of delight. Finally, there came an actual female voice. "Jason! Don't ever stop, Jason! Never, never, never stop!" Then a long sequence of Blair Lawton panting and squealing again, all out of control.

Coley sat the earphones on a table. "Nice of her to identify him by name. Looks like we've got some evidence. I think we ought to let the tape recorder go for a while longer. What do we do now, Willy?"

"Did you rent this room for the night?"

"Sure did."

"We better split up for a while. The missing kid has to come first. You stick with the recording here in the room. I'll leave and contact the Pennsylvania State Police. Maybe they'll have someone in the area. If they split before I get back, follow Granger."

Coley nodded. "Willy, I still find this all hard to believe. Where do you suppose he has the boy?"

Willy shrugged in deep thought. "Stay close to him, Coley. We've got to find out." Willy looked at the tiny tape recorder on the carpet, picked up the earphones and listened for a few moments. "By the time they crawl out of the sack, I don't think we'll have to spend any more time building a case for Amanda Granger. I think they are acting out the entire *Kama Sutra* in there."

Coley shook his head. "I just can't figure it out. If Granger kidnapped the boy, how can he push it out of his mind and spend the day like this?"

Willy shrugged, opened the door and made his way quietly down the hall. Maybe the police would know something.

25

Willy parked in front of the building marked PENNSYLVANIA STATE POLICE. He hesitated for a few moments before leaving his car, pondering the best way to approach them. It was imperative that he immediately establish his credibility. Explaining why he had robbed the rural mailbox was taking a chance. To be sure, police were understandably irked by private investigators who took any liberty that would be taboo for themselves. The ransom note could be tainted evidence. After all, what business did he have exploring the farmer's mailbox?

But what the hell, there could be a kid's life at stake. The authorities had to know what he knew. This is one time he hoped some of his professional fame would be recognized. On many high-profile cases he had worked prudently close to the local jurisdictions.

Inside, an officer faced him from behind a small, cluttered desk. "Yes, sir. What can I do for you?"

"Name's Willy Hanson." He pushed his private investigator credentials in front of the officer and watched him study them carefully. "I have some information that I ran across while investigating a routine divorce case. It's about the boy who supposedly drowned in the Delaware River near here."

Officer Evan Knight sat erect in his chair and looked sharply at the man standing in front of him. If the name Willy Hanson meant anything to him, he didn't show it. "Supposedly drowned?" questioned Knight. "Tell me, Mr. Hanson, how do you come to know anything about young Tad Houston?"

"All I really know about the investigation is what I've read in the papers. Is the boy still missing?"

Knight continued to stare at him. He sipped from a steaming cup of coffee before saying anything. "If you don't mind, Mr. Hanson, I'd like you to get on with your story. No one around here has had a decent night's sleep since it happened. We've done everything but dredge a twenty-mile stretch of the river. There's been no sign of the boy as yet. Where's this partner you talk about?" Knight set the cup down precisely on a ring stained into the wooden table, obviously a regular repository. "Just a minute before you go on." He turned toward an open door to an adjoining room. "Hey, Leonard! Get in here for a minute."

Another trooper walked in. He wore heavy boots and khaki work clothes. His outfit was rumpled and stained. The man looked exhausted. He rubbed at his eyes as if he had been sleeping, then slumped into a chair.

"Maybe you better hear this, Lenny. This man here is a P.I., name's Willy Hanson. He claims to know something about Tad Houston." He turned again toward Willy. "I don't mind telling you we've had a lot of people call in about the boy. There's been a lot of kooks and self-styled P.I.s. But we're still searching the river. Lenny here has been out there since dawn. Now go on, Mr. Hanson."

"My partner's doing a shadow job right now at a place

called the Crestview Hideaway up on the ridge. It's a divorce case. A man up there is breaking his marriage vows." Willy grinned, but if either of them thought what he said was funny, they didn't show it. "We're hoping to have the case wrapped up today."

"That's all very interesting to you, I suppose. If the walls to that old hot-pillow joint could talk, half the people in these hills would be in trouble. What's all this got to do with the boy?"

Willy looked at the two men, now edgily alert. Maybe he should have gone a little further with the case before talking to the police. "Well, it turns out that man we are following, the fellow that's cheating on his wife right this minute, could be a kidnapper. He might know where Tad Houston is."

Eyes riveted on him, the two men quietly waited for him to finish. Finally, Evan Knight prodded him to go on. "Mr. Hanson, that's a serious accusation. I hope you have something to back it up."

Willy produced the envelope holding the ransom instructions from his pocket and slid it across the desk. "We've been careful to touch only the edges of the note. In the course of following our philandering husband, I saw him put this envelope, containing the message just as you see it, into Sonny Houston's rural mailbox up near Milford."

Evan Knight held the ransom note gingerly by its edges. He waited until his partner, now standing behind him, had read the message. "How did you come into possession of this?"

"I took it out of the mailbox real fast and continued to follow the man to Crestview Hideaway. There was nothing else in the mailbox. It seemed a safe enough thing to do. The mailbox is a long ways from the house, which is at least a quarter of a mile away in a grove of trees."

"What on earth possessed you to do that, to steal the note from the mailbox?" The trooper was now really scrutinizing him, as if trying to find an obvious flaw in his story.

He turned to his partner. "Call the captain. He ought to get over here right away."

Willy felt his credibility was in question. "You've got to understand that we've been on this case only a couple of days. This guy, Jason Granger is his name, leads me from a hotel in Manhattan to the Crestview Hideaway. He detoured about twenty miles for no reason other than to put the note in Houston's remote mailbox. It seemed out of character. After all, he has just been appointed vice president of a big insurance company in New York." Willy paused, facing their stony silence. "I got curious. I lifted the note."

"What makes you think you weren't spotted by Granger or his lady friend?"

"The woman wasn't with him. She had driven to the Crestview Hideaway earlier in the day. My partner followed her. I met him there. She had already checked into a suite. I don't think Jason Granger ever became suspicious of me. It was an easy tail. He drives a red Corvette. It's like following a neon light."

"What do you drive, Mr. Hanson?"

"A BMW Z3 roadster."

"Good thing, Hanson. If he decided to speed, he would have lost you with most anything else. I'm still surprised you could keep up." The words were the first spoken by the officer named Lenny. He was a tall, lean fellow who never blinked while Willy gave his story.

"Do you think there's a chance that they've got the boy in the Crestview?" Evan Knight asked.

"I don't see how. My partner tailed the woman from her hotel in Manhattan to the Crestview. She was alone. He watched her check in and go immediately to her room. We know from our investigation that the woman, Blair Lawton, has an ongoing shack-up history with Granger, among others."

"Sounds like a busy bimbo. She must be some dish."

Lenny scratched at his unshaven face. "How about your client, the man's wife. Could she be involved in the kidnapping."

"I seriously doubt that. Both my partner and I have spent some time with her lately. Her knowing anything about this seems out of the question. Seems to be a classy woman, pregnant, and filled with disappointment at Jason Granger."

Knight looked again at the note now lying on his desk. "You'll have to leave this with me, Hanson. The boys will want to run it through the lab. You about finished with your surveillance of Granger?"

"My partner should be wrapping it up about now."

Lenny looked intensely at Willy. "Your partner's name is Coley Doctor, right?"

Willy was shocked, but quickly felt pleased at his identification. "Yes . . . How do you know that?"

Lenny broke into a half-smile. "I pegged your name right away, Mr. Hanson. You got a million dollars worth of publicity when you and Coley busted that Hong Kong murder case." Lenny looked at the note on the desk. "To tell you the truth, it would have been a hard story to swallow if it have been someone else."

"Where does this Jason Granger live?" Knight asked.

"He and his wife live near Harrisburg. Supposedly he's on his way there to pick up some personal stuff. His wife isn't buying the Manhattan move. She's staying in Harrisburg."

"Where are you going right now, Mr. Hanson?"

"I'm going back to the Crestview. If Coley feels he has our case wrapped up, we'll be heading back to Manhattan."

Lenny spoke up. "Something bothers me about the wording of the note." He leaned over Knight's shoulder and pointed. "It says here, 'Put the two hundred thousand'. . . . and so forth. 'The two hundred thousand' makes it sound like there has been a previous communication. Maybe we'd better talk to the Houstons. Remember how odd he acted?"

Willy had to ask one question. "Aren't you going to pick up Jason for questioning?"

"Maybe later in the day." Knight looked thoughtful. "I'd like to question Sonny Houston first. We can tell him that we've been getting phone tips about a possible kidnapping. How he reacts will determine whether or not we have enough to bring him in for further questioning. Meanwhile, we'll have our own shadow on Granger the minute he checks out of the Crestview. The boy is the main consideration. If he is alive, maybe Granger will lead us to him. After all, there may have been two ransom notes."

"Yes, maybe. Mind if I make a suggestion?" Willy spoke in a low voice, almost tentatively.

"You run true to form, Mr. Hanson. All P.I.s love to make suggestions. Okay, shoot." Knight kicked a heel up on the edge of his desk and folded his arms.

"I'd make a copy of the note and then slip it back into the mailbox. Then I'd keep tabs on Houston's vehicle starting Wednesday, like the note instructs, and try to nail the guy when he picks up the two hundred grand. Of course, this might depend on whether Houston can raise that much money."

"We'll get right to work on the evidence, Mr. Hanson. There might be fingerprints on the note. No telling what else the lab might turn up."

Willy nodded, deep in thought. "By the way, call me Willy. The only one alive that calls me Mr. Hanson any more is my lady when she's furious with me. Better yet, why don't you just make a Xerox of the note and put it in the mailbox? Houston would still get the message, and you'd have your evidence, which is a bit tainted, I'd say." Willy paused to let them consider the ramifications of what he proposed, and then spoke again. "As far as I'm concerned, every single action should be taken with the welfare of the boy in mind. If he has been kidnapped, time might already be running out."

"Willy, I appreciate your suggestion, and I like it, but the chief may have other ideas. Meanwhile, I strongly suggest that you back away from this investigation and keep out of the way. When you've finished gathering your evidence on Jason Granger today, we'll make it our business to keep track of him." Knight looked again at the note on his desk. "I'll tell you something, Willy. We appreciate this lead. What we do with it will remain confidential. I don't want you poking around Houston's property again. We could get in each other's way and blow the whole thing."

Willy nodded and then handed Evan Knight his card, which listed himself, Coley Doctor and Penny Wine. "I hope the boy is alive and you find him. If we can help somehow, give us a call." He pointed at the card. "We work together. Talking to one of us is like talking to all of us. Good luck. You know where to find me."

As Willy left, Evan Knight called out to him. "Oh, by the way, Willy, I have one bit of news that might make you feel better about the boy. In view of the ransom note, you've got to keep it under your hat." Knight hesitated. "The boy might have escaped. An Amtrak conductor spotted his picture in the paper a couple days after his canoe turned up empty. He swears the boy was on his train when he arrived at Hoboken station that night. The conductor took him in tow. Says he planned to call his parents when he got to Hoboken, but the kid ran away. He thinks he ran downstairs to the PATH train and might have gone to New York."

"Really? Have the New York police been notified?"

"Yes. So far he hasn't turned up. Finding a lost kid in metro New York ain't no piece of cake. We think it is more likely he would try to get back home, unless the boy is deliberately trying to run away. Of course, the conductor could be mistaken. The kid called himself Eddie Foxworth. The conductor even wrote it down. I talked to the trainman myself. He claims the kid was a dead ringer for the boy in the paper. I'm telling you this just to let you know there may be real hope that the boy is alive."

"Thanks. Have you talked to Tad's parents about this yet?"

"As a matter of fact we told Sonny Houston when we were winding up the search down on the river. It was eerie. He just stared at me for a while, and then said it didn't make any sense. He didn't say another word."

Willy walked out to his car feeling uneasy. He had a gut feeling that the police were dragging their feet. If it were him, he would be tearing away to Milford right now to set a trap for Granger and question Houston. After all, the boy's life might be at stake. He decided right then he would nose around the case a little bit more.

He hated the endless parade of sordid divorce cases that had occupied their time lately. Finding the missing boy, if he were alive, would be a meaningful pursuit. Many times his routine business failed to produce the satisfaction of doing something really worthwhile. He couldn't wait to talk to Coley. If the boy were alive, he had to be found before it was too late.

26

"So my sis didn't bake me an apple pie. I figured it would be coming out of the oven about the time Bessie and I got here." Sonny Houston looked genuinely disappointed. He frowned at his sister.

Sarah looked at him questioningly. How could her brother be thinking about apple pie so soon after Tad had vanished? She looked at Bessie and shrugged. Bessie's eyes were all swollen and red. The woman looked as if she had been weeping for days. "Bessie, darling, why don't you take a nap? Sonny, she looks like she hasn't rested in days." She hugged Bessie close and patted her gently on the back, and then turned to Sonny. "Is there anymore news about Tad? Why haven't they found him?"

"Look, Sis, don't you start asking stupid questions. That's a mean river this time of year. The boy's dead and that's that. Both of you might as well get used to it. Hell, I've done been in New York and talked to the insurance company. Nice folks! They're getting ready to pay us fifty thousand dollars."

Bessie moaned and slumped in a chair, her eyes welling with moisture. "Sonny, how can you even think about things like that? Sometimes you act like you're glad he's gone."

"Shut up, woman! Whine, whine, whine . . . somebody's got to keep a level head around here." He turned to face his sister, now gaping at him.

"Sonny, you just leave Bessie with me awhile. It's gonna take some time for her to adjust. Little Tad was such a sweet boy."

Sonny Houston scowled at her. "You just don't know, sis. The boy had become an ungodly liar. Destructive, too! Bessie better get over it. The boy is better off in heaven."

Sarah put her arm around Bessie. She squeezed her and then led her from the room onto a sunporch, which held a large sofa. "Bessie, lay down here for a while." Then she whispered, "I'll get rid of Sonny. I can tell that he wants to leave, anyhow."

When she reentered the living room, Sonny was already putting his leather jacket on. "Gotta get goin', Sarah. I'm working on our defense perimeter."

"Defense perimeter? Now what might that be?" Sarah looked at her brother, puzzled. She didn't understand much about him anymore. He had come home from the army with a dishonorable discharge and hadn't been the same since. He had denied the dishonor once, but she had once seen the papers hidden upstairs, before he married Bessie.

"It's man's work, Sarah. You wouldn't understand, but you damn well will someday when we stand behind that perimeter. They're going to close in on us someday."

"Who, Sonny? Who is going to close in?"

Sonny shook his head in disgust. "You never was much for havin' common sense, Sarah. You'll find out when the time comes, and then hightail it up to the farm. You'll need protection. You'll see." With that said, he zipped up his jacket, gave his sister an exaggerated version of a military salute, and left.

Sarah breathed a heavy sigh, thankful that he was gone. In recent years her brother had become very hard to understand. She was actually afraid of him, but she didn't really understand why.

She tiptoed into the room where she had left Bessie and was surprised to see her sitting erect with her eyes wide open. "Is he gone?" she whispered.

"Yes. I'm worried about my brother, Bessie. I don't know how you stand being around him all the time. Poor thing, can I get you a cold drink or something?"

"That'll wait, Sarah. First I have to show you something." Sarah opened the large purse she had kept at her side since she arrived. She unzipped an inner pocket and produced the ransom note she had found buttoned in Sonny's work clothes. She passed it to Sarah.

Sarah's eyes grew large. The short, stocky woman glanced at Bessie in disbelief for a moment. She read the note again, aloud. "Who in the world sent this, Bessie? What does Sonny say about this?"

"Oh, Sarah, I found it buttoned in his overalls. He's never once mentioned it to me. He could have had it for a few days. I'm so afraid of him, Sarah. What should I do with the note. Little Tad might be alive somewhere!" Bessie burst into tears again. "But we . . . haven't got that kind of money. What can I do, Sarah?"

Sarah sat on the sofa next to her, reading the note again. "We'll have to go to the police with this, Bessie. Or maybe Sonny has already."

"Oh, no, I'm sure he hasn't. Only a couple of days ago he went to New York and tried to cash Tad's insurance policy.

He has never mentioned the note. I'm sure he is hiding it from me." Bessie sat in silence for a moment and then looked wide-eyed at Sarah. "You know what I think? I think Sonny doesn't ever want to see my Tad again. I think he'd rather have the insurance money."

Meanwhile, Sonny Houston sped homeward. It was a big relief getting rid of Bessie for a while. He couldn't stand her whining all the time. He realized the time would come when he would have to beat some sense into her again.

Nearing his farm, he spied the backhoe he had rented from Smitty's Equipment Company in Port Jervis. They had parked it in the grove of trees next to the house, just where he had asked them to. The big backhoe would make digging the trenches along his defense perimeter a snap. He figured to dig them fifty feet within the strand of razorwire that now protected his property line. To a casual observer it would seem to be an irrigation ditch fed by the old well at the north end.

He parked his van next to the house, went inside and rushed upstairs. There was still a lot of daylight left. He donned the spanking clean pair of coveralls that Bessie had washed and hung in place on the door. He reached above the door and grasped the Marlin and then walked from room to room upstairs.

At each window he paused and tracked the Marlin along the line of posts marking the strand of razorwire. He grinned with satisfaction at his workmanship and squeezed the trigger as the crosshairs passed each post. He was satisfied that from the upstairs windows his complete perimeter was well within range.

He returned the hunting rifle to its rack above the door. Before going downstairs he paused to look at the backhoe parked in the grove of trees. He determined exactly where he would start his project of the day. Then he smiled.

The Casualty Memorial Park would be situated behind

the grape vineyard next to the woods. It was imperative that several graves be dug now. Once casualties were incurred they had to be taken care of immediately. Anyone who was ever in a battle knew that.

At first he had thought of digging four graves, side by side, regular cemetery size, but then he decided they might look strange. So he decided to excavate a similar area as one cubical. It could always be passed off as a basement for a new building or the start of a new pond. Off in the heavy brush near the razorwire marking the northern perimeter, he would dig a single grave away from the others where it could easily be obscured by the brambles.

Downstairs now and out of the house, Houston walked over among the trees and climbed aboard the backhoe. He turned the ignition and the powerful engine rumbled to life. He pulled it slowly out of the grove of trees and pointed it toward the grape arbors to the rear of the property.

"Mr. Houston! Mr. Houston!"

Houston turned abruptly in his seat and saw the small boy running behind the backhoe. It was Eddie Foxworth. "Now see here, boy. Can't you see that fence over there? That's for keepin' people out. You understand that, boy?"

Eddie stopped and gaped at the big earthmover as Houston brought it to a halt. "Sorry, Mr. Houston, I just wondered if they have found Tad. My mom was wondering, too."

Houston shook his finger at him. "Now I want you to get it straight, boy. Tad's dead. There's no use pestering anyone in this house anymore. Now git!"

Eddie turned and walked toward the front gate, then quickly started running toward home as fast as he could.

Sonny Houston watched the boy until he was out of sight before he continued toward the grape arbors. "Dumb kid," he mumbled aloud to himself. "He's too stupid to know how dangerous it is to be inside a defense perimeter. If he ain't careful, he'll find out someday."

He looked up at the sun, still high in the afternoon sky, then slammed the jaw of the backhoe into the wet soil and lifted out the first big scoop of earth. He grinned appreciatively. The grave site would be a reality before sunset.

In the distance he watched a mail carrier's truck pause at his mailbox. He sat quietly for a moment as a scowl creased his brow. He idled the backhoe for a moment as his hand went to his left rear pocket and slipped inside. There was nothing there! He looked down at his clean coveralls, wondering if they were the same ones he had worn before. He decided they were. Maybe the note had been destroyed in the washwater. But then, maybe it hadn't. Then his frown turned to a smile as he slammed the backhoe into the earth again. Hell, he thought, Bessie wouldn't have the guts to show the note to anyone.

27

Empress Carlota sat quietly in the old Ford Escort and started her second pack of cigarettes. She was weary of her vigil of never once dropping her eyes from the row of buildings in the small strip mall. She could see both exits to the mall. The chain-link fence to the rear of the mall was at least six feet high. She couldn't imagine little Tad managing to scale it without her seeing him. Beyond the fence were broad green lawns of a residential neighborhood.

Perhaps Tad had managed to slip away during the first several minutes of his escape from her. But how? She had taken only a few seconds to look inside McDonald's before backing her car to her present vantage point. Carlota inhaled deeply and then squashed the cigarette out in the brimming ashtray.

More and more cars were now entering the mall. Soon it would be lunchtime and the traffic would make it easier for Tad to hide his escape from her. She was disappointed in

Tad. She felt a rapport. Maybe his obvious displays of affection for her had been an act.

She caught a glimpse of herself in the rearview mirror. Harsh lines showed on her face, the makeup smeared from dabbing at occasional tears. "My God," she exclaimed in a whisper to herself, "I look like what I am, an old whore." No wonder the boy had run away.

She lit another cigarette and decided to wait a little longer. Her eyes swept the fast-filling parking lot again before coming to rest on an antique fire truck parked near an entrance to the mall. A sign above the truck proclaimed that a fireman's picnic would be held two weeks hence at some local park.

Her heart leaped as she saw movement in the old truck. Then Tad's face appeared at it's open window. He was obviously staring at her car. Tad climbed though the window and lowered himself to the ground. She froze as she saw him walk slowly toward her, afraid of making any move that might frighten him away. As if in answer to her silent prayer, he kept coming until he stood a couple of feet from her window.

"I'm sorry, Aunt Carlota. I don't ever want to go home. I'm sorry I ran away. I really am."

"Tad, get in the car, please. We'll go back to the city. This whole trip was just one of my bad ideas. I guess we'll have to figure out something else. Come on, Tad!"

Tad circled the car, opened the door and climbed in. Carlota circled him with her arms and hugged him close. "Oh, Tad, what am I going to do with you?"

"You don't have to do anything, Aunt Carlota. I'll be fine."

She tried to hide and brush away those damn tears that kept coming. "Tad ... for one thing, what about your school? You've missed several days, haven't you?"

"Yep. But that's okay, I'm already pretty smart," he assured her.

"Tad, I've got an idea. When we get back to New York,

we'll go down to Barnes and Noble and get you some books to read. Do you like to read?"

"Oh, sure! That would be great."

"We'll pick out some books that you like. Then you can read them when I go out to work once in a while and we can talk about them when I get back. How's that sound?"

His head bobbed decisively in agreement. "I like books about airplanes and boats. Someday I'm going to have an airplane," he said, as if it were sure to be true.

"I bet you will, Tad. You just keep on thinking about that. Keep dreaming about what you really want."

"What do you want, Aunt Carlota?"

She shook her head, wondering what she had any right to want or hope for. She had sunk to the subbasement of life. It had been a long time since she had wished for anything other than her next meal, her next month's rent and a fervent hope that her next trick didn't have AIDS. She glanced at Tad, now rapt with attention as they sped through the Lincoln Tunnel and into Manhattan.

She did know for sure that right now there was one thing she wanted most of all. She prayed that she would find the way to point Tad in the right direction. The Ninth Avenue walk-up, with her gone frequently, was no place for the boy. Carlota wondered idly whether the naive boy had any inkling of her profession.

28

"You look like hell! Do you know how terrible you really look, Jason? When are you going to start working out again? I'll bet you haven't jogged since you left the hospital." Blair Lawton scrutinized her bed partner, naked and disheveled, looking up at her with bloodshot eyes. Her tummy furnished a pillow. They had collapsed in exhaustion after hours of wild exertion.

"The doc say's jogging still a no-no. You know, he said the concussion was real bad." Jason squirmed his way up next to her and pulled the champagne bottle from the now-tepid water in the bucket. He took several swallows of the warm champagne, then rolled over and drooled a mouthful between her breasts.

Blair abruptly swung her legs to the floor and sat up on the edge of the bed. "Jason, it's over! I have to get back to the office and you must get on to Harrisburg. Remember? Or do you remember anything at all this morning?"

"Of course I remember. But why do we have to be in such an all-fired hurry? . . . Ohhh, my head! For a moment I thought I was going to pass out." Jason propped himself on an elbow and held his forehead as he grimaced.

"You're a mess, Jason. What would the good doctor say about mixing champagne, coke and all-night sex? I would think he'd put that on the list of no-nos with jogging."

"Didn't say anything about it. He thinks I'm an all-American boy. Doc's kind of stupid. He still thinks coke comes out of a bottle."

"I doubt that, lover. You'd be amazed at the information they can get from a blood test." Blair stood up and began to make her way to the shower, then paused and looked at him again. "By the way, Jason, we both left New York about the same time. How come I beat you and your fancy Corvette here by over an hour?"

Jason now sat on the edge of the bed and held a throbbing head in both hands. "Beats me," he mumbled. "I guess I got lost." He watched her turn and walk toward the shower. He thought momentarily that he would join her, but thought better of it and slumped back on the bed.

That was a good question, he thought to himself. Why was I so late? Then the early morning came back to him. He had gone far out of the way to put the note in Houston's mailbox. He felt uneasy. Maybe he ought to forget the vendetta or at least lay off for a while. His thoughts ran back to the day on the turnpike when Houston had left him for dead. The thought of it still caused the rage to build inside of him. He would make him pay for what he had done. He would do it someday, when Houston would least expect it.

Jason stood, walked to the window and steadied himself by putting his open hand on the sill. He knew the feeling all too well. Mixing cocaine and booze always left him this way. But he knew how to fix it. He walked, head throbbing worse than ever, to the open purse Blair had left on the dresser. He methodically rifled the contents. Where in the hell did she keep the stuff? The bitch was hiding it somewhere. He felt himself stirring again, aching to have Blair's legs clamped around him.

He was swept by a spasm of nausea. He retreated to the bed and sat rigidly until the feeling ebbed. He listened to the sound of water still running in the shower, slumped back onto the bed, burrowed into a pillow and passed out.

Meanwhile in the adjacent suite, Willy had returned to find Coley stretched out on the bed, earphones on and the tiny recorder doing its work. Coley nodded at Willy, then put a finger to his lips urging silence. Willy closed the door gently and sat next to him.

"The walls are paper thin," he whispered. "I got lots of good stuff. She's in the shower now. I haven't heard a peep out of him since the last orgasm. I think he finally conked out. We've got a solid case for Amanda. How'd you make out with the police?"

"They're taking over, putting a tail on Granger. They are going to see if he'll lead them to the boy." Willy furrowed his brow. "It just doesn't make sense to me. Granger is in there banging away and having a grand old time. What in the hell has he done with the kid?"

"Willy, I know how you feel about hunches, but after tailing this guy around for two days, I get the gut feeling he's no kidnapper. Hell, this guy doesn't get out of sack long enough to be riding herd on some ten-year-old."

Willy nodded. "Well he's the state police's problem now. By the way, an Amtrak conductor says he saw the kid in Hoboken alive and well. The police say the conductor is damn sure of himself."

"Let's hope so, Willy. Hey, the shower has stopped." Coley held the earphones tight to his ears. "There isn't any conversation now at all. She keeps thumping things around. I think she's getting dressed."

The two of them sat in silence for fully ten minutes before Coley heard Blair Lawton's voice again.

"Good-bye, Jason! See you tomorrow night in New York. Hey! Are you awake?" Blair's voice was clearly audible to them through the thin walls, even without the earphones.

Jason gave an unintelligible reply that came out mostly as a grunt. The door to the adjacent room slammed and they heard Blair's heels clicking down the hall.

Willy jumped to his feet. "I'll follow her, Coley. Keep after Granger until you know for certain that the police are on his tail. See you soon."

Willy hustled out the door and got downstairs just in time to see Blair entering the white Mercedes.

The woman sat for the longest time after she started the engine, preening in the rearview mirror. Willy marveled at the woman's appearance. You would never think she had spent the last half day balling Granger. He followed her eastward until she had crossed the Delaware and proceeded high speed toward New York on Route I-80. She was rapidly putting miles between her and her lover.

Willy slowed down and pulled onto an off-ramp. He made a U-turn and headed back toward the Delaware. He rang up Penny on the cellular and filled her in. She was flabbergasted at the news of a ransom note. Like Coley, she had read of the canoeing accident on the Delaware several days ago and then lost track of the story.

"Willy, Granger is a miserable, lying, cheating bastard, but I can't imagine him as a kidnapper. So what are we going to do?"

"Zilch, kiddo. We've got Amanda's adultery charge nailed. We're about done with the case. The kidnapping, if there was one, is a problem for the police."

"Shucks. I hope they find the kid. Do you suppose he did drown?"

"The odds are he is a goner. The ransom notes just might mean that for some unexplained reason our man Jason has become a sleazy opportunist bent on tormenting Houston."

"Hey, that fits! A sleazy opportunist is a perfect description of Jason Granger. Now that I can imagine. By the way, Willy, Amanda is going to check in by phone soon. Shall I tell her that you and Coley have nailed the bastard?"

"Yep, might as well put her at ease. And while you're talking to her, bounce the possibility of Jason being a kidnapper off her. After all, she knows him better than anyone."

"Gotcha! I thought we had turned all that kind of stuff over to the police, Willy."

"Life is a continuum, Penny. Ideas move in and out of our conscious thoughts as changing data accumulates. Understand?"

"Of course I understand. That means we are going to keep poking around in the case until the boy shows up either dead or alive."

"Hey, you're a smart kid. That'll get you in big trouble some day. By the way, keep your eye on the papers for any more follow-up stories, and tell Coley to do the same thing. With two tabloid junkies working we shouldn't miss a thing."

Willy hung up the cellular and proceeded toward Harrisburg. He couldn't get Jason Granger off his mind. The thought of him stuffing the ransom note in a mailbox defied any logical explanation. How in the hell did he even know where the Houston's lived, and why would he drive so damn far out of the way to do such a thing? Somehow, he had to learn a lot more about Jason Granger.

Amanda had mentioned that Jason had been involved in a beating at a turnpike rest stop and had been hospitalized for several days near Carlisle. As soon as he was again on the west side of the Delaware, he gunned the engine of the Z3 and sped west on I-80 as fast as he dared. He turned south on Route 33 until he reached the turnpike and again roared west.

It was afternoon when Willy arrived at the hospital. He sat in the parking lot reviewing the notes Penny had prepared after their discussion with Amanda Granger. He found the name of Dr. Philip Lavin. He had been on duty in the emergency room when Jason had been brought in.

Inside the lobby of the hospital he sat in the waiting room and dialed the Granger residence on his cellular phone hoping that Amanda would be home. She wasn't. He then turned his attention to the reception desk.

He was lucky. The doctor was in, but he would have to wait. "Please tell the doctor I will wait. It has to do with a patient of his, Jason Granger. Amanda Granger has asked that I talk to Dr. Lavin." It was a lie but he would fix that as soon as he reached Amanda.

Willy sat down in the small waiting room and reviewed the day, which had started before sunrise. A lot had happened. The ransom note, the police, the surveillance at the Crestview Hideaway, and three hundred miles of driving in between had understandably made him weary.

"Mr. Hanson, I'm Dr. Lavin." Willy opened his eyes and realized that he had been dozing off. "Mr. Hanson," the voice persisted, "I'm sorry I kept you waiting so long, but it's been a busy day in the ER."

Willy jumped to his feet. "Thanks for seeing me, Doctor, and thanks for taking so long. I got a much-needed nap." Willy handed him his card. "I'm investigating a case involving Jason Granger on behalf of Mrs. Granger. She tells me he was taken here after being badly beaten in a turnpike rest stop."

Lavin was a tall, angular man with penetrating blue eyes that studied Willy for several seconds before he replied. "Oh, yes. Jason Granger had a narrow escape. I hope he is taking it easy. He persisted in his desire to leave the hospital from the moment he came out of a mild coma. How is Jason?"

Willy stared at the doctor, wondering what he would think about Granger's sexual marathon with Blair Lawton. That hardly qualified as taking it easy. "Seems to be doing quite well, Doctor. You do good work. Can you tell me anything about his arrival at your hospital?"

"I suppose Mrs. Granger has told you the story. For a time after he woke up he had periods of delirium. He couldn't let go of a peculiar phrase. Let's see, he kept mumbling something like 'git-go' very clearly over and over again. He had us worried for a while. But that's in the past. I guess we'll never know. Glad to hear he's doing well. But then he is young, and was in marvelous shape before this incident. That all helps."

Willy took time to make a note of the puzzling "git-go" nonsense. He had come a long way for nothing much. "Doctor, is there anything about his stay here, especially when he was in and out of a delirious state for a while, that would give an inkling as to why he was beaten?"

The doctor hesitated for a long time before he spoke, apparently in deep thought. "When a person comes in here with the extensive trauma that he showed, we run a lot of different tests, Mr. Hanson. Because of his coma, he could tell us nothing in the beginning, so we ran many tests, including extensive blood work. There was a possibility that we would have to operate." He stopped for a moment as if contemplating his next words.

"And, what about the blood work, Doctor?" Willy prodded.

"Well, there are some things that should be discussed with Mr. Granger. He has stayed completely out of touch since leaving here. Tell me, will you be seeing him soon?

"Certainly. Any message I can deliver to him?"

"Mr. Hanson, as a private investigator, I am sure you know that his medical report is privileged information. Just tell him that I would like to review his tests with him." Dr. Lavin stood up. "I'm sorry, I have work to do. I wish you a lot of luck, sir. My patient took a terrible beating."

Willy watched him until he disappeared down the corridor, wondering all the time what was in the medical report that was all that hush-hush. The police would have better luck if they pursued a kidnapping charge. Then he had another thought. Perhaps Dr. Lavin would release the report to Amanda. Then again, maybe the report wouldn't help him at all.

29

"I saw him, and then this morning I saw his picture in the *News*. I swear I did. I can take you to him right now. He's living with a whore. We got enough wrong with this neighborhood without whores teaching youngsters that kind of life. No telling what goes on in that woman's flat."

Detective McCutcheon eyed the unkempt lady warily and then opened the file in front of him. There was precious little on Tad Houston in it beyond the original newspaper account of his possible drowning. That morning, however, there was a small news item in two tabloids under a picture of Tad Houston. The headline on one read, POLICE LOOKING INTO KIDNAP POSSIBILITY FOR LAD BELIEVED DROWNED.

The story gave absolutely no further details. McCutcheon's experienced eye told him that the story was quite probably a fishing expedition, a plant by some police jurisdiction or perhaps the FBI. The boy's picture was the same as used with the original story of the possible drowning.

"So, Mrs. Bates, where did you see the boy?" The obese woman's frizzled gray hair seemed to grow in every direction. McCutcheon decided it hadn't been combed or cut in months.

"I was wondering, is there a reward for information?" She almost whispered, leaning toward McCutcheon, sending a wave of garlic breath his way.

"Not that I see here, Mrs. Bates, but I'll make a record of your inquiry and check into it. The boy has been missing over a week now. If you have information, Mrs. Bates, it could save the boy's life." The woman frowned, obviously wanting to hear that there was a reward.

"Mr. Policeman, what do you think about a whore being in charge of a little boy like that. You think that's okay?"

He looked thoughtfully at the woman. Her credibility was rapidly waning in his eyes. "Okay, Mrs. Lottie Bates, where is the boy? And how do you come to know about him?"

"I make it a point to mind my own business. There's too much going on these days to do anything else." Though there was no one within earshot, she leaned over his desk again and started to whisper, sending another billow of garlic breath his way. "The boy is being held by a common streetwalker. Everybody on the block knows just what she is. The way she parades around in practically nothin' in front of that poor boy is a scandal. And I'll betcha she's not his aunt either. The lad was too scared to tell me what she really is."

"This lady is the boy's aunt?"

"No way! Carlota's been on my block for years. Everybody knows she ain't no kin to respectable folks. That young lad is a very polite one."

"And you know where he is?" McCutcheon was trying not to sound impatient.

"Sure! He's right down the block. She makes him stay in the flat while she parades up and down the street showing what she's got to all the old fools." Again she leaned over his desk to whisper. "Half the times her skirt don't even cover her underwear."

"Right on your block? All right, Mrs. Bates, let's start at the beginning. What is your address?" Detective McCutcheon started writing down her response, then picked up the phone with his other hand. "McCutcheon here. I have a possible sighting of Tad Houston. We should get a unit over on Ninth Avenue at Fortieth. The possible kidnap victim is ten years old, blond hair, blue eyes, fair complexion, short haircut. Stand by at that location until until further instructed."

McCutcheon continued to talk on the phone, staring at Lottie Bates, now sitting across from him with eyes as big as saucers. "Mrs. Bates, what is the exact address where you saw the boy?"

She looked panicked, shaking her head negatively. "I don't know? It's a third-floor apartment, down the street from me, near Fortieth Street."

McCutcheon again turned to his telephone. "Stake out the area. I'll have the eyewitness identify the flat."

"Mrs. Bates, how do you know exactly where the boy is being held?"

"I took him there. The boy was lost. He came up to my flat. I had to take him home. When we got there, there was that woman standing in the doorway with practically nothing on."

"He went inside willingly?"

"Oh, yes. He said that she was his aunt. I'll tell you, she was a disgusting sight, parading around in front of a youngin' like that."

"Okay, Mrs. Bates, we want you to help us rescue that

boy. Do you mind coming along right now and pointing out that apartment to me?"

"Sure, I get a ride home, even if there ain't no reward." Lottie Bates frowned at McCutcheon.

"You'll get your reward in heaven, Mrs. Bates. Now come along with me. I'll tell you what. I'll pop for a dinner for you and your husband if we can locate the boy."

Lottie Bates continued to frown as she followed McCutcheon from the office. "Mr. Bates has been dead twenty years," she muttered just loud enough for McCutcheon to hear.

When you work on the street as long as Empress Carlota, doing what she did, you acquired a sixth sense about cops. Sometimes a sixth sense wasn't required. She had driven the dusty old Ford Escort right past her apartment so that she could return Suzie's car to the lot on Eleventh Avenue. Tad was curled up sound asleep on the seat next to her.

She spotted two plainclothesmen who had hauled her down to the precinct house several times in the past. They were standing on the sidewalk in front of her building. There was also a police cruiser at each end of her block. Some other men idling in the area looked like fuzz to her. She tensed, hoping that Tad would stay out of sight.

Luck was with her. The light turned green on Tenth Avenue, so she didn't have to pause at the corner. It looked like a bust for sure. But why the army? Usually it was only one or two cops. She glanced down at Tad, now stirring restlessly. She'd face the music if he weren't along. Hell, she had learned long ago that the quickest way to deal with the cops was to do what she was told. It came with her territory.

Tad sat up and looked out the window. "Hey, we're about home." He looked at Carlota. "I'm sorry Pops was at my Aunt Sarah's house. I'm really sorry, Carlota. Hey! Where we going?"

Carlota had turned abruptly southward on Eleventh Avenue, away from the parking lot. "Tad, I'll bet you are as hungry as I am. How about hamburgers and french fries? I know a great place."

"Sounds good to me!" Tad enthused.

And then what? Carlota wondered to herself. She couldn't afford getting busted with Tad along. Right now the boy needed her.

Carlota was lucky enough to find a parking space on Thirty-sixth Street, just around the corner from McDonald's. It was far enough from her neighborhood that she felt it safe.

Tad was famished and dug enthusiastically into the tray of burgers, fries and cokes while she paged idly through a copy of the *News* left by a previous customer.

For an instant she thought her heart would stop. There, buried deep in the paper, was a picture of Tad. POLICE LOOKING INTO KIDNAP POSSIBILITY FOR LAD BELIEVED DROWNED.

Carlota folded the paper carefully and stuffed it under her buttocks. She gaped at Tad, hungrily attacking his food. What was she going to do now? She began to review all the things Tad had told her about himself and wondered if he was being completely honest with her. She couldn't help but wonder if Tad wasn't the reason there was a small army of fuzz on her block. She didn't dare go home now.

"Tad, darling, I want to show you something I just read in this here newspaper." She produced the paper and began leafing through the pages until she came to Tad's picture over the brief news item. Tad shoved a ketchup-laden french fry into his mouth and took the paper from her hands.

"Hey, that's me!" he squealed as he slowly read the headline aloud. "That's crazy, Aunt Carlota. I didn't drown and I wasn't kidnapped."

"Ssh! Tad, not so loud." Carlota glanced around to make sure no one had overheard. "Tad, baby, are you sure you been telling me the truth about how you got to New York?"

"Honest, I've told you everything. I really have." Tad gaped, wide-eyed, at her. Disappointment transformed his face as he held back tears. "The paper's crazy, Aunt Carlota. Really!"

Carlota sighed heavily, wondering what to say next. "Tad, we've gotten ourselves into a real pickle. When I drove past my place, there were police all over. I betcha they were looking for me. We can't go home, Tad. They would take you away from me and send you back to your folks."

Tad shook his head. "I won't, Carlota. I just won't go. Mom and Pops would have a big fight, and then he would whip me somethin' terrible."

Carlota began to fish around in her purse. "I have about fifty dollars left, Tad. That won't get us very far."

"I got some money. You can have mine." Tad dug two crumpled dollar bills from his pocket and tried to give it to her.

Carlota forced a smile. "That won't even buy us breakfast, Tad. You put that back in your pocket."

Carlota read the short item in the paper again. Then, for the first time, she had a frightening thought. Those police weren't looking for her. There were too many of them. They were looking for Tad! Her thoughts went back to the contemptuous look on the face of the obese woman who had brought Tad home when he was lost. She would bet money that the woman saw the same picture of Tad in the paper that she did. She had told the police where to look for the kidnapped boy! If that were true, she couldn't go home, and she couldn't take Tad there.

"Tad, honey, we made a big mistake. We should have waited until your dad's van left your aunt's house. That's what I wanted to do, but then you had to go and run away on me. We got to go back, Tad. We'll make sure your Aunt Sarah is alone. Your kinfolk can deal with you better than I can."

Tad squirmed on his seat. Carlota spotted the same wide-eyed wild look on his face that she had first seen when she rescued him from the pervert in front of the theater. She took his hand and led him from the hamburger palace back to Suzie's old Ford. She became aware that she was holding on to him. He was not the one eagerly grasping hands as usual, nor was he saying a word.

Once inside the car she drove slowly down Thirty-sixth Street, circled the block, and then paused for a stoplight across from Macy's. Herald Square was jammed with the usual pedestrian traffic. Tad sat quietly except for a nervous jiggling of his legs. She wished that he would say something, anything. It was out of character for Tad to sit still for very long without saying something.

The traffic light turned green and she moved cautiously across Broadway only to become ensnarled in a traffic gridlock. Without saying a word, Tad swiftly flung his door open and jumped from the car. He ran behind the car, through traffic and then onto the pedestrian island in the middle of Herald Square.

Carlota opened the door, screaming at him. "Tad! Tad!" Horns started honking all around her as the traffic started to move. She watched helplessly as he disappeared from sight into the crowd. Then she caught one final glimpse of him as he darted into a subway station stairwell.

Carlota got back into the car and parked it next to another subway station entrance across Broadway. She ran down the steps as fast as she could and continued running the entire length of the station. It was hopeless. The huge station had rows of tracks with subway cars passing constantly, obscuring any clear view, and level after level of tracks. As a last effort she reached the sublevel where PATH trains left regularly for New Jersey. She paid her way through the turnstile and searched her way through the several trains lined up side by side, peering through each window, but Tad was nowhere to be found. She was exhausted and in tears when she sat down on a bench, trying to catch her breath. Finally she rose. She walked back through the station, out to the Ford, still parked, its engine idling.

"That's a miracle," she said aloud. "That fool kid could have made me lose Suzie's car." Then she sat quietly behind the wheel and broke into tears.

"Hey! Move it, lady. You can't park here. Can't you read?" The policeman bellowed at her from a few inches from her window.

Carlota jammed her foot on the gas pedal and drove down Thirty-fifth Street, wondering where to go. She began to wind her way back and forth on several cross streets, hoping to catch a glimpse of Tad. Finally she went south on Eleventh Avenue. She parked Suzie's old Ford in the lot where they had picked it up.

Reluctantly, she began to walk down the long block toward her flat. It was the only home she knew. Maybe, by some miracle, Tad would show up there. But deep inside, she didn't believe it.

Ahead, she saw a police car parked near her apartment. She hesitated for a moment before entering her block and then decided to face the music. Perhaps they weren't looking for either her or Tad. She deserved a little luck, she thought. After all, she really hadn't done anything wrong.

As she neared the steps to her walk-up, a policeman she recognized got out of a squad car and approached her. "Empress, you ain't looking so good." His eyes roved up and down her baggy, rumpled garb, "Not the usual duds for Empress Carlota."

"Please leave me alone. I've had a rough day. And believe it or not, I haven't done anything wrong." The policeman blocked her path to the steps.

"Empress, we got to have some answers. This ain't the usual bullshit. The boys downtown want to talk to you, Empress. I gotta take you in. Where's the kid?"

"What kid?" she said icily.

"Have it your way, Empress, but we gotta take you in." The tall policeman was joined by two others, and they led her to the waiting squad car. She took one last look up and down the block, hoping to see Tad, and then climbed in.

30

Coley stirred, awakened by the noise in his earphones. He had dozed off waiting for Jason Granger to make some sort of a move. He heard water running. Then came a few curses and the readily identifiable sound of Granger puking his guts out. Granger called the desk to verify the time. He let out a long string of invective and began to move around. Clothes hangers rattled in the closet, and Coley decided he must be about ready to vacate the room.

Coley peeled away the tape holding the antenna sensor to his wall. He stuffed everything into his duffel bag and took a quick look around to make sure he didn't leave anything. He slipped out the door, shut it gently and went downstairs.

There were just a few cars in the wooded parking area north of the veranda. Granger's red Corvette was parked closest. Out next to the woods, a Chevy Malibu was now parked next to his own economy vehicle. The driver's-side door of the Malibu opened as he approached his own rental car.

"Sir, you have to be Coley Doctor. It can't be anyone else." The man eyed his lean six foot seven frame and stuck out his hand. "I'm Luke Forrest, Pennsylvania State Police."

"I figured you guys would be out here." Coley grasped the plainclothesman's hand. "Better get yourself ready for the chase. Granger's getting ready to bail out. Our boy's got quite a hangover this afternoon."

Forrest grinned. "How about the babe?"

"She checked out this morning." Coley's experienced eye told him the man carried a weapon under the light poplin jacket. "I understand that you're going to have all the fun now chasing that red Corvette."

"Yep, the boys upstairs sent me. Wish they'd considered something other than this dinky Malibu. It's got nothing under the hood to match that." The policeman nodded at the Corvette. "Anything I ought to know?"

"I hope Granger can keep that baby on the road. I figure he's still pretty pukey. Between all the screwing, the champagne and the coke, it might be a problem."

Forrest nodded and then climbed into the car. He rolled the window down for some last words with Coley. "Where are you headed?"

"I guess I'll get back to New York. My partner and I have our divorce case nailed." Coley tapped on the duffel bag that held the tape recorder. He then leaned down to the window of the detective's car. "Any news about the boy?"

The detective shook his head negatively. "We haven't found him yet. Do you really think he's the answer?" Luke Forrest nodded toward the Corvette.

Coley shrugged. "He doesn't seem to fit the mold. But who knows? I guess you know the mailbox story."

"Yep. Very strange, unless lover boy is some kind of nut."

"Good luck, pal." Coley climbed into his car, started the engine and backed out of the parking area. He nodded to the detective, and pulled out onto the narrow blacktop road leading toward Milford. Officially, he was off the case.

A few minutes later Jason Granger stepped outside on the veranda of the Crestview Hideaway. He stretched his arms and took a few steps around the long porch. His head was still pounding. Of course, Blair's Mercedes was gone. In fact, there were only a couple of cars left in the guest parking area. He had blown the day.

He tried desperately to think. He was pretty sure that Blair had gone back to New York to await him later in the day. By now, he should have been in Harrisburg and picked up some clothes and his laptop. Amanda was to have brought those with her, but then Amanda was not being too cooperative these days. He dreaded the drive to Harrisburg with his pounding head and queasy stomach.

He walked to the Corvette and sat inside. He ran his fingers along the console and noticed that the screws holding the receptacle inside were still missing. Hopefully, he yanked the box from the console and slid his hand inside.

Nothing! Nothing was there. Blair had taken every last packet of the cocaine. He probed deeper into the opening and snared one videotape. He inspected it and found it unlabeled. And what about the rest of the videotapes? Where in the hell were they? He sat quietly, trying not to move a muscle. He felt better now, from time to time. But he still couldn't focus. There were big blank periods of time missing. He couldn't remember having a hangover like this since his college days. He never wanted to taste champagne again. The champagne, and the insatiable Blair, had wiped him out.

He started the engine. After staring at the tach needle for a while, he pulled onto the road and soon was heading west on Route 730. Still in a half-stupor, he crawled along. He realized that he needed sleep too badly to try to reach Harrisburg. A single car appeared behind him in his rearview mirror. He looked at his speedometer, which read forty miles per hour, and then floored the accelerator when the car in his mirror drew nearer. Within seconds the other car was no longer visible on the winding road. About ten miles later the I-84 intersection loomed ahead. Granger remembered the motel cluster a few miles north. He had passed this way once before, the day he had followed Houston all the way to Middletown and put that lovely scratch in his van. He swerved into the on-ramp leading north toward Milford.

Behind him, Luke Forrest's Malibu was no match for the Corvette on the crooked road. He hadn't actually seen the Corvette racing ahead of him for several minutes. When he reached I-84, he didn't once hesitate in getting on the ramp leading south toward Harrisburg. He got on the cellular phone and tried to reach a highway patrol car, thinking that he might be able to stop Granger and let him close the gap. Finally he got through to a cruiser twenty miles south of him. The patrolman hadn't yet seen the Corvette but would keep his eyes peeled. Forrest breathed easier now and concentrated on getting all the speed he could out of the overmatched Malibu. If all else failed, some of the boys down the pike near Harrisburg would pick up the trail on Granger. That was the contingency plan.

Coley drove slowly through the pine woods on the winding blacktop road that led to Milford. He stopped for hot coffee at a diner on the main drag of the quaint little town. The street was lined with antique shops and sporting goods stores that featured lots of boating and fishing gear. The quiet village would be a much busier place in the summer when engulfed by tourists and sportsmen.

Coley carried a container of hot coffee and a couple of bagels back to his car and began to sip cautiously at the steaming hot coffee. He had tried twice to get through to Willy on his cellular phone, figuring he must be in Harrisburg by now. He decided to try once more. The third time was the charm.

Willy had little information. Amanda was still not home and the doctor at the hospital could shed little light on Jason Granger. "The doc did tell me that the man took a severe beating. He was definitely in a coma for a while and delirious from time to time when he came out of it. Granger kept spouting some gibberish over and over again. The doctor claimed it sounded like 'git-go, git-go.' All in all the day was a waste of time. The doctor was perfectly within his rights not to show me Granger's medical report. I'll ask Amanda to pick that up for us."

"So I guess we get the hell off the case," Coley murmured in disappointment. "The Pennsylvania police left the

Crestview tailing Granger in his Corvette. They ought to be in Harrisburg in a couple hours. So I guess I'll head back to the city. We got Granger cold on his shenanigans. At least Amanda will be happy."

"Good work, Coley. I'm heading back to New York myself as soon as I talk to Amanda." Willy hung up, leaving Coley to his restless funk.

While sipping coffee, Willy scrutinized a map of the area in his road atlas. He had placed a tiny dot on the map identifying the approximate location of Sonny Houston's farm. He felt vaguely uneasy and disappointed. The story of the young boy who may or may not be alive, or may or may not be drowned or kidnapped, would not leave his mind.

Granger's hot and heavy tryst with Blair Lawton had nailed him for sure. Amanda with her expected baby had all she needed to take him for a bundle. Still, Coley didn't feel the usual elation about having been so successful so quickly. It was definitely the unresolved matter of Tad Houston that bothered him.

He looked at the map again, tossed the atlas in the seat beside him and drove slowly in the opposite direction from New York toward the penciled dot on the map that represented Houston's farm. His restless curiosity had to be satisfied. He simply had to take a quick peek at the Houston property. After all, Willy had seen it when he had taken Granger's note from the rural mailbox.

He turned off the main road. The area was heavy with stands of pine. Here and there were small clearings with a house or a barn tucked away on a hillside. Usually the small farms were in a poor state of repair. He wondered what would grow in this country. The soil in the hills was filled with outcroppings of underlying rock in contrast to the lush, fertile land in the valley along the Delaware. A few horses and cows eyed him occasionally from along the fences.

The road widened ahead for a hundred yards or so. A large rural mailbox sat on a wooden post with the name

HOUSTON on it in big block letters. He passed it slowly and then made a U-turn. The flap was hanging open on the mailbox. It was empty.

He looked up a long driveway which wound up the hill. Houston's house was nestled in a wooden copse. Only parts of the second floor were visible.

He heard a noise clearly audible over the idle of his engine. It was the sound of some sort of motor coming from somewhere to the east of Houston's house. Now and then he caught a flash of bright orange amidst the brush on the hillside.

Coley took a small pair of binoculars from his duffel bag and focused on the bright orange machinery. It was a backhoe. He could see it start to slam down into the earth now and then, and looking more closely, he saw a pile of earth and rock above the level of the underbrush at one point.

A fresh ditch had been dug behind the fence immediately to the right of where Coley had pulled over. It was only a couple of feet deep and ran for about a hundred feet alongside a single strand of wire. It had been freshly dug, and the earth had been dumped haphazardly back of the long excavation. Houston was evidently working on some kind of a drainage ditch. It looked pretty sloppy.

He watched the backhoe rise again and again to dump more fresh earth on the pile behind the trees. Someone was working feverishly on the project. Coley laid the binoculars in his lap and pulled further down the road. He could see a bit more of Houston's old house at the driveway's end. A large SUV, probably a Cherokee, was parked next to the house.

Coley lifted the binoculars for one last view. GITGO 7 jumped at him from the license plate like a neon sign. Coley stared in disbelief for a long time. It explained the nonsense words Granger had spoken in his delirium at the hospital. Perhaps Houston had something to do with the beating he took! That would explain a lot of things.

He put the binoculars away and drove back to Milford.

He tried several times to reach Willy on the phone, but got no answer. The revelation of the meaning of "git-go" was interesting, but it didn't seem to shed any further light on the disappearance of Tad Houston. He began to drive slowly down the Delaware Water Gap toward Route I-80. He decided to look for a place to stay the night. He couldn't wait to bring Willy up to date on GITGO 7.

31

Jason Granger tossed in his bed in the roadside motel just off the Milford junction with I-84. He looked at his watch. It was six P.M. That was good news. He had gotten several hours sleep. He got up and doused his head with water from the cold tap. His mouth was cotton-dry and still tasted of cigarettes and champagne. He ripped the cellophane from a plastic cup and gulped the cool water.

Jason gaped at his unshaven visage in the small mirror. He looked terrible. Amanda would be disgusted for sure. The thought of Amanda surprised him. Why the hell should he give a damn what she thinks? His head pounded as thoughts of Amanda from the old days refused to leave his mind. Hell, I might as well tell her to have the baby, he thought. My life couldn't be any more screwed up than it is.

His thoughts returned to Blair. Life was a continual sensual blast with her. She had arrived on the scene a couple years ago and slowly taken over his life. Actually, unknown to the company, she had taken over his job. He had become lazy. The gin, the dope that Blair got somewhere, and that flawless, sensual, insatiable body possessed his thoughts. Amanda, so perfect, so good, so beautiful, mysteriously invaded his mind with fleeting memories of their past only in his most sober and lonely moments. It was weird that he was thinking of her at this moment. Hell, first chance I get, I'll tell her to go ahead and have the damn baby, he thought.

Jason paced restlessly in the tiny room and wondered what Blair would think when he didn't show up in New York tonight. The thought of Blair began to stir him physically. There was nothing more compelling than a horny hangover. Blair had once agreed with him about that. Blair knew all those little things that could drive a guy crazy. He picked up the telephone and tried to reach her at her hotel in New York. She wasn't there. He left a message. "Sorry, doll, where are you when I need you? I conked out for a while. You're right, there's nothing like a horny hangover. Thank God there's tomorrow night."

Jason hung up without leaving his name on her room voice mail. He began to dress. The tiny room was driving him nuts. He might as well continue to Harrisburg. He estimated that he had slept over four hours. Besides, he needed some cigarettes. Staring in the mirror, he had a thought, the same thought that had crossed his mind before he had dozed off. He was only a half dozen miles from Sonny Houston's farm. He probably wouldn't have the time to come this way again. Now was the time to stick one last needle into the son of a bitch.

Jason sat at the desk printing block letters on a small scrap of soiled paper. He finished quickly, and reread the note. IF YOU DON'T COUGH UP THE MONEY AS YOU WERE INSTRUCTED, YOU GET THE BOY'S EARS IN THE MAIL. That would be sure to stir up the old bastard, he thought. He wondered what effect the note would actually have on Houston. He wondered if it would begin to equal the suffering he had gone through after the beating. After all, he could have died. Houston probably had left him for dead.

It was almost dark when he checked out of the motel and drove down the lonely road toward Houston's farm. The headlights reflected on the name HOUSTON as he approached the mailbox at the end of the road to his house. Houston's van was parked just a few feet from the main road. It faced the house at the end of the winding driveway. He parked by the mailbox and doused his lights.

There were lights up the hill near the house and he heard the sound of machinery of some sort back in the woods. Granger thought about the last teasing note that he had left. Could the guy have been so stupid as to leave the money in the van to accommodate him?

For a moment he froze with fear. What if Houston had gone to the police, and they were waiting for him to show up? He'd have a tough time convincing the police it was all a joke. He sat quietly with the windows rolled down. He stretched his arm to shove the note into the mailbox, only to feel the hard steel barrel of a shotgun prod him in the ribs from the passenger-side open window. The shock of the intrusion caused him to drop the note short of the mailbox.

"Don't move unless you want your guts all over this fancy car." Sonny Houston moved into the seat beside him. The barrel stuck deep into Granger's side. "Now we're going to take a little ride. Drive right up the hill to the back of my house. There's a nice quiet place there where we can talk. Be careful when you pass my van. I don't want any more scratches on it."

Granger looked for a way out. The man had the shoulders of an ox. Taking him on physically at this moment was out of the question. He began to sweat profusely. For a moment no words would come. Then another firm prod of the barrel forced him to speak. "No . . . no! I can explain all this. It's all so simple. I didn't really mean anything—"

"Shut up!" Houston thrust the shotgun deeper into his side. "Now get on up the hill there. If it's all so simple, you can just tell me about it some other time." Houston started to chuckle softly and soon bellowed out a maniacal laugh as he again jabbed Granger hard with the barrel.

Reluctantly, Jason began to drive up the hill. Houston directed him to go beyond the house toward a light that filtered through the trees. The low-slung Corvette scraped bottom several times on the rocky tire tracks that led through the woods.

"Not much of a vehicle you got here. A man like you should know better than to take one of these things out here in the woods. Not exactly a proper vehicle for a military mission." Again came the nervous, derisive laugh from Sonny Houston.

Soon they came upon a small clearing behind several rows of grapevines. The orange backhoe towered above them. The engine of the mud-caked machine was idling noisily. "Now I want you to drive up in front of the backhoe and shine your lights down into the excavation."

Granger obeyed, still racking his mind, trying to pick the right time to make some sort of a move. "Oh, my God!" he gasped as the headlights beamed down into a crude excavation. The backhoe had cut a deep gouge in the earth about ten feet wide and twenty feet long. The front of the Corvette now pitched forward on the steep incline the backhoe had carved into the pit. The bottom of the pit was a standing pool of muddy water.

"Now I want you to listen carefully. This here is the Houston Memorial Park. You should be honored to be the first to see it."

"Memorial Park?" Granger squealed and gaped at what surely was a madman beside him.

"Now I'll make you a deal. I want you to drive this powerful fancy car right down there to the bottom. If it's God's will and you can drive it back out, you can leave here a free and happy man." Houston climbed out of the Corvette, now parked on the muddy incline into the pit. He held the shotgun across his chest.

Granger, seeing what he figured to be his last chance, slipped the Corvette into reverse and stomped on the gas pedal. The engine roared as the front tires plowed into the deep mud, spinning the tires ferociously, forcing the vehicle backward for several inches before slipping further into the pit than ever. He screamed once and then felt one burst of unrelenting pain in his chest. Then Jason slumped over the wheel, motionless. His foot was still jammed on the accelerator, keeping the tires futilely spinning in a monotonous drone against the wet mud.

Houston studied the situation for several seconds. He hadn't fired a shot. The man had collapsed behind the wheel all on his own. He walked quickly to the backhoe and climbed aboard. The machine rumbled onto the incline. Sonny rammed the giant claw into rear of the Corvette, persisting until the car was as far into the pit as it could go.

For the next couple of hours, he worked methodically at scooping earth from the dirt pile nearby and pushing it back into the pit. Once the pit was filled, he carefully mounded more earth over it. In the light of morning he would come back and push brambles and old timber over the mounded area. And there was still work to do on the individual burial sites. The only one completed was the small one, about half the size of the other two.

Houston picked up the shotgun, climbed out of the backhoe and started to walk down the hill to his house, stopping once to look back and assess his work. Getting rid of the Corvette was a stroke of genius, he reasoned to himself. He had not only defeated his enemy in battle but had eliminated the flashy red car that would have caught the attention of any support troops his foe might have. His defense perimeter was secure.

What pleased him most was that he had won the battle without firing a shot. He pictured his enemy slumped over the steering wheel, encased in mud. He was obviously a coward. He should have never gone to battle in the first place.

Sonny again walked toward the house. Once he turned and saw the unfamiliar bulge in the landscape silhouetted against the night sky. He snapped to attention and executed a proper military salute in the direction of Houston Memorial Park. Then his deep voice boomed out in the cool night air, "Lord, I promise to mark this spot with a suitable monument when the last battle is done and the last grave is filled."

32

Empress Carlota was trembling. She had always played ball with the cops. She had taken her deserved lumps in the past. Always, the cops had soon permitted her return to minding her own business. This time was different. She sat on a wooden chair in the precinct house. She was surrounded by four policemen, including a lieutenant she had never seen before in the precinct. He was doing most of the questioning.

"Where's Tad Houston? What did you do with the kid? Empress, we know you have him. Let's make this easy. We have a witness who saw the boy. The boys say you know how to cooperate."

"He's gone. He ran away." Carlota spoke softly, feeling that nothing she told them would be accepted.

"When did he run away? What did you do to him that made him run away?"

"Nothing! I treated that boy like a brother . . . even like a son." Carlota's voice broke as she thought of Tad.

"Now, come on, Empress. I'm sure you know how to treat a young man. Why would he run away?" The detective leered at her.

Carlota glared at him, struggling not to lose her temper. "I treat him like a fine, sweet young boy, which he is. Some creep was trying to drag him into a porn house when I took him away from him. You, Mr. Policeman, should be putting that creep in jail instead of bothering me." Carlota stuck out her chin defiantly, her eyes flashing.

"Okay, Empress, that's enough! It's time we get down to business." The lieutenant stood and shook his finger at her scoldingly. "Who paid you to hide the kid?"

"Paid me? I haven't got this month's rent! I found him

several days ago, just like I said. I didn't know who he was for the longest time. He was afraid to go home."

"Empress, without rent money, I can easily see why you tried to make money with the boy. It was a dumb move, Empress. Do you know the penalty for kidnapping?"

"Kidnapping! Do I look like a kidnapper?"

"You look like a whore. Whores will do anything to pay their rent." The lieutenant paced around in front of her. "You might as well level with us. Like I say, we have a witness. Where's the boy? Did you kill him?"

"You are a bastard! I love that boy!" Carlota sobbed uncontrollably. Finally she managed a few more words. "I've told you the truth . . . God knows that."

"You better start praying a lot to that God of yours. You're in a real mess now, Miss Empress Carlota." The lieutenant looked at the others. "Why is it that whores always invoke God when they get caught red-handed?"

Carlota sat erect, tense in her chair, eyes tightly closed.

"Flannery, you stay here with Empress, and try to get her to talk some sense." The lieutenant walked to the door of the room, telling the others to leave with him. "I want posters of the kid's picture all over the West Side. Use the shot from the paper. I want him found before he leaves Manhattan, if he's still alive."

The lieutenant left with the others, leaving Detective Flannery alone with Carlota.

Flannery sat quietly for a few moments before speaking softly. "Come on, Empress, you and I go back a long way. You've always told the truth before. You're in one big hell of a mess now. Do you understand that?"

She shook her head in agreement and then opened her eyes and stared at Flannery. The detective must have hauled her in a dozen times, and considering the job he had to do, he was usually civil with her. "Tad ran away only today. I was going to take him to his aunt's house in New Jersey, but the boy was afraid that his father would be there. He said that he beat him a lot."

Flannery started to take notes on the yellow pad now in front of him. "Tell me all about it, Carlota, from top to bottom."

A few blocks away, at the Thirty-third Street station, Tad watched the dollar bills disappear as people stuck them into a slot next to the turnstile. One by one they paid their dollar, pushed on the gate and then raced to the PATH train on the other side. He remembered taking the PATH train before. It had first brought him to Manhattan from Hoboken. He knew it went to New Jersey.

He pulled a crumpled dollar from his pocket and tried to push it into the slot. But every time he tried, the dollar, hopelessly crumpled from being in his pocket so long, would pop right back at him, rejected by the machine.

The rush-hour crowd behind him was getting impatient. "Hey, kid, we're going to miss the train! Just duck under the gate," one of them yelled. Tad didn't need a second invitation. He ducked under the turnstile and raced into the open door of the nearest train and got in just in time to beat the closing door behind him. In less than fifteen minutes he was in the Hoboken terminal.

Hoboken looked familiar. The station was jammed with people waiting to board the many trains lined up in the terminal. He walked past the boarding gates warily, remembering the conductor that he had escaped from. He certainly didn't want to see him again.

He looked up and saw the sign next to one gate that read PORT JERVIS. That was perfect! Then he remembered again his trouble with the conductor. He didn't have a ticket, nor did he have enough money to buy one.

An attendant moved the big iron gate, allowing the rush-hour commuters to surge through and board the train. Tad moved with the flow of people and found a seat by the window in the train car that was filled, leaving quite a few people as standees. The train pulled out of the terminal. Tad spotted a conductor taking tickets from passengers, working toward him from the end of the car. It was not the conductor who had caught him before.

He squirmed in his seat and looked out the window, trying to ignore the conductor. Then he slumped in his seat and feigned sleep. Soon he felt a trapping on his shoulder.

"Let me see your ticket, son."

He opened his eyes and stared at the conductor. He began to put on a show of searching frantically through his pockets. "Shucks, I must have lost it."

"Where you headed, boy?"

"Port Jervis, that's where I live, Port Jervis." He shook his head affirmatively, hoping the conductor was as nice as he had looked so far.

"Oh, you've got a long ride, haven't you, Son. You keep hunting for that ticket. I'll check back with you before we get to Port Jervis. That's the last stop. You and I will be the last folks off the train. If you haven't found that ticket, we'll have to call your folks when we get there, okay?"

Tad shook his head again. "Thanks, sir. That's fine with me. I'll keep looking." He again started digging his hands through his pockets, as the conductor moved on through the car.

The man sitting next to him was busy reading a newspaper. Tad began to watch the towns flash by his window one by one. It wasn't long before the train was half empty. A couple of times the conductor passed him again. Once he even winked and gave him a friendly smile.

He began to think more and more about his plan as the train raced through the wooded countryside. Pops had made him break his arm, but maybe he didn't mean to. He thought about the day when he had crashed against the milk can. He looked down at the arm and realized he was using it all the time now, and he sometimes didn't even remember it had been broken. He thought of the times he and Eddie Foxworth would go off and do things Pops didn't like at all.

He had lost his shoes swimming in the greeny pond once, and Pops had got out the strap for that one. But, he thought to himself, he did lose his shoes, and they do cost a lot of money.

His plan was to go back to the farm. He would go through the woods along the Delaware and sneak up to the back of their property. He and Eddie had done it a hundred times during the summer. He'd get where he could see their house from the back, and wait until Pop's van was gone. Then he would run down and talk to his mother.

His plan was for her to tell Pops that he was sorry for all the trouble he had caused and that he would never break any rules again. After all, Pops did win the war, and the rules were mighty sensible, most of the time. He really didn't know how that big scratch got on the van, but he would confess anyway. Since Pops thought he did it, he knew he would never be able to change his mind. He would "own up to it, and be a man," as Pops was always telling him. He'd promise he'd never be a "sniveling little crybaby again." That seemed to irritate Pops the most. He was always calling him that.

So his plan was to get Mom alone and tell her his plan so she could tell Pops all about it first. He couldn't wait to talk to Mom about it. But then, what if Pops still got out the strap and beat him again for running away? It was easy for him to visualize Pops doing that at least once before he accepted his plan.

Where else could he go? Maybe he could go over to the Foxworth's place for a while. His mom was real nice. Sometimes when he and Eddie were playing together, she would say, "Why don't you ask your folks if you can come and visit Eddie for a few days?" But then, Pops would never agree to that. And he probably wouldn't agree to his plan either.

Then he thought of Carlota, and how she would hold him close and be so good to him. It was bad for him to run away from Carlota. He absolutely knew it would make her cry. But Carlota was so busy with her work. It wasn't fair of him to stay. He vowed that someday he would see her again.

"Sussex! Next stop, Sussex!" The conductor's voice boomed over the intercom.

Sussex! He knew where Sussex was. It was across the Delaware, just a few miles from home. Pops used to take them to a farmers' market near Sussex.

Several people lined up at the end of the train car to get off in Sussex when the train stopped. He quickly rose and ran to the end of the car to join them. They were getting near Port Jervis and he didn't want the conductor to call his folks. That would ruin his plan.

The train stopped and Tad followed the others down to the platform. Then he took off down the street as fast as he could run. He thought he heard someone yell, but he didn't stop to see if it was the conductor yelling at him.

He didn't stop running until he was well out of town. He knew that the narrow road led west toward Dingmans Ferry. There he could cross the Delaware and be only a few miles from Pops's farm. Maybe he could hitch a ride part of the way. He and Eddie Foxworth used to do that a lot. When Pops found out, he would always get out the strap. Suddenly he felt afraid and wondered if his plan would work. Hitching rides was another thing he would have to stop doing. Pops must have a hundred reasons for giving him a beating, he thought.

He turned and looked back toward Sussex and then to the south along the farmland. Tears came. Somewhere way back there he would bet that he had made Carlota very sad. He began to walk very slow, thinking more and more that his plan wouldn't work.

33

It was eight P.M. Blair Lawton opened the door to her hotel room half expecting to find Jason crashed out inside. "Damn," she exclaimed aloud when she faced the empty room. He hadn't called her at the office all day and she had canceled a late dinner date with Dillon Archibald.

Her message light was blinking. She picked up the phone to audit her voice mail. Jason's voice came loud and clear, too loud and too clear. He still sounded smashed. Their night at the Crestview had wiped him out. The call didn't make much sense to her. He said he was holed up in a motel, but didn't say where. He did say he would see her tomorrow night. She figured he was probably staying in or near Harrisburg.

Blair dialed Dillon Archibald's private line at the office. He picked up on the first ring, still at his desk. "Dillon, you workaholic, you're still at it. I thought I was bad, but you take the cake."

"Just checking over the stuff Jason left me. The proposal is all in good order. I'll bet you contributed to that."

"Between you and me, Jason just hates the word processor. He may be the thinker, but I'm the perfectionist on this team."

"Ah, I knew you put this report together. Don't sell yourself short in the thinking department. You had a couple of great ideas the other night. Too bad we aren't having dinner. Since you actually put this proposal together, I'd like to discuss the report with you. I can't seem to find Jason. I just got off the phone with Amanda in Harrisburg. He's not there yet."

"That bad boy! I'll bet he's on the nineteenth hole at

some golf club. He believes that all work and no play make dull boys."

"Really?" Dillon paused for a moment, wondering if she realized that her remark could be interpreted as a dig at her boss. "Well, if that's what he did, I think he deserves the day to himself. Obviously you share that philosophy about the all work and no play routine." Then, in a low whisper, "You were magnificent the other night, my dear. Too bad we had to cancel this evening. I would relish another session like that."

"Dillon, shame on you. Are you still free for dinner?"

"Of course. I hope you've changed you mind?"

"No, you just did it for me. You must promise you won't spend too much time on business. You've got me thinking a lot about the other night, Dillon. I think we should pick up right where we left off. Do you remember what you were doing, Dillon?"

"You don't mince words, do you? You are a very decisive woman, Blair. I like that. I'll be right over. Give me about twenty minutes."

Blair hung up the phone and gazed at her image in the mirror. Dillon Archibald was certainly deserving of her attention. Even Jason had encouraged her to butter up the old guy. "Any means to an end" was very much a part of Jason's philosophy.

She flirted with herself in the mirror and began touching up with a makeup brush. It wasn't fair, she thought, but as far as Dillon Archibald was concerned, he was no match for her weaponry. The old fool had an Achilles heel that ran all the way up to his swelled head.

At the most important time in his business life Jason was out there someplace nursing a binge. As a loyal assistant it was absolutely her duty to carry the torch. She stood up and twirled in front of the mirror, then started to undress, deciding that there was something else that would be much more appropriate for Dillon Archibald's taste.

Blair fingered the the tiny leather miniskirt. Perfect, she thought, perfect for some dark little out-of-the-way place in the Village.

Dillon was on time. She didn't give him a chance to ask to come up to her room. "I'm ready, Dillon. I'll be right down."

Emerging from the elevator, she spied Dillon standing in front of the concierge desk, his eyes fixed on her every step as she walked toward him. She became aware of other heads turning as she walked toward him. The leather mini was just the right length, she thought to herself.

"Exquisite, my dear, exquisite! For years I've yearned for a vice president who presents herself as well as you do." He brushed her cheek with a greeting kiss, grasped her hand and led her toward the cabstand.

"Vice president, Dillon? That kind of talk will get you anywhere. You really shouldn't joke about things like that. I might choose to believe everything you say, Dillon." She beamed a smile at him, now very much aware of the side glances directed at her from passersby outside the hotel. Maybe the mini was too damn short.

"Joking? Who's joking, my dear. Just keep it to yourself until I spring it on Jason. I've decided you will work side by side with Jason, rather than together. Actually, it was my wife's idea. Very practical woman, Cora," he mused as they climbed into the taxi. "She figures she can better keep her eye on you as a VP than if you were an obscure assistant tucked away in some cubicle."

"Dillon, that's hilarious. Now you are joking. Cora is such a doll," she lied. "I absolutely know she couldn't be that devious. That's mean of you, Dillon."

"Trust me, dear. Trust me, I know my Cora."

As he spoke the words "trust me," she felt his hand probing the accommodating high hem of the leather mini. The mere act of sitting down in the cramped space in the taxi eliminated any possibility of modesty.

The Gray Area was aptly named, thought Blair, as Dillon Archibald led her into the currently trendy Village hideaway just off Ninth Street. The dimly lit bistro was done in various shades of light gray, which slowly darkened to charcoal black in the corners of the room. Once the eyes became adjusted to the dimness, the patrons in the corner tables became barely visible. An obese piano player near the bar, cigarette dangling from the corner of his mouth, played soft jazz.

Blair clasped his hand firmly, not from any intent to show affection, but to stop his incessant probing in the darkness. "Dillon, how ever did you discover The Gray Area? Do you bring all your women here?"

"All my women? You mean Cora? She'd think I was insane if I brought her here." Blair released his hand and he resumed his stroking.

"Of course, you are insane, Dillon. She is right." She planted a quick but firm kiss on his cheek. Might as well let the old boy have his kicks for a while, she thought. He was setting the stage perfectly for the rest of the evening.

Dillon ordered a couple of Scotches from a scantily clad waitress who faded unobtrusively in and out of the dim light. Then he turned toward Blair. "Where do you suppose that scoundrel Jason is tonight? Since he's not in Harrisburg with Amanda, and he's not here with either of us, it makes me wonder what sort of priorities he sets for himself. Do you suppose I made a mistake in promoting Jason?"

"Of course not. He's very talented, you know." She paused for a moment before slipping a verbal stiletto into Jason's fair-haired-boy image. "But you do have to give golfers space to play their silly little game."

Archibald nodded his silent assent, staring off into the dark recesses of The Gray Area. A diminutive woman, well groomed, with a boyish bob sat drinking alone at the bar. She was sleek and attractive, but primly dressed for the usual patron of the Gray Area. He noticed several times she seemed to be looking in their direction. Archibald wondered idly whether or not the attractive woman was intrigued by Blair. He nudged Blair. "I think the young lady at the bar is ogling you. Perhaps she would enjoy being our toy for the evening."

"Dillon! You amaze me. Doesn't your mind ever get away from sex? How did you ever manage to build Harmony Mutual?" She squirmed an inch or two away from him. "I'm insulted. What makes you think I would be interested in her? Am I boring you already, Dillon?"

"Relax, my dear. You know much better than that. I suppose I was trying to say that if there was anything you really desire, I want to know about it. We'll be working closely together. It's important that we are totally frank with each other."

Blair closed the space between them and circled her arm around him. "If you really mean that, Dillon, take me where we can be alone. You don't have to sell me on Dillon Archibald. I think you are one in a million, Dillon. We don't need to fence with each other like two teenagers. We both know exactly what we want." She pressed against him and probed aggressively into his mouth with her kiss.

Archibald called for their tab. A few minutes later they headed for the exit and passed close by the attractive young woman at the bar.

Penny Wine, caught by surprise at their sudden departure, found herself exchanging glances with the couple as they passed by. Dillon Archibald smiled openly and Blair Lawton flashed a sheepish grin. It was as if the couple where sharing some private joke.

I wonder what that was all about? she mused to herself. Penny took a sip of her Perrier, slid a tip across the bar and followed them out of The Gray Area in a matter of seconds. She ran a few paces up the block to where her taxi still sat, with the off-duty sign lit.

"Quick! Follow that cab up ahead of us. I don't have an

address." Penny wasn't surprised when their taxi pulled up in front of Blair's hotel. She waited until they had entered the hotel before exiting her cab. She felt vaguely uncomfortable. The smiles she had collected from both Archibald and Blair Lawton were a bad sign. She had a strong intuitive feeling that they must have been talking about her. Putting herself in the position of being so easily noticed had violated one of Coley's basic rules of the chase.

Nevertheless, she entered the lobby just in time to see the pair enter an elevator together. Penny looked at her watch and then spent another fifteen minutes window shopping the fancy shops just off the hotel lobby before deciding to call it a night.

From the moment Blair and Dillon entered her suite on the security level, Dillon pawed at her aggressively. The leather mini dropped to the floor as Blair pressed against his exploring hand. Blair tilted her head back and moaned, offering no resistance. "Dillon, you mad devil. I knew you'd like my skirt," she whispered. "Perhaps you should get one for Cora."

Dillon paused for a moment. "Cora? I don't think they grow cattle that large." He maneuvered her to the long plush sofa.

"Dillon, that's absolutely cruel. What do you say about me behind my back when you're making love to someone else?"

Dillon, now kneeling, traced kisses over her bare midriff and leered up at her. "Nothing, you crazy sexpot! Nothing. We never speak of each other to anyone. Is that clear?"

"Perfectly clear, Dillon. And speaking of perfect, keep doing what you are doing." Blair moaned appreciatively and threw herself back on the sofa.

Several minutes later Dillon moved over her, preparing to enter her. He paused for a moment as Blair's eyes met his, and she spoke. "Dillon, there is something you should know before you do this."

"What's that?" he gasped hoarsely.

"If I become pregnant, it's yours. Do you understand that, Dillon?"

He stopped for several seconds, smiled, then met her unblinking eyes with his own. Then he thrust himself into her, permitting her legs to lock cooperatively behind him.

34

Willy Hanson sat facing Amanda Granger in the living room of her home. She looked puzzled. Jason's laptop computer and a box containing several files sat on the coffee table between him. "Jason said he would drop by to pick them up last evening. When it comes to business, Jason almost always does what he says he is going to do. Archibald Dillon called her twice looking for Jason. Blair Lawton called and left a message, which I chose not to answer. She was also looking for Jason."

Willy chuckled. "That woman's got a lot of brass. She has her nerve calling you under the circumstances. I'm sure all communication from her will stop once she knows she's been named as correspondent. This miserable ordeal will be over soon, Amanda. You can count on it."

She forced a weak smile. "Oh, I'm getting used to my decision, Willy. All my tears have gone now. I just want to get this whole messy thing over with and go on with my life—and the life of my child. Now, what can I help you with?"

Willy pondered what question to ask first. He dreaded bringing up Jason's possible link with a kidnapping. The woman had enough problems already. "Well, first of all, do you have any idea where Jason might be? He was last seen heading for Harrisburg yesterday." Willy nodded toward the laptop on the coffee table. "Obviously, he never got here."

Amanda shrugged. "I haven't an inkling. In fact, when it comes to matters of business, it is very out of character for Jason not to do what he says he will do. If I were to guess, I would suppose he is out there somewhere with that woman."

"The last word I had is that Blair Lawton is back in New York. Jason was driving alone toward Harrisburg the last time we saw him. After getting all the evidence we needed, we dropped our tail on him." Willy decided not to mention the involvement of the Pennsylvania State Police for the moment.

"I have just a couple more questions, Amanda, and I promise I'll get out of here. First of all, the emergency room doctor who treated your husband after his beating wouldn't turn over Jason's medical report to me. I want you to request a copy of it."

Amanda looked puzzled. "I'll call him today. But why on earth do you need that now?"

"We think that Jason might be involved in the use of cocaine. We would like to be certain." Willy watched the look of disbelief cross Amanda's face.

"I'll ask Dr. Lavin for the report, but I think that you are barking up the wrong tree. Jason is a real physical fitness nut, you know." Amanda shook her head. "And that leaves one more question. I hope it is as easy as the last one."

Framing the question was a problem. There was just no easy way to ask about what seemed absurd. "Amanda, there is a reason to believe that Jason could be involved in the kidnapping and ransoming of a young boy. Can you shed any light on why there may be such suspicions."

Amanda stared, dumbstruck, at Willy for several seconds. Obviously his question came from so far out in left field that she was having trouble with it.

"That's preposterous. At a time like this I am willing to

accuse Jason of almost anything, but this is totally unthinkable. Jason wouldn't do such a thing. Whoever told you that is horribly mistaken or a liar."

"Okay, Amanda. I believe you. Just forget I asked the question. The state police are nosing around and thought they had a lead. I guess they haven't."

Willy got up and prepared to leave. Amanda walked him to the door in silence. Willy suspected that she was having trouble with his own credibility because of his last question. "Amanda, thanks for considering what must seem to be stupid questions. We'll be turning the evidence over to you so that you can present it to your attorney. We'll meet with him at his convenience. Under the circumstances I would be very surprised if Jason contests the divorce."

"Let's hope you are right," she said softly. Then she broke into a warm smile. "Thank Coley for me. I think you have a fine young man there."

"I will. Coley's tops in his field." Willy walked to his car, started the engine, then looked at his watch. Jason had been missing for over twelve hours now. It was perplexing how the conspicuous red Corvette could just vanish into thin air.

Willy drove eastward and pulled onto the Pennsylvania Turnpike at his first opportunity. He decided to try Coley again on his cellular phone.

"Hello, beautiful," Coley's sleepy voice answered his own cellular on the second ring.

"Sorry to disappoint you, Coley, but this isn't 'beautiful,' it's Willy. Where the hell are you?"

"Let me see. I'm at the Delgap Sportsman's Lodge about ten miles north of Route 80, and have I ever got news for you! Are you sitting down or standing up?"

"I'm driving. I'll hang on to the wheel real tight. What's your news?"

"I've solved the 'git-go' mystery. Guess what? It's Sonny Houston's license plate number. It's G-I-T-G-O, then the number 7. I saw it with my own eyes as I just happened by chance to pass his farm."

"Isn't that interesting. That is news! I hope the feds or the state troopers don't see you poking around up there." Willy paused for a moment, mulling over the implications of Coley's information. "I figure I must be about two hours away from the place where you're staying. We'd better have a little think tank before we decide what to do. That all you got?"

"Nope, I got more. Penny just called. Dillon Archibald and Blair Lawton did the Village last night and wound up in Blair's sack. Wherever Jason is, he's being cheated on big time. We better have a serious talk with Penny, Willy, she's beginning to do stuff on her own. She's taking her private eye apprenticeship seriously."

"She's got some brains back of that cute button nose, Coley. She's bound to break the rules now and then, but I'll talk to her. What do you think we ought to do with her information?"

"Easy! Maybe it's time to talk to Cora Archibald and rustle up some fast bucks from another millionaire."

"That's a real noble suggestion, Coley. Why don't we just open a whorehouse out in Nevada and blackmail all the guys who are cheating on their wives?"

"Cool down, boss, cool down. I'm sorry, but you asked me what to do with Penny's info, and me being me, I thought of the obvious joke. The only constructive thought I get from Blair's two-timing is that Jason Granger is behaving like an erratic fool and is a lousy judge of character. Swapping a class act like Amanda for a bimbo like Blair makes him plain crazy in my book. Of course, I would have to get both of them in the sack to truly assess their appeal to Jason Granger."

"Coley, please eighty-six that last idea before you think it's a good one. I think we can assume that Sonny Houston may have had something to do with Jason's beating on the turnpike. Why else would 'git-go' have been etched on his mind. I still can't really believe that Jason would kidnap someone. It's far out of character for him. Yet the kidnapping is all we really care about at this point. The kid, Coley—we've got to find the kid."

"Willy, I think we've got to confront Sonny Houston and find out what caused the bad blood between him and Jason."

"Good thinking, Coley, but we have to be careful how we do that. If the boy is harmed, it could be our fault. Think about it, and think about how much we should share with the police."

"Police?"

"Yes, Coley, the police. They're trying to locate the kid, too. We've got to be careful. Just think about the welfare of the kid all the time, and we'll be okay. Call Penny and bring her up to date. Keeping an eye on Blair in New York is a good idea. There is always the chance she can lead us to Jason. See you in a couple of hours, pal."

Coley hung up the phone and stared at the Delaware River from his window. A half dozen shad boats stretched in a line across the river. He trained his binoculars on the fishermen. They wore similar shoulder patches.

He focused his glasses on the nearest boat. The group was comprised of a unit of the Pennsylvania State Police continuing the search of the river. He was actually heartened by the sight. As long as the search went on, and they didn't find anything, there was a chance that Tad Houston was still alive.

Coley opened the desk drawer and took out several sheets of stationary. He proceeded to itemize the people involved in the case and list the information known about each. He was consumed with a feeling of urgency. When Willy arrived, they had to formulate a plan of action as quickly as possible.

35

The hike to Dingmans Ferry was longer than Tad had figured. He recalled that when Pops drove it by car it took almost a half hour. It was well into the afternoon of the next day before he crossed the Delaware and plunged into the woods on the other side. Cutting through the woods, he figured he was still a three- or four-hour hike from home. Eddie Foxworth had once made the hike with him, but they had started quite a distance to the north of Dingmans Ferry.

The more he thought about his plan, the more fearful he became of the possibility of facing Pops when he was alone. He decided to make sure that only Mom was around.

He was really hungry when he came to the familiar trail along a series of waterfalls that fed the creek winding behind him to the Delaware. Tad sat on a rock and munched the last of a candy bar he had bought at Dingmans Ferry. He now had no more money. He had been to the waterfalls before and knew now that he was only a couple of hours away from home. He was excited at the prospect of seeing Mom. But when he imagined his planned conversation with Pops, he became upset. If Mom were not with them all the time, he guessed that Pops would get out the strap and wallop him for running away.

The candy bar now gone, he again started pushing through dense underbrush, now feeling real pangs of hunger as he climbed to the high ridge ahead of him. At the top of the ridge his heart began to beat faster. He gazed across the wide expanse of woodland leading to the next ridge of the Poconos in the distance. Home was now just the other side of that ridge. It wouldn't be long now before he would see Mom and get something good to eat.

About halfway to the next ridge he came upon several crude lean-tos. Deer hunters had constructed them as blinds during the hunting season. It always made Pops mad when they built them too close to his property. He stopped and inspected one of them. It would be a great place for camping with Eddie Foxworth. He made a mental note of exactly where they were. One of them was next to a narrow stream, so narrow that it would probably dry up after the spring rains were over. Still, it would be a great place to camp.

Now, really weary, he reached the top of the ridge and found himself on the back edge of Pops's farm. Beyond the strand of wire that Pops called his defense perimeter stood a giant backhoe. A long ditch led along the back of the farm, obviously freshly carved by the backhoe. The dirt from the ditch had all been piled into a huge mound behind Pops's grape vineyard. He climbed up the mound of dirt and looked down. The whole farm was visible. He could see the house clearly, and the driveway that led to the main road in the distance. The new mound was kind of neat. It would be a great place to come and sit once in a while when grape picking began.

Off to the right, near the edge of the property, were two small but deep excavations, separate and close together. They had also been scooped out by the backhoe. Tad shook his head as he peered into them. Pops had a big project going. Maybe he would tell him about it, and he could help him finish it.

He again climbed to the top of the newly built mound, lay on his stomach and peeked out toward the house. Pops's SUV was nowhere to be seen. It was not in its usual parking place by the barn, or out near the front gate where he parked it once in a while. He gave a big sigh of relief. Mom might be alone.

Now he was really excited. If Mom were there alone, he could explain his plan to her. Avoiding the high brush, Tad ran directly toward the house. Within a couple of minutes he was pounding on the back door. Usually it was only locked if no one were at home. His spirits sank. Mom was not home. He went to the side porch and looked through the screen. The window was not latched. In fact, it was open just an inch or so. It didn't take long to find a long ten-penny nail in the barn. Poking carefully to make sure he didn't make a big hole in the screen, he managed to loosen the single hook, causing the screen to hang open. He lifted the window and scrambled inside.

"Hi, Mom," he yelled, hoping to hear her voice. He looked in the downstairs rooms and then ran upstairs. No one was home. Then he remembered how hungry he was.

He opened the pantry, found the jar of peanut butter, and untwisted the bit of wire from the end of a fresh loaf of bread. He found a dinner knife, smeared a slice of bread heavy with peanut butter, and ate it as fast as he could. Then he repeated the process, taking time to pour and gulp down a glass of milk.

He walked into the living room and looked down the long driveway. Pops was getting out of the van to pick up the mail. Mom was not with him. He froze for a second, contemplating meeting alone with Pops when he got to the house. He decided against it.

Tad grabbed the loaf of bread and the jar of peanut butter and scrambled back through the open window, pushing the unhooked screen back into position. Careful to keep the house between himself and the van so as to block Pops's vision, he ran up the hill as fast as he could. He sprawled on the ground behind the newly built mound and peeked back at the house. Pops parked the van where he always did, walked to the rear door and disappeared inside. Tad's heart was pumping so loud he could actually hear it. There was no way he could gather the courage to face Pops without Mom.

Tad made his way back through the woods for about a half mile before he relocated the hunters' blind next to the small stream. He curled up inside and decided that he would check every now and then to see if Mom was home. He had seldom known Pops to go very far into these woods. If he did, Tad doubted that he would walk as far as this lean-to.

He sat the jar of peanut butter and the loaf of bread on a rock beside him. At least he had food and he could get a drink from the small spring whenever he wanted to. He and Eddie Foxworth had done that a lot of times.

Now in the house, Sonny Houston put the grocery bags he had carried from the van on the kitchen table. He had almost completed putting them all away before he noticed the dinner knife in the kitchen sink, all smeared with peanut butter. He stared at it a long time before picking it up. There was no way that he had left that in the sink before leaving that morning. He picked it up gingerly and stared around the room. A small bit of a crust of bread lay next to the sink. He had been invaded!

Sonny walked to the gun rack in the front hallway and removed a shotgun from its hooks. He quickly checked to make sure it was loaded, as it always was, and then began to make a room-to-room inspection of the entire house.

Satisfied that he was alone, he walked back into the kitchen. "I'll bet it's that damn Foxworth kid," he muttered to himself. "I wonder how he got in? I'll have to set that boy straight." Eddie was a little thief, he thought, and he had invaded his property line again despite his warning.

Tomorrow morning he would go pick up Bessie. He decided she had stayed far too long at Sarah's. After all, there had been an invasion just because she wasn't there to protect the premises while he was gone. Kids were running wild these days. Bessie just had to stay home and watch the perimeter when he was gone. If she thought otherwise, he'd have to beat some sense into the woman.

Sonny began to wash the dinner knife under the tap, staring at the unfamiliar mound at the rear of his property. He broke into a smile. There was ways of taking care of people when they got out of line, he thought. Hell, that's what Houston Memorial Park is all about. Bessie would just have to shape up. He should have disciplined her long ago when he first found out Tad was a little bastard.

36

Agent Mark Whitcomb of the FBI sat in the backseat of the van with Empress Carlota. Whitcomb was now coordinating the investigation of the disappearance of Tad Houston, which now encompassed parts of three states. Detective McCutcheon of the NYPD and Lance Carver of the New Jersey State Police sat in the front seat as the van slowly circled several residential blocks in Morristown, New Jersey.

"There! I think that's it. It's the white house with the green trim." Carlota pointed at the house as the van drove slowly by. "These houses look so much alike, but I'm certain now this is the right one. When Tad and I saw it before, his father's van was parked right there in that driveway." She pointed again at the prim little house, shaking her head up and down with conviction.

"And the boy wouldn't go in because he was afraid to face his father? That's what he told you?" questioned Whitcomb.

"Oh, yes. Tad started shaking and ducked down in the car, terrified that someone in the house would see him. His father broke his arm, you know."

Whitcomb watched the prostitute closely as she spoke. So far the woman had shown no indication of being devious. In his estimation she had been sincere. "You're saying that had his father's van not been there, you would have taken the boy inside to his aunt."

"Oh, yes. Tad was prepared to go in. He likes his Aunt Sarah."

"Do you think he might have found his way back here by himself and that he might be in the house right now?" Whitcomb asked.

"Oh, I hope so. I really hope so." Carlota's eyes grew moist.

"Okay, boys, let's have a look-see. Get the other unit around in back of the house." Another van soon appeared, and circled the block. Two men emerged and approached the house from the property in the rear. "McCutcheon, you stay here with Empress. Lance and I will say hello."

Carlota watched the two men approach the front of the house, praying that Tad would appear in the doorway after they knocked. But he didn't. There was a brief conversation with a woman who she supposed was Sarah, and then they entered the house.

Agent Whitcomb eyed Sarah Houston carefully. She must have been in her late forties, maybe fifty. She seemed pleasant enough, hair speckled with gray, completely unflustered at being confronted with the search warrant.

"I hope you're here with news about young Tad. His mother, my sister-in-law, is visiting, and we are both worried sick about him. Please tell me you have found him and that he's okay."

"I wish I could, ma'am, but we're hoping to find him here." Whitcomb looked around. It certainly wouldn't take long to search the tiny cottage thoroughly. "Those are my men at the back door. Mind letting them in, ma'am?"

"Oh, my, the place is kind of a mess now. Bessie and I have just been sitting and talking about young Tad all morning. He's not here. You're certainly welcome to look. Bessie is taking a nap on the back porch. I'll go get her." She walked quickly through the small house and opened the door to allow two additional investigators inside. Bessie was already sitting up on the sofa when they entered.

"Bessie, these officers are here to talk about Tad. I'm sure they'll want to talk to you."

Bessie sat rigidly, trying to figure out what was going on. One of the men had stationed himself just inside the back door, blocking any entry or exit. "Tad? Oh, my God! They've found him in the river." Tears started streaming down her face, her eyes pleading with Sarah to tell her she was wrong.

"No! No! Bessie. It's not that at all. They think he might be alive." Sarah sat next to her on the couch and put an arm around her, trying to calm her down. In the background they could hear the other men ascend the stairs leading to the two rooms upstairs. Soon they came down and went to the tiny cellar below the house.

Within minutes, Whitcomb and Lance Carver joined the two women on the storm-windowed porch. Whitcomb introduced himself to Tad's mother. "Mrs. Houston, we were hoping that we would find Tad here. We haven't found him anywhere yet, but we have talked to several people who claim to have seen him as recently as yesterday afternoon."

Whitcomb paused as Sarah whispered something in Bessie's ear. He supposed it to be words of comfort, but the other woman looked extremely distressed. "There is something I must tell you, however. The boy might be alive and well, but there is this possibility that we may be dealing with kidnappers."

Bessie wailed, losing all composure. "I know, I know." She looked at Sarah and then began searching through her purse.

Sarah again put her arm around her. "Show them, Bessie. It's the only thing to do."

Whitcomb became impatient. "Show us what? Look here, if either of you know something we don't know, you'd better tell us."

Bessie produced the ransom note from her purse and steeled herself to speak. "I found this in Sonny's work clothes. He doesn't know I have it. If he remembers where he put it, he probably thinks it was lost in the wash." She handed the note to Whitcomb.

Whitcomb read the note and passed it along to Carver. "I have a copy of another note from this bastard. The printing looks very similar. The Pennsylvania State Police picked it up a couple of days ago." Then Whitcomb turned toward Bessie Houston. "Why didn't you discuss this with your husband, or did you?"

"I . . . I don't know."

"You don't know!"

"She's afraid of him!" Sarah interjected in a shrill tone, totally out of character from her prior demeanor. "My brother isn't a man you bring up any unpleasantness with." She shrugged and looked squarely at Whitcomb. "I know that's hard for you to understand, but I do. That's why Bessie came here, to talk about the note with me. We had decided to go to the police before you got here."

"Mrs. Houston, is that right? Do you have a problem asking your husband about this note? For instance, who gave it to him?" Whitcomb waited patiently for an answer.

Bessie shook her head, trying to find words. "He kept it from me. That means he didn't want me to see it. You have to realize that Sonny is a very difficult person. He was injured some way in the war."

"I'm sorry, Mrs. Houston, but your son is evidently in danger somewhere, and every hour we have lost by not knowing about this note has made finding him more difficult. Where is your husband right now? We've got to talk to him."

"He's on our farm up in Pennsylvania. He called this morning and said he is coming for me. He didn't say exactly when." Bessie dropped her hands in her lap in a hopeless gesture and turned to face Sarah. "Oh, Sarah, please, I don't want to go back up there. It's so nice and restful here. It's not the same at home without Tad."

Sarah held the sobbing woman in her arms while speaking to Whitcomb. "I'll talk to my brother. She really should stay with me a while longer. Maybe they'll find Tad, and then things will be better up there. I doubt if he'll listen to me, though. When Sonny makes up his mind to do anything, he never changes it."

Whitcomb and Carver looked on silently as Sarah tried to calm Bessie. One thing seemed obvious to both of them. They were terrified of Sonny Houston and probably knew nothing else about the kidnapping of the boy.

"Mrs. Houston, I'm going to leave one of my men in the area to keep his eye on things. If Tad Houston does show up, we want to know immediately." He handed Sarah a small, flat box designed to fit on a key ring. It had a single button recessed on one surface. "If Tad shows up, or if you want one of my men here at any time over the next couple of days, just push the button. My man will be here in less than five minutes."

Sarah took the pager and stuck it in the small pocket of her sweater. "I'll take good care of Bessie and try to talk some sense into my brother, but I doubt if it will do any good."

Whitcomb and Carver said good-bye and walked back to the van out front. Carlota still sat there with Detective McCutcheon. Whitcomb spoke quietly to the detective. "Why don't you take Carlota back to her apartment in New York. Given his past history, by some miracle the kid might show up there. Tell your boys to keep an eye on the place. Carlota, I must advise you to stay put until we say otherwise."

Carlota groaned. "How am I supposed to make the big bucks? I'm behind in my rent now. I don't get no paid days off in my business, you know."

"Relax Carlota, we'll think of something," Whitcomb assured her, without going into detail. "You're dealing with your Uncle Sam here."

Whitcomb walked away and rejoined Carver. "I think it

is time for us to go up to Milford and fire some questions at Mr. Sonny Houston. How far is it?"

"Hour and a half at the most."

"Let's break the record. I got a feeling this is urgent. We also got to find this Jason Granger character. He's got to answer some questions." Whitcomb smiled wryly. "Then there's Willy Hanson and his partner Coley Doctor, the famous private eyes. They keep pussyfooting around on the edge of this case. I wonder why?"

37

Coley Doctor could hardly contain himself when Willy showed up at the Delgap Sportsman's Lodge. Using a road map of the area, he marked every confirmed sighting they had of Jason Granger until he disappeared.

"Willy, I think that Jason Granger just might be the kidnapper. I think he's keeping the kid someplace up here." Coley swept his hand across a portion of the map north and far west of Milford, near the New York state line.

"How in the hell do you figure that? Jason's specialty in life is fancy derrieres, not kidnapping. He doesn't have time for both."

Coley pointed at the map again. "The Pennsylvania cops lost him right before reaching I-84. I managed to complete a call to the Pennsylvania cop who picked up the tail on Jason when I had to drop it. He verified that. Nice guy, but he didn't have the horsepower to keep up with the Corvette. Since everyone believed he was headed for Harrisburg, they reasoned Jason would go west on I-84. The cops had a half dozen cars between him and Harrisburg, figuring he would go the fastest route. Nobody spotted the red Corvette."

"Why do you suppose that is, Coley?" Willy asked, realizing that it was improbable that Jason would elude so many police cruisers on the interstate, especially since he had no real reason to believe he was being followed. Of course, he might have tried to elude the police if he were the kidnapper.

"Maybe he turned east instead of west." They both stared at the map. "He could have gotten off at the Milford junction. That's also the cutoff for Houston's farm. Maybe he wanted to pay him a visit." Coley traced his finger along the map. "I'm going to go up around Milford and take a look, if you don't mind."

Willy nodded. "There's also a bunch of little motels at that interchange. According to you, the guy didn't get any sleep for twenty-four hours. Check around there for the red Corvette. Maybe he just decided to crash for a while."

"We gotta find him, Willy. How's Amanda going to get her divorce papers served if we can't find him?" Coley grinned at his own observation.

"That's very funny, Coley. The SOB is a bad apple. He'll turn up sooner or later." Willy paused, deep in thought for a moment. "I know the real reason you want to check out Milford is to get another peek at Houston's place. Be careful. We promised Knight we wouldn't butt in. As long as you are going, check out the motels. Maybe you'll find the Corvette. Of course, he might have just kept moving up I-84 into New York State. Hell, he could be in Canada by now."

"Not a chance, Willy. He's too hooked on Blair Lawton to fly the coop. Also, the bastard has too damn much to lose, as I see it. His big new promotion has got to mean big bucks. The guy has spent his whole career pointed toward this promotion."

Willy's cell phone beeped. It was Penny. "Amanda just called. She said Jason hasn't come by to pick up his stuff after you left her. She's got a locksmith coming in to change the locks. Says she'll leave his laptop and files on the porch. And guess what?"

"I'll bite, what?" Willy decided that he would have to speak to Penny about her habit of saying "Guess what?" before saying something important.

"She talked to Jason's doctor. It turns out that he was high on cocaine the day he got beaten up. She's really pissed off. Amanda said that she had suspected it sometimes, but always pushed it out of her mind. That's really why she's having the locks changed."

"I don't blame her. I still don't see why he should just vanish, considering the big new job and his hots for Blair. Everything is coming up roses for the guy. Penny, I want you to pick up your tail on Blair. There's a damn good chance she might lead us to Jason."

"That's easy, Willy. She'll come out of the building with Dillon Archibald. They will go about six blocks to her hotel, spend three or four hours in there doing whatever it is that they do, and then go out for a late dinner. Then it's back to the hotel again to do it some more. About four A.M. he'll go home to Cora. If Cora knew what we know, I'll bet she'd be seeking a divorce. Hey! She'd make a fine client!"

"Penny, you are beginning to think like Coley. We don't give a damn what they are doing in the sack, but we must talk to Jason. That's your goal, to see if Blair will lead us to Jason."

Willy hung up feeling they were stymied. It could be that Jason Granger might be on some business mission that Blair and even Archibald might be aware of. "Okay, Coley, we've got to split up. I'm going to barge in on Dillon Archibald and ask a few questions before Jason's trail gets any colder. I'll just tell him I'm working on a case and that he has some information I've got to have. It isn't exactly a lie."

Coley nodded. "Good. I get to have all the fun. I'll go up to Milford and look for the red Corvette. I'll take a peek at Houston's farm. I've always wanted to buy a little spot in the Poconos. Great deer hunting up there, Willy."

"Not the kind of 'dears' you care anything about, Coley.

Go ahead, but just keep a low profile." He always wondered when he said it how the six foot seven black detective would manage a low profile.

Outside the Delgap Sportsmans Lodge the two men split. Coley watched Willy head south toward New York and then pulled slowly onto the road leading north. Soon he made a left near Dingmans Ferry, figuring he would return to the Crestview Hideaway and follow the system of rural roads that Granger might have used to get to the Milford junction.

He reached I-84, where Granger was supposed to have turned west toward Harrisburg, and took the eastern on-ramp toward Milford. In ten minutes he arrived at the interchange featuring a half dozen small motels and several fast-food joints. He decided to start with the small motel that was nearest the off-ramp. If Granger had been fighting fatigue, he would probably pick the first one that looked decent.

Coley described Jason Granger to the clerk, who stared at him, tight-lipped, as he talked. "This guy drove a new bright red Corvette. His wife is quite concerned about him and asked me to inquire around." Coley fingered a twenty dollar bill thoughtfully as the clerk began to riffle through an index file of registrations.

"I remember the car. Rain was predicted, but this guy was so tired that he left the top down." Coley peeled off another twenty and the clerk's memory began to improve greatly. "Here's his registration, a Mr. Jason Granger."

Bingo! Coley couldn't believe his good luck. And he had used his own name! The idea that Jason might have been a kidnapper became even less valid. What kidnapper on the run would use his own name?

The desk clerk, happy with his windfall, showed Coley the registration card. "Oh, yes, I remember him quite well. He didn't even stay for the night. He left here at about six o'clock the same day. He said something about driving to Harrisburg."

"Really?" Coley was sorry to hear that. Now he was right back to square one.

"Except that when he drove away, he didn't get back on I-84 at all. He drove in toward town. Of course, he might have been hungry. We don't have a cafe right here."

"Thanks, buddy, you've been a big help." Coley saw the man looking at his hands, probably trying to figure out what he could say that would produce another twenty.

Twilight was closing in when Coley reached Sonny Houston's farm. He drove past it, then made a U-turn and pulled up short of his mailbox. Coley got out of his car and walked down the road along the single strand of new wire that marked Houston's property. A crude ditch had been dug that paralleled the wire for a short distance. Walking back to his car he noticed a scrap of white paper, folded neatly in the middle, lying among the tall weeds around the mailbox.

He leaned over and picked it up. The message was clearly legible in the dim light

IF YOU DON'T COUGH UP THE MONEY AS YOU WERE INSTRUCTED, YOU GET THE BOY'S EARS IN THE MAIL.

It was handprinted in block letters similar to those used in the other note Willy had taken from the box. Since Willy had witnessed Granger putting the other note in the box, it seemed logical that Granger might have just done it again after leaving the motel at the junction. But why was it lying here in the weeds?

Coley stuffed the note into his shirt pocket and suddenly became distracted by the sound of a vehicle coming from the direction of Houston's house. Houston's van, the same GITGO 7 that had caused Granger's nightmares in the hospital, came roaring down the long driveway, kicking up a cloud of dust all the way.

Coley waved at him as he neared, deciding to see what the guy was really like. Houston pulled the van within inches of where Coley stood. Houston opened the door and climbed out. Coley estimated there must be almost three hundred pounds of the man. He had broad shoulders, a barrel chest and thick arms. His face was scarred and totally without expression when he began to speak.

"I've been watching you. I saw you walk all along my fence staring at my property, staring at something that's none of your business. Now, what the hell you doin' here?"

"Mr. Houston?" asked Coley, pretending to read the name off the mailbox. "I think your farm here is awfully nice. I like the way it's tucked away off the beaten track. I've been up in these parts for a few days looking to buy something like this. You know of any property for sale around here?"

"Hey, I'm asking the questions. You got that clear? I'm damn sick and tired of you city folks coming out here and causing trouble. If you ever cross that property line, I'll give you plenty of trouble." Houston waved at the single strand of barbed wire. "We're in mournin' in this house. I lost my boy to the river. Now get outta here."

"Okay, okay. I hear you. Sorry about your boy. I think I read something about it in the papers. I'm sorry I bothered you. I hope my friend didn't bother you. He's been up in these parts, too, helping me find some property. He drove a fancy little red Corvette. I'll tell him to stay away from here."

Houston stared icily at Coley. "A red Corvette? Ain't seen nothin' like that around here." Houston's face contorted into his version of a smile. "When you find him you can tell him that this property ain't for sale."

"I'll do that. Hey, by the way, I read just this morning in some paper that the police think your son might have been kidnapped. I'll be praying for him to turn up."

"Praying? Just keep your praying out of my business. You see, I ain't sure what God you'll be praying to. My God don't do the impossible. The river's got my boy. It's no concern of yours at all. God's done called him home."

For a second, Coley considered whipping out the ransom note he had just found in the high weeds near the mailbox, but decided against it. For one thing, Houston was an imposing mountain of flesh, and his own weapon was locked in the trunk of his car. And more important, he reckoned that Willy would hardly approve of him making such a move. The note should be turned over to the police and compared to the other one in the police lab.

"Mr. Houston, I'm one of those people that never gives up hope. Wouldn't it be wonderful if your boy turned up alive?" Coley watched Houston's eyes narrow and then scrutinize his rental car. "If I were you, I guess I would feel like no news is good news."

Houston walked past him and peered into the open mailbox. Then he spun around to face Coley, showing amazing agility for one of his massive frame. "You seen my boy?"

"No, but according to the papers, other people have."

"My property ain't for sale to anybody, and it's off-limits to everybody. You got that straight, Mr. Black Man?" With those words he strode past him again, brushing against him as he walked back to his van. He reached into the backseat and quickly produced a gleaming 12-gauge shotgun. He held the butt under his shoulder and let the barrel hang loosely over his wrist, just high enough to wave gently back and forth over Coley's midsection. "Now if you don't mind, I'm gonna hunt some rabbit along the fence row. You git outta here. I don't like an audience when I hunt. I just might have a bad accident."

Coley realized the ominous presence of the shotgun tilted all the odds in Houston's favor. It didn't take much to see that the guy was probably nuts. He cautiously backed away several steps and then climbed into the car. He turned on the ignition, waved casually at the scowling Houston and then drove slowly away.

Once out of range, he breathed a heavy sigh of relief. He had heard of people going completely off their rockers in a time of tragedy. Maybe that was Houston's problem. Perhaps the man needed help. To lose a young son would be a terrible trauma. Maybe the passage of time would help. Still, he couldn't figure out why the man wouldn't accept any hope that his son might still be alive.

Coley decided to stay in the area. He would hole up in one of the motels along the interstate near Milford. The odd confrontation with Houston had produced another ransom note, but nothing further to solve the problem of Jason's disappearance. The fact that he had found the ransom note in the weeds in front of Houston's farm might well indicate the last known spot where Jason Granger might have been.

Coley called Willy to bring him up to date. Luckily, Willy had just arrived at the marina in Weehawken. Coley proceeded to tell him about the events of his day.

"He pulled a shotgun on you?"

"Well, not exactly. He said he was going rabbit hunting. The man's crazy over the loss of his son, Willy. He's a ticking bomb up there in the woods. I told him I had read about a possible kidnapping in the paper. He would hear none of it. He insists the boy is drowned. It just don't make sense, Willy."

"I talked with Evan Knight this afternoon. They've given up looking in the river for now. He tells me that our old FBI friend, Agent Whitcomb, is coordinating the investigation, assuming that there was a kidnapping. They want Jason bad. They've put out a national bulletin on him. The first thing we've got to do now is turn over the new ransom note. I want to stay on this case, pro bono, until they find Jason and the kid."

"Willy, the missing Corvette is a mystery. By this time the cops must have stopped every red Corvette east of the Mississippi."

"It's not that easy to find if Jason is really on the run. He could have ditched it somewhere, or garaged it and switched vehicles. I doubt if he could have gotten into Canada with it."

"What the hell would he be running from? He has a new big job, a gorgeous wife, a beautiful home, and a fancy piece of tail on the side. That's what I call living life in the fast lane. What's he running from?" The obvious answer came to Coley just as Willy spoke.

"The only reason I really see him running is that he must be the kidnapper. He has the boy and somehow keeps him holed up someplace. Otherwise the whole thing doesn't make sense."

"What about all these people, like the train conductor and the hooker in New York, who say they've seen the kid? The only thing that makes sense is that the hooker is tied in with Jason on the kidnapping. A real enterprising broad might have well got her hooks into our cokehead playboy."

"Logical, Coley, but the police all say the prostitute's story stands up. They've turned her loose and are keeping her under surveillance."

"In that case, there is only one move I can think of. We've got one more base to touch. Blair Lawton knows more about the day we lost track of Jason than anyone else. We've got to pry open the head of that hot chick and see what's inside."

"Be my guest, Coley. I think that's your department. Check with Penny before you scope out Blair. Penny can give you a list of her habits. By the way, Penny's beginning to think just like you. Just this morning she told me that Cora Archibald would probably be interested in her investigation. Tell her to cool it, Coley. There are much more useful and nobler endeavors for P.I.s than chasing from one bedroom to another."

38

Blair Lawton was furiously searching her office for more information. Jason had been missing for two whole days now. She had blown the day trying to reconstruct the new financial plan locked securely in his missing laptop. She had managed to talk superficially about the program to Dillon Archibald, but it was Jason's brainchild. She tried desperately to remember everything Jason had said before leaving the Crestview Hideaway on his trip to Harrisburg. But she could recall nothing that indicated he had any other plans than to pick up the laptop and meet her back in New York that night.

Steeling herself for an unpleasant conversation, she dialed Jason's home in Harrisburg. Amanda picked up on the first ring.

"Amanda, I'm so glad I caught you at home. I'm worried sick. Your Jason is being a bad boy. I've been sitting in on all his meetings for two days and haven't heard a word from him. Dillon Archibald is getting a little testy. By the way, you made such a hit with Dillon. He's raved about you ever since our dinner at the Water Club."

"I can't say I can return the compliment, Blair. I found him a presumptious, boring, horny old goat." Amanda became silent, as did Blair. Her candid slap must have stunned her for a few moments.

"Amanda! You are a wonder. I don't know how many times that same thought has crossed my mind. I guess I'd better keep my eye on him. I really called about Jason. Is he there?"

"I haven't seen Jason since the morning after the Water

Club dinner. Actually, I don't intend to. You see, Jason doesn't live here anymore. He flew the coop. I thought you of all people, would know where he was."

"Oh, you poor dear. You must be going out of your mind."

"Not really. I feel much better about my life than I have felt in months. Frankly, I don't give a damn about Jason. I meant it when I said he doesn't live here anymore."

"Oh, my God! You've got to be kidding. You and Jason are the perfect couple. He'll show up. There is some perfectly logical explanation. There always is with Jason."

"Blair, if we are the perfect couple, what are the three of us, the perfect triple? Look, kiddo, I've packed his business stuff that I found lying around into boxes. He knows where I live if he wants the stuff. I'm sure you'll pass along that information." Amanda slammed the phone into its cradle. She had said enough, maybe too much. She decided she wouldn't talk to the woman again.

Back in New York Blair sipped at her morning coffee, deep in thought. She had dialed twice trying to reach Amanda again, only to be met by an answering machine.

Blair remembered the morning she had left Jason at the Crestview. He had a serious hangover. If he tried to leave soon after she had left, he could well be in some jail, or worse, in some hospital. But then why wouldn't Amanda know, or Harmony Mutual for that matter? Jason had all kinds of identification on him.

The loud voice of Dillon Archibald raging at someone down the hall interrupted her thought.

"Cancel the meeting! We'll schedule it again as soon as we get all the players together, the old players *and* the new ones."

She was sitting in Jason's office, now aware that he was stomping down the hall toward her door. It swung open. A red-faced Dillon Archibald then slammed it behind him. "What the fuck is going on around here?"

Blair startled. "Dillon, you poor man, I'll bet you couldn't sleep last night. I couldn't either, you know. The day had been a total washout. I just kept thinking about us and wishing you had stayed."

Dillon flopped in the chair in front of Jason's desk and stared at her. "Forgive me. I had forgotten all about last night. You mean you haven't heard?"

"Heard what, Dillon?" she said, expecting that he had heard the news about Amanda leaving Jason.

Archibald stood up and pulled a *Daily News* from under his arm. He placed it on the desk and opened it to page two. An ample headline screamed, NY INSURANCE EXEC WANTED FOR QUESTIONING ABOUT KIDNAPPING.

Awestruck, she read the story. It mentioned Harmony Mutual and Jason Granger by name. The FBI had entered the search. Granger was described as the suspect in the kidnapping of a Tad Houston near Milford, Pennsylvania.

Milford? Vaguely she remembered seeing signposts pointing the way toward that town when she had traveled to the Crestview to meet Jason. It was the morning that Jason had arrived late and never really explained why.

"Dillon, this is preposterous! Can you imagine Jason as a kidnapper? It's nonsense."

"Nonsense? Is it nonsense that we haven't seen Jason for two days and nights? Is it nonsense that the FBI is sending an agent up here to talk to me? What in the living hell is going on? Tell me, have you seen him since that night at the Water Club?"

Blair stared at him, remembering the trysts in the hotel and at the Crestview. If an FBI agent wanted to talk to Dillon, would there be any chance that he might also want to talk to her? But then how would he have her name? "Yes, but just for a few hours the next day. He was on his way to Harrisburg to pick up his laptop and some files. Hey, why don't you try Amanda?"

"Blair, call Amanda for me, will you? I'm going into my office and try to forget this day every happened."

"Sure, boss, I'll get right on it." That would be a simple task with no need for a lot of conversation. Amanda wasn't answering the phone right now.

She picked up the newspaper and read the brief article again word by word. Impossible! Nothing could come of the story, because it just wasn't true. Between his job and their torrid affair there was no time for any such thing as a kidnapping. Jason had many talents that were a little offbeat and perhaps illegal. But a kidnapper? Not in a million years. She could easily banish that thought from her mind.

Jason's unexplained disappearance was certainly an inconvenience right now, but in the long run it might play right into her hand. If Dillon did fire him, that would elevate her. After all, Jason was still struggling with a household budget. Archibald Dillon had millions. She would have no problem faking at her new position until she could start tapping those millions. Her next thought was really a wish. Maybe that damn Corvette was lying in some ravine along the backroads somewhere with Jason pinned under it. That would really simplify things.

The last time she had looked through the bars of a prison at her own father, just a few weeks before he died, he had winked at her and said, "You're gorgeous, honey. When your time comes, you can get anything you want." Maybe her time had come.

39

Sonny Houston watched the red apple roll along the kitchen floor until it came to a stop in the corner. Bessie had left the room in pristine condition. She was a flawless housekeeper. Everything had it's place in her kitchen. Sonny respected her for that.

He had kicked the apple by accident when he had entered the kitchen. He was sure of two things. It was not there yesterday when he had found the peanut-butter-smeared knife, and he had not eaten an apple since placing them in the pantry. He opened the door to the pantry. The brown grocery bag storing the apples was sitting in its proper place. He had bought a dozen apples. He always bought a dozen apples. He picked up the bag and carried it to the kitchen table.

There were nine apples in the bag. The one on the floor made ten. Two were missing! He looked warily around the room. Everything else seemed to be in its place. But there was no question about it. He had been invaded again.

Sonny walked to the gun rack at the end of the hall and removed the 12-gauge. The work on the perimeter would have to wait awhile, until he had completed a thorough search of the entire house. He walked upstairs and searched the bedrooms and closets, crouching low on the floor to peer under the beds. He climbed the small stepladder inside the closet and pushed the panel in the ceiling out of place with the barrel of his shotgun. Then climbed high enough to scan the entire attic.

He continued searching every nook and corner of the first floor. He looked last in Bessie's sewing room, his eyes finally coming to rest on the window.

The screen was not quite parallel with the window frame. A close look revealed that the hook was undone and the window was unlocked. He bent low and saw the tiny hole in the screen where the mesh had been pulled apart. Tad! It wasn't Eddie Foxworth at all. Tad had done that once before when they had been locked out of the house. Sonny remembered distinctly taking an icepick and bending the tiny wires of the mesh back into place after they had boosted Tad inside to open the door for him and Bessie.

"Tad!" he bellowed loudly. Then he ran upstairs, gun in hand, and circled through the rooms again, scanning every foot of the perimeter around their ten acres from every upstairs window.

Now downstairs again, he eyed the apple he had removed from the floor and set it on the kitchen table. Only he and Tad ate the apples in this house. And Tad was always required to ask permission. Then he spoke aloud in an almost angelic voice, "Tad, my son, you have broken the rules." Then in a bellowing roar that gained volume with every word he screamed, "For that you will be beaten! Do you hear me, Tad?"

Sonny decided that the trip into Morristown to pick up Bessie would have to wait. He would now have to search outside and try to locate Tad, the invader.

It was a gray day, heavily overcast. A steady drizzle limited visibility beyond the defense perimeter. He slipped on the drab olive poncho he had bought at the military surplus store for days such as this. Then he made a tactical decision, deciding to put the 12-gauge back on the rack and take a rifle. The Winchester would give him more range and effectively widen the perimeter.

Sonny took the apple with him as he started walking down the driveway toward the mailbox, the Winchester hanging loosely over his arm as he bit into the apple. That little bastard, he thought, Bessie had brought the bad seed into their life, and as Tad grew older he acted more like the devil himself every day. Now here he was, penetrating their very own defense perimeter, ripping away at the hands that fed him all the years since his bastard birth.

He plodded through the deep wet grass, starting westward along the single strand of barbed wire. When he reached the southwest corner of his property, the road was clearly visible along the wire, but the house could only just be seen in the distance through the heavy mist. Then he turned up the small grade, north, along the ditch he had started with the backhoe but had stopped because of an outcropping of limestone. Blasting powder would definitely be needed to complete the work. The north edge of the property ran through some light underbrush that led to the hundreds of acres of dense white pine that ran on and on to the New York state line.

The rainfall now grew heavier, obscuring any view of the house in the distance. Now he trampled through the dense woods, occasionally circling fallen tress, trying to keep the northern perimeter wire in view. A deer bounded in front of him, flushed from hiding by his tramping through the brush. He instinctively lifted the Winchester to his shoulder, but held his fire and let the whitetail vanish into the thick pine grove.

Now the rain became torrential, narrowing his range of view to a few scant yards. Sonny plunged ahead, changing direction frequently in search of the barbed strand. He stumbled over a crude lean-to and cursed at the deer blind crafted by some hunter in opposition to the frequently posted NO TRESPASSING signs. He saw other blinds in the distance, then lifted the Winchester and fired warning shots high into the air over each of the blinds. The smell of gunpowder hung in the thick air.

"You bastards! All of you cowardly bastards. Come out and fight." Now completely disoriented by the downpour, he spun around and squeezed off a volley of shots until the magazine of the Winchester was empty. A sound of something crashing through the underbrush in panic came from the distance. He froze and listened. Probably another whitetail, he thought.

Now the acrid smell of spent gunpowder filled the air around his sudden volley. As he reloaded, his eyes rolled from side to side trying to identify shadowy images in the woods.

Houston huddled down to blend in with the clumps of thorny briar. Now he was transported to another time, to a remote soggy ridge in Southeast Asia where gunfire raked the landscape in the distance. Screams of warning ahead of him and now behind him echoed against the far ridges as he flattened and cowered against the wet ground. Members of his unit charged by him into the certain deadly fire that lay a mere few yards ahead. He let the fools pass, uttering no warning for fear of revealing his protective niche.

Now the battle was over. The day brightened and he saw the perimeter wire a scant few yards to his left. He had won the day! Sonny rose confidently and strode back inside his perimeter until he approached Houston Memorial Park. He climbed atop the earthen mound. His boots left deep imprints in the mud. There was a flicker of a smile as a fleeting image of Jason Granger molded to his fancy car ten feet below passed through his mind.

The adjacent two empty graves that he had chiseled into the ground looked to be half full of muddy water from the downpour. No problem, he thought to himself. Their mouths were open and their function still intact. His forage beyond the perimeter had brought in no casualties. But his defense had held, and his farm was secure.

He made his way down the mound, peered one last time into the unused graves and then made his way to the house. Perhaps he would pick up Bessie late in the day.

A quarter of a mile away, young Tad huddled in a soggy lump underneath a leaky deer blind. Some of the shots from the barrage of gunfire had whistled ominously low over his head. He had heard Pops bellow and curse. Once in a swirl of mist he had seen him just for a second stumbling past him less than fifty yards away. Tad froze until he could no longer hear the footsteps.

He trembled from the cold, raw dampness. The blind had long ago become saturated, permitting the water to drop down on him, soaking his clothes with water. He thought about the long trek behind him leading to Dingmans Ferry and Sussex. He doubted that he could find his way in the heavy mist.

It had been stupid of him to run away from Carlota, he

thought. At times now he trembled uncontrollably. The remains of the loaf of bread he had pilfered had become soggy. He had eaten the two apples immediately. He screwed the top from the peanut butter jar and dipped his finger inside and then licked the glob from his finger. The peanut butter no longer tasted good to him.

The rain was ebbing and the sky was now much brighter. Tad crawled from the dank blind and sat on a long trunk of a fallen tree, wishing for the warm sun to come out.

Slowly he formulated a plan. He would work his way back to the high mound next to the backhoe and peek through the weeds at their house. The next time Pops left to go anywhere, he would return to the house for dry clothes and more food. Then he would try to make his way to the train station back in Sussex and return to Carlota's place in the city. He slid from the log and propped his back up against it. He imagined he was snuggled in Carlota's sofa and then passed out in a deep sleep of total exhaustion.

40

Penny Wine, short dark hair bobbing saucily, strode rapidly down Ninth Avenue. Her diminutive trim figure caught the low whistles of construction workers sitting on the curb taking a midmorning coffee break. Willy had called and told her he was puzzled about the press reports on Empress Carlota. The authorities claimed a kidnapping, and yet the woman who had actually harbored Tad Houston in her home was allowed to go free. Why? Willy had instructed her to try to question Carlota and follow up any leads that might bring more information.

As she neared Carlota's place, the two policemen sitting

in the patrol car paid no attention to her, nor did the plainclothesman garbed as a homeless vagrant sitting on a stoop near the steps to Empress Carlota's building. She walked right up the steps and into the building just as if she lived there.

Penny walked up to the third floor and knocked on Carlota's door. She could hear movement inside the apartment and then finally the release of a deadbolt. The door opened to the length of a restraining chain and the dark eyes of Empress Carlota stared at her.

"Carlota?"

"Yes, honey, but I ain't buying nothing and I ain't selling nothing. Who sent you here?"

"I've come to talk to you about Tad Houston and Jason Granger." Carlota was starting to close the door, but hesitated at the mention of Tad.

"Tad and who? I don't know anybody named Jason. You a cop? You must be a cop or one of them pesky reporters. I told the police all I know. They say I don't have to talk to anyone else. You better get going, baby, or I'll get the police up here."

"Please, Carlota. I'm real worried about Tad. Maybe you can help. I'm a private investigator, working for someone trying to locate Jason Granger. He's a man who might have kidnapped Tad. Let's talk for a few minutes."

"You? A private investigator?" Carlota looked Penny Wine up and down and smiled. She looked more like a high school cheerleader. "Honey, I'm a whore. Now, I've told you the truth. You better do the same with me." Carlota let the security chain drop from the door and opened it to let Penny inside. "First of all, that dear boy hasn't been kidnapped at all. He was right here all the time the police said he was kidnapped. If his old man would just stop beating on the boy he would have never run away in the first place."

Carlota closed the door behind her and restored the chain. Penny looked around the small apartment. It was very clean and neat. Carlota was something else, sporting a low-cleavage gauzy blouse, a miniskirt that barely reached her thighs, and black stockings. She indeed looked like what she had proclaimed she was. "Look, honey, are you what you say you are? I got enough trouble in my life. I don't need any more cops or any more reporters."

"Carlota, I give you my word of honor. My name is Penny Wine." Penny stuck out her hand and grasped the one that Carlota extended tentatively. She fished her P.I. credentials from her purse.

Carlota grinned at the unlikely private investigator. "I swear, I don't know why I'm talking to you. You might think it's strange or something, but it's probably because I love that little boy. All I did was try to help him. If I had it in my power to help you find Tad, I would. He didn't even tell me who he was in the beginning. He told me he was Eddie Foxworth. He just said it right out and I believed him." Carlota shook her head at Penny.

"Eddie Foxworth? That's an unusual name to blurt right out."

"Well, later he told me Eddie Foxworth was his best friend up there in the country where he lived. Tad and I developed a pretty good relationship. Odd, isn't it, a sweet boy like that and a no-good whore like me." Carlota's eyes became moist, as they always did when she talked about Tad. "All I wanted to do was help him. He has no business roaming the streets of the city. When I found him, some creep was trying to drag him into a porn movie house over on Eighth Avenue. I'd like to give that father of his a real piece of my mind."

"You seem sure that he wasn't kidnapped. How can you be certain?" Penny asked, watching the woman tug at her skirt, trying to bring it down to a respectable length.

"Honey, he was with me all the time. We talked about his mom and his pop. We even talked about his Aunt Sarah over in Morristown. Hell, I even took him there, and he ran away when he saw his dad's van in the driveway. His dad beat him up all the time. He broke his arm, you know."

Carlota hesitated, realizing that she was breaking the request of Detective McCutcheon not to talk with anyone about the boy. "Look here, Miss Penny, you could get me in big trouble. Here I am running off at the mouth just like I ain't supposed to do. I think you'd best leave, Miss Penny. I got enough trouble with the police. In my business it comes with the territory."

"Trust me, Carlota. What you tell me is just between you and me." Carlota shrugged and moved toward the door to let her out. "If you love the boy as much as you say you do, it's best that you trust me. It might help find him. At least more people that care will be looking for him."

"I hope so, Miss Penny. Now I think I have blabbed all I know. I wish you would leave. That ain't no homeless man on the stoop next door. That's a cop. Whatcha gonna tell him if he asks you why you came upstairs?" Carlota was nervous.

"I'll tell him I'm a friend and that we work together sometimes."

That brought a grin to Carlota's face. "Honey, he'd never believe you. If you were in my business, our paths would never cross. You'd be strictly Upper East Side, at five hundred a pop."

"Hey, thanks for the compliment, I think." Penny chuckled at the notion. "Maybe something you told me will help us find Tad." Penny handed her a card. "Let me know if you can think of anything else. No one will answer at this number. When you hear the tone, just leave your message. Okay?"

Carlota took the card, nodded her head slightly and closed the door. Penny heard the heavy deadbolt slam into place. She believed Carlota. Despite the woman's obvious profession, Penny couldn't believe that she wasn't really broken up about the boy she had befriended.

She walked swiftly down the block, careful not to make eye contact with the plainclothesman on the stoop. She looked at her watch. It was not yet noon. It was a delightful day and there was plenty of time left to follow up on the Eddie Foxworth lead by driving to Milford. She felt buoyant. Willy had actually given her an assignment out of the office. She would find out if Eddie Foxworth was a real person, and if he was, what he had to say about Tad. She had a gut feeling that if they were to find Tad, they would have to know more about the boy himself.

Penny walked south and turned down Thirty-third Street where she garaged the little red Miata that would be hers after only forty-eight more payments. Within minutes she was on the Henry Hudson Parkway pointed north toward the George Washington Bridge. There was a nagging twinge of conscience—she had not checked with Willy or Coley first. But, then, Willy had told her to follow up, and he was always advising them never to let the trail get cold on any new lead.

She pressed down on the accelerater and wove the peppy Miata in and out of traffic, making it to the bridge in minutes. There she picked up Route I-80 and began the one-hour drive to Pennsylvania. This was a real treat. It was seldom that she got to enjoy the Miata while on the job.

Penny reached for her cellular phone and then remembered that she had left it in her office. In her haste to get to Milford she hadn't returned to pick it up after leaving Carlota. There would be plenty of time to bring Willy and Coley up to date later when she would already be in the Milford area.

Less than an hour later she parted company from I-80 just after crossing the Delaware and proceeded north along the river all the way to the Milford cutoff. The Miata had her cruising the main drag in another forty minutes. She pulled into a parking space in front of a general store that could have come from an old Norman Rockwell cover illustration.

There was a public phone within an outside alcove. Great, she thought to herself, as she spied a local telephone directory, yellowed and ragged from exposure to the elements, jammed underneath the phone. She walked quickly to the phone. Casting a glance around her first, she pushed the small directory under an arm beneath her sweater and walked back to the Miata.

There was only one Foxworth listed. It was on Mountain Road. She flipped through the phone book and located a Sonny Houston on the same Mountain Road. Penny sat in the Miata scrutinizing a road map. She knew from her talks with Coley that Mountain Road was just off Route 6, which snaked through town. She decided to go west. The eastern portion wound through the Delaware Gap National Recreation Area.

Penny took a deep breath. Now was the time to bring Willy and Coley up to date. She returned to the phone and called her office to check for messages. There were none, so she decided to leave a message with Coley, who was somewhere in her area. "Hi. I talked to Empress Carlota. She told me that Tad Houston told her his name was Eddie Foxworth when they first met. Tad later told Carlota that the real Eddie Foxworth is a school pal of his, who lives down the road from him. I plan to talk to Eddie or his parents as soon as I can get there. According to my notes, it's the only new name that we haven't checked out. I'll check back in an hour or so. My new office is a phone hanging outside the Milford General Store." She read the number from the posting on the phone. "See you later, Coley. By the way, I ran off without my cellular. I'll check in every hour or two. Okay?"

Now having brought Coley up to date, Penny drove through the countryside, feeling exhilarated. Soon she turned off Route 6 and drove slowly down Mountain Road, a narrow blacktop that led past several small farms. In front of the Houston farm, the mailbox bore the name in large print.

Penny slowed the Miata and looked down the long

driveway. She saw no people or vehicles. The house was mostly hidden by a grove of pine trees. She picked up speed and followed the road until it turned sharply to the right. The name FOXWORTH stood out boldly on the first mailbox she met. There were two pickup trucks parked in front of the house, which stood less than fifty feet from the road. Without hesitation Penny pulled in next to the small trucks and climbed out of the Miata.

Mrs. Foxworth came to the door before she got there.

"Hello, I'm looking for the Foxworths."

"Well, you've found them." The woman smiled slightly as she studied the pert-looking young woman. "What can I do for you? I'm Elsie Foxworth."

"I'm Penny Wine. I'm a private investigator. I'm looking for a Jason Granger, who disappeared in these parts. Maybe you've read in the papers that he might have kidnapped Tad Houston."

Elsie Foxworth stared suspiciously at the tiny woman, who certainly didn't fit the description of any private investigator she had seen on TV. "Really?" She paused to study the identification Penny held in front of her. "I'll tell you what I think, Miss Wine. I think the boy is drowned. I spoke to Sonny Houston myself one morning and he sure thinks the boy drowned. He got real mad at my son, Eddie, when he went over there one morning. I think he wishes folks would leave him alone. I told Eddie to stay away from there. Eddie and Tad were good friends. My boy has taken the news very poorly. He lost his best friend."

"I'm sorry about that, Mrs. Foxworth. But we think the boy might be okay. Quite a few people claim to have seen him."

Elsie shook her head slowly. "I wish I could believe that, but I think that's just newspaper stuff. You know you can't believe a thing you read anymore. They've got Sonny so worked up that he's carrying a shotgun around all the time.

Eddie saw him with it. Yesterday we heard him shooting up in the woods. I think people should leave him alone. I feel sorry for Bessie. She's Tad's mother. Sonny runs a very strict house. He's an old military man, you know."

"Is Eddie here now?" Penny ventured.

"Eddie," Elsie turned and called into the house. "Come here for a minute." She turned toward Penny again. "Eddie's busy working on a model airplane. He and Tad used to build them together. He sure misses the boy."

A small boy appeared beside his mother. Wide dark eyes and a thick bowl-cut mop of black hair made the muscular boy look older than his age.

"Eddie, this lady is an investigator looking for a man who might know something about Tad. She thinks Tad might be alive."

Eddie shook his head vigorously. "No, he ain't. He drowned in the Delaware. His pop told me so."

"When did he tell you that, Eddie?" Penny decided to keep him talking about Tad before discussing Jason Granger with them.

"The other day I went over to Tad's house. His pop is doing a lot of digging up on the hill back of their house. He was running a big backhoe. He had a hole in the ground big enough to be a swimming pool and had dug ditches all around his farm. He got mad when I asked about Tad and told me to get out." Eddie paused as if trying to picture the hostile scene that day. "I hope Tad just ran away. His pop is a mean son of a gun."

Elsie Foxworth looked at him sharply. "Now Eddie, you are just a boy. I don't want to hear you talking about our neighbors that way. The Houstons have lived there for years and never bothered us. Bessie is a fine woman. Now, you go on back to your model airplane."

Eddie wandered slowly out of the room. Mrs. Foxworth didn't speak until he was out of earshot. "Sonny Houston is a bitter man. Bessie says he's been that way since he came home from the war years ago. She says he got a lot of medals and was quite a hero. I suppose the war changed a lot of men."

Penny wasn't quite ready to call him a hero. "Is it true what I've heard about how he treated Tad?"

"Well, as they say, Tad is a handful, but I never personally witnessed Sonny mistreating him. But the boy does tell some whoppers about the mean things he does."

"Did he break Tad's arm?"

"Can't say that I really know. Eddie thinks so. But he just knows from talking to Tad. I do know that Tad has a big, big imagination. Who knows whether it's true or not? Bessie says Sonny should have made a career out of the army. He's just a natural-born military man according to her."

"Well, we sort of got sidetracked talking about Tad. I guess you've never heard of Jason Granger. He's spent some time in these parts. He's in his thirties, dark-haired and very athletic in appearance. He drives a red Corvette, a kind of a sports car."

Elsie Foxworth shook her head, deep in thought. "No, can't say that I have. I don't pay much attention to the cars that drive by."

"I betcha I saw it." Eddie chimed in, eavesdropping from the next room. Suddenly he was standing in the doorway. "I saw it two days ago."

Elsie Foxworth turned toward him. "Eddie, are you sure? You weren't supposed to be listening, you know."

"I'm sorry, Mom. You were talking so loud. I know a Corvette when I see one. Remember I once built a model of one. You bought it for me."

"Where'd you see it, Eddie?" Penny was getting excited.

"It was just whizzing down the road about sunset. We don't get many cars on our road, and I'd know a red Corvette anywhere. I know a lot about cars," he boasted.

"I bet you do, Eddie." Penny studied the boy closely,

wondering if what he saw was really a red Corvette. "Did he stop along the road? Did you see him stop at Tad's farm?"

Eddie shook his head. "Nope he just went zooming by. A Corvette is a very fast car," he assured her. "I've read all about them."

"Thanks, Eddie." Penny looked at his mother as she turned toward the door. "I guess I'll be going now. Thanks for your time. I hope they find Tad, so Eddie will have his friend back."

Elsie walked with her to the front porch. "We'll all pray for that, won't we?"

Penny handed her a card with her answering service number on it. "Please call, Mrs. Foxworth, if you hear anything about Jason Granger or Tad."

Penny climbed into the Miata and proceeded slowly down the road. In the rearview mirror she saw Elsie Foxworth standing on the porch watching her until she rounded the curve a quarter mile away. She looked at her watch and decided that she still had time to check out Sonny Granger before checking in with Willy and Coley. If Elsie Foxworth wasn't afraid of him, why should she be?

Just a few yards up the long driveway that curved through the field toward Houston's house was a giant oak. She could read the NO TRESPASSING sign posted on the trunk from where she had stopped near his mailbox. Bravely, she decided to ignore it. Despite the poor evaluation others had of the man, she preferred to judge him for herself. After all, the man had just lost a son. Such a misfortune might well make anyone bitter for a long time. And maybe young Tad was addicted to telling whoppers, just as Elsie Foxworth had said.

She drove slowly up the long gravel driveway. Just as she turned into a parking place alongside the old farmhouse, she saw Houston's big SUV, parked in the rear of the house. Just the tail end, with the license plate bearing GITGO 7, was visible.

She stopped, not yet willing to turn off the engine of the Miata. She felt her pulse racing at having seen the plate number that Jason Granger had repeated in his delirium in the hospital. For the first time, she felt apprehensive about the task she had undertaken. Taking a deep breath, she fabricated a smile, switched off the Miata, climbed out and walked toward the front door of the Houston's house.

Penny rapped gently on the door at first, after discovering there was no doorbell. Then she began to rap with vigor on the big oak door.

"Hey, woman! I would advise you to stop that right now. Can't you read? This land is posted. Now get the hell out of here!"

Penny stopped abruptly at the sound of Houston's booming voice and turned to face him. He stood at the corner of the house, glaring at her with dark, squinty eyes. His massive frame must carry at least three hundred pounds for sure, she thought. She felt herself grow tense as he fondled the barrel of the rifle slung under his right arm.

"Mr. Houston?" she asked, ignoring his invitation to leave for the moment.

"That ain't none of your business. I quit talking to newspaper reporters, and I've said all I'm gonna say to the cops." Houston paused, staring her up and down for an uncomfortable length of time, and then turned to focus on the red Miata convertible, walking a few steps to read the name of the small sports car. He again turned and faced her, just staring, his eyes roving up and down her small frame.

Penny wished that for that moment she could be ugly as sin. She didn't like the way he gaped at her legs. She made a move to get back into her car. After all, she could talk to him sitting down.

"Just one second. You ain't going nowhere till you tell me why you're here."

"I'm looking for a Mr. Jason Granger. He drives a red

Corvette." She briefly described him, drawing on the memory she had of him that night at the Water Club.

"Ain't no such person around here. No fancy car like that red Corvette either. You city folks with your fancy cars would do well to stay away from here. You ought to be taught a lesson."

Again he stared, focusing unmistakably on her well-conditioned legs. "In fact, I'll have to ask you to come with me." He now held the rifle waist high, pointing it directly at her.

She again moved to get into the Miata, but Sonny Houston, showing exceptional agility for a big man, quickly moved between her and the car. She looked hopefully back toward the road in the distance and then all around her. She was trapped. Barring some miracle, she was at his whim and mercy.

"Now you git around back of the house. No funny stuff or those fancy clothes will be full of holes." He waved the rifle menacingly, inches from her face.

"Mr. Houston! Will you put that gun down, please! Before there is an accident. What do you think you are doing?" Penny froze as he prodded her belly with the barrel. "Please, please . . . I meant no harm," she stammered. "I only want to help find your boy."

"He ain't my boy, damn you! Now get yourself over by the cellar door." This time he prodded her firmly with the barrel and pointed to the open metal cellar door pitched at low angle, opening on a stairway leading under the house. He jabbed at her with the rifle until she began descending the cellar steps. Finally she reached the bottom and turned to face Houston, who was still outside above the celler steps.

He now held the rifle in one hand and pointed emphatically at her with the forefinger of the other. "I'll have to hold you for the proper authorities. You will be charged with invasion and considered a prisoner of war."

"War?" Penny stepped back a few paces and gaped at

what surely was a madman at the top of the stairs. "Oh, my God! Please! I'm only trying to help. I'm sorry I bothered you ... just let me go. I won't ever bother you again." Penny's voice wavered as she realized he was paying no attention to her.

She saw Houston grasp the steel door and then let it slam closed on its concrete casement with a mighty clang. She heard him close some sort of latch and then walk away. Now she was alone in the darkness. The door up the cellar steps was outlined by a dim frame of light around the casement. Somewhere behind her there was a ray of light that came from a tiny window.

She took a couple of steps and stumbled over something that went rolling away in the darkness. Penny heard herself whimper in the darkness. She was terrified, and resolved that she would stand motionless until her eyes became adjusted to the near-darkness. What did the madman mean by saying he would "call the authorities"? At that point, she would welcome the sight of anyone.

Above ground, Sonny Houston walked to the side of the house and squeezed his huge frame into the Miata. He turned the key, forced the car into gear and pointed it up the muddy tire-track road that led through the underbrush toward Houston Memorial Park.

Once there, he concealed the Miata among the trees so that it could not be spotted from the distant road. He climbed into the backhoe and quickly selected a spot of ground that looked fairly free of stones. Measuring the Miata with his eye, he began tearing huge chunks of earth from the ground, preparing a suitable trench for a final resting place for his new prisoner.

He glanced at the darkening sky and grinned broadly. He figured the entire project would be completed in the morning.

As he toiled with the backhoe, his thoughts went to his prisoner down the hill in the cellar. She was a pretty thing, he thought. He had never had a woman as sleek and fine as she was. She could have stepped right out of the ads in the Sunday paper. He felt himself becoming aroused. He wondered if the Lord would forgive him if he used her like a woman just one time. He would have to think about it. The more he thought about it, the more aroused he became. It looked like the Lord was giving him the answer he wanted.

41

Blair Lawton shoved the heavy briefcase onto the floor. She watched wild-eyed as the contents spilled out in disarray over the carpet in her hotel room. "Damn! Damn!" She cursed loudly in a fit of temper that had been threatening to burst out for many hours. "Jason, you simple fool! How dare you treat me this way!"

It had been three days since she last saw Jason at the Crestview Hideaway. Except for the single phone message that same afternoon telling her he would see her the next day, she had heard not a word from him. She looked at the digital clock. She had watched the numbers roll by all night long. It was now after seven A.M.

Reluctantly, she picked up the phone and dialed Amanda in Harrisburg. She had been quite abrupt in her one previous phone call, and had volunteered little information, except that Jason was expected two days ago to pick up his belongings.

Amanda Granger picked up the telephone after several rings. "Hello," she answered in a subdued voice, barely audible.

"Amanda, is that you? I can barely hear you, dear. Are

you alright. This is Blair." Blair was trying very hard to sound civil.

There was a heavy sigh. "Blair, do you know what time it is?"

"I'm sorry. I'm an early riser. I wouldn't call if it weren't important. I'm trying to locate Jason. Our presentation at the office has been rescheduled for this morning. I just tried his hotel again, and he's not there."

"Really!" There was a long pause. "Blair, I have no idea where he is. The FBI, the police, among others have been calling. I told them all the same thing. Really, Blair, I figured if anyone knew where he was, you would."

Now it was Blair's turn to hesitate. "Why the FBI and the police? Really, Amanda, that doesn't make sense. What in the world did they want?"

"I don't feel I have to discuss that with you. You'll have to ask Jason."

"Well, I haven't seen him for days. Dillon Archibald is throwing a fit. By the way, did Jason ever stop by to pick up his computer and the files?"

"No. I sat them out on the side porch. I think it rained. They might have gotten wet."

"Wet! Amanda, why . . . ?"

"Because Jason doesn't live here anymore, dear." The "dear" came out derisively. "Blair, please never call here again." Amanda clicked the phone down softly in its cradle.

"That bitch!" muttered Blair as the dial tone buzzed in her ear.

She rose from the desk and paced nervously around the room. The truth, and she was well aware of it, was that Jason, at this stage of the game, was the business genius. He had engineered the new budgetary plan, and her cursory knowledge wouldn't get her to first base in the meeting with the directors of Harmony Mutual. Her rapid ascendancy to assistant VP was not the result of any depth of knowledge about insurance and actuaries. Blair realized that more than anyone. "Jason! Where the hell are you?" she groaned as she paced.

She glanced at herself in the mirror. She leaned close to her image and became more enraged at what she saw. There were lines there she swore she didn't have yesterday. The meeting was at nine o'clock. It would be a major job pulling herself together in that short a time. She picked up the dress she had intended to wear, tossed it on the bed and started rummaging through the closet. Something tasteful, yet adventurous, she told herself, but soon she had rejected everything she had brought with her.

The phone rang, sounding shrill and very loud, interrupting her concentration on clothes. "Hello," she said tentatively, hoping by some miracle that it might be Jason.

"Has he shown up? Have you heard from the bastard?" It was Dillon Archibald. She thought for a second she could hear other people talking in the background.

"Dillon, you sound like a real bear this morning. Shame on you!" she said, trying to coax him down to a conversational tone.

"Listen carefully, Blair, we've got some talking to do. I want you front and center here in the office in forty-five minutes."

"Oh, you poor man. You're worried about the meeting. I haven't head a word from Jason. I've just had a chat with Amanda, and neither has she. Now calm down. I'll be right over and we'll wing it through the meeting."

"Meeting!" he shouted. "Bullshit! I've canceled the meeting again! Do you really think I would let you get in front of knowledgeable people and make Jason's presentation?" There was a slight hesitation before he went on in a whispered voice. "You're hot stuff, kiddo, but your specialty has nothing to do with the new concepts Jason discussed with me, and you're smart enough to know just what I mean."

"And what is my specialty, as you call it?" Blair felt as if she had been slapped. The nerve of that old fossil.

"Look, Blair, I'm sorry I'm impatient, but there have been developments that seriously affect the public image of this company. I want you over here in a few minutes so that we can discuss them," he said, raising his voice dramatically. Now she was sure that there were people sitting at the conference table at the other end of his office. "By the way, Blair, have you seen the *Daily News* this morning, or the network TV news? There are follow-ups on yesterday's story."

"No, to tell you the truth, I just woke up. I did call Amanda Granger. She was kind of bitchy."

"She didn't tell you why?"

"No, not really. She said the police had been pestering her."

"And for damn good reason! Flip on Channel Four right now and be prepared to give us your input as soon as you get here." Dillon Archibald slammed down his phone before she could ask another question.

Blair picked up the previously rejected dress from the bed, rejected it again and selected a tight-fitting short silk suit with a silk blouse. If the time became right, she could take the jacket off when the others left the meeting. Minus the jacket, the outfit should keep old Archibald's mind off of business and on her "specialty." She clicked the TV on as she passed by. The first words she heard had to do with Jason Granger. She sat on the bed, spellbound, as the story developed.

Jason, missing for three days, was believed to be on the run as a kidnapping suspect! Listeners were told to be on the lookout for a red Corvette bearing a license plate number that was repeated several times. It was believed that he might be traveling with, or know the whereabouts of, a small boy by the name of Tad Houston.

Blair listened in total disbelief. There were practically no details other than speculation by the newscaster that there might have been a ransom note delivered to the boy's home.

She felt uneasy. Things hadn't been the same with Jason since the terrible beating he had taken at the turnpike rest stop. He had been more aloof and on edge of late. She had supposed it stemmed from trouble with Amanda.

She surprised herself with a sigh of relief. At least the morning meeting had been canceled. She could wing it on her new job for a while longer, at least until Jason returned from wherever he was. Jason had a lot of weirdo flaws that she knew only too well. But the thought of him being a kidnapper was ridiculous.

Upon her arrival at Harmony Mutual, she immediately sensed a state of turmoil, not at all the usual staid conservative atmosphere. She saw several clerical types in a cluster around the watercooler. She imagined that almost everyone gave her a quick glance, and then turned their eyes away. She was quickly hustled into Dillon Archibald's office by his assistant.

Surrounding her at the conference table were a group of people she did not recognize. A uniformed police officer closed the office door behind them and proceeded to stand guard at the door.

Dillon began speaking without any personal greeting for her. "The gentleman is Mark Whitcomb of the FBI." Whitcomb nodded stiffly as Dillon introduced the others. "This is Detective McCutcheon and this is Detective Flannery of the NYPD. Mr. Hanson here is a private investigator working on the case."

She focused on Willy Hanson. His was the only warm face of the group. He at least nodded civilly and flashed a quick, fleeting smile.

Archibald addressed Whitcomb. "Mark, feel free to ask any question you wish of Ms. Lawton. She is a trusted and loyal member of the Harmony Mutual executive team, and the missing man's working colleague."

Whitcomb got right to the point. "Ms. Lawton, Jason Granger has been seriously implicated in an apparent kidnapping. It is necessary that we confirm his whereabouts up to the time he disappeared. Do you think you can help us with that?"

Blair shrugged, shaking her head in disbelief. "Forgive me for saying so, but I think someone is terribly mistaken. Jason Granger would never get involved in a kidnapping. I'm sure of it."

"Let us be the judge of that, Ms. Lawton. There is ample evidence or we wouldn't be here." Whitcomb stared at her coldly, secretly taken a little aback by her strong defense of the man without knowing the facts. "Tell me, when did you last see Jason Granger?"

Willy turned in his chair to face her directly. If she were going to lie, it might be a temptation to do it now. Of course, thanks to the work of Penny and Coley, he knew the answer to the question.

"Let me see," Blair moved forward to look at a calendar on Dillon's desk. "It was on the morning of June tenth. I left him at the Crestview Hideaway in the Poconos."

Bravo! thought Willy, she's at least telling the truth up to now. It was Dillon Archibald who almost choked on a sip of coffee.

"The Poconos?" asked Dillon in disbelief. "What on earth was he doing there?"

Blair avoided eye contact with Dillon, and looked Whitcomb right in the eye. "We wanted to celebrate with a dinner. Jason and I were extremely happy about our promotions. Jason said he knew about this delightful restaurant at the Crestview. He was on his way to Harrisburg to pick up his PC and some papers. He just loves to drive his new red Corvette. I told him I would meet him there for lunch on the afternoon of the ninth."

Willy became rapt at her honesty this far. Was she going to tell the whole sordid story that Coley had on tape? He wished Coley were here to share this moment.

"The afternoon of the ninth?" mused Whitcomb. "That means you both spent the night there."

Dillon, red-faced, swiveled around in his chair and stared out the window. You could have heard a pin drop in the room.

Blair started again. "Well, kind of." She hesitated and then decided to go on with a perfectly logical explanation. "Jason became very drunk. I'm afraid our celebration was a bit too much. He was in no shape to drive on to Harrisburg. Actually, I am well aware of Jason's determination. The simple innocent truth is that I put him to bed. He passed out immediately and slept like a rock. I waited until early the next morning before leaving. You have to understand that Jason is a good friend. It was unthinkable for me to leave before knowing that he was in condition to drive on to Harrisburg."

Willy listened and marveled at her story. With the cards stacked against her she had managed to come off like Jason's guardian angel. This was some sharp woman. She had turned their drug, sex and booze marathon into an errand of mercy.

"Good thinking, Ms. Lawton." Whitcomb said it with his usual stone-faced expression. If he thought Blair was playing with the truth, you couldn't tell it. "And you haven't heard from him since?"

"I've haven't talked to him. When I got back to my hotel in Manhattan that same day, he had left a message on my phone. Said he was still too tired to drive, and that he had crashed out in some motel and would go on to Harrisburg to pick up his computer and his files later. I haven't heard from him since." Blair dabbed at a tear she somehow forced from the corner of one dazzling blue eye.

"Do we know if he ever got to Harrisburg?" Whitcomb persisted.

Blair shook her head and again dabbed at her eyes. "I talked to his wife this morning. Poor thing, she was so upset. He never got to Harrisburg."

"Mark, do you mind if I ask Ms. Lawton a question?" Willy asked. Whitcomb gently nodded his approval while furiously taking notes on a yellow pad. "Blair," Willy asked, using her first name and trying to be as gracious in tone as possible. "I'm trying to account for all of Jason's time over the last few days. I realize that you drove separate cars, but did you both leave New York City about the same time?"

"Yes, but I got to the Crestview almost an hour before he did. We kidded about it. He drove his new Corvette very competitively. He said he lost his way on some of the back roads up near Milford." Blair evinced a weak smile. Though her answer was plausible, Blair became aware of several seconds of dead silence by her inquisitors. They were all looking at her, as if they wanted to hear more.

Finally Whitcomb spoke. "Ms. Lawton, I thank you for telling us all you could. If you think of anything else, or if you hear from Jason, by all means let me know immediately."

"I will. Jason is such a fine man. I know there must be some simple explanation." She dabbed at her eyes again, rose and prepared to leave the room.

"Oh, yes, there is one more thing." Whitcomb again looked straight into her eyes. "Are you aware that Jason Granger has a chronic problem with cocaine?"

Willy saw her flinch, almost imperceptively, and cast her eyes downward from Whitcomb's stare. Several seconds passed before she said anything. She had managed to fill in with little white lies now and then during her story. He wondered at what she would come up with now.

"That's preposterous! That's almost as preposterous as your kidnapping accusations. Dillon, may I leave now?"

"Yes, I think you'd better. Thanks, Blair. Is that alright with you gentlemen?"

No one protested. Whitcomb stared straight out the window at the canyons of skyscrapers beyond. Most of the other eyes couldn't help glance at the subtle movement of the tight silk skirt, slipping here and there over her well-toned derriere as she left the room.

Dillon Archibald excused himself for a few moments and

followed her down the hall, leaving the others at his conference table.

Agent Whitcomb broke his fascination with the scenery and turned to direct a comment at Willy. "What do you think?"

"The framework of her story is true. We know that. But she embellished it with lots of little lies and omissions. As I have told you before, our investigation lends no credence at all to her petition for sainthood. The man I feel sorry for is Dillon Archibald. Imagine having someone like that digging their claws into your perfectly fine company."

Whitcomb shrugged and then nodded his agreement. "Fools are made, not born, and Dillon Archibald, along with Jason Granger, has been made: turned into a pitiful dupe."

McCutcheon broke into a broad grin and looked at Whitcomb. "Hey, did you catch the equipment on that babe? She can dupe about anybody she wants any time she wants to. I think you've got to give her credit for her talent."

Mark Whitcomb waited until he was walking down Sixth Avenue alone with Willy before he spoke again. "So, as far as the kidnapping goes, it looks like we're still on square one. Right?"

Willy pondered the question for a few more steps. "We didn't get much out of her. I honestly believe that she thinks the idea of Jason being involved in a kidnapping is preposterous, and I'm beginning to think the same thing myself. It was perfectly logical for her to try to cover up their hanky-panky. If Coley hadn't given us the real goods on her, we'd all be willing to give up and call her an angel."

"You trust Coley implicitly?"

"You're damn right, with my life and yours, too."

"Where you headed, Willy?"

"Pennsylvania. I'm not sure why, but I think this whole thing will play out in Pennsylvania."

Agent Whitcomb parted company with Willy after a couple of blocks. Willy stopped for a pedestrian light, looked at his watch, stepped into a vacant doorway and pulled out his cellular phone. During the morning he had tried to reach Penny four times, spread over a period of five hours.

The last time he had heard from her was the message that she was calling from a General Store in Milford late yesterday afternoon. The sharp young woman was the epitome of efficiency. Something had to be wrong. In the several months she had apprenticed with them, not once was there an incident like this. His first thought was about the Miata zooming around unfamiliar roads in the Poconos. Yet she had plenty of identification. If there had been an accident, somebody would have probably called.

He checked his voice mail and there was nothing from Penny. About an hour ago there was a one-liner from Coley. "Where the hell is Penny?"

Willy looked at his watch. It was a long shot, but he decided to call Coley on his cellular. There was no answer. He called the office again and left a recorded message "Coley, has Penny checked in with you? I'm calling Knight. They've got to put out a search for the Miata. Something's happened to her, Coley."

Willy hung up, feeling worse than ever about Penny's disappearance. Yesterday's message from Penny was dated four P.M. She was missing nineteen hours now, counting the overnight time. His worries about the kidnapped boy were shoved on the back burner by a problem it was impossible to ignore. Where the hell was Penny Wine?

42

Tad worked his way slowly through the underbrush toward the top of the ridge. He scratched at his arms and legs almost without cessation. Mosquito bites, spider bites and red scratches from the brambles had made sleep almost impossible. The remains of the peanut butter and the water he had scooped from the spring only seemed to make him hungrier than ever.

The mound of earth Pops had scooped into a pile was just ahead of him. He approached it slowly, careful not to go to either side and make himself visible from the house below. He scrambled up the mound and lay flat against the ground. He peeked over the top, then jerked his head down quickly. Pops was standing in the back of their house, carrying the old double-barrel 12-gauge shotgun.

Cautiously, he peeked again. This time his eye caught an amazing sight about a hundred feet to his left. A tiny red sports car sat in a small clearing. It looked brand new. Behind it was a deep, wide trench that had been chiseled out by the backhoe, which was still parked at the end of the trench. What was the red car doing on Pops's property? He always made fun of cars like that.

He tore his eyes away from the unlikely find and looked back toward the house. Pops still stood in back of the house about two hundred yards away. The gun was broken to expose the breech, and he appeared to be inserting shells into the chambers. Then, as he watched, Pops sat down on the metal cellar door. Every now and then he rapped the stock of the gun on the door several times. The loud noise carried all the way up to where Tad pressed against the earth.

Then Pops got up and walked quickly to the corner of

the house. Tad expected him to turn right and head for the fence row along the property line, where he usually went to flush rabbit for the kill. Instead, he turned left and began walking directly toward Tad, up the hill toward the mound.

Keeping his head low, Tad backed down the mound and ran to the barbed-wire strand and crawled under it. Then he dashed into the woods and ran as fast as he could, careful to keep the mound to his back until he was obscured by dense foliage. He soon came upon one of the makeshift deer blinds and lay flat on his belly underneath it. He could feel his heart pumping under him as he tried hard to muffle the gasps from his deep breathing. He prayed that Pops wouldn't come into the woods. He seldom hunted there, preferring to walk the high weeds along the fence rows.

Tad huddled silently for a long time. Now his breath came easier and he began to think about the red car. If someone were visiting, why wasn't the red car parked down below? He was reminded of the red Corvette Pops had scratched at the turnpike rest stop. This car was different. He just couldn't figure it out.

His thoughts were interrupted by the rumble of the backhoe's engine coming to life. He breathed a sigh of relief. That meant that Pops wasn't looking for him. He had come up the hill to do more work on his project, the defense perimeter.

Tad crawled out from under the deer blind and scrambled to the base of a large pine tree that had been toppled by the wind. From his vantage point behind a small opening in the dense tangle of fallen limbs, he could see Pops working back and forth with the backhoe, gouging out the trench in the earth. The sound of the constant scrape of metal against rock told him that he had dug the trench as deep as possible. Pops let out a string of curses unlike any Tad had ever heard before.

Tad stepped on a fallen limb so he could see what was going on, careful to keep his body hidden behind the pine trunk. Pops had positioned the backhoe directly in back of the sports car and was pushing it slowly down into the newly chiseled trench. The shiny red sports car, with its top down, disappeared slowly from view. In seconds, all Tad could see was the tip of the radio aerial.

Tad huddled, awestruck, as Pops then moved load after load of dirt onto the shiny red car. Within an hour the trench was filled. Then Pops turned the machine around and began to plow additional earth over the top of the trench until he had a small mound, very much the same in appearance as the other one.

Tad felt sick to his stomach. He didn't know why, except that the whole thing didn't make much sense. Why would he bury a brand new car? He felt tears running down his cheek that he couldn't explain. Pops is sure crazy, he thought to himself. Pops is really crazy.

Tad watched as Pops inspected the new mound for a couple of minutes. He walked a few steps and inspected the two much smaller holes in the ground that he had made earlier. Then Pops turned away and picked up the shotgun, which he had leaned against a tree next to the excavation. He took one last look at his handiwork and then walked down the hill toward the house. Tad watched him every step of the way.

When he got to the house, Pops slammed the butt of the shotgun against the metal cellar door again, causing metallic clangs that he could hear easily. Tad heard him vent another string of loud curses, then bang the cellar door once more. He seemed to be talking to himself down there. Finally he went into the house.

The remarkable scene that Tad had witnessed had left him terrified. More and more he wondered what he was going to do. He had heard about boys who had run far away, all the way to California. Just going to Aunt Sarah's wouldn't be any good. Sooner or later, Pops would make Aunt Sarah send him home. Carlota would help him, he thought. But the police seemed to hang around Carlota. And the police would find him and just make him go home.

He scratched again at the insect bites. His clothes were soaked and torn. He knew enough to know he wouldn't be safe anywhere looking like this. He had to get back to the house one more time, clean up in fresh clothes, steal some food and steal some money from Pops's tobacco jar. Then he would go back to the train in Sussex and keep going, maybe all the way to California.

Tad once again left the woods, took his vigil on top of the mound and peeked down toward the house. The van was still parked in its place. He decided he would stay there every minute until Pops drove away someplace. Then he would run down the hill and do the few things he had to do.

His eyes caught the newly constructed mound that had buried the sports car. It was less than a hundred feet away, and though smaller, it was very similar to the mound he was now lying on. He felt uneasy. The thought crossed his mind that something else must be buried beneath him. He knew one thing. Pops had lied to him. He had told him it was going to be farm pond.

Then Tad had another idea. Why didn't he just go to the Foxworths' house. He could go back into the woods and take the next trail over the ridge. It was a long way around but he would be hidden from anyone's view the whole way. He had only to cross the road when he got near the Foxworths' house. He headed back into the woods, stumbling several times. He felt very tired, and once in a while he felt dizzy. Sleep had become almost impossible in the soggy deer blind the night before. He and Eddie had once taken a shortcut to his house through the dense woods. It was a long ways back to the trail over the ridge.

He would tell his story to Eddie and his mom. I'll bet she would fry me up some bacon and eggs in a hurry, he thought. Eddie's mom was always trying to feed him. But then he frowned. She might feed him, but then she would march him right up to Pops's house. Whenever he would tell her something Pops did, she would just laugh and poke fun at him. Nobody ever believed Pops was really as mean as he made out.

Still, maybe he would see Eddie outside and get his attention. He would bring him food and stuff, and his mom would never have to know Then he could come back and wait for Pops to leave, just like he had planned. Pops always went someplace in the van every day.

Tad scratched at the insect bites. Some of the scratches were pretty bloody. He was a mess. He groaned aloud. There was no way that Eddie wouldn't tell his mom about him. Eddie's mom would turn him over to his folks right away. He was sure of that. Reluctantly, he turned back toward the mound. He might as well wait there until Pops drove away. There would be plenty of food in the house.

Tad stumbled again and fell to the ground next to a broad outcropping of limestone. Then he realized that he was very tired. He stretched out on the slab of mossy limestone and allowed his eyes to close. He would nap, just for a few minutes, he thought. There was no reason he couldn't nap.

Exhaustion overcame him. He couldn't believe how good it felt when he closed his eyes. He drifted off to sleep, quickly interrupted by a vivid dream. The image of Pops sitting on the cellar door and banging the butt of his shotgun on it, and screaming curses, woke him just for an instant. Then he curled up in a fetal position on the soft moss and fell into a deep, exhausted sleep.

43

Penny Wine slid the heavy oaken chest of drawers a few feet along the wall, positioning it nearer the source of light. Her eyes had become accustomed to the meager light that filtered through a small window. If there was a light switch anywhere in the cellar for the single bare bulb hanging from the ceiling, she couldn't find it. She decided that she probably wouldn't use it, anyway. Apparently the only exit from the cellar was the one from outside the house through which she had been forced to enter.

Except for Sonny Houston's maniacal pounding and cursing at the cellar door once in a while, he had left her alone. But the heavy steel door remained locked. She had tested it with all her strength on several occasions and it would not budge.

She opened a drawer on the heavy chest and used it as a ladder. She removed several small cartons from the window ledge, allowing more light into the dark cellar. The cartons contained large building nails and pieces of heavy, miscellaneous hardware.

Penny carefully measured the dingy glass pane with her eye and then her fingers. She figured it to be about nine inches in height and perhaps fifteen inches long. She could find no way of opening the window. The pane of glass had been mounted in the wall of the house. The window looked out on the left side of the house as one faced it from the road. It was about twenty feet from a small grove of pines standing on the side of the house that was not used as a driveway.

Penny scrambled down from the chest and backed away several feet. She looked down at her small figure. Getting her shoulders and chest through the window space seemed unlikely. And then there were her hips and fanny, a little rounder than she always wanted them to be. But it seemed to be her only shot at escaping. She had to try.

At one end of the cellar was a small pile of scrap lumber. She selected a piece of two-by-four about a foot long and returned to the top of the chest. She sat silently, listening for any signs that would indicate Houston was in the house. There hadn't been any for a long time.

Then she rammed the end of the board into the pane of glass causing a shattering noise that sounded louder than crash of thunder to her. She climbed again on the top of the old chest. The opening she had made in the window had left a ring of glass shards all around the edge. There was no way she could crawl through them.

She stood atop the chest on her knees, and began to pick the glass shards from the window frame, dropping the pieces of glass behind the old chest. It was slow going. And now that she was close to the potential opening, she still wasn't sure that she would fit through the small window. When she had cleared one corner, she tried to slip an arm and shoulder through and opened a nasty gash on her forearm. There was still a lot more work to be done.

A grinding of tires on the gravel driveway and then the sound of Houston's SUV stopped her work. Quickly she stacked the small boxes she had removed from the window ledge back into the window, trying the best she could to conceal what she had done.

Soon Sonny Houston's heavy footsteps sounded over her head. He quickly exited the back door and she heard the rattling of a padlock against the cellar door. He swung the big door up and back, letting a dazzling stream of sunshine into the cellar, which reached her where she sat on a stack of packing cases. The silhouette of Houston included the shotgun.

Houston descended the cellar steps and paused at the

bottom staring at her sitting motionless on the boxes. "Whew! It smells awful in here."

"I'm sorry. Nature called," Penny blurted, surprised at her own quick retort. "Have you come to take me out of here and let me go?"

"Not so fast, young lady. I suspect you will have to stand trial before the tribunal before we can do anything like that."

"Before who!" Then Penny became silent, now surer than ever that he was mad.

"My, you're a pretty thing, aren't you? Look what I brought you." Houston walked close and placed a sack from a fast-food chain next to her. She could see the round top of a soft drink carton. She craved liquid. He then walked back to the cellar steps and sat down and stared at her. "Yes, ma'am, you sure are a pretty thing."

Penny looked down at herself. There was the smear of blood crusted on her arm. Her clothes and her body were filthy from poking around in the dark cellar. If he thought she was a pretty thing, he was indeed crazy. "Look, Mr. Houston, I have a lot of friends, and they are all looking for me. And they are very good at it. You'd better let me out of here right now!"

"Yep, you sure are a pretty thing. I ain't never had nothing like you," Houston said, totally ignoring her demands. "How'd you cut your arm?"

"Stumbling around in the dark. It's okay." Penny assured him quickly, afraid that he might come closer to examine her. She looked him in the eye and decided to use the only gambit that she thought might work. "You know, Mr. Houston, your boy is still alive, and we're about to find him."

"Liar! Liar!" Houston bellowed. "My boy's dead! In fact he never was my boy," he added in a whisper. Then he broke into a broad grin. "But we got better stuff to think about haven't we? You understand, don't you, that I never had anything like you. Not in my whole life."

Penny could hear her heartbeat, afraid that anything she might say would set him off. She pulled the carton containing the soft drink from the sack he had put next to her, removed the plastic lid and took a long drink.

"Now, that's being nice. You just sit here and enjoy your dinner. I went all the way to the junction to bring you that. I have some business to tend to up at the Memorial Park. But don't worry. I'll be back soon."

Memorial Park? What was he talking about. Nothing much he said made any sense to Penny. "Mr. Houston, will you do me a favor and talk to the tribunal about letting me out of here or at least letting me wash up and eat my dinner upstairs?"

"Of course, I'll just do that. The boys on the tribunal are all my friends. You just sit right there and I'll put in a good word for you." The grin quickly changed to a scowl. He was staring at her body, undressing her with his eyes. Then he slowly backed up the cellar steps, eyeing her all the way to the top. The heavy door clanged down and she heard him put the padlock in place.

She couldn't stop trembling. The sight of the burly three-hundred-pound madman was overpowering. If he had rape on his mind, what could she do? Neglecting to carry the small handgun that Coley had her qualify for was stupid. But how was she to know Houston would turn out to be what he obviously was? All she wanted to do was ask a few questions and cheer him up with the idea that they might find his son. She realized that leaving her cellular phone in the office had also been stupid. She pictured Coley when he had pointed a finger at her and insisted she carry it all the time.

Not really hungry at all though she hadn't eaten for hours, she opened the bag of food. Inside were two hamburgers and some french fries. She pulled one of the burgers from the sack and opened the cold burger for inspection. She smelled it and then took a small bite. It seemed okay. There was no use weakening herself further for the ordeal ahead, whatever it might be. She ate the burger and then half of the other one, and set aside the french fries for a future meal.

Then she climbed back up on the chest and started picking at the shards of glass, digging them out one by one with one of the nails from the cartons. Finished now, she realized that the opening was smaller than she had earlier thought. But she would still try. Now she sat quietly on the chest hoping to hear Houston take the van down the hill on some expedition off the property. The sound of the powerful engine of the van as it moved on the gravel driveway was always quite audible. She had even heard him drive the Miata somewhere behind the house before he returned to confront her. That's another stupid thing she did. She left the keys in the Miata. Of course, maybe that was best. Houston would have probably beaten her to get them. Also, if he dared drive the Miata on the open road, there was a good chance he would be picked up.

She made up her mind to sit on the chest until nighttime came. If Houston didn't come back to the cellar all day, she would make a break for the woods at night. She figured that would be her best bet and prayed that he wouldn't come back to the cellar anytime soon.

If only Coley or Willy would come looking for her, she thought. The red Miata would stand out like a neon sign anywhere around Houston's house.

Her thought process was interrupted by the sound of the back door slamming, and then the heavy footsteps of Houston walking around in the house. The audible pounding of her heartbeat began again. All her life she had heard about rape, read about rape, and been told what to do if confronted. Now she could think of nothing helpful at all. The imposing mass of Houston's bulk was terrifying.

The cold hamburger started to churn in her stomach, threatening to come up. She turned slightly and ran her fingers along the window frame behind the cartons she had restacked in their place. There were still tiny bits of glass here and there. But, by God, she would try it anyway, if only the madman would leave the house.

44

Blair Lawton inverted the small travel bag over the bed in her hotel room and four videotapes tumbled out. She shook the bag again. It was empty. There were supposed to be five.

She picked them up one by one and searched the cassette holders for some sort of identifying markings. There were none. She looked at them thoughtfully for a moment while sipping at a Perrier she had taken from the small guest refrigerator. Yes, there had been five. Now she recalled that quite clearly. There were five when Jason had slipped them into the console of the Corvette. She must have left one there by mistake when she had cleaned out the Corvette before leaving it at the hospital for Jason.

She slid one into the mouth of the VCR beneath the TV set in her room. Quickly the image of Jason, totally nude, appeared on the TV screen. He was strutting around with a tremendous erection, a promenade he was given to during long evenings of booze and cocaine. Soon the redheaded prostitute he had hired in Columbus appeared and they began what would be a long and degrading exhibition, all quite amateurish.

Blair pressed the eject button, removed the tape and inserted another. It was basically the same orgiastic display. These were tapes that Jason had claimed to have made long before she knew him. The last two turned out to be the same thing, except featuring a different long-legged blonde companion, statuesque, but mechanically following Jason's lewd instructions.

"Damn! Damn! Damn! It's gone!" she exclaimed loudly

to herself. Quickly she jammed the four tapes back into the travel bag and tossed it into a large piece of luggage in her closet.

The one tape she sought was not there. It was a tape that she had made with Jason in the conference room back in Columbus one late night when they were alone in the building. Jason had put the video camera on a tripod and they had put on an X-rated performance the likes of which very probably had not been seen before or since on the polished mahogany surface of that conference table. The tape was as embarrassing to her as it was to Jason.

On several trysts after that, he had played it over and over again. That tape and a couple spoons of cocaine were Jason's mood music for their steamy times together.

The tape had to be in the Corvette. In her haste that day she had left one tape, and it was the only one that she had appeared on. The rest of the tapes didn't matter. She had to find the Corvette before anyone else did, especially Amanda. "Where the hell are you, Jason, you bastard!" she shouted again, furious that she not been more careful.

She sat quietly on the edge of the bed for a moment, pondering what to do. Of course, the missing tape probably was still in the empty space beneath the console. It might go undiscovered for a long time. Calmed by that thought, she settled down and thought about locating the Corvette. The police all over the country were not having much luck.

Next she rummaged through the bulky Manhattan Yellow Pages and found Willy Hanson's name under "Private Investigators." She dialed the number, and the resonant voice of Willy Hanson answered almost immediately. "Willy here."

"Mr. Hanson, this is Blair Lawton. I want to thank you so much for being so civil in Dillon's office. I felt that the others acted like they were holding some sort of an inquisition. You were quite a gentleman and I appreciated it."

"Well, thank you, Ms. Lawton. I really think you have nothing to be upset about. They were just policemen, and very good ones, trying to do their job. There may be a small boy's life at stake here and they are understandably impatient."

There was a short pause. "I suppose so, but I have been thinking about the meeting ever since, and I would like to talk to you about it. Can I come and see you? I would like to do that as quickly as possible."

Willy glanced at his watch. He really wanted to leave for Pennsylvania as quickly as possible. "I'm heading out of town, Blair. In fact, when you called I was about to go get my car. Are you at your hotel now?"

"Yes, I plan to stay here until I hear from Jason."

"Tell you what. I'll meet you in the hotel coffee shop in fifteen minutes. We'll have to make it short. Can you do that?"

"Wonderful, I'll be waiting for you. Thanks so much, Mr. Hanson."

"Call me Willy. It's a deal, Blair." Willy hung up immediately, not wanting to waste any more time. He was intrigued by what the woman might have to say about Jason that wasn't already said. After all, the couple had spent a lot of time together. There must have been some common ground besides business, and their incendiary X-rated stuff on Coley's audiotape.

When he arrived, Blair was already seated at a far corner table in the coffee shop sipping at a cup, still wearing the silk suit. She made a perfect picture for a late spring day.

"Blair, thank you so much for being on time. I'm really in quite a hurry." He sat down quickly and signaled the waiter for a cup of coffee. He looked across the table and found Blair's wide-set blue eyes fixed unblinkingly on his own. At his close vantage point he noticed a tired, slack-jawed appearance. She was still dazzling, but not quite flawless, as she had appeared earlier. She looked a bit nervous, not quite so sure of herself. "So what can I do for you?"

"Find Jason Granger for me. I'll pay you whatever your going rate it. I hear you are very good. I must find him as quickly as possible." Blair paused, studying his reaction. "Perhaps I am selfish, but my career is tied up completely with Jason's success. I have no idea why Jason disappeared now, but Dillon Archibald is furious. He's ready to fire Jason, and me, too, I think."

Willy stared back into her still-unblinking eyes. He thought of Penny and Coley's reports of old Dillon cavorting in her suite on several occasions. He seriously doubted that Dillon would be willing to fire her, risking the possibility that Blair might take her wrath to Cora Archibald. "Blair, It's quite flattering of you to have all that confidence in me. But in my case you can save your money. My people are already doing everything they can to locate Jason. We couldn't be working any harder than we are now. I can only promise you that when we find him, you will be one of the first to know." His eyes remained glued on hers until she finally broke her gaze. She pushed her chair back slightly from the table and crossed her endless legs, bobbing her dangling foot up and down impatiently. The sensuous woman was a natural flirt. He doubted if she could act otherwise for any length of time.

"Willy, quite frankly, there were some things that I hesitated to say at the meeting this morning. I know how important all those people were. But I felt that it was unfair to expect me or any woman to bare her intimate soul in front of all those people. Can I tell you something in complete confidence, just between you and me? It might help you find Jason."

She resumed her eye contact with him. Finally, he looked away from her and stared off into the coffee shop for a few moments before he shrugged and began to speak. "Blair, I am already committed to working on this case involving Jason, and in a significant way, yourself. I will try to share confidentiality with you, but if things become critical, I may have to pass along anything you tell me. The life of a young boy might be at stake here, you know."

"But you'll at least try to protect my privacy?" She persisted.

"I'll try. That's all I can promise."

"Okay. That will have to be good enough, I suppose." Blair stopped, opened a small purse, withdrew a pack of cigarettes and lit up.

Willy waited in suspense as she went through the ritual. Until then he had had no idea that she smoked.

"Jason and I are lovers." She paused and looked again at Willy. If he were shocked or surprised, she couldn't tell by his face. "Also, Jason has a problem that I have been helping him to work out. He is hopelessly, big-time, addicted to cocaine."

Willy's face remained expressionless. After all, she hadn't said anything that he didn't know. But why was she telling him this? "Blair, this morning you said quite the opposite. You told everyone that Jason having a cocaine habit was preposterous."

"Of course. Can you imagine me being candid about this in front of Dillon Archibald? It would have ruined Jason right then and there. Harmony Mutual's drug policy is quite unforgiving."

Willy nodded his head. Still, she hadn't told him anything he didn't know. She wasn't protecting Jason. She was protecting herself, however. For a woman so in love with Jason, she was spending a hell of a lot of time in the sack with Dillon Archibald. He pondered asking his next question, feeling himself tense up as he thought about it. But, he couldn't resist. "Was Jason on a cocaine high when you left him at the Crestview?"

Blair's eyes dropped. "Of course. When I left him he was in hopeless condition. All the champagne didn't help, either. I know Jason very well. I was sure he wouldn't leave the Crestview until the next day. I went into New York to cover for him." Blair shrugged. "I was a fool to leave him like that."

"Some party!" murmured Willy, trying to sort out the

fact from the fiction in her account. He decided that most of it was probably true. "So, what do you think happened to him?"

"I am sure of one thing. Even if he checked in for a couple hours of sleep someplace, he couldn't have gotten very far. Jason and I are very close. He never misses communicating with me for more than a few hours. Something terrible has happened to him. He's run that toy of his off some mountain road, perhaps into a river or creek. The backcountry up there around the Crestview is pretty wild, you know."

"I know," replied Willy. I've explored a bit of that country myself over the years." Willy was disappointed. Is this what she wanted to talk to him about? He couldn't believe that she wanted a conference with him to tell him the obvious. "Blair, I really am in a hurry. I don't see how that me knowing you are having an affair with Jason will help us find him."

"Willy, have you ever been in love, superintimate with someone to the point that you can almost crawl into their mind?"

"Crawl into their mind?" Her phrase brought a smile to Willy's face. He thought of Ginny and their idyllic life together aboard the *Tashtego*. Despite their intimacy, an aura of mystery still surrounded her at times. He couldn't say that he was always able to crawl into her mind. "Blair, I'll accept that intimacy breeds predictability between people to a certain degree. What's your point?"

"Remember when I told the policemen that Jason said he was an hour late getting to the Crestview because he got lost? He was lying! I know it. Also he was over an hour and a half late. Take a look at a map. The area is really very compact up there. Jason is brilliant with details. He's never late. That's just Jason."

"So? If he was lying about being lost, how did he turn a one-hour trip into two and a half hours?" Willy thought to himself that dropping off the ransom note wouldn't take all that time. "What if I told you I think he is holding Tad Granger hostage for ransom in some hideaway in the Poconos?"

"I'd say you were insane to believe such a thing, Mr. Hanson." Blair smiled and then added, "It's more likely another woman. Jason is rather insatiable in that department."

"So you want me to find Jason, and find him with another woman. What would you intend to do with that information? The last I heard there were no laws against cheating on a mistress." Willy returned her smile and looked into her dazzling blues again. He was now getting very antsy to get on his way. He felt he was wasting valuable time listening to the plaints of a very vain, scorned woman.

"Willy, just find him! Just find him and that stupid red Corvette, and I'll give you anything you want. Anything! Do you understand, Mr. Hanson?"

"I believe I do. If I can help you it will be my pleasure, pro bono. Okay?" There was something about her remarks that prodded at his sense of logic. Her emphasis on the "stupid" red Corvette was strangely puzzling. It was almost as if she was jealous of it. Willy pulled away from the table, stood up and extended his hand to her. "I've got to be on my way. Let's hope we can bring you some good news soon, Blair."

To his surprise she stood up, grasped his hand and pulled herself close to him. She kissed his cheek gently, lingering for an uncomfortable second or two before thanking him for his effort to help her. Willy pulled away quickly and strode to the door, impatient to be on his way. The subtle hint of her lilac essence persisted as he walked in the open air. He decided Blair Lawton needed a lot of help, most of it on some therapist's couch.

When Willy reached his Z3 in the garage, he tried one more time to reach Penny. There were no messages. Something had to be wrong. The young woman prided herself on her frequent informative communications.

He called Mark Whitcomb at his high-priority number

and was patched through immediately. "Mark, Willy Hanson here. Any news about the boy, or my operative, Penny Wine?"

There was a long pause before Whitcomb said anything. "Nothing new on the boy. Tell me about Penny Wine."

"She's the third operative in our firm. Penny took it upon herself to drive to Pennsylvania and check on Eddie Foxworth, a neighbor kid Tad Houston buddied around with up on the farm. She got the name from Empress Carlota."

"We know about Foxworth. He was the kid's alias when he talked to the conductor that day."

"Mark, we haven't heard from Penny for over a day. She is religious about checking in every couple hours. Coley is on his way to retrace her steps. He should be at the Foxworths' house any time now. I'm about ready to leave for the area myself."

"My, my, my . . . for being under instructions to stay off the case, it looks like you're in with both feet. Willy, I guess I'll have to slap a pair of cuffs on you."

"Do whatever you want to, Mark. My first responsibility is for all my people. I'm still trying to locate Jason Granger. He, the kid and Penny are all missing up there. Please try to understand, Mark."

"We'll talk more about that when we have time. While you've been poking around, getting people lost, I've gotten a search warrant for Houston's property. I have a half dozen men meeting me there at six P.M."

Willy looked at his watch. It was a couple minutes after four. "Mark, I heading for the Foxworths' right this minute. Why don't we meet there?"

"I insist on it, Mr. Hanson. Don't get any bright ideas. If Coley beats us there, instruct him to wait for us if you can reach him. I want our search of Houston's property to be a total surprise."

"Do you need the location for the Foxworths' farm?" Willy asked, eager to get started.

"Willy, I remind you that you are talking to your FBI. Do you really think I would agree to meet you somewhere I couldn't locate? Just to put you at ease, we've called the Foxworths. They expect us. They even told us about Penny Wine's visit." Whitcomb paused a moment, "I would appreciate a description on Penny Wine."

"She's about five foot two, short brunette pageboy, brainy and strong as such a teensy little person can be. A real looker if you like miniatures."

"Does she carry a piece?"

"Not all the time. She probably wouldn't have it on her person just to interview the Foxworths." Willy knew that she abhorred carrying a gun.

Whitcomb groaned. "We lose a lot of men who neglect to carry their weapon, Willy. We do need to talk. See you in Milford in about an hour and a half, at the Foxworths'."

Bastard! Willy muttered after he hung up. Whitcomb was a fine agent, as fine as you could get, but totally unforgiving and humorless.

Within minutes Willy had the Z3 speeding along Route 80 toward the Delaware. He wanted to get to the Foxworths' first. As far as he knew they could have been the last people to see Penny Wine.

45

Coley Doctor drove the rental Malibu off the road, which consisted of two tire tracks heavily overgrown with underbrush. He decided he really needed a four-wheel drive if he were to get much further. He hid the Malibu from view in the dense brush, emerged and spread the road atlas out on the roof of the car. As nearly as he could tell he was about two and a half to three miles from the back side of Houston's farm. He strapped on a holstered nine-millimeter Glock, figuring that he would make better time than if he carried a rifle.

Looking southward across the thick pine forest running down through a deep valley, he could see a high mountain ridge of the Poconos that stretched for many miles in each direction. If he had it figured right, Houston's property was just over that ridge. He estimated the hike would take over an hour. After he cased Houston's property unseen from the rear, he would walk around the bend to meet the others at the Foxworth place.

Coley hiked due south, looking at his compass frequently. His camouflage togs seemed to blend in well with the heavy underbrush. Once he was startled by a couple of deer that raced past him and then disappeared into the woods. At one point he came upon a clearing that gave him a fine view of the high ridge, which was his goal. He figured he was making better time than he had planned.

Over the ridge at the Houston farm, Penny sat huddled against the oaken chest that had been readied as a stepladder in her planned escape. She had studied the narrow window opening and decided that she could squeeze through if she had a chance.

All at once came the sound of tires spinning on the gravel of Houston's long driveway. The sound was getting farther away! It was music to her ears. It was the sound she had been waiting for.

Penny scrambled to the top of the old chest. She pushed her arms and then her torso through the narrow opening. She squirmed and pushed until her hips cleared the window, and then dragged her legs through. She was free! Feeling pain, she glanced down. A slash along one calf was bleeding freely. She must have left a tiny shard of glass in the window frame, and it had made the ugly gash. She put pressure on the wound with her open hand, but the blood kept coming.

She glanced around. The wound would have to wait for attention until she was hidden by the woods. She stood for a moment contemplating the run across the field, over the strand of wire, into the beckoning trees.

She began her short sprint and was able to see the entire front of the property. Houston's van was parked at the huge rural mailbox. He was standing by it, reading something! Just as she hurled the barbed-wire strand, Houston glanced up, probably attracted by her movement.

"Hey!" came the shout, loud and clear, just before she plunged into the woods.

Once in the woods she found herself ensnared by thorny berry bushes that seemed to be everywhere. She plunged on, trying to find an open space through them to the pine grove ahead of her—to where the trees actually began. In the distance she heard the roar of the SUV, its wheels spinning up the gravel driveway. Then she could actually see it racing toward the woods. It plowed through the single strand of wire and finally came to stop a few feet from her.

She was trapped and she knew it. She had unknowingly made a poor choice of entry into the woods, especially dressed as she was.

Houston got out of the vehicle and came toward her carrying the shotgun. Finally he stood just a few feet away, saying nothing. He watched her as she bound the gash on her leg with a strip of cloth she tore from her blouse.

Finally he spoke in a low voice, sounding concerned and almost civil. "That needs attention from the medical unit. Unfortunately they are way behind the lines. It will take awhile for them to get here."

Penny's hopes sank lower as she tried to make sense of his spoken gibberish. "Don't bother with them. I'll manage quite well. Please just let me go. I'll be just fine."

"Now that would be against the articles of war, wouldn't

it? You have to help the wounded, even if they're on the other side."

She glanced up to find him grinning at her, staring at her legs, which she had elevated in order to tend to the wound. She quickly flattened them against the ground and smoothed her clothing close to her. The gash from the sliver of window glass was bleeding much less now. She glanced around her, wondering if she had enough stamina to sprint past him when she stood up. He surely wouldn't actually shoot her with that shotgun, would he? Catching his leering visage once again, she decided he would.

"You've made a terrible mistake, young lady. The tribunal had approved your request to come upstairs in the house and live with me. When they hear about what you've done, they'll no doubt rescind those orders."

"Why don't you let me talk to the tribunal. I can be very convincing." Penny, trying to get as much time to rest as possible, made up her mind to try to humor the madman.

He moved a step closer and then stopped, seeming unwilling to push into the snarl of brambles that surrounded her. "You've got yourself tangled up in my wild blackberries. Bessie makes fine pies out of those."

"I'll bet they're good. Where is Bessie now?" Penny wished for a miracle, for Bessie to have returned to the house, but realized she had heard no one else walking the floor above her.

"She's off on special assignment." Houston answered, and then broke into his big friendly grin. His eyes were unblinking as he gaped at her exposed legs as she struggled to her feet. "You and me got the place all to ourselves."

"You aren't going to put me down in that old cellar again, are you? That wasn't very nice of you, Mr. Houston." Penny began to work her way out of the brambles. She moved slowly, eyeing the open field, now only a few feet away. She thought that surely she could outrun this hulk of a man if only she got the chance. He just kept staring at her, seeming momentarily oblivious to the shotgun, now with it's butt on the ground, held loosely in his hand by the tip of the barrel.

"Well, the tribunal's already said that you can come upstairs with me. A pretty thing like you shouldn't have to live in the cellar."

"Hey, that's good news!" As she spoke, Penny looked down at the last few strands of the blackberry bushes ahead of her. Just as she stepped free, she burst to his right with all the strength she could muster.

For a second, she thought that she had made it past him, but then he moved quickly and grasped her arm with a vice-like grip. He jerked her against him and bear-hugged her to his massive frame. Even kicking and struggling as she was, he managed to slobber a drooling kiss firmly on her cheek. She fought at him, managing to dig her fingernails into the flesh of his face.

Then he slapped her hard with his massive open hand and she fell, stunned, to ground. He picked her up easily, carried her to the SUV and tossed her onto the rear seat. Houston shut the door and turned to look all around him, scrutinizing the narrow blacktop road in the distance. Not a half dozen cars a day came down his road, and he was satisfied that no one had seen him.

He got into the van, started the motor and drove back across the sagging barbed-wire strand. He drove rapidly across the open field. He stopped for a second at the back of his house and glanced over his shoulder at the now-unconscious and bruised Penny. "You had your chance, young lady. I gave you a chance to join up with my forces, but you had to have your way, didn't you?" He reached his arm over the seat back and twisted her face toward him. If she was alive, he couldn't tell it.

He put the SUV into low gear and bounced up the road toward Houston Memorial Park.

* * *

A hundred yards away, Tad groaned and moved slightly, roused by the sound of the SUV racing up the rocky hill in back of his house. The boy lifted himself on one elbow and then dropped back down on the mossy flat rock, curling into the boulder that blocked his view of Houston Memorial Park.

46

Willy Hanson sped by Sonny Houston's farm without easing up on the accelerator of the Z3 roadster. A quick glance spotted Houston's van making its way up the winding road across the pasture to the rear. It took all the willpower he had to pass it by and go on around the bend to the Foxworths'. He glanced at his watch and found that he had made incredible time. There would no doubt be a wait for Whitcomb and his entourage.

He was met at the door by Elsie Foxworth. She studied him for a moment before unhooking the screen door. "You must be Willy Hanson. Agent Whitcomb called and told me to expect you." Willy nodded and she led him inside. "This is my husband, Byron, and this little fellow is my son, Eddie."

"Nice meeting you folks. I hope this isn't too much of an imposition. Whitcomb and his boys should be here soon. Do you mind if we talk a bit before they get here?" Elsie surely seemed friendly enough, but Byron, tall and lean, had a stern look on his face that was anything but gracious. It was he who spoke first.

"Do you mind telling me what this is all about? We get along real fine with all our neighbors up here and don't want to start any trouble with any of them."

"Mr. Hanson, I've made a pitcher of iced tea. Would you

like some?" Elsie asked, quickly injecting herself into the conversation. "Byron is as upset as I am about the drowning of the Houston boy. Of course there have been reporters around, policemen, and the young woman yesterday who was a private detective. Nobody stops by for months and all of a sudden all these people, asking questions."

"The young lady, Penny Wine, she works for me," Willy interjected. "When did you last see her? Was she okay?"

"Penny was a fine young lady. She got on real well with my son, Eddie. Byron wasn't home when she was here. She left here late yesterday afternoon."

That confirmed the worst news Willy expected. It meant Penny had been unaccounted for for a full twenty-four hours. "When she left here, did she say where she was going? Do you know whether she went back toward Milford or out toward the junction?"

Elsie Foxworth paused in thought. "She didn't say where she was going."

Eddie, who had been all ears up to now, quickly chimed in. "She went back toward Milford. I watched her all the way around the bend. She had this keen Mazda Miata."

"Eddie, you speak only when you're spoken to, young man. How can you be sure of that?"

"I watched her, Mom, I watched her!"

Willy puzzled over the information. That meant that if she drove toward Milford, she had to pass Sonny Houston's farm. If she got to Milford, she would have checked in from the phone at the general store, like she promised them in her only message. Willy felt uncomfortable with the information. He could only think that curiosity had gotten the best of her, and she might have stopped to talk to Houston.

"Thanks, son." Willy patted the young boy on the back as he sipped at the iced tea. The thin line of probability suggested that Penny had disappeared somewhere between where he stood and the town of Milford, somewhere around Sonny Houston's farm. They were interrupted by the beep of Willy's cellular phone. It was Coley.

"Hi, pal. Any word from Penny?" From the tone of his voice Coley was just as worried as he was.

"Not yet. I'm here at the Foxworths'. Whitcomb's guys should be here any minute. Elsie Foxworth says Penny left pointed toward Milford about this time yesterday. Where the hell are you?"

"I'm taking a hike through the poison ivy and brambles along the ridge back of Houston's farm. I must be less than a mile from his property now. It's a steep climb from here, but when I get there I should have a bird's-eye view of the whole place. Willy, I'm worried about Penny. If she got to Milford we would have heard from her yesterday."

"I know just how you feel. When you get a vantage point up there, don't actually move onto Houston's property until you see us moving in from the south. Whitcomb is very much in charge. We don't want to tweak him any more than necessary. Of course if it is an emergency, like spotting the red Miata, use your own judgment. We'll begin our search as soon as Whitcomb gets here. Are you carrying a weapon?"

"Yep, the Glock."

"Good. I can't imagine needing it, but I'm glad you have it. Was Penny armed?"

"Probably not. You know how she feels. I instructed her to carry her .38."

"No doubt she conveniently forgot it. We've got to raise some real hell with her, Coley." Willy hung up, feeling more impatient than ever. Whitcomb should have been there by now.

Willy downed most of the glass of iced tea and then decided to go ahead and begin questioning the Foxworths. "You would say that Sonny Houston has been a good neighbor?"

Elsie readily agreed. "Well, he does keep to himself. He's a retired military man, you know. He raises a few vegetables, grapes and melons, which he sells on a stand down the road a ways. He'll really miss Tad. The boy helped him a lot."

Byron interrupted. "We all mind our own business up

here. If you want to know any more about Houston, I suggest you ask him. He's home most of the time. I think he would be happy to speak to you."

"Sometimes he's an old grouch, Dad. He ran me off the other day. All I wanted to do was ask about Tad and find out what he was doing with the big backhoe."

"Backhoe?"

"Yep, it's a big digger. It's got a plow on one end and a big scoop on the other end. It's fun to watch him work it. He was digging a new farm pond. But he must have decided he put it in the wrong place. So he filled it up and dug another one. He got mad and ran me off when I asked about it."

Byron shook his finger at the boy. "I told you to stay away from there, and I mean it. That's hard work he doing, and no man likes to be pestered with silly questions when he's hard at work."

"Silly! I think he's the one that's silly, digging a big pond and then filling it up again."

"That's enough, young man! You don't call your neighbors names, especially your elders. Now you go in your room or outside. We've heard quite enough from you."

"You've got a fine boy there," observed Willy, when the boy vanished into the next room. "Obviously he has a good head on his shoulders. You should be proud of him."

"He is a good boy," agreed Elsie. "But he has been upset terribly by the loss of his friend. He and Tad Houston were together all the time."

"It'll take time for him to get over it. To lose a best friend in such a tragic way at his age must be a terrible experience. But hopefully," Willy added, "the boy will turn up somewhere."

They all were distracted by the sound of a car pulling into the driveway. A black Chevy Lumina followed by a black Blazer pulled up next to Willy's Z3. Mark Whitcomb climbed out of the Blazer and came to the door. The other personnel in the vehicles stayed put. Willy went to the door to meet Mark and introduced him to Byron and Bessie.

Willy rapidly briefed him on the chat he had had with the Foxworths, including the remarks offered by young Eddie, who seemed to be more knowledgeable about Sonny Houston than his parents. "Mark, I don't think we should waste any time. Let's get up there with the search warrant and make sure everything is the way it should be."

Mark nodded, pausing to decline a glass of iced tea from Elsie Foxworth. "Willy, I want this search to proceed quickly and courteously. We have no hard evidence that Sonny Houston is anything other than the simple farmer he appears to be. Now, let's get it over with." Whitcomb began to walk back toward the Blazer with Willy alongside.

"How about GITGO 7, Mark? We have evidence that Houston might be the one who beat the hell out of Jason Granger."

"The evidence is anecdotal and circumstantial. We've got to regard Jason Granger as a possible kidnapper. At this point I am more worried about your Penny Wine. Maybe Houston knows something we don't know. Let's get on with the show. I'd like to wrap this up before it gets dark."

Whitcomb turned once more before he climbed into the Blazer to wave good-bye to the Foxworths. "Sorry to inconvenience you. Thanks for the information you gave to Mr. Hanson."

The three-vehicle caravan pulled out of the driveway and turned down the road toward Sonny Houston's farm. Just before they made the bend in the road that would make them visible from Houston's property, Whitcomb had them pull over and study the eighty-by-ten blowups of an aerial photo of Houston's ten acres one last time. He had been supplied with the prints by his lab only that day. Sure enough, to the north end, the scars on the earth from all the digging as reported by Eddie Foxworth were clearly visible. The man's effort to tap mother nature was probably unimportant, but the photo did give credence to Eddie Foxworth's comments.

47

Up on the hillside, in Houston Memorial Park, Sonny Houston positioned his van alongside one of the two small graves that he had scooped out with the backhoe and then chiseled at them with a shovel until the sides were vertical. He figured they were a little over six feet deep. Water was still standing in the bottom of both pits due to yesterday's heavy rain.

He had parked the van so that any of his activity around the excavation would be blocked from view from the road. He glanced back at Penny Wine, still lying motionless where he had put her. He opened the rear door and pulled her from the vehicle. He carried her to the nearest grave site and lowered her into the pit, finally letting her drop the last couple of feet. Her legs bent under her as she settled into the muddy water, leaving her in a semisitting position.

Now heading for the backhoe, he became distracted by movement from the road below. Alongside his property, just west of the gate, three vehicles were lined up. There was a small sports car, a black sedan, and black Blazer. Two men had exited the vehicles, and both of them were carrying rifles.

Houston ran to the backhoe and started the engine, while continuing to watch the men. They certainly didn't look like the usual hunters that came by occasionally. He clawed a partial scoop of dirt from the pile next to him and maneuvered the scoop over the open pit. He glanced down at Penny. He stared at her. Had she moved? One hand was positioned over her face. He didn't remember that. Quickly he tripped a lever to dump the dirt into the pit.

Glancing down, he could see that parts of her were still visible.

There was movement down by the road. All three vehicles had lined themselves up inside his property. Two men had gotten out of the cars and were stretching a wide yellow tape across the mouth of his driveway.

He began to panic. He looked again at the partially covered form of the young woman. He jumped out of the backhoe and ran into a pile of scrap lumber, most of it the remains of an old barn that once stood near there. He dragged a section of an old barn door over to the pit and positioned it over the top. If the men were to come up the hill, there just wasn't time to do what he had to do. He decided to go down right now and run them off his property.

Once again, he climbed into the backhoe and moved it toward the slab of wood covering the unfinished grave. He eased the big metal scoop down until it pressed against the wood. No way anyone could move the old barn door without moving the backhoe. Now the excavation was totally sealed. The old barn door sagged under the weight of the metal claw.

Houston took one last quick look around him and then climbed in his van. He put the loaded shotgun on the seat beside him and drove down the winding road. By the time he got to the house, the black Blazer had started moving up his driveway. The Blazer stopped about fifty feet in front of him and two men got out, both wearing shirts emblazoned FBI. Another man in a state trooper's uniform joined them.

The trooper walked briskly to him. "Sonny Houston. sir, we have a warrant to search your property."

Houston slowly climbed out of his SUV and planted his massive frame in front of the trooper. He scowled at Evan Knight. He had dealt with him a couple of times before during the search for Tad. "You back again? I told you the river got my boy. No use hunting for him around here. He sure ain't here. You got no right to come in here like this."

"Mr. Houston, it's a court order. We do have a right, sir. Now if you just stay here with me, while the officers go about their business, we can get this over with in a hurry." Knight glanced inside Houston's SUV and spotted the rifle. His hand moved swiftly to draw his sidearm. "I'll have to take care of that for the time being. Is it loaded?"

"Sure it's loaded. Varmints been gittin' my chickens. Been trying to put 'em out of commission." Houston stood rigid and scowled as one of the other officers lifted the gun from the SUV. "It just ain't fair. There's no point in looking. There ain't nothin' here. My wife Bessie is waiting for me to pick her up down in Morristown. I was on my way when you guys come in here like a bunch of fools."

Whitcomb had sauntered up to monitor the conversation. "You were going to drive to Morristown, in another state, with that loaded gun in your front seat? Really, Mr. Houston, I'd say we did you a big favor by showing up when we did. Now do you want to let us inside your house, or do you want us to break down the door?"

Houston scowled at Whitcomb. Unlike the others, he wore a fancy business suit, black hair all slicked back, not a single hair out of place. "Big fuckin' big shot, ain't ya? I served in the big war and paid my taxes all my life, and what do I get? I get a fuckin' big shot in a suit treatin' my home like dirt."

Evan Knight listened in amazement. He had never heard the reclusive Houston put so many words together. They all watched as Houston dug his keys out of his pocket, twisted his house key off the ring. He tossed it at Whitcomb, who fielded it easily, accompanied by one of his rare, slight smiles.

The group followed Houston down the hill. He walked over to a big flat rock which jutted from the ground in the side yard and sat down on it. He pulled a pack of cigars from his pocket and lit one up. Knight shrugged and looked at Whitcomb.

"Oh, hell. Put a man on him and let him sit there. I get

the distinct feeling we're barking up the wrong tree. I think we'll be out of here in a few minutes."

Knight knew better. This thing was going to take a few hours. Whitcomb had said what he did strictly for the ears of Sonny Houston. He wanted to put off any more trouble with the big man as long as possible.

The search inside the house progressed rapidly. There were three small rooms upstairs and four downstairs including the kitchen. Knight noted that Bessie Houston was a meticulous housekeeper. There was very little accumulation of junk anywhere.

Whitcomb spent some time at the gun rack hanging in what passed for a family room. There were two high-powered rifles—a .30–30 and a .30–06—a lever-action .22 and three shotguns of different gauges. It was quite an arsenal, but not unusual for a serious hunter living in this remote location. Whitcomb inspected the guns one by one. They were as meticulously cleaned as was the house itself. None were loaded. The .30–06 looked as if it had been freshly cleaned, but it had a faint residue of gunpowder residue on the tip of the bore.

Within twenty minutes Whitcomb, Knight and Willy Hanson all met in the kitchen. Whitcomb was again studying the aerial shot of the premises. "Okay, let's move outside. There is a cellar door out in back. I can't find an access from inside. Let's take a look."

Willy exited the front door, deciding to circle the outside before meeting the others. There was a narrow window at ground level on the west side. The pane of glass was missing. He stooped to look at the opening, noticing immediately a deep brownish red smear on the white paint of the house. It extended from a tiny shard of glass embedded in the sill and fanned out to the far outside edge. He tried to look inside, but it was pitch black.

He turned away from the window. There was a small grove of young pines close by. Beyond that was a meadow which ran some fifty yards to a single strand of barbed wire, which ringed the ten acres. At one point the barbed wire was twisted and pushed to the earth. Crushed weeds formed a set of tire tracks than ran past the barbed wire into the dense brush beyond. Curiosity got the best of him and he began hiking quickly across the field.

The tire tracks stopped abruptly amidst a dense thicket of thorny underbrush. He was about to turn away when he spotted a small strip of yellow cloth snagged on one of the branches. He plucked it from the thorns and examined it closely. It was saturated with a bright red stain. He ripped a sheet of paper from a small notebook, wrapped the scrap of cloth in it, then tucked it into his pocket. It may mean nothing, it may be something, he thought to himself. But it was the only thing his part of the search had yielded that was even mildly interesting.

As he started climbing the sloping meadow back up to the house, he became aware of a noisy ruckus coming from the rear of the house. Loud bursts of heated conversation and curses came from the group just now becoming visible to Willy. Sonny Houston had abandoned his seat on the rock where he had sat through the whole search up to now and was confronting the others. His arms waved wildly as his foot stomped repeatedly on the metal cellar door.

"You have no damn right to go ripping away at my house. Bessie knows where the key is, and she'll be home as soon as I get her." Houston promptly sat himself down on the cellar door, reached into his shirt pocket and produced another cigar.

Now joining the others, Willy could see the cause of the consternation. One of the agents had backed the Blazer up near the cellar door. Another agent was stooping down to attach a metal chain from the Blazer to the steel eye that held the padlock. The obvious objective was to yank the entire cellar door from the concrete casement.

Willy got Whitcomb's attention and walked him around

to the side of the house. He pointed to the open window. "There is a way to get someone inside the cellar without ripping the door off."

"I saw that! Don't you think I'd look for an easy entry before we tear the cellar door off? There also isn't a man among us that could squeeze through that window."

Sometimes Whitcomb was unsufferably imperious. But he was also right this time. "Just wanted to make sure you'd seen it and the smear of what looks like blood on the sill."

Whitcomb became very quite for a moment. "Very observant of you, Willy. I saw that, too. I've also sent for some lab boys to come out by copter." He huddled close to Willy, making certain the others couldn't hear. "Notice how Houston there throws a conniption fit every time we talk about opening the cellar? Willy, brace yourself. God knows what we'll find in that cellar!"

Willy felt his heart pumping as the two officers advanced to remove Houston from the cellar door. God, I hope Whitcomb's instincts are wrong this time, he thought. He prayed that the smear on the cloth and on the window not be Penny's blood.

48

Coley stopped his hike up the rugged mountainside to take a good look around him and checked his compass again. The terrain was getting much more free of dense undergrowth. He figured he was only a couple of hundred yards from the top of the ridge, which he could see in several places ahead of him. Not long ago he had heard a noise that sounded like the loud throb of a powerful engine. He had altered his course just a trifle to zero in on a tall tree that sat atop the ridge that seemed the source of the sound. His progress was hampered by the lack of any kind of trail. He had to trample his own path through the pesky underbrush.

To his left a small spring trickled from an outcropping of stone and formed a cleft in the hillside. The tiny creek pooled here and there to form an idyllic scene that he would relish under other circumstances.

He easily jumped across the small creek and rounded a large boulder covered with lush green moss. He glanced down at a hollow next to the boulder, and gasped! A small boy, eyes wide with fear, huddled there.

Coley stopped, searching for words. He did not want to further frighten startled the boy. "Let me guess," said Coley, trying to be as unthreatening as possible, "I'll bet you're Tad Houston."

The boy shook his head negatively and backed against the rock. His eyes darted from side to side like a trapped animal desperately seeking an escape route. Then he staggered to his feet. In a burst of energy he tried to run past Coley, only to be stopped by a long arm, which scooped him easily into Coley's grasp.

The boy made an effort to break free, but after one last burst of energy, he collapsed at Coley's feet, where he sat breathing heavily, staring off toward the top of the ridge.

Coley took stock of the lad, who was obviously suffering from exposure. He was covered with mosquito bites and red scratches from the thorns. His clothes were ripped and he was caked with dried clay. He had evidently fallen into the creek at one point. Still, Coley could recognize the boy in front of him as the same one pictured in the newspapers.

"Tad, my boy, do you know how happy I am to see you?"

"I bet my pops sent you out here hunting for me." Tad's voice quivered as he spoke. "You can just tell him I'm living with Aunt Sarah and Aunt Carlota. I was just hiking around out here. You let me go or I'll . . ." The boy's voice faded and his eyes closed as he slumped at Coley's feet.

Coley dropped to the ground next to him and pulled him

into his arms. He felt his pulse. It felt strong enough, but no doubt the boy was suffering from exposure and physical exhaustion. He wondered how long he had been out here in the woods and when he had last eaten.

Coley pulled the small cellular unit out of his pocket and called Willy. It seemed to take forever before he answered.

"Willy, I've got him! I've got Tad Houston. He's alive but just passed out on me. He's suffering from exposure and hunger, I would guess. We'll need a medical unit to take him to the hospital to be checked out."

"Where? Coley. Where are you?"

"We're just over the ridge, probably less than ten minutes from the north edge of the farm." Coley glanced down at Tad, who had opened his eyes and taken a viselike grip on Coley's big hand. "I guess I can carry the boy the rest of the way up there. Get hopping on the med-vac unit, okay?"

"I read you, Coley. Just a second." Willy called out to Whitcomb, still with the group arguing with Houston over the cellar door. Whitcomb left the discussion and joined Willy at the corner of the house. "Coley's found Tad. He's up on the ridge on the north rim. The kid's okay, but suffering from exposure. We'll need a medical evacuation unit."

"Good work, Willy! We'll get right on the medics. I'll inform Houston. Maybe that will calm the crazy son of a bitch down." Whitcomb called one of his men over and got him to work on procuring the medical unit and then turned back to Willy. "Willy, the idea of having Coley search the woods to the north was a stroke of genius. I compliment you. I thought this thing was going to drag on all night long."

Willy nodded. "You can credit Coley with that idea. There's still a lot of unfinished business, Mark. We still haven't heard from Penny Wine or Jason Granger. I think we should push that search warrant to its limit."

Whitcomb, turned slowly around, eyeing the entire perimeter of Houston's farm. "Willy, I fail to see a red Corvette or a red Miata anywhere."

"Mark, for God's sake, people don't vanish into thin air. Penny Wine is as reliable as they come."

"Relax! Take it easy, Willy. We've still got some time before the lab boys and the medics get here." Whitcomb stared at Houston, still smoking his cigar, his huge frame slumped on the cellar door. "Don't worry, I'm still going to rip that cellar door out from under his fat ass. First, let's tell the bastard we've found his son. I want to see how happy he gets. Want to join me?"

"Thanks, Mark. I wouldn't miss that for anything."

Willy and Whitcomb joined the others, who were still trying to get Houston to abandon the cellar door voluntarily. "Okay, boys, listen up." Whitcomb called the group together as he stood with one hand on the shoulder of the recalcitrant Sonny Houston.

Whitcomb bent low and spoke with his face a few inches from the scowling father. "I've got good news for you, Mr. Houston. We've found your son, and he's okay."

They all saw not one bit of elation on Houston's face. He continued to scowl while moving his head, looking between members of the group of agents and policemen around him. "So where is he?"

"He's just over the ridge, right behind where you've been digging up there. He's scratched up a bit and covered with bites and he's real hungry. We'll bring in a copter to take him to the hospital to get checked out. But your ordeal is over. Would you like to go inside and call your wife?"

"My wife? Now why would I want to do that? She'll find out when I drive down there later to pick her up. That'll be soon enough."

Willy looked stunned. "I take it you want to surprise her, and I don't blame you."

"Surprise! Now that's a crock. That woman's already

been spending the insurance money." Houston rose from the cellar door, walked a few paces and then stopped. He stared at the ridge beyond, where bits of the bright orange backhoe showed through the trees. "Okay, you found my boy. So get all your troops together and get them off my land. I don't want the boy going to any hospital. Bessie will take better care of him than anybody. Now git!"

Houston spun around, looking at his ring of captors one by one. His face was beet red and his fists were clinched at his side. Unarmed as he was at that moment, he still was an intimidating force. "I'll tell you once again. Git out of here. Git out beyond my defense perimeter. I warn you." He waggled his finger at them. "Get out of here or you'll all be reported to the tribunal."

"The who?" asked Whitcomb quietly, scrutinizing the man who was going completely insane right in front of them. He had become more angry than ever after learning his son had been found. He seemed to be furious that he had been found.

"Mark," Willy said softly, "we're wasting time. Let's pop the cellar."

Whitcomb glance at his driver in the cab of the Blazer, and nodded. "Okay, now!"

The powerful Blazer leaped forward. It wrenched the steel cellar door from its frame with a loud bang, and a screech as the door was dragged along the gravel.

Houston watched it all happen, not budging an inch from where he stood. He pulled another cigar from the pocket of his overalls and lit up. Then he turned his back on the group and walked over to the big flat rock and sat down. Between puffs his lips were moving with barely audible gibberish richly laced with obscenities.

Whitcomb assigned two of his agents to watch him. "Let him sit there. If he makes any move at all, put him in cuffs. I think he's an emotional time bomb. Watch him!" He motioned to Evan Knight and Willy. "Let's get on with it."

Whitcomb led the way down the cellar steps. The cellar

floor was almost barren except for a few boxes and an old chest of drawers by the paneless narrow window. On one of the boxes was a sack from McDonald's. Willy picked it up gingerly and sniffed at the contents. Inside were the remains of a hamburger and a few french fries. He touched the bun on the hamburger. It was still soft to the touch. He peered into the soft drink container standing on the box. It was almost empty. Then he saw the bright red ball cap lying on the floor in front of the chest.

"That's Penny's cap! It came with the Miata, she wore it into the office the day she bought the car." whispered Willy. "Oh, my God! That miserable son of a bitch."

49

Coley Doctor reached the top of the ridge near where the backhoe stood between two mounds of earth. Young Tad was still perched on his shoulders when the farm came into view down below. They were immediately greeted by the sight of the black Blazer jumping forward and dragging the cellar door from its casement.

"Wow, look at that!" exclaimed young Tad, "What are they doing that for?"

"Well, Tad, that's my boss and the FBI. I'm sure they have their reasons." Coley let the boy slip down from his shoulders and they retreated to a point where they could peer through the brambles and not be seen easily by those a quarter mile away. The climb up the ridge carrying Tad was more exercise than he had anticipated. "Now let's just sit here for a minute and catch our breath. We'll sit right here on this mound and have the catbird seat. Keep your head down. We don't want them to see us until we know what is going on down there. Don't you get any ideas about running away. I want you to stick with me, pal, okay?"

"Catbird seat? My mom says that all the time." Tad sat cross-legged on the mound and peered through the tangle of brush. He was obviously exhausted but still gave his rapt attention to the scene below.

Coley looked at the spectacle with wonder. Willy and Whitcomb had disappeared into the cellar the instant the door had been ripped from its foundation. They had been down there for several minutes. Adding to the mystery was Sonny Houston, sitting on a boulder a hundred feet away from the house, calmly smoking a big fat cigar, under no apparent restraint. Two FBI agents were standing nearby with rifles covering Houston. They were all evidently waiting for the two men to exit from the cellar. Coley pulled the cell phone from his pocket but decided not to interrupt Willy for the moment.

Coley felt Tad trembling next to him, and then saw him wiping tears from his eyes with the back of his hand. The boy had his eyes fixed on Sonny Houston, perched on the rock between the two FBI men who now had moved closer to him. "Just calm down, son. Say, did you ever take a ride in a helicopter?"

Tad looked up at him, but had something else on his mind. "Pops is going to whup me good. I hope he don't break my arm again."

"Now, you don't have to worry about stuff like that," Coley assured him. "I promise that we're going to take good care of you. You ever shoot hoops, play basketball?"

"Sure! Eddie Foxworth has a hoop in his backyard. We play all the time. I'm pretty good, too."

"Mind if I shoot some baskets with you sometime? I used to be pretty good, too." Coley kept trying to distract the boy from the scene below and gain his confidence. "I was an All-American once."

"Wow, I bet your autograph is worth lots of money."

"Maybe about a nickel, I guess." Coley grinned at him. "But I'll give you a whole stack of them for nothing."

Tad started kicking at the dirt in front of him. "I betcha don't know what this is."

Coley looked at his sneaker now pushing at a shiny wire sticking out of the mound. "Well, I guess its a coat hanger, or maybe you buried an old fishing rod there."

"Nope, it's a radio thing." Tad shook his head up and down confidently."

"Radio thing? Oh, you must mean an antenna."

"Yep. I was back in the trees right over there." He pointed over his shoulder. "And I saw Pops bury it there. It's on a neat little red car. Sometimes Pops does stupid things."

Coley stared at the boy, wondering if he had heard him correctly. He leaned over and gave the wire a tug. It wouldn't budge. He rubbed at it. It was shiny like chrome or stainless steel. It had a little round metal cap on the end. It looked like a radio antenna for sure. He looked up at the backhoe and the tire tracks running back and forth from the end of the mound. A chill ran down his spine. "You saw him bury a real little red car here? A real automobile?" Coley grasped him firmly by his shoulders. "When?"

Tad winced and squirmed away from him. "Yesterday night. It was so dumb. I don't know why he did it."

"Tad, I want you to think about it, and tell me exactly what you saw. Was there anyone in the car?"

"Nope. Pops ain't that crazy. It was just dumb, that's all." Tad shook his head and kicked at the wire. "He made this big hole, kind of a trench, with the backhoe. Then I saw this red car, with the top down, parked right over there. I could see real good. There was no one in it. I don't even know how it got there. He took the backhoe and pushed it down into the ditch and covered it up. It was really dumb!"

Coley jumped to his feet and looked all around, searching for a shovel or anything else that might dig through the loose earth beneath his feet. He walked over to the ruins of an old barn and found a piece of scrap lumber. He brought it back to the where the antenna protruded. Then he began to tunnel furiously into the mound of earth.

Tad was watching. "It ain't very deep. The radio thing was only about this high." He made a measurement of about a foot and a half with his hands.

Coley dug straight down along the aerial with his makeshift shovel, scraping away a trench until he hit a firm object. He cupped his hands and scraped at his hole until he could see the chrome fixture that was attached to metal that was unmistakably red, even in the waning light of day.

"Tad, I want you to just sit right there and stay out of sight. I'm going to be right here until the helicopter comes. But we have some business to attend to."

"Sure. Do you think the car will still run?" Tad started to dig more dirt out of the hole that Coley had started.

"Hey, save your energy, boy. I don't want you conking out on me again." Then the same fear he had before came back to his mind. What if Tad were wrong and Penny was still in the Miata? "Now stop digging, Tad. We'll get some tools and some muscle up here or get someone who knows how to operate that backhoe."

Coley saw Whitcomb and Willy emerge from the cellar and turn their backs on Houston, still sitting on the rock. They were engaged in conversation they evidently wanted to keep confidential from the rest of the group. Coley decided that now was the time to call him.

"Was Penny in the cellar?" Coley asked.

"No, but her red cap was," Willy said softly. "You know, the one she got to match the new Miata."

"Oh, Jesus! She might have been buried in the Miata. It's buried up here on the hill next to where you can see the backhoe. Tad is with me. He's a great kid! He saw his dad bury the car. He is sure there is no one in it. We need some strong hands and some shovels up here quick. It would help if somebody could run this damn backhoe." Coley paused while Willy repeated the news to Whitcomb.

"Coley, Whitcomb is working on your request. He says he can run the backhoe if no one else can. Keep Tad under wraps with you. We're getting ready to slap the cuffs on Houston, all three hundred pounds of him. Whitcomb says not to worry. The two agents assigned to him are some kind of black belt experts. First we're going to try to be nice, but we've got to quiz him directly about Penny. Keep the boy out of sight till the copter comes to pick him up. We'd rather Houston not be distracted right now. My God, Coley, if Houston killed Penny, I'm going to take care of him myself."

"I don't even want to think about it, Willy. All the answers I come up with are horrible. Hey, Willy, light a fire under Whitcomb. We've only got about forty-five minutes of daylight left."

Coley hung up and turned his attention to Tad, still laboriously scaping dirt from the Miata with his hands. Now you could see about a ten-inch-square area of the vivid red sports car. "Tad, take a rest for a while. Let me have a crack at it." Coley began tunneling relentlessly toward the spot where the driver's seat would be located. There really wasn't much room inside the small car. In a few minutes he would know whether Tad was right.

50

Willy and Whitcomb wandered off some distance from the others to discuss the pending interrogation of Houston. "The way I see it," said Willy, thinking aloud, "For some reason Houston locked Penny in the cellar. She must have been in there some time, long enough for him to go to buy her some food up at the junction. She must have smashed the window and freed herself from the cellar, cutting herself as she squeezed through. She ran for the woods. He took after her with the van and caught her out beyond the fence. There are tire marks right out across that little ditch and into the woods. I found a bloody makeshift bandage at the point where the tire tracks end."

Whitcomb looked at him questioningly. "That's a small window. Certainly you or I couldn't get through it. Maybe a small kid could."

"Penny is very petite. I think she could make it." Willy stopped to allow Whitcomb to answer his cell phone. It was from the guards stationed at the entrance to Houston's driveway. Looking toward the gate, they saw three vehicles lined up. One of them carried a TV CHANNEL 10 logo.

"Who let the cat out of the bag?" Whitman yelled gruffly at Trooper Evan Knight, still at a distance and talking on his own cell phone.

"I haven't the slightest idea, but we already have three carloads of newspeople down there claiming that they had heard there was a break in the kidnapping case."

"Hold them right there. We've got no time for questions. The Houston property is off-limits until we complete the investigation. You can tell them the boy is safe but they'll have to wait for details."

Whitcomb glanced down the hill toward the gate and could see state police cars arriving one by one. He turned back to Evan Knight. "Tell your new arrivals down there to form a security line along the road. Nobody gets in here until the lab boys are finished. It'll be a long wait, because they're not here yet."

Whitcomb and Willy walked over to confront Sonny Houston, still sitting as if in a trance, staring off into the distance, puffing on the big cigar. The two agents assigned to him were standing on either side of him a few feet away.

"Where's Penny Wine?" Willy bent low and spoke only inches from Houston's face.

"Who the hell is Penny Wine?" Houston asked, staring at the open cellar door.

"Is she buried in that little red sports car up on the hill? Is that where you took her after you caught her over in the woods?" Willy nodded toward the mound a quarter mile away.

Houston scowled and squinted at the place where he had buried the red Miata. He made out the movement of someone beyond the brambles. "I found that piece of junk on my land and decided to get rid of it right away. There ain't nobody in it. Don't know how it got there, but I found it parked at the side of my house. The vehicle had invaded my property."

Then Houston unexpectedly grinned broadly. "I bet that little bastard, Tad, told you it was buried there, didn't he? I saw that little sneak running around the woods up there earlier when I was working. He thinks he's getting away with something."

"Bastard? Sneak? Is that what you call your own son?" Willy was aghast at his remarks.

"He's no son of mine. Who told you that? Everybody round here knows his father is a drunk down in Williamsport. Tad's been sneakin' around the woods up there for a couple days." Houston scowled again and became very serious. "Tad's a little traitor, you know. He's been down here, crawling through windows, stealing peanut butter and apples." Houston shook his finger at them and then smiled. "I've already reported him to the tribunal."

"The tribunal?" Willy approached him again, nose to nose. "You're crazy! You big, fat, filthy slob, you're crazy! Where's Penny Wine?" Willy cuffed him hard, slapping the cigar from his mouth.

"Stop! Willy!" Whitcomb muscled his way between the two, shoved Willy away from Houston and then whispered hoarsely in Willy's ear. "We've got this bastard nailed. Don't pollute the case!"

"Pollute the case? Mark, this guy knows what happened to Penny!"

"Cool it, Willy. We'll soon have about a hundred men

here. If she's alive, we'll soon know. If she isn't . . ." Whitcomb's voice trailed off, not wanting to say, what to him, was the obvious.

Whitcomb picked up the questioning of Houston. "Mr. Houston, what about the ransom notes? Why didn't you report them to the police?"

"I don't know what you're talking about. Even if I did, I don't see how that's any of your business. The boy wasn't kidnapped. That stuff is just a lot of bullshit. You keep nosing into my business and I'm going to have to report all of you to the tribunal. Now git the hell off my property!"

Houston moved to the other side of the rock. He turned his face totally away from them and focused his scowl on the buildup of media people down in front of his house. He reached into his pocket, produced another cigar and lit up.

Whitcomb motioned to one of the agents guarding Houston to join him and Willy out of earshot of where Houston sat, glaring at the crowd of people.

"The guy is crazy and he's strong as an ox. When he gets distracted by something, slap the cuffs on him and read him his rights. We already got enough on him to put him away for years. Willy and I are going on up the hill and see what's happening. Call our boys down below and tell them we need about six men with shovels."

Willy grimaced. It was obvious Whitcomb felt the answers to their questions would be found in the excavation up on the hill. If Penny had escaped the property, she would have made herself known by now. Reluctantly he joined Whitcomb in his climb up the hill.

"Are you sure about the red ball cap?" Whitcomb asked as they walked.

"Mark, I guess there must be zillions of red ball caps in the world, but along with all the other evidence, it's hard to come to any other conclusion.

The thump-thumping of a helicopter grew louder and

louder as they climbed the hill. The pilot, searching for a level piece of ground, was zeroing in on a spot about a hundred yards from the mounds at the top of the hill.

Young Tad jumped to his feet, fascinated by the incoming copter. Coley withdrew from his tunnel in the mound, which had reached the steering wheel. So far there was no sign of Penny. He glanced down the hill and saw Willy and Whitcomb striding rapidly through the pasture toward him followed by a half dozen men with shovels in the distance.

Coley turned around and saw Tad sitting on the claw of the backhoe, mesmerized by the circling chopper. Then, all of a sudden he scrambled down off the claw and lay flat against the old barn door upon which it rested. His head was turned away from Coley, and he lay perfectly motionless. Coley shouted at him but was unheard over the din of the landing chopper. Coley climbed off the mound and ran to the boy.

Tad pointed beneath him. "There's somebody down here!"

Coley flattened himself against the old barn door next to Tad.

"Help me! Help! Help!" The thumping of the rotors in the distance stopped as the pilot cut the engine, and now the cries for help beneath the old slab of wood came out loud and clear.

"That's Penny! My God, that's Penny!" Coley tried to peek into the darkness below through a crack in the wood, but could seen nothing. "Penny, this is Coley! Hang tough. We'll have you out of there in a jiffy."

Coley leaped up and struggled for a second with the iron claw that pressed into the wood. The giant iron claw was immovable. Willy and Whitcomb popped into view, followed by the agents with shovels.

"Willy, Penny's down under this piece of wood and she's alive. Penny, can you hear me?"

"Yes, Coley. Of course I can. Just get me out of here. If Sonny Houston is up there, grab him. I want to kill him."

"Don't worry about that son of a bitch. We've got him," assured Willy, now kneeling and tugging at the old barn door.

Whitcomb began giving instructions to the men with the shovels. They began digging along one edge of the wood, rapidly digging downward and then tunneling in underneath. Within minutes, Penny's face became visible. Soon she extended her arms and the agents pulled her from her intended grave amidst the cheers of the dozen people who now surrounded her.

Coley held her close for a few moments. Then he carried her to a grassy patch in the meadow and laid her down. The usually sleek and fastidious Penny Wine was hardly recognizable. "You're going to be okay. Don't worry about a thing," assured Coley, amazed to see a flicker of a smile cross her face. He wondered if the realization that she had almost been buried alive was yet clear to her.

"Water, please, some water," she pleaded hoarsely.

Whitcomb spun on his heels. "Water, damn it. Water! Somebody go get some damn water!"

Penny stared at the unlikely man in the pressed business suit with black hair slicked back impeccably, still shouting for water. "Who in the world is that?" she asked quietly.

"That's Agent Whitcomb of the FBI," answered Coley. "He gets a little dramatic once in a while. But he's our favorite cop."

"Then he's mine, too," mumbled Penny, now inspecting herself closely. "God, I'm a mess," she exclaimed, suddenly aware of the growing ring of people surrounding her.

"Well, it's not every day they see someone crawl out of a hole in the ground," said Coley. "Hey that's a bad-looking leg you've got there." He pointed at the leg she had scraped over the shard of glass, now badly inflamed and caked with blood and mud from the bottom of the pit.

"I want you to meet someone, Penny." Coley motioned Tad Houston over to where she lay. "This is Tad. We found him. And he's the one who first heard you under the wood. He found you."

"I betcha that hurts." Tad stared at the injured leg.

"It'll be okay. Thanks, Tad, for finding me." She struggled to a sitting position and gave him a hug.

"Tad, you're going to have company on the copter. Penny's going to fly to the hospital with you," Willy informed them, as a medevac unit arrived with stretchers.

"Willy, I'm going to be fine. I hate helicopters," protested Penny.

Willy shook his finger at her. "This time you are going to follow instructions. You are going to the hospital!"

"Okay, boss, you win. Hereafter, I promise to carry my cell phone, carry my weapon and go to the hospital whenever I am told to."

Willy knelt down to hug her, marveling at her sense of humor. "You had a close call, kid. Welcome back."

Whitcomb, Willy and Coley followed the stretcher bearers to the helicopter, watched and waved until it took off and rapidly disappeared from sight.

51

Sonny Houston measured the distance to his house carefully with his eyes. The two agents guarding him had shed their jackets so their side arms in shoulder holsters were in full view. He figured that if he picked his moment, he could sprint the twenty-five yards to the house, get inside and reach his gun rack before they could stop him. They wouldn't dare shoot him in the back in front of all these people. Feds didn't do things like that, he reasoned to himself.

Picking an instant when both agents were glancing skyward toward the rising helicopter, he bolted from the rock and sprinted toward the house.

Within a few steps one of the agents flattened him with a flying tackle, and the other pounced on his back, shoved his head into the gravel and twisted an arm behind his back. Within seconds he was handcuffed and being hustled back to the rock.

"Thanks, pal. We were waiting for you to make a move. You made it easy. Now you sit quietly or I'll finish busting up that face." The agent feinted a punch near his nose, which was already pouring blood from its encounter with the gravel driveway.

Houston spat at him and glared at the several men who had left the ridge and were walking his way. "Every damn one of you will have to face the tribunal. I guess you know what they do with traitors." He spat again at them, then twisted and yanked at the cuffs until a stream of blood ran down his fingers. The tall black man whom he had seen the day before, the one who had professed to want to buy his property, reached them first.

Coley saw the smashed nose and the blood still streaming down and grinned appreciatively at the agent. "Nice work, Officer. I only wish I could take another shot at him."

Coley stood close to Houston. "You tried to bury my partner alive. You tried to bury that tiny five-foot-two lady alive and couldn't get the job done. It's a good thing you didn't." Coley stuck his fist near his chin. "If we hadn't found her, I'd make sure you'd be a sorry, helpless cripple the rest of your life."

"Coley!" It was Whitcomb roaring at him as he came running down from the ridge and saw Coley menacing the handcuffed Houston.

"I know, I know! Don't pollute the case! Don't worry, I

wouldn't think of giving this sorry bastard any kind of an out." Coley backed off a couple of paces as a tow truck, lights flashing, roared up the gravel driveway.

"We're going to pull the Miata out of there, take some photographs and videotape the excavation," Whitcomb explained to the others. He turned to one of the policemen. "Let's read Mr. Houston his rights and get him booked. It's been a long day."

"Just one minute, Mark. I've got one more question for Mr. Houston." Coley bent over until he was nose to bloody nose with Houston. "My information is that you dug a big pond up there and then filled it up a couple days ago. Then you dug another pond, and planted that pretty little Miata in it. Would there, by any chance, be a brand new red Corvette underneath that other mound of dirt up there?"

Houston answered his question with a big bloody mouthful of spit.

Coley stepped back, grinned and looked down at the mess on his camouflage pants. He turned toward Willy, who had just arrived on the scene. "Willy, I think Mr. Houston has just answered my question in the affirmative."

Evan Knight turned to one of his men. "Boys, it's been a long day, but let's get it over with. Drill a few test holes in that other mound of dirt."

Sonny Houston was led away by Whitcomb's men and placed in a waiting police car.

Lights flashed on top of the ridge and shined on the red Miata. The work party had strung lights so they could continue their work on the other mound into the darkness.

Willy, Coley and Mark Whitcomb stood near the flat rock that had become their command post. If Jason Granger and the Corvette were not buried up near the Miata, none of them could come up with an idea of where they might look next.

After a very short time, there was a shout from up above, and Evan Knight came jogging quickly down the hill. He stopped in front of them for a moment to catch his breath and then spoke. "We've just called the coroner. You can add homicide to all the other Houston charges. Would you believe there is a red Corvette under there, with a man still at the wheel?"

"Jason Granger, no doubt," murmured Coley.

Willy Hanson sat down on the rock and shook his head in disbelief at the grim news. "Our case is shot to hell, Coley. Amanda doesn't need a divorce anymore."

52

After the body of Jason Granger had been extricated from the cockpit of the Corvette and turned over to the coroner, Evan Knight was left with the task of retrieving the Corvette. It was past midnight before the Corvette was pulled from the excavation and sat alongside the Miata, both awaiting tow trucks to take them to a security garage in Scranton. There they would be gone over by forensic experts and held until the disposition of Sonny Houston's case was clear.

Willy and Coley hung around until the excavating job was completed. They circled and inspected the two vehicles, still filled with dirt. Surprisingly, the Miata seemed basically unscathed, except for the filth. The Corvette had been heavily damaged in the rear, probably by the backhoe, and might not be salvageable.

Coley scrutinized the Corvette. The intended coffin for Jason Granger was practically new. In the glare of the floodlights set up for the workers, he noticed a long scratch on the driver's side running from the front headlights to the rear bumper. It was the only blemish on the forward part of the car.

"What a shame, Willy. It's got less than three thousand miles on it. I always wanted one of those."

"I suggest you be patient. I'll bet Amanda will sell it to you real cheap."

Coley shook his head slowly. "No thanks! Even if they could fix it up like new, I don't think I'd ever get over the sight of Jason Granger, dead as a doornail with his hands still gripping the wheel."

Willy dialed Harrisburg again. Amanda hadn't picked up her phone all evening. He wanted to talk to her before she heard the news elsewhere.

"Yes." The one quietly spoken word told him that she had already heard what he had called to tell her.

"Amanda, this is Willy Hanson. You've heard about Jason?"

"Yes. I turned on the news about a half hour ago. I couldn't sleep. I . . . I really didn't expect anything like this."

"Neither did any of us. I'm sorry, Amanda. Are you okay?"

"Oh, yes. My brother, he lives in Harrisburg, and his wife are on their way over. I'll be fine. Jason went off the deep end long ago, but nobody would wish this on anyone. I guess I actually feel somewhat guilty. It's hard to explain."

"Not at all. It is completely understandable to feel that way. Look, the police have taken the Corvette to a garage they use near Scranton. It's probably totaled. I'll follow up and keep you informed."

"Oh, I think it was registered to me. I'll probably hear from them. Thanks anyway, Willy, and thank Coley for me."

"You have my number, Amanda. Call me anytime day or night."

"I will, when things settle down. You can bet on it." Amanda hung up the phone, walked into the living room and sat down on the sofa. Outside, a bright sliver of a new moon silhouetted the trees bordering the golf course in the distance. Golf was Jason's favorite diversion, and their home's proximity to the club was probably the biggest factor that had led to the purchase of their house. Yet, recently, golf had become a minor part of Jason's life. His passion for the game seemed to ebb when she began to hear the name "Blair Lawton" bandied about.

Unexpectedly, tears bursted forth, running down both cheeks. They kept coming as she recalled their earlier years—not so long ago—when they were making all their plans and were so excited about the new home. Everything seemed so right, almost perfect.

But recently she noticed that Jason was often restless. He had confided that he was unhappy with Harmony Mutual—in fact, that he found it incredibly boring. He aggressively pursued the transfer to New York, thinking that would rejuvenate his excitement for the work. She had volunteered to postpone her own dreams of a family to accommodate the prospective move. That was a mistake. Without those plans and dreams, she slowly discovered they had absolutely nothing in common. "What a handsome couple you are." She had heard the comment from others a hundred times. It became a compliment without meaning for her. The excitement of the first years, of marrying the handsome linebacker, was gone.

She used to laugh when Jason would tell her, "All the fun is in the fast lane, baby." But it was no joke. He meant it. And then Blair Lawton entered his world, and he turned into a man Amanda didn't know.

Her hand dropped into her lap, so near the baby who would never know its father. In fact, it need not know anything about the details of the real reasons for their ceasing to love each other. That would be good, much better than a gossipy record of a divorce. She dabbed at the tears now with a tissue. They stopped coming. The doorbell rang. That would be her brother and his wife, Carla. She rose from the couch and walked to the door, feeling strangely refreshed.

* * *

There was something about the tone of Amanda's voice that told Willy she was desperately trying to shut the door on that part of her life. He really never expected to hear from her again.

Willy looked at his watch. It was after 1:00 A.M. "Coley, lets grab a few hours sleep at one of those hot-pillow joints over near the junction. They've taken Penny and Tad to the hospital in Scranton. We'll get up early and visit the hospital. Penny looked terrible."

"Yep, but she could still crack a smile now and then. She's a tough cookie. It's the kid I worry about. Physically, he'll be okay. But how does he handle something like this emotionally? You can't escape the fact that the man he called father buried someone alive. I know you always harp about not getting emotionally involved in our cases. But I'll tell you, Willy, I'm going to break one of your damn rules. In the future, I'm going to help Tad every way I can."

"Bravo, Coley! When it comes to you, it's not helping little kids I worry about. It's your penchant for the bimbos of this sleazy world."

After a few hours sleep, Willy and Coley walked through the doors of Scranton Hospital. Penny was sitting up in bed with a heavily bandaged leg protruding from the covers. Aside from the bandaged leg, she looked amazingly like her usual perky self.

Willy tossed copies of the newspapers that he had picked up at the junction onto the bed. They all featured the Houston case prominently. "Take a look at page four, kiddo. I'm going to get a blowup of that and put it on the wall in front of your desk."

The news photo of her being pulled out of her muddy intended grave had been taken by a telescopic lens from quite a distance. Her mud-caked figure looked like nothing alive or human. "Oh, my God! Is that really me?"

"I think it looks pretty natural," teased Coley. "Tell me, were you totally unconscious very long?"

"Not for long. I really wasn't in the ground for very long. He had just found me running away in the woods, cuffed me pretty hard, and took me up the hill in his van. I vaguely remember him dropping me down in that pit. Then all of a sudden he covered me with the planks and left. He didn't have time to finish me off. You guys must have showed up down below."

"In the last nick of time. God! That was close. You still like being a private investigator after all that?" Coley asked. "Did he keep you in the cellar all night?"

"Yep. I think he had some weird ideas for a while. He kept telling me what a pretty little thing I was." She hesitated before confiding, "I was sure he had rape on his mind. He said he had never had anything like me before. Then he talked about getting me a pardon from the tribunal, and I knew he was nuts for sure. I was petrified, guys. I'm ashamed of how afraid I was."

"Ashamed? Nothing to be ashamed of," admonished Coley. You got down to a life and death situation. Any sane person would be petrified. That'll teach you to stay close to the thirty-eight."

"I left it in the lockbox at home," confessed Penny.

"It figures," murmured Willy. "You know, you might need that thing only once or twice in your life. But there's no substitute when you do."

"I've learned that. Let's talk about Tad. Now there is a kid who has his head glued on straight in spite of all he went through. Isn't he something!"

"Whitcomb called us this morning," Willy said. "They are having him picked him up in the morning and dropping him off with his mother and Aunt Sarah in Morristown. He likes it there, at least for the foreseeable future."

"That's wonderful. The doctor said that I could get out of here in the morning, too. Maybe the big FBI guy in the funeral suit and greasy black hair will arrange for me to ride along with Tad's escort and then drop me off in the city. I'd like to spend a little more time with Tad."

"Sounds great," agreed Willy. "I'll clear it with Whitcomb. You'll even have time to get to the office for a meeting with another client, Blair Lawton. She called on our cell phone driving over here."

"Blair Lawton? What does she want?"

"I made a deal with her to find Jason and the Corvette. Jason, of course, is history. But she wants a peek inside the Corvette."

"A peek? That's strange."

"It's not only strange. It's impossible right now. The car has been impounded and is being given the once-over by the FBI lab boys. Her highness will be in the office at two o'clock tomorrow. Hey, look who's here!"

Tad Houston walked in accompanied by a nurse. "Hi, Coley. I'm feeling pretty good today. Do you know my Aunt Sarah has a basketball hoop on the side of her garage?" He ran over to Coley, who promptly lifted him up to eye level.

"Hey, that's great. We can shoot buckets once in awhile." He walked over to Penny, still carrying Tad. "Here's the lady you found yesterday. She cleaned up pretty nice, didn't she?"

Tad bobbed his head up and down. "Yeah, she looks nice." He pointed to Penny's leg. "Does that hurt?"

"Not a bit, Tad. Everything is going to be fine. I'm headed back to New York in the morning."

Coley lowered him to his feet and Tad walked over and stood next to her bed. "Mom and I are going to live with Aunt Sarah in Morristown. It's not that far from New York. I have an aunt in New York, too. She's Aunt Carlota. She's real nice." Tad cast his eyes toward the floor. "Well, I guess she isn't a real, real aunt. But I liked her a lot."

Penny quickly recalled the interview she did with the Ninth Avenue hooker. "You know Tad, I've met your aunt Carlota, and it was awfully nice of her to take care of you.

Maybe we can go see her some day. Now you've got to promise me that you won't go running off to the city by yourself again, though."

"You don't have to worry about that. I sure don't want to cause any more trouble." The boy looked around at all the others, his face flushed for a moment, embarrassed at all their attention. He took the nurse's extended hand and waved an awkward good-bye as they left the room.

53

Willy arrived early in his office the next morning. His E-mail was piled high and his telephone message light was blinking. There was a call from Blair Lawton, who sounded a bit impatient at not having reached him, confirming again their meeting of that afternoon. Willy groaned to himself and wished he had turned her over completely to Coley. If there was any follow-up work to be done based on what she had to say, he wanted Coley to pick up the details.

Willy then called Ginny Dubois, whom he had left sound asleep at the marina near Weehawken. He had arrived at the *Tashtego* in the early morning after the drive from Scranton, and they had spent very little time together. His call found her busy at readying the *Tashtego* for their summer sail to the Maine coast. Both yearned to return for a while to their idyllic existence on the great ketch.

It had always been normal for Ginny to join him on important investigations. What he had expected to be a simple and rather trivial divorce case had caused him to agree with Ginny—the *Tashtego* needed her help more than he would for a few days. She hadn't seemed to mind that at all. Sometimes he was actually jealous of the showy ketch. The *Tashtego* was an important third party in their long affair.

"Willy, why don't you bring Mark Whitcomb and Coley along for dinner tonight? I'll get a window table at the marina. I'm anxious to be brought up to date. I still can't believe that you got involved in a murder and a kidnapping case and let me miss all the fun," Ginny teased.

"It wasn't very much fun, Ginny. We almost lost Penny."

"So I heard. Was she armed, Willy?"

"She left the thirty-eight at home. Remember when you did that? You babes all have to learn the hard way."

"Be sure to bring Mark and Coley along tonight, Willy. We can talk about old times, from Hong Kong to Nyack, okay?"

"Okay, but I warn you, I haven't slept much in days. Last night didn't help much. You've got to do all the talking."

Willy hung up, feeling buoyant for the first time in a long time. But Ginny always affected him that way. He leaned back in his chair. It was twenty minutes until two. Maybe he could nap for a few minutes before Blair Lawton showed up. He knew that Coley and Penny would be on time. He was hoping that Blair Lawton would forget all about it.

At two o'clock sharp he was startled awake by a knock on his office door. He figured he had slept for about ten minutes. He stared through the reception room at the front door of the office. Penny turned the key and entered. Blair Lawton and Coley followed her into his office.

"Willy, you're here! Why didn't you give a yell when I knocked?" Penny was back to her old exuberant self. Slacks covered the bandaged leg, and sans mud, she was as sleek and perky as always. "I found these two guys in the elevator."

"Good! We're all right on time. It's business as usual again." Willy popped one leg up on the corner of the desk while Penny slid a chair under Blair Lawton. Then she and Coley took the two remaining chairs. Blair crossed her legs and the flimsy summer dress slid carelessly up her legs. "Ms.

Lawton, this is your meeting." Willy folded his hands, met her eyes and waited for her to speak.

He could see right away that Blair didn't expect a crowd. She glanced at the others, raised her palms upward and shrugged. "Well, now, I hardly expected to make a public speech. I expected to talk to you in . . . privacy." It took her awhile to get the word out.

"Blair, you will never in your life have more privacy than you have right here. That's the trademark of our firm. You talk to one of us, you talk to all of us. It saves a lot of paperwork. Trust us. You are paying for our trust. Now, how can we help you?"

Coley had to turn toward the window. He almost choked on his coffee watching Willy deadpan his employee rules to include the beautiful client. Then it hit him. Willy was actually trying to run the woman away. He didn't want her business.

"Mr. Hanson, I think this is ridiculous. I don't care one whit how you operate your company. I need you because I honestly believe that you are the only person in the world who can help me. I have something very personal to say, and I'm going to say it. I only hope that you are certain that what I have to say stays in this room."

No question about it, thought Willy, it was a beautiful speech. He toyed for just a moment with giving her the privacy she wanted. Had she waited him out just a little longer, he probably would have. But she began to speak again.

"Jason Granger and I had a very intense affair," she began.

Willy saw Penny grab for the inevitable yellow pad and ballpoint pen. "No notes! Please, Penny, no notes. I'm sorry, Blair. Please continue."

"Well, one day we did something very foolish. We had spent a long workday in the boardroom. It was a successful day, and after everyone left, we felt the urge to celebrate." Blair paused, trying to find the words. "Well, Jason had this miniature camcorder. He put it on this little tripod, and we sort of lost our heads in that boardroom. I can't explain such foolishness. Perhaps you've loved someone as much as Jason and I did. We went on and on in front of the camera. Our feelings for each other just exploded."

Penny grew red-faced, slipped out of her chair and began to water the window plants with the small pitcher she kept on her desk. Coley rubbed his chin thoughtfully, trying desperately to maintain decorum.

Willy finally broke eye contact with her and decided that the time had come for a merciful interruption. "That is quite enough, Blair. I think you've made everything quite clear. There is no need to go on. My question is, What can we do to help you?"

"It's that damn red Corvette. There is a compartment underneath the console box. The videotape is in there. The car has been impounded by the Pennsylvania State Police and the FBI. I fear that if they clean the car they might find the tape under the loose console box. I told you all along I wanted to find Jason and the Corvette. You've helped do both. But what I really want, I can't get."

"Blair, what you want is probably impossible to get at this point. I'd say that there is a good chance that the tape will never be discovered." Fat chance, Willy thought as he said it. The FBI would take that car apart bolt by bolt.

"Willy, look at it this way. If Amanda Granger ever came across that tape, it would be very cruel. Her affection for someone she loved would be destroyed. I can't sleep, thinking about the effect it might have on such a wonderful person." Blair began dabbing at the corner of her eyes.

"Blair, I believe that all of us understand the depth of your concern. I can't promise you anything, but I'll try to do something. Sorry I can't be more helpful. I think you'd best wrap yourself up in your job at Harmony Mutual and hope for the best."

"Willy, I'm afraid that's impossible. I'm leaving Harmony Mutual. The thought of working there without Jason is unbearable."

"Really! Do you have any plans?"

"Oh, yes. Dillon Archibald is backing me in a little venture I've always dreamed of. We're doing a high-fashion and gift boutique in Palm Beach. Dillon was so kind as to help me get started someplace where I can be busy and stop brooding about the tragedy here."

"He's a kind man, isn't he," observed Willy. "He's married to a wonderful woman. Cora is her name, I believe."

"Isn't she a doll!" gushed Blair. "How did you come to know her?"

"Oh, our paths crossed somewhere once," Willy lied. He showed Blair to the door, walked her a few steps to the elevator and soon returned to the office.

"Willy!" Penny was churning with excitement when he returned. "Blair Lawton is a wicked, lying woman. I thought I was going to throw up. How could you be nice to her?"

"Well, I really wasn't too nice, was I? We put her through quite an inquisition. Of course, her reason for recovering the tape is hardly to shield our dear Amanda. That's bullshit. She's afraid it will show up somewhere and ruin the relationship with Archibald, her new meal ticket. The sad thing is, I don't think she realized we had her number."

"So what are we going to do?" asked Coley.

Willy shrugged. "Probably nothing. I consider our relationship with Blair Lawton at an end. I may make one pass at Whitcomb to turn over the tape for the very reason Blair professed. I don't think Amanda deserves another kick in the gut by having the tape turn up later, either in private or in public."

When Blair Lawton left the elevator in the building lobby, she stopped for a moment to primp a bit in front of her reflected image in a shop window. She looked terrible, she thought. She had actually shed tears at the news of Jason's demise, and it puzzled her. She couldn't remember such a spate of tears since she was a child. No man had affected her that way.

There would never be any tears for Dillon Archibald. He had sat there in sheer terror when he had listened this morning to her lie about being pregnant. After that, the Palm Beach proposal was an easy sell. In fact, he had approved the location without many questions. It was conveniently distant from New York. Learning the boutique business was more up her alley. Had the insurance business not been so dreadfully boring she and Jason wouldn't have found time to get in all that trouble. Poor Jason, she thought. It would be best if I not hang around for the funeral.

54

Mark Whitcomb met Willy and Coley at the New York Waterways Ferry Terminal on West Thirty-eighth Street. The commuter facility serves New Jersey commuters traveling from Midtown New York to Weehawken, New Jersey. From their vantage point at the terminal they could easily spot the *Tashtego* across the Hudson River.

"Mark, I thought we'd have cocktails aboard the *Tashtego* and then have dinner at the marina. Ginny deserves a night out. She's been working like the devil to get the *Tashtego* ready for our summer vacation."

"Sounds good to me, Willy. We've all earned a night out." Instead of going inside the ferry's cabin, Whitcomb suggested they enjoy the ten-minute voyage outside along the rail. It was a rare, low-humidity, clear evening.

Standing between Willy and Coley, Whitcomb reached inside his jacket pocket and produced a small envelope. Whitcomb looked all around them. When he was sure they were not being observed, he opened the metal snap at the end of the envelope and let them peek inside. It contained a videotape. He tapped the envelope with his finger. "Blair Lawton's performance," he whispered with no elaboration.

"That was quick work, Mark. I'll have a satisfied client," Willy said, waiting for him to offer him the envelope.

Willy watched as Whitcomb once again peered inside the envelope. Then, very calmly, and deliberately, he turned the envelope upside down. The cassette slipped from the case, fell the few feet down to the water, created a tiny splash and slipped from view into the murky chop of the Hudson River.

"Mark! Why?" Willy shouted almost in reflex to his action. Then he saw the same quiet smile he grown to expect from Whitcomb over the years when he was very satisfied with something.

"Trust me," he said, still smiling. You're dealing with your FBI here."

The three men watched the water swirl around the stern of the ferry. The lights of the towers of Manhattan began to sparkle against the evening sky. "I've often thought that this is the most beautiful perspective of Manhattan," said Coley. "Everything is shining and perfect from out here."

"But when you dig into things," observed Whitcomb, "it's a world gone mad. Take your case that we just closed, for instance. It started with some guy cheating on his wife. The same guy cutting off somebody in the fast lane of the turnpike. Then, if we are to believe little Eddie Foxworth and Tad, a scratch on a fancy car and a beating. Then revenge, one-upmanship, corporate greed, vanity run amok, drug abuse, child abuse, kidnapping, insanity and then murder. And we know about it only because Amanda paid you to nail Jason. In a selfish, amoral, me-first world this stuff has become common every time you bother to dig into people's lives. And you ask why I threw the cassette away. Is it really necessary to dig any deeper?"

Willy nodded in agreement. "Case closed. I don't want to know any more about these particular people."

"Now wait a minute," said Coley. "I meant what I said about looking after Tad now and then. And you know what else I'm going to do?"

"I have no idea, Coley."

"I'm going to help Empress Carlota find a day job."